Dying For Coal

A story of sacrifice and resilience in the South Yorkshire pit village of Denaby Main

Carol Ann Bullett

First Published in 2024 by Carol Ann Bullett
Written by Carol Ann Bullett
Editing by Anne Grange Writing
Copyright © Carol Ann Bullett 2024
Cover design © Ian Bullett 2024

All rights reserved. No part of this publication may be reproduced, stored in a retrieval system, or transmitted in any form or by any means, electronic, mechanical, photocopying, recording, or otherwise, without the prior permission of the author.

This book or any portion thereof may not be reproduced or used in any manner whatsoever without the express written permission of the publisher except for the use of brief quotations in a book review or scholarly journal.

ISBN: 9798346644828

Dedicated to the men and boys who lost their lives whilst working down the mines in the pursuit of coal.

Also, to their families who suffered the heartbreak of losing them.

ଔ

This is a fictional story based on both true and fictional events. The lives of both fictional and historical characters are woven into the story.

A huge thank you to my sister, Lesley, who painstakingly computerised my handwritten manuscript with great care and attention.

The Call of Coal

By Carol Ann Bullett

Down in the mines where the shadows crawl,
Men dig deep, giving their all.
With picks in hand they toil and strain,
Hewing black diamonds through sweat and pain.

But danger hides, it lurks and prowls,
Snatching and grabbing in Earth's black bowels.
A spark, a flash, a fatal fall,
Men are taken by Death's final call.

Widows weep and children cry,
But life moves on, though loved ones die.
They pick up the pieces, their lives torn apart,
Carrying on with heavy hearts.

For the coal still calls beneath the ground,
But the pain of grief is the only sound.
In mining towns still stories are told
Of men who lived and died for coal.

Introduction

Mary watched the flames in the fire frolicking along the cobbles, rising and falling as if dancing.

Recollections flew around in her mind like dandelion seeds floating on the breeze, looking for a place to settle. Her failing body housed a myriad memories, each of which could be highlighted and expanded, like sparkles from a diamond turning to catch the light. A full spectrum of emotions could be summoned from the events of her life, shaped and moulded by her environment, Denaby Main, a South Yorkshire pit village.

This "company owned" village was dedicated to the getting of coal – at any cost. This unstinting pursuit choked and sooted hopes, aspirations and ambitions as much as any hands or lungs.

The relentless grasping of the valuable treasure, coal, with all its inevitable consequences pervaded the lives of all who lived and worked there. But that was how it was. Men and boys were commodities to augment the wealth and power of bosses, easily replaced by others desperate to earn a living wage.

Women had to watch this brutal, uncaring attitude and try to pick up the pieces, sometimes literally, for the sake of their families. Mary had learned to be strong in order to exist, just like the other women.

Coal was money, money was power, and power restrained the rising demands of the working class. They, too, wanted better living and working conditions, adequate food to nourish bodies and souls, and a sustained feeling of security for their families.

Blood, breath and bones were given in the attempt to gain a better standard of life and to balance inequality. The trouble was, it was the sons, fathers and husbands who were sacrificed in villages like Denaby. Women had to grieve, but still carry on.

Mary sighed a shallow breath. Tears sprang beneath her closed lids. So many tears over the years, so much regret for what could have been.

PART ONE

Chapter 1
1881

The body had been left in an old wooden barrow, upturned against the sooted brick wall. A gnarled, blackened hand jutted upwards, as if summoning help. A booted foot dangled, as if resting.

Mary's sore eyes narrowed as she approached her house. She rubbed at the sticky mess that clung to her lashes, trying to focus on the strange object that waited by her front door. She kicked her flapping boot soles harder, staring intently at the nearing hand. The middle finger had no tip, the little finger was completely missing.

It was her grandfather's hand. So many times, it had created shadowy shapes of animals and monsters, made to entertain her and her brother and sisters. That hand had been the recipient of many accidents, but Grandad George had thanked the Lord that his thumb was intact; a shovel or a pick could still be held and used.

Ominous fear squeezed her insides as she peered into the barrow's contents. She instantly recoiled at the sight of the contorted figure, only partially covered by the piece of cloth. Her ears heard the screams departing her throat; they could not be stopped. The nine-year-old little girl had witnessed a dead body before, but this was her beloved Grandad, broken and bloodied.

The door was yanked open, revealing her grumbling mother, Sarah. Her gaze swept from the child to the hand in the barrow, then up to the smoky sky. She had been a miner's daughter and wife long enough to instantly realise the situation.

'The bastard gaffers have dumped him.'

* * *

Sarah tried to stem the steady flow of tears. Her swollen eyes could hardly focus upon the coffin lying on the living room floor. It still felt so unreal, that the body of her much-loved father lay inside it.

He had been removed from the indignity of the barrow by neighbouring menfolk, also miners, only too willing to help in any way possible, while women friends comforted her with soothing words and cups of tea.

She had carefully washed and dressed George, grief thankfully numbing the horror of seeing the mutilated body, cut and crushed by stone and coal. The undertaker had brought the coffin, together with his murmured condolences, as soon as he was informed of the accident. Yet another life lost to mining. She and her husband, Albert, had tenderly arranged the body into as natural a pose as possible, given the unnatural state of the injuries inflicted.

Anger joined sorrow as they acknowledged that the mining company bosses had delivered the body in such an unseemly way, devoid of sympathy or respect. The death of a miner was of little importance to them, as long as work was not interrupted. The value of an old man's life could not compete with a possible reduction in the tonnage of coal extracted.

Sarah's gaze dipped to her father's face, no longer rosy and smiling. His temperament had always been so warm and friendly. All who knew him considered him a loyal, decent man. She felt proud that she was his daughter.

George had always been hard-working, firstly in local quarries, then in nearby mines. He had met and married Sarah's mother, Annie, when they were both twenty, both smitten with each other. Sons and daughters had been hoped for, but nature had other ideas. Finally, their prayers were answered when Sarah was born, the image of Annie. They were so thankful for their only child, and felt very close bonds.

As she'd grown up, Sarah worked in service at a Conisbrough farmhouse where she'd met Albert, a farm labourer there. The attraction between them was instant, and George and Annie were delighted when the couple married. Albert was the youngest of ten children, so his family life had been very different to Sarah's.

Children came along quickly: four girls, then a boy, much to the pleasure of Annie and George, who doted on their grandchildren. Both George and Albert had worked at Kilnhurst pit and Warren Vale pit in Swinton, pleased to earn better money than at their previous jobs, though not always as consistent.

Sarah and Albert had moved into a newly built house in Denaby after Denaby Main pit opened, while George and Annie continued living in Mexborough. Both miners were pleased to have work closer to home; work was hard enough without a long walk to and from it. Everything had changed when Annie died suddenly and unexpectedly.

It happened one Sunday afternoon when she and George were walking towards the River Don, intending to cross on the ferry to Denaby. They were looking forward to visiting Sarah, Albert and the children. Annie had just called out to the ferryman to bring his boat over, when she collapsed. George could not believe what had happened and what he saw, but there she lay on the riverbank, gone. His beautiful, beloved Annie, gone.

The inquest was later held at the George and Dragon public house in Mexborough. The coroner stated a verdict of 'Death in a fit of apoplexy'. Some kind gentleman explained that it was a bleed on the brain, symptom of a stroke. All George knew was that the sun had left his world.

He had moved into his daughter's home almost immediately, not minding that he had to squeeze into the already full household. The children were delighted to have Grandad George living with them.

Sarah looked on, hoping she could help her grieving father. He hid his emotions well, but she could see the difference in him since her mother's death. She worried that at his age, sixty, the strain and dangers of pit life would become too much. He'd had several accidents in the past, some at the quarry, some at the pit, all of which had affected his hands. But he laughed off her concerns.

'There's work left in me yet,' he would say.

Work will fill the loneliness in me, he would think.

* * *

A steady stream of people had visited Sarah and Albert to pay their respects over George's death. Deaths due to accidents and disease were commonplace there, but fear and sorrow were always keenly felt. People knew the possibility, if not probability, of similar situations lurking around their whole community. It could affect any of them at any time.

Mary and her brother and sisters felt the oppression of gloom and sadness that shrouded their lives at that time. They missed their Grandma and Grandad. Childhood innocence and naivety were crumbling away, leaving scars of harsh reality and developing disillusion. They craved happiness and laughter – and their Grandma Annie and Grandad George.

Two of the visiting miners, Fred and Harry, had expressed condolences to Sarah, then silently beckoned to Albert for a quiet word. He listened in silence as they related the facts of George's "accident", guessing the outcome even before they had finished.

'We were just walking to our work district underground. George was chatting away as usual when he pulled up sharp, moaned and fell to t' ground,' Fred explained, turning his cap round and round in his hands, as though propelled by the anguish in his words.

'He died there and then, right in front of us,' Harry pronounced. 'Must 'ave been a heart attack,' he added, sadly.

Albert stared at them, understanding slowly unfolding. George's body was broken and mutilated – no heart attack did that. Fred and Harry nodded, answering the unspoken question in Albert's eyes.

'He was already gone. Nothing could be done, but we're his mates, so we did what we 'ad to do,' Harry continued in a measured tone of voice.

Albert nodded agreement and understanding. 'Don't tell Sarah,' he warned.

The two men nodded briefly to each other; no other words were necessary. As Albert watched their retreating backs, he pictured what had happened.

No compensation was ever given if a miner died of natural causes in the workplace, in fact, bosses were reluctant to give any compensation, even for accidents.

Lately, a compromise had been decided between workers and bosses, that if work was not interrupted by a death occurring, some form of compensation would be given. Whatever money was collected by miners for the bereaved family, the Company would match it, meagre though the final amount usually was.

The custom of stopping work out of respect for the dead had to be abandoned. But other measures had been adopted by the men. A miner dead due to natural causes might well suffer a different "death" in order to gain some kind of compensation for the family. This was usually by organising a "fall of coal", made to look like an accident.

Miners did this brutal action out of duty and respect to fellow workers and their families, harsh though it was. Albert vowed that Sarah would be spared this knowledge; she was wounded enough. He shook his head, unable or unwilling to accept the gulf between gaffers and workers, between rich and poor.

Mary's painful memory of finding Grandad's body dumped on the doorstep would remain with her always, but so would her love for him.

Chapter 2
Early 1880s

Bridie Flannagan was Mary Cooper's long-time friend as well as neighbour. They had grown up together in Denaby, playing in the "backs", going to school, giggling and sharing secrets.

They could be mistaken for sisters, both having thick, chestnut-gold hair, grey eyes and luminous, freckled skin. Their families endured similar lives, but they were essentially from different backgrounds.

Mary's family, the Coopers, was one of Denaby's oldest. They had lived and worked in the village when it was a rural hamlet, with only a few hundred residents. It was surrounded by fields and woods, nestling in the Don Valley with the Crags looming above. Life was slow and agricultural, but all that changed when coal was found.

John Buckingham Pope and George Pearson rented land in Denaby from the affluent Fullerton family in 1863. They were hoping to sink a shaft, the furthest east in the Yorkshire coalfield and the deepest, trying to reach the rich seam of high-quality Barnsley bed coal. Poor quality coal had earlier been mined near the surface, but the new, successful sinking struck "black gold", and a new era of growth and prosperity began.

The Denaby Main Company began producing coal in 1867, providing work for hundreds at the Denaby Main pit. Mary's father and grandfather were two of the few local miners there at that time; the rest were recruited from far afield: Cheshire, Derbyshire, Scotland and Ireland.

The Company had found the pit's ideal location. The South Yorkshire Railway ran along its south side, and just to the north ran the River Don and the South Yorkshire navigation canal. The getting of coal soon flourished.

One of the Irish immigrant families was the Flannagans. Originally from County Galway, the effects of the earlier potato famine had eventually persuaded them to emigrate, first to Liverpool, where Willie Flannagan met his future wife, Hannah, then on to South Yorkshire with the opening of Denaby pit.

Many new houses were being built for the new workforce and the Coopers and the Flannagans moved into two of the first ones built on Doncaster Road, only yards from the pit and adjacent railway. They were tied houses, built and owned by the Company, so the miners were liable to eviction at the whim of their landlords, who were also their bosses.

Rent was stopped from the miners' wages as insurance of payment, but conditions were bad. There was no gas, no water and no proper kitchens, together with overcrowding and poor sanitation. The houses were literally thrown up in haste, with little care or thought. Yet, the lure of a new house and a job was great.

Mary was fascinated by her friend's family. She loved their loud, lilting voices, so unfamiliar in tone to her own broad, guttural Yorkshire accent. A constant stream of words filled the house, as well as the many inhabitants – three adults, six children and even a lodger.

'Sure, we could do with the extra rent,' Hannah, Bridie's mother, stated casually.

The house strained at the seams, but Mary liked the stories of Irish folklore that they told. They whisked her fanciful imagination into thoughts of imaginary people and places. She liked their playful teasing and quizzical protestations that left her wondering if they were telling truths or just "kidding" her. Laughter and jollity jostled alongside brawn and brashness, making hardships somehow easier to bear.

Her own family was, by contrast, more serious and realistic in tone. Unnecessary words were unspoken, as if conserving energy. Overt expressions of feelings or ideas were not encouraged, preferring to concentrate on long-held accepted notions of behaviour. Their house, too, was overcrowded, but that was the norm. Everyone was the same, just like the houses. One key could fit nearly all the houses, but that was accepted.

Thus, a close bond was established between the two little girls, cemented by shared secret hopes and longings, whispered to protect themselves from outside mocking.

Mary would often remember, in later life, the hook at the bottom of the stairs in Bridie's house.

'That's where naughty children are hung until they can behave,' Willie Flannagan told Mary in a low whisper, eyes twinkling.

It was a long time after that when the impressionable Mary found out it was for hanging a dead pig on.

Chapter 3
1882

Sarah banked up the roaring fire with yet more cobbles; she needed the room to be hot. Mary and her sisters, Gertie and Ivy, watched a haze of steam and smelled the caustic lye rise from the wet clothes draped around the room.

'Washday Mondays!' sighed Sarah. 'Roll on spring and summer when we can dry the washing outside!' she added with heartfelt longing.

'At least you'll have more room with us out at school,' Mary replied.

Her father, Albert, was on the morning shift, and her eldest sister, Betty, was already at work at Kilner's glass works. Bob, their two-year-old brother was playing on the hearth rug. The girls wrapped their shawls around their heads and bodies, in preparation for their journey to school. They were not really sorry to leave the suffusing humidity and pungent aroma of the room.

'Are you sure you'll be warm enough?' Sarah called to her daughters. 'You can take my shawl if you want.'

'We'll be all right, Mam, we'll run to get warm,' the girls chorused, waving goodbye.

The freezing air made them gasp as they walked along the back of the row of houses. Bridie and her brothers were waiting for them, stamping their feet and puffing out icy breaths.

Sooty clouds of steam hung above the children as they walked the short distance from homes to school. The disappearing steam locomotive momentarily blurred their vision. The imposing headgear of Denaby pit soon reappeared, looming over their school, a small building situated alongside the pit and the railway.

The girls chatted as they crossed the lines and Dermot, Michael and Martin, Bridie's younger brothers, followed behind. The chilly air stabbed through their clothes. The Flannagan children had paper wrapped against their skin for extra insulation, but Mary and her sisters refused to crackle and rustle as they moved, so they felt the cold.

'Where's your Paddy?' Mary asked Bridie about her eldest brother.

'Oh, he's waiting for his turn for the boots,' Bridie explained. 'He'll help Mammy in the house then do some errands. He never was one for school, says it's a waste of time when he could be working,' she laughed.

'Well, he's only got another year to wait, he'll soon be thirteen,' Mary replied.

She loved school, even though it was difficult to hear and concentrate with all the commotion of chugging trains and pit noises so close by. She liked how her mind could explore other pathways at school. Looking at maps of strange lands, the dreaming up of stories, the writing about Kings and Queens, all these breathed new life into her narrow world of poverty and hardships.

The school children varied in age and size, but shared the common knowledge of harsh times, especially if there were lay-offs or strikes at the colliery. They were dressed and shod as well as their families could afford. Threadbare clothes, patched beyond recognition of the original garment, were commonplace, even bare feet in the most deprived of families. Jacket sleeves were completely shiny from being wiped around sweaty faces and runny noses.

Most children suffered the same poverty and hardships, so deprivation was not highlighted so starkly. It was all the children knew. Occasionally, incidents occurred which demonstrated humiliating aspects of poverty. Mary remembered a recent event at school.

Walter Smith, a small, shy boy, had been sent to school wearing a home-made pair of trousers, hastily stitched by his busy mother. Unfortunately, as the day progressed, the stitches loosened until the trousers became a skirt.

Mary felt genuine pity for him as he was mocked and teased by some giggling classmates. Walter fought back angry tears at his predicament, and was greatly relieved when his friend, Jim Walker, had stepped in, to quietly but firmly, defend him and halt the teasing. A close friendship was forged that day between the two boys. Mary also realised her growing admiration for Jim.

Chapter 4
Early 1880s

Mary had always felt that Jim was different to the other boys that she knew. From being at school together as young children, she gradually grew to recognise that he had a curious blend of strength of character, with a sensitive vulnerability that was foreign to the other rough and tumble boys. His manner was positive but gentle, his speech minimal but of substance. He was a child with an increased maturity and sensitivity that Mary could readily identify with and admire. In short, he was a kindred spirit.

Jim was acutely aware of his difference to other children. They all had mothers and a conventional place within the family, which he did not. Despite all the hardships and conflict that overcrowding could bring, he longed to belong to a normal family. He was, however, intolerant of anyone's probing or questioning about his parents, becoming fiercely dismissive of any special attention or treatment doled out to him.

His pride forbade any overt show of sympathy or taunting from his peers, although some rough boys would frequently attempt to, especially Tommy Prince, the bully.

Mary felt Jim's unease and saw his quickened reactions when anyone alluded to his different family life. In later years, she realised her love for him had been born and developed from their early school years.

* * *

Jim couldn't really remember his mother, even though he often tried. He had vague memories of folding chubby fingers onto long skirts, being held against a warm, cushioned chest, wrapped around with a shawl and receiving kisses from soft, plump lips. But all that had stopped when his mother, Catherine, left him and his father, Richard.

His parents had moved to Denaby in 1871, the year that he was born. The promise of a new house and a job at Denaby pit had resulted in them leaving Derbyshire where they had lived with Catherine's parents. Dick had little experience of mining, having previously been an agricultural worker, but his humble manner and willingness to work hard to support his family soon taught him to learn the ropes. Many men had similarly relocated, tempted by regular work and money, but Dick had another reason for moving to Denaby. His sister, Hilda, had married a Denaby man, and lived in the village.

Jim was born a few months after moving, in a new house only yards away from the pit and the railway. Noise, soot and steam had invaded Catherine's life, as well as a new baby. Increasing unrest and hatred of her new environment overwhelmed her, causing bitter arguments. Within two years, she had left, returning to Derbyshire to live with her family. She left her husband and young son.

'Why did Mam leave us?' Jim asked his father when he was old enough to feel the sting of abandonment and rejection.

'She could never settle, lad,' was the slow, sombre reply.

'Won't she ever come back to us?'

His father's face had crumpled, then he turned away. Jim never did get an answer.

Chapter 5
Early 1880s

Life was difficult for Dick and Jim. On a practical level, it was nigh on impossible to manage a job, a house and a baby without a woman. Dick had to work, so Jim and the house had to take second place. Although Dick was a loving man, he felt the stigma of rejection. It eroded his confidence, replacing it with a sad resignation to a solitary life. He did not want another woman.

Jim's Aunt Hilda became his replacement mother. She was a strong woman with a bubbly laugh and welcoming nature. Jim led a split life; a quiet, almost solitary life with his father, and a cosier time with Aunt Hilda and Uncle Edmund. They shared their love with their own children, but always having some left over for Jim. Yet he always felt on the outside looking in.

In later life, he could be reduced to tears when thinking about Hilda, with her wiry, curly hair, smooth white skin and crinkly laughing eyes, such was his love and gratitude towards her. Uncle Edmund looked on, quietly supportive and encouraging.

This strange upbringing shaped Jim's nature in both good and bad ways. He was introvert, content with his own company, even withdrawn at times. His father cared for him physically as best he could, but the constant sadness in him was almost a barrier between them. It was understood that they shared a limited relationship, not wanting to overstep each other's boundaries of affection.

Self-sufficiency became second nature to Jim, however. He could make and mend fires, cook simple meals and tidy up in a fashion. He developed a great love of roaming the surrounding woods and fields, considering nature his companion. Whittling and carving wood became a hobby, a passion.

Uncle Edmund had given him an old pen knife and shown him how to fashion wood into objects: a catapult, a sword, even a handled walking stick. His hands enabled him to express his feelings as no words could.

The one pastime Jim shared with his father was poaching: rabbits, hares, game birds, anything that could be eaten. Dick had been taught the skills by his own father in the Derbyshire valley where they lived. Although Dick had become a man of few words, the knowledge he passed on to Jim was both an emotional bond as well as a practical one in times of food shortages.

The frequent strikes and cutbacks at work necessitated all manner of means to gain essential food. It was no surprise that hungry miners increased the number of poaching offences dramatically during long strike periods. There was never-ending conflict between the workers and the bosses. But most miners saw it as fair game, saying:

'The landowners rob us of fair wages in return for the wealth we've given them from coal, so we're only taking what's owed us. The land belongs to us all, rich or poor, hungry or full.'

Dick and Jim justified their method of survival in times of great need.

'They'll not miss a rabbit or two,' was their shared opinion.

Chapter 6
July 1884

Jim and Walter's footsteps fell in with the rhythmic clomping of boots on cobbles made by the stream of miners heading to work. It was a summer's morning; the boys' first day working at Denaby pit. The sun was almost breaking through the blanket of smog that hung above the village, courtesy of hundreds of smoking fires and belching chimneys. Both Jim and Walter had reached their thirteenth birthdays the previous week, and their first day down the mine had arrived.

Although both boys were secretly nervous, even afraid, of coping with their new jobs, neither would admit it. Older miners did not openly discuss the severe nature of the work, preferring the young lads to become enlightened through experience rather than hearsay. Jim's fingers eased the thin muffler scarf around his neck, and he felt the tension of the string tied at the bottom of his trousers. His rough, woollen jacket and open-necked vest already felt scratchy, prickling his skin with a film of sweat.

Walter was similarly dressed, both wearing flat caps and carrying snap tins. Walter's mother, Peggy, and Jim's Aunt Hilda had seen them off, despite the early hour. The women showed proud smiles and almost shy admiration for the boys' newfound status as workers and earners.

The lads cast sidelong glances at the other men, who were greeting each other with the familiar 'How do?' but saying little else as minds and bodies were roused into action. Walter was reminded of the old superstition that his grandad frequently related. If a miner saw a woman on the way to work it was a bad omen, and some would return home, refusing to work.

'Many's the time money was lost and wives would go mad at their men for this waste, but no matter,' Grandad explained. 'I'll have a day of sun and sky instead, they would say.'

'A day laiking, more like,' their grumbling wives muttered under their breaths.

Nearing the pit, some men darted into the nearby field, each having a particular spot to leave some items. Tobacco, pipes and matches were stashed into crevices and crannies until they could be retrieved later.

Jim and Walter reached the pit and, with fast-beating hearts, embarked on a day that would be forever imprinted in their memories, an assault on their senses.

Blackened, weary faces of the night-shift workers briefly acknowledged the waiting miners with nods and 'Ay-ups'.

The cage rose and fell with a clanging of bells, a clanking of metal and a whooshing of wind. Out spilled groups of departing miners, in shuffled the new shift, lamps in hands. Comments were directed to the new boys by a few of the men.

'Na then, lads, don't be missing yer mams.'

'No roarin' in t' dark.'

The boys felt the sudden drop as they stood in the cage. Hearts leapt, stomachs dropped, whistling rang in their ears. Then, strangely, partway down, was the sensation of the cage rising rather than descending further, a common experience as they later found out.

The cage juddered to a halt. The doors cranked open, revealing an unexpected large space, busy with people ready to head off to their work districts.

Jim's recollections of that first day, from then on, blurred into a kaleidoscope of emotions and sensations. Later, his memories fragmented into splintering highlights – darkness, dirt, dust, dread. The exhausting shovelling of dust into tubs and the stumbling on the uneven ground were compounded by the feeling of never-ending blackness. Creaking supporting timbers strained to preserve the space for life to move and breathe. The feeling of being in the very bowels of the earth, alone at times, was overwhelming.

Even more frightening, was the dawning realisation that this was repeated day after day by men in order to provide food and lodgings for their families. This would be their lot, too.

Few words were spoken as the boys walked home, each trying to compute their thoughts and feelings. They felt a mixture of relief that the first day was over, and pride that they were now earners. They had left their homes as boys and returned as young men. Jim even thought he detected a new look in his father's eyes. He hoped it was pride and respect.

Chapter 7
Spring 1886

The girl strained and panted. Stifled screams expanded in her throat and widened her eyes. Searing pains scored her body. In the dim, dusty gloom of the cellar, bloodied water burst from between her quivering legs, splashing the earth where she knelt.

The heavy load pushed relentlessly until it left her body, ripping and tearing flesh. Her dirty hand dabbed at the soft skin, slippery and finely downed, almost luminous in the shadows of the crumbling stone walls.

A thin, complaining wail pierced the silence, but overwhelming fatigue engulfed the shocked girl. She lay still, uncaring, lethargic. Cold and damp clung to her, but she felt nothing. Her eyelids drooped, a deep sigh spilled from her dry mouth. More feeble cries punctuated the chilled air, eventually rousing her into action. She knew what she must do.

Stiff fingers reached the hem of her skirt, pulling, until a strip of ragged cloth detached itself. Calmly winding it around her baby's neck, looking to one side, gentle pressure was applied, enough to carry out her wish. The strange, muffled whimpers – from both her and her baby – gradually subsided, until silence once more.

A few teardrops fell upon the lifeless body, making his skin glisten as it grew cold and stiff.

Chapter 8
Spring 1886

Mary reluctantly left school when she was nearly fourteen. She had loved the new school recently built in Rossington Street; it was so much cleaner and quieter than the old school that was so close to the pit and railway. The children had flourished in their new surroundings.

She still yearned for further education, for the expansion of her mind and her love of learning. Yet that world was literally a closed book to young girls and boys of her status. Ambitions of the mind had no place in the harsh reality of coping with immediate, practical duties. Even within herself, she felt a dichotomy, in some ways still naïve and child-like, yet in most other ways, a strong, maturing young woman.

Her older sisters, Betty, Gertie and Ivy, had all left school at thirteen, so in some respects she felt grateful for the extra year. They had quickly gained jobs at Kilner's Providence Glass Works, situated on the border of Denaby and Conisbrough.

Their wages provided some security and insurance for the family, especially when their father, Albert, was on short time or on strike at the pit. Sarah regarded Mary as a great help in the family home, as well as looking after six-year-old brother Bob.

'Our Mary's such a good lass,' praised Sarah. 'I don't know what I'd do without her.'

* * *

Mary shrieked gleefully as she rolled down the sloping grassy banks in the grounds of Conisbrough Castle. Faster and faster, blue sky flashing, warm sun beating, breath mingling with saliva, as the feeling of space and freedom bathed her soul.

Precious time away from never-ending chores allowed her to luxuriate in the thick, warm grass. Spring had been a long time arriving after a dismal, dreary winter. It now truly felt like new beginnings with warmth, light and the rebirth of nature. Squinting up at the frothy white clouds, her contentment was punctuated by a long, nearby wail.

'Bloody hell! I've landed in a pile of nettles!' screeched her friend, Bridie.

'Get some dock leaves, then,' Mary laughed. 'You'll survive.'

The girls had slowly adjusted to the fact that they were no longer schoolchildren. Both shared the feeling that the future was obscure and indistinct beyond the ritual of daily chores. But their adolescent emotions were arousing optimism for thrills, excitement, even passion.

Bridie led a similar life to Mary. She too was expected to take on strenuous household duties, as well as child minding. Her house was so full that her mother, Hannah said:

'It's a good job the middle boys are on nightshift, or I don't know where we'd all sleep.'

Beds were in constant use, rotating weary bodies. Space was continually sought, as was the stale air circulating, such was the proximity of human flesh and breath.

Bridie had confided in Mary that she disliked these conditions more and more as she got older, resenting the prospect of probably never having any future improvements in life. Mary was worried by her friend's increasing disillusion, even though she understood her despondency.

Still, today they were enjoying the freedom of laughing and joking, like little girls again. Chattering, they linked arms and ran down to the Castle gates, then onto the roadside leading from Conisbrough to Denaby.

'Let's cut down Burcroft Hill and go down to the river,' suggested Bridie. 'It's ages since I was down there.'

They sauntered to the bottom of Burcroft, a small hamlet, passing by Booth's Sickle Works, a long-established business.

'Ted and Will got taken on as apprentices here.' Mary talked about their old school friends. 'They say they like it here, and it's not bad pay.'

'Well, if you can sit down to work at a grinding wheel, I reckon that's better than killing yourself down the pit!' declared Bridie.

'I wouldn't want to pull a snake out of a sack of wood, though,' shuddered Mary. 'That's what Ted did the other day.'

'As long as it's dead!' Bridie retorted.

The old brick walls bordering the Sickle Works provided welcome shade from the unexpected heat of the sun. A fresh, stirring breeze signalled that the River Don was not far away, although its smell wasn't welcome.

The remains of an old derelict stone cottage came into view as the girls rounded the corner onto the lane approaching the river. The building was roofless, with exposed rooms and no door. Its forlorn appearance seemed incongruous in the warm, peaceful atmosphere.

'Wonder who used to live here,' mused Bridie. 'It's all so old and ramshackle.'

'No idea,' Mary replied. 'But it feels cold and creepy even in this weather.'

Propelled by curiosity, Bridie stepped into one of the shadowy rooms. Her eyes adjusted to the murky gloom, finally distinguishing an old set pot in one corner. She turned to leave when something caught her eye. There was an old sack to one side of the metal cauldron, partly concealed by a clump of withered, dried grasses.

She stepped closer. The sack was open, with a strip of cloth protruding at one side. Mary watched as Bridie bent over, peering intently into the sack. Her sudden shriek resulted in a startled jump by Mary.

'There's something inside – it looks like…like a baby!' cried Bridie.

Shocked, they both stepped back, unsure of what to do.

'Is it alive?' whispered Mary.

'I don't know, you look,' Bridie answered.

Mary carefully opened the sack wider, her heart thumping. Her sad expression informed Bridie. The baby lay still and stiff, eyes closed as if sleeping. Smears of dried blood mottled and contrasted with the blueish tinge on his skin. The fuzz of reddish down outlined the shape of his head. The tiny fingers were spread wide, as if reaching out.

The strip of calico was wound around his neck, the knotted end covered his mouth. Mary shook her head slowly, unable to believe what they were seeing. Bridie stared, all the colour gone from her face. Shock rendered her speechless.

* * *

Mexborough and Swinton Times, 28th April 1886

Shocking revelations were made at an inquest held at The Station Hotel, Conisbrough, relative to the death of an unknown male child, whose body was found in a sack at a disused building in Burcroft, Conisbrough.

In connection with the affair, a fifteen-year-old girl is in custody charged with 'wilful murder' and at the inquest, the coroner (Mr W. Scott) committed her for trial at Leeds Assizes, and, at the express wish of the jury, severely censored the girl's mother and sister, who according to the evidence, made no preparation for the girl.'

Mary read the local newspaper's report of the inquest, then closed her eyes. She had experienced repeated flashbacks of the recent events. Images and memories paraded like thunderbolts before her eyes: running up Burcroft Hill, informing the police, accompanying Sergeant Llewellyn to the derelict building where Bridie stood guard and explaining how they had found the body.

They had been questioned at length and required to give statements, then told to attend the inquest to give evidence to the coroner and jury. All these things had been upsetting and stressful.

They found out that the police had arrested a girl not long after the discovery of the baby's body, and word soon spread about her identity. Her name was Edith Parks and she was only fifteen years old, not much older than themselves. She lived down Burcroft, not far from the derelict cottage and close to the Sickle Works. Will and Ted, the new apprentices, soon informed Mary and Bridie about these facts, as another worker there, Jacob, a grinder and polisher, knew the girl and her family. It wasn't until the inquest, however, that the full distressing facts were revealed.

Sergeant Llewellyn gave evidence that, after the discovery of the body, he had made enquiries at nearby houses. One of the houses, an old stone cottage, was the home of Mrs Elizabeth Parks, a widow, as well as her fifteen-year-old daughter Edith Parks, and another daughter, Minnie Hill, her husband Fred Hill and five children.

When questioned about the dead baby and its mother, Edith Parks had stated she would only tell the truth if her mother was not hurt. She then admitted that she had given birth in her mother's cellar, then had put the baby in a sack with the cloth wound round its neck. She had taken the sack to the derelict cottage nearby.

'I only did it for my mother's sake, to save trouble,' she repeated.

The Sergeant had identified that the strip of calico in the sack was the same cloth as her skirt.

Mary and Bridie gave evidence how they had found the baby's body, stating that they had only looked around the derelict building purely out of curiosity; they had never expected to find anything.

Edith said she had "been with" Fred Hill, her sister's husband. Mrs Parks stated that she knew Edith was "in trouble" but had not accused Fred Hill when Edith told her about him. Instead, she had told Minnie, his wife, who confronted him. He denied it, and so nothing else was said.

Neither Edith's mother, nor Edith's sister discussed the baby again. They maintained that they did not know that Edith had given birth, saying they presumed she had miscarried. They denied knowing anything about the dead baby or the sack.

The medical evidence was provided by Dr Forster. He had made a post-mortem examination of the body and found it to be that of a fully developed male child, weighing 6lb 10oz. The face was congested and there were two compressed marks round the neck as if something had been tied round it. The lungs suggested that they had actively respired. A valve in the heart was closed, indicating that the child lived up to birth. In his opinion, the child lived and breathed and had a separate existence. There was no natural cause to account for death, and in his opinion, death was due to strangulation.

The coroner summed up by saying there was conclusive evidence, and he addressed the jury to find a verdict of wilful murder against a child of fifteen years. He stated it was a pathetic case, particularly from the fact that the mother and sister, who should have looked after her, seemed to have done everything they could to conceal the fact, although they knew of her condition and what must have taken place.

He also stated that a certain punishment could not be passed upon her due to the Children's Act. She would, if the Assizes held the same opinion as them, be sent to a home where she would get helpful assistance and become a respectable member of society.

It was not their business to enquire into whether Fred Hill was the father of the child, but they knew that the mother, who had given birth to twelve children, and the sister, with five children of her own, made no preparedness for the girl's confinement.

The jury returned a verdict of wilful murder against Edith Parks but were also unanimously of the opinion that the mother, Mrs Elizabeth Parks, and the sister, Mrs Minnie Hill, should be severely censored. Addressing the girl, the coroner said:

'You will take your trial at Leeds Assizes. You are only a child and must be judged as a child.'

* * *

Mary and Bridie listened to the verdict. They both felt a mixture of emotions. Mary had some sympathy for Edith Parks, as did Bridie, but they both felt they would never forget the horror of finding a dead baby. Bridie would have many nightmares about seeing his poor, still body.

Chapter 9
1888

Jim matured quickly after starting work, both physically and mentally. Shoulders broadened, sinewy arms strengthened, he even had the makings of a moustache. Time was regarded as 'above' and 'below' ground. His craving for light and open air resulted in him wandering the surrounding countryside in all weathers. Subtle changes of seasons were keenly noted. New buds of foliage, the first buzz of a bee or the ripening of berries were happily acknowledged.

He looked for suitable pieces of wood to whittle and carve, spending long winters' nights shaping and coaxing them into objects of pride. His thickset, calloused hands, clumsy and awkward performing some finer tasks, transformed into dexterous, productive tools when handling wood. Its touch was solid, comforting, its smell sweet and natural.

To his surprise, he developed a love of cricket. The Company had built and formed a cricket club in the village, and Jim's natural solitary state of mind emerged into an enjoyment of being a team member. The thwack of leather on willow, the sting of catching a flying ball, all done on springy green grass beneath sky and sun, recharged his soul and spirit, depleted by exhausting subterranean work.

Walter had also developed after starting work, although in a different way. His once rather slight schoolboy frame suddenly burgeoned into a compact, sturdy body of a young man.

He laboured long and hard underground, at first struggling to adapt to the relentless conditions. But the more his body succeeded in carrying out the strenuous tasks, the more his confidence and self-worth grew. It was as if his muscles were straining to display their growing might, so boxing was a natural progression to allow this avenue of ambition.

Bare-knuckle fighting was a rough, rugged sport which fed his desire for combat and competition. Within his own large, rather dysfunctional family, he had felt almost anonymous as a child, just another mouth to feed. Walter felt the need to stand out, to be an individual now.

Boxing granted him occasions to prove the strength of both his body and personality; it fed his ego, even though cuts and bruises were often his souvenirs. Most of all, it gave him a newfound status within his peer group. Boys who had previously taunted his weaknesses were now silenced, confronted by an assured, almost aggressive person who could defend himself.

He was victorious in a series of local fights, tackling older or much heavier opponents at times, such was the lack of rules and regulations. The pinnacle of his boxing achievement was his fight with Tommy Prince, the brash bully from his school days, who had often targeted Walter for unkind teasing and taunting, as well as thumps and rough pushes.

The fight was on the Crags where crowds of people gathered, eager to shout and bay their clamouring for serious fisticuffs. Walter was the underdog, not expected to beat the gifted, brawny Tommy who was older, taller and stronger, a stalwart boxer of the area. But Tommy had underestimated Walter, overconfident that his own reputation would be enough for victory.

They each came up to the scratch in the ground and adopted the fighting stance. At first, Walter failed to make his mark, literally, on Tommy, instead receiving plenty of cuffs and punches that sucked the wind out of his body. But the more he received, the more he was determined to succeed, drawing on hitherto unknown reserves.

'Go on Walt, give him one!'

'Get stuck in, lads!'

'Wallop him, Tommy!'

'Don't give up, Walt!' were cries from the excited crowd. Walter was in such a dazed state, after many lengthy bouts, that at first, he didn't realise that he had thrown the winning punch. Tommy had wheezed and gasped, and had failed to come up to the scratch. Loud cheering rang in Walter's ears as his own body buckled.

The children who had been standing guard in the distance also cheered. They had no further need to watch out for the police. The illicit gambling on the match was over.

Jim watched all this with a mixture of excitement for his friend, but also a feeling of unrest. Walter had changed so much recently, hopefully for the better in future, but doubts niggled in Jim's mind, not to say what the reaction of Tommy Prince would be after being defeated and humiliated.

* * *

Tommy Prince did not like losing. His life, so far, had been largely lacking in setbacks. As an only child, his natural expectations had always been that he should gain anything he wanted, attain success at everything, and disappointment or defeat should not be tolerated.

His father's position, as a senior deputy at Denaby Main Colliery, further reinforced his feelings of superiority. His parents did nothing to curb his assumptions, preferring to boost his ego. Their pride in him overlooked any unpleasant attributes of his character. Thus, arrogance was allowed to dominate; he thought he could do no wrong, and he expected others to agree.

His recent defeat in the boxing match with Walter Smith had both surprised and angered him, so unaccustomed was he to being beaten, both literally and figuratively. His black eyes, cuts and bruises were fading but his injured pride and resentment at losing were quietly smouldering and festering, resulting in irrational, inflated thoughts of revenge on Walter. He would bide his time, but he would make sure he was the winner next time, in whatever competition came his way.

PART TWO

Chapter 10
Easter 1889

Crowds of people strolled along Doncaster Road, heading for The Station Hotel at Conisbrough. Some were local Conisbrough and Denaby families; some had walked longer distances from nearby villages including Swinton, Mexborough, Cadeby and Edlington. A few had even arrived by train from Sheffield and Doncaster, Conisbrough railway station being conveniently situated close to The Station Hotel. The good weather and the fact that it was Easter combined to create a mood of high spirits and pleasurable anticipation.

It was Good Friday, one of the two days each year that Ticklecock Fair was traditionally held in Conisbrough. Year by year, it had grown so much in size and popularity that it had recently been moved from the Castle grounds to the areas of land surrounding The Station Hotel, where it was larger and flatter, better able to accommodate the attractions.

People welcomed the change of routine at Easter, a brief occasion for enjoyment rather than work. Excited children dashed from stalls to sideshows, eyes shining, hoping to coax a few extra pennies from unusually relaxed parents. Older children, on the cusp of adulthood, revelled in the opportunity to see and meet new people. Coy smiles and sidelong glances were frequently exchanged, daring and thrilling.

Mary was there with her sister Gertie, Bridie and three of Walter's sisters, Ellen, Beatie and Ada. They chatted excitedly, caught up in the holiday atmosphere. Even Bridie seemed in better spirits, which pleased everyone.

As they wandered around the different areas of the fair, Mary heard, then saw Tommy Prince just ahead, standing with a group of his cronies. As usual, he was the loudest and most vociferous, staring at the passing girls, exchanging cheeky comments that flew in the air, back and forth.

Mary was just about to move away when Tommy spotted her. She knew he would stare, lips parting to reveal a wide grin; he always did that.

'They undress you with their eyes,' the girls would say about such forward boys, and Tommy knew no bounds. He felt his usual basic arousal when he looked at Mary. Her thick, golden hair, grey-green flecked eyes and glowing complexion belied her unhealthy environment. Her upright stance and elegant stride belied her age. She seemed at once girlish, but mature for a sixteen-year-old. He, at eighteen, felt just right for her.

'Having a nice time, girls? My, you do all look pretty. Fairs must suit you, they do us, don't they, boys?' he quipped. 'You'll not mind if we walk with you,' he stated rather than asked. He advanced towards Mary, a leer rather than a smile on his face.

As he pressed his body closer to hers, she caught the smell of beer on his breath, and realised that alcohol was making him even more brazen than usual. She glanced around uncomfortably, embarrassed by his uninhibited behaviour.

'Come on, Mary, let's take a walk together. Let me make this a day you'll remember!' he drawled, grabbing her arm. She pushed him away, causing him to sway and stumble. His pals laughed and cheered at this, inciting Tommy to save face by grasping her hand roughly and smearing his lips onto her face.

'Just a kiss, then,' he laughed.

'Leave me alone!' she shouted. 'I don't want your kisses and I don't want you! Find some other girl. Mind you, you should sober up first!'

'Aye, he'll have his brewer's droop, right enough!' guffawed Eli Shaw, one of his mates. He, too, was obviously inebriated. The coarse comment shocked the girls, but more howls of laughter erupted from the men, this time annoying Tommy rather than amusing him. He lunged at Eli. The two tussled, arms flailing, dust flying, until they were separated by the other men.

The girls watched all this with a mixture of unease and intrigued attention. Mary's competent handling of the situation drew their admiration, enjoying the way Tommy was rebuffed.

Ellen, however, looked on, experiencing other emotions. Despite his bad reputation, she had always been very attracted to Tommy. To her mind, his bold, forthright confidence was a positive feature; it excited her, not to mention his dark, handsome looks. She had often allowed her imagination to meander to possible future scenarios with him, though she knew this was probably wishful thinking. She didn't feel special enough for him, but she wished she was.

Chapter 11
April 1889

Ellen's thoughts tumbled and churned. The more she tried to blank her memories of what had happened, the greater her fixation. She shook her head as if to physically clear her mind, but the events would not be shifted. They bore through, taunting and tormenting, refusing to be dismissed. That day replayed itself over and over.

Ellen and her younger sisters Beatie, Ada and Alice had worked hard to complete the chores that their mother expected them to do. They wanted to go for a walk and a picnic.

The unseasonably good weather had continued after Easter, so even though Ticklecock Fair had moved on, the mood of the people remained lifted. Smoke and smog still hung in the air, there was no change there, but warmth and hazy sunshine promoted a feeling of wellbeing. It made the many outside jobs that were necessary a little more bearable to accomplish, a blessing for the harassed women and girls involved in them, day in day out.

Hours were spent queuing and fetching water. There were only two taps in Denaby, one at either end of the village, and these had to serve the hundreds of houses newly built for the miners by the Company. Water was, therefore, precious, although not always clean and pure.

No wonder the pitmen chose to drink so much beer; it was cleaner and safer to drink than water, less inclined to cause upset stomachs and infection. Few miners could afford the time off work.

The girls had brought the water earlier that morning, joining in the conversation with the other women.

'It's a nice day for queuing,' the women agreed.

'But I wish they'd hurry up,' one old lady grumbled. 'I've still got washing to do.'

'You can hang it out in the "backs" this weather,' Ellen replied.

'Aye, it's a mercy not to have to block out the fire with all the wet washing. It's bad enough without all the steam and fusty smells,' agreed another young woman.

Toilet facilities and coal houses were all outside, as well as yards for children to play in, so the fine weather aided spirits as well as aching muscles.

'Just think if we had running water in the houses,' one woman mused.

'You'll have a long wait, love!' retorted the old lady.

* * *

'Are we all ready?' Ellen asked her sisters.

'I've made the egg sandwiches,' Ada replied.

'And I've got the cold tea,' added Beatie.

'I'll take a cloth to sit on,' Alice decided.

'Good, I'm looking forward to a bit of peace and quiet,' their mother interrupted.

The menfolk were either at work or sleeping. She could have a bit of time to herself, Lord knows that didn't happen very often.

The girls walked down their street onto Doncaster Road, passing the Co-op. It had been built as a Company store but had recently become part of the Co-operative Wholesale Society.

'Everyone says it's really good having a Co-op,' Ada said.

'I know, it's got a grocery department and a beer-off,' agreed Beatie.

'Mam says it's even got a Post Office now!' Alice added.

Ellen laughed. 'One day you might have a savings book if you save up your pennies.' Alice smiled in agreement.

Just ahead, across the road, loomed the headgear of Denaby Main pit and the railway lines. They had all attended the first school there, except for young Alice, but they were thankful for the newer school in Rossington Street. Ada was due to leave the school in a few months, and Beatie had one more year.

As they approached the pub opposite the pit, The Reresby Arms, a few men were leaving, passing comments to each other, wiping drops of frothy beer from their moustaches with the backs of their hands. They were still in their pit clothes, obviously slaking their thirsts as soon as their day shift had been finished.

This was the only pub in the village, although there were rumours that a new one was going to be built by the Company. The Reresby Arms, or "The Pig", as it was affectionately known, was one of the few buildings in Denaby not owned and run by the Company.

Mr Lowe, the landlord, was standing outside, watching the group of raucous men shouting parting comments and other more blasphemous remarks. For once, he had emptied his house without complaints and trouble from drunken customers. The next opening session might prove more difficult if experience was anything to go by. Night-time drinking seemed more intense compared to the afternoons.

He stood beneath the pub's sign that displayed the Reresby coat of Arms, depicting a boar. No wonder the pub had "The Pig" as its nickname. He wiped his hands down the apron that descended past his knees. Time for a cup of tea and a snooze, he decided to himself.

The girls were turning onto Denaby Lane when one of the men called to them. Ellen turned when she heard her name, then realised it was Tommy Prince. She stopped, shocked that he had spoken to her. He approached the sisters, smiling, his eyes playful and welcoming. His rugged good looks stunned Ellen. She felt herself blush, overcome by a sudden shyness. She was almost breathless.

'Hello, girls,' he greeted them. 'I thought it was you, Ellen.' He spoke in an almost confidential whisper.

The sound of his voice speaking her name made her even more flustered and faltering.

'We're just going for a walk and a picnic to Vinah's pond,' she blurted out, then wished she hadn't. She sounded like a silly schoolgirl, even to her own ears. Tommy's dark eyes lit up, dwelled on her face, then lowered to her body. She was a well-developed girl, with an hour-glass figure more usual in a mature woman. This close, almost intimate scrutiny resulted in a deep spreading blush on her face and neck. Yet, secretly, she was thrilled.

Tommy chuckled, his ego flattered. He recognised all the signs and reasons for her embarrassment. He also recognised that she was Walter Smith's sister. An idea clicked in his mind.

'I was just fancying a stroll myself. Mind if I join you?'

Ellen's brain instantly registered a divided response. Yes and no sprang to her lips, but her sisters' shy looks, and her own disbelief that he could actually want to share their company, resulted in a blurted:

'Yeah, if you want.'

Ellen's mind was racing, her thoughts dancing, as she walked in their little group, self-conscious and incredulous that he was interested in being with her. Her sisters threw her frequent glances, unsure of the situation. They knew all about Tommy Prince.

A short walk along Denaby Lane brought them to Vinah's pond, a local beauty spot popular with residents from both old and new Denaby. It had been created forty years earlier when the railway company isolated a bend in the river Don during the building of the South Yorkshire railway.

The old, established oak and elm trees that skirted the pond produced a calm, secluded atmosphere. The surrounding meadows were green and peaceful, ancient and rural compared to the sprawling, industrialised rigidity of the Company village. It was an oasis.

Tommy chatted, confident and almost charming in his manner. He was so nice to them that Ellen's sisters queried the reasons for his bad reputation.

The picnic had been eaten and drunk resting on the thick grass, gazing at the glinting surface of the water. Ducks darted amongst the rushes that outlined the pond, a pair of buzzards exchanged their plaintive calls, high in the sky, gliding and soaring, outstretched wings barely moving. A kestrel hovered in the distance, waiting to dive for its prey.

Ellen felt almost detached from her surroundings though, such was the impact of being so close to Tommy. She scanned his face, although work-stained, noting the wave in his dark brown hair, the masculine heavy eyebrows, his full mouth, the way he licked his lips. She still felt rather plain and gauche, but never before had she experienced feelings of such magnetic attraction.

'It's time to go home now,' Ada stated, breaking into her reflections. 'Are you coming?'

Ellen hesitated, reluctant to end this dream-like afternoon. She glanced towards Tommy, he settled his gaze on her, grinning. 'Why don't you girls go on ahead, we'll follow you in a minute,' he suggested.

It was their turn to hesitate this time, but they stood slowly, gathered their few belongings, and looked for Ellen's reaction.

'Yes, you make a start, we'll follow on soon,' she murmured. 'It still seems too nice to go home yet...' her words faded away. Her sisters nodded, said their farewells and began walking back.

It felt strange to be alone with Tommy. Ellen fell silent, her mind suddenly bereft of casual conversation. Tommy stood up, offered his hand to her, and smiled.

'Come on, let's walk a bit further round the pond.'

Ellen took his hand and stood up, enjoying the sensation of his touch. They strolled, hand in hand. The young woman thought she had never been happier than at that moment. Her dreams had become reality. She could not believe it.

They reached a copse with dappled shade. Overhanging branches displayed their developing buds of foliage. Clumps of daffodils decorated the ground here and there. All was quiet.

Tommy stopped and gently leaned her against the trunk of a sturdy oak tree. His eyes fixed on hers, he pressed his body on hers.

He felt the swell of her feminine figure, shapely and curvaceous, through her cotton blouse. His basic male instincts were aroused.

Ellen lifted her face to his, smiling, closing her eyes, wanting her sense of touch to be intensified and defined. She felt his fingers tracking the contours of her face, then her neck. His brief kiss, barely more than a brush of lips, she found exquisite. She pressed her body against his, hardly aware of the movement. Tommy's reaction was immediate; he was enjoying the arousal he was experiencing.

He pushed Ellen to the ground, her long skirt gathered upwards. Tommy's hands continued searching, pulling and pushing at undergarments, probing for that special place, secret and seductive. His actions became rougher, alarming Ellen, jolting her into stark reality.

'Tommy, no, you're hurting me!' she managed to cry. But he didn't listen, he didn't speak, he didn't stop.

'No, stop, stop!' she screamed, panic stifling her breath.

One final tug at her underwear revealed the part he desired. He stared at her nakedness, dazing him momentarily. His eyes never wavered as he untied his belt and dropped his dirty, work-stained trousers.

His strong arms pinned her to the ground. He lowered his body onto hers. She felt his weight and began to struggle, squirming, pushing and groaning with the effort of resisting. Heavy breathing mixed with rhythmic panting. His weight suffocated her senses, her undulations intensified his excitement. Her resistance suited his love of competition; he liked a fight.

Ellen cried out in pain as he penetrated her body. With swift, rapid movements, his breathing intensifying with every thrust, he continued until he reached his desired climax. He groaned with pleasure; she cried with pain.

* * *

She lay still long after he had left her. Shock, dismay and humiliation rendered her immobile. He had looked down at her, aloof but smirking.

'Let's keep this our secret,' he warned, his tone threatening, yet persuasive. 'I think that would be best for everyone. You wouldn't want anyone to know what you've been up to.'

He strode away, whistling, jaunty, pleased with himself. It pleased him to think he was the winner this time. He had found a way to inflict revenge on Walter Smith, even though he wouldn't know.

Ellen said nothing, but she saw the coldness in his eyes and the callousness of his smile. She understood now, all right, why he was not liked, why his reputation was so bad. But she could not understand why he had treated her like this, or what she had done to deserve such treatment.

How could she have been attracted to him? Could she ever trust her judgement again?

* * *

She arrived home, trying her very best to act as if it was just a normal day. She wanted it all to remain a secret; her shame and guilt required that. She also feared the consequences if her father or brothers found out what he had done to her. But she hadn't realised that her suffering was not over.

Chapter 12
August 1889

Sweat glistened in the folds of her skin and trickled down her flushed cheeks, yet Ellen shivered and shook as if cold and chilled. She lay on a bed sheet, already damp and fetid, writhing periodically in unison with the stabbing pains.

Fear gripped her, realising she could do nothing but try to tolerate the agony. She was frightened, as was her mother, Peggy, who leaned over the terrified girl, trying to smile reassuringly, but only achieving anxious looks.

Peggy had given birth to seven children, each time painfully but with no serious complications. She felt a certain pride in her own strength and achievement, especially as her husband, Alf, gave little support to her or the children.

Alf worked as a miner but did not consider any further assistance his responsibility. That was women's work. Beer, baccy and a little gambling suited him. Peggy had been forced to bear the heavy burden of responsibility for everything. She now had to watch her daughter's suffering.

Ellen had been adamant that she did not want to keep the baby. She had revealed enough to convince her mother that it would affect the whole family, and for the worse. She begged her mother to help her get rid of it, and eventually Peggy agreed, but with mixed feelings. Ellen was little more than a child herself, but she knew the trouble that would erupt if she went on to have the baby, given the circumstances. Better if it was kept a secret.

At first, mother and daughter had tried traditional methods of terminating the pregnancy. Ellen had been subjected to lifting and heaving weighty items, doing copious vigorous movements and downing plenty of neat gin. All of these had been difficult to carry out in secret, not wanting anyone else to know Ellen's condition.

But all of them had failed. Time was causing increased urgency, as the pregnancy was still at an early stage, but progressing. They knew they would have to seek the help of Nellie MacArthur, the local abortionist, as well as midwife.

Nellie used the front room in her house to perform her "procedures". Living only a few streets away, Ellen and Peggy had slid into her house in darkness, allowing Nellie to take charge. She had done this many times before, sometimes successfully.

The aged Scottish woman was brusque in her speech and mannerisms, but her practical, unemotional attitude bolstered their acceptance of the situation. She had a reputation for liking her drink, as the glaze in her eyes and the bloom on her cheeks confirmed, but she got things done. They would have to settle for that.

Ellen screamed a primeval howl as the knitting needle was inserted, overwhelmed by intense fear and pain. Her senses had clouded, thankfully numbing her agony momentarily. Waves of shock radiated throughout her body, spiking and perforating her consciousness. The penetration felt like contamination, alien and foreign within her being.

Afterwards, she had been helped to stand, Nellie issuing practical instructions for future necessary actions. Poor Ellen had been so dazed, she heard little of all that. It was all she could do to remain conscious and standing, such was the trauma experienced. She just prayed that the outcome would justify the suffering.

Back home, Ellen writhed with fever for two whole days and nights. The rest of the family believed it to be caused by an infection, probably dirty water, so common were the symptoms.

Ellen flailed and thrashed, grasping her mother intermittently for comfort. Peggy stared in anguish at the distressing state of her daughter, guilt and regret combining with anger and resentment that such drastic action had been necessary.

In the outside privy, Ellen deposited the remains of her pregnancy into the ashpit, shovelling cinders over it to conceal the gruesome sight. She felt relief but also bitter resentment. How could she have been so stupid? She no longer felt like a child, but a violated woman.

Chapter 13
August 1889

Bob felt the sun warming his face, the breeze licking his hair. How he loved being outside, away from the cloying presence of too many people squeezed into too little space. His sister, Mary, had agreed that he could take his new puppy, Rex, for a walk. She trusted the nine-year-old to be sensible.

He breathed in deeply, trying to cleanse and ease his tight chest. His mother worried about his wheezing and coughing, always wanting to slather goose-grease poultices on his chest. She and his sisters worked tirelessly to subdue the dust and moist, stale air that shrouded every part of their house. It was a losing battle, considering the poor quality of floors, and walls that fought to gape, uncomfortable on their cinder, shingle foundations.

Bob felt the sting of being different, small for his age, often sickly, but his spirit was strong and robust, to the point of recklessness and stubbornness, as though compensating for attributes of himself he could not change.

His natural affinities were with nature and animals rather than people. His sisters often teased him about the birthmark on his leg, a group of raised, brown freckles in the shape of a donkey. He secretly hoped that one day, when inevitably he worked down the pit, that he could handle the pit ponies. He'd like that.

School summer holidays stretched ahead; excited anticipation bubbled inside him. He broke into a run, his puppy responding likewise. Rippling tall grasses waved by; the trees' foliage blurring into a green flash. They slowed down, panting and gasping. The next deep breath wasn't so pleasant as the putrid stench from the nearby River Don invaded his nostrils. Rex tugged at the rope that tethered him to Bob, eager to investigate the mysterious water.

'No, no, boy, you can't go in there, that'd be the death of you!'

Children were warned never to play in the dirty, stagnant water. Even in its industrial environment of choking smoke and polluted air, the river was taboo. Smells and odours invaded all aspects of Denaby life, hardly surprising with the open middens filled with every kind of waste.

Bob's lips twitched with amusement as he recalled the recent morning inspection by Miss Jackson, their teacher. The children had stood in a line as she walked up and down, slowly and majestically, peering at each child with a stern but caring eye. Her lofty figure had halted and leaned over Billy Evans, her nose slowly descending towards his slicked down hair.

'What's that smell, what's on your hair?' she asked abruptly.

'Lard miss,' was Billy's prompt reply. 'Mi mam says it's only way to stick it down,' much to the mirth of his classmates. Miss Jackson again paused as she reached Bob in the line. This time she retreated rather than advanced towards the odour.

'Goose-grease, Miss, for mi poultice,' Bob explained before being asked. 'Only thing that helps mi chest, mi mam says.'

Even the sober features of Miss Jackson settled into an amused but understanding acceptance.

Loud, jibing voices travelled in the air, interrupting Bob's thoughts and spoiling the blackbirds' cheerful songs. He recognised the group of older youths, idly tossing stones into the river, dispersing the green film momentarily. Bob's reaction was to retreat and avoid them, especially as Tommy Prince and Eli Shaw were amongst them. Too late: Rex had sniffed their scents and yapped playfully.

'Well, if it in't Bob Cooper, Mary's little brother!' guffawed Tommy. He remembered how Mary had rejected him at the fair, how she had made it clear she wanted nothing to do with him. She'd shown him up in front of his friends. Tommy had seen her from time to time, but he was always ignored. Irritation bubbled up inside him. He wanted to hurt her now.

Bob turned away, silently striding, but Tommy was enjoying taunting and goading.

'That's a nice puppy. Let's have a good look at this dog of yours,' quipped Tommy. 'Looks to me like he's wantin' a dip – dogs like water.'

Bob spun round, alarm flashing in his eyes, just the desired response that produced a satisfied smirk across Tommy's face.

'Nah then, pup, fancy a bath?' laughed Tommy, scratching behind the dog's ears.

'Leave him alone!' cried Bob, yanking at the makeshift lead.

'But he's hot, he wants to cool down,' joined in Eli.

The other youths jeered and suddenly pounced on Bob, wrestling the rope from his hand. The frightened animal yelped and whimpered as it was tugged away roughly by Tommy, down the slope of the riverbank. Bob strained and struggled through the melee of arms and legs that pinned him down. He heard a gentle thud and saw Rex thrashing in the contaminated water.

'No, no!' shrieked Bob, but no mercy was shown.

'He wants to join him, lads!' roared Tommy.

Bob's flailing arms and legs could not stop them. He was manhandled down the bank and shoved forcibly into the deep, murky water of the Don.

Gurgling, cold darkness washed around him. Panic pressed into his throat, constricting his breathing even more. He was sinking, he couldn't swim. Stinging pressure squeezed at his lungs; his ears pounded. Then the thrashing of limbs started, writhing and clawing.

The urgency to breathe penetrated his terror, but there was almost a resigned acceptance that he could do nothing to save himself. His mind flashed to sun-drenched grass and warm earth; his body was relaxing into a soporific dream world of welcoming tranquillity.

Suddenly, shimmering light and fierce tugging pierced his senses. His weakening body was miraculously being lifted, his craving lungs snatching air, starting the coughing and spluttering. Vile-tasting water spilled from his mouth and nose. The lifting sensation continued until he realised that someone was helping him out of the water. A voice stated:

'Let's get you out before you bloody drown yourself.' Bob's stinging eyes squinted to focus on the face near him. It was Jim Walker, Mary's friend.

'Yon buggers have scarpered,' Jim nodded towards the disappearing group of laughing youths.

'Say hello to Mary for me!' jeered Tommy, waving goodbye.

'That Tommy Prince is a nasty piece of work,' Jim muttered. He looked at Bob, gently pushing plastered hair from the boy's face. 'Are you all rate? What happened?'

'Rex, Rex, where is he?' wailed Bob, still unable to stand.

Jim quickly reacted. 'Wait here, get your breath back.'

Rex was found only a hundred yards away. He was still attached to his rope-lead which had wrapped itself tightly around a wooden prop jutting from the water. Rex's still body rested gently on matted debris that clung to the prop. Nothing moved, everything was stagnant. Bile rose in Jim's throat, produced by bitterness, not the river. He despaired of such a cruel, callous action.

Looking up, he saw Bob staring at the awful sight of his precious puppy now still, dead. As they walked home, sorrow, defiance and bitterness flicked through Bob's mind in swift succession. Jim followed the young lad, carrying the sagging body of Rex with a protective gentleness.

Chapter 14
August 1889

Mary winced as she knelt on sore knees. Clouds of dust stung her eyes and clogged her throat. Four bucketfuls had been swept from their small backyard, another bucketful had swirled beneath the door, depositing a clinging layer inside. It was a thankless job, but only one of the many she had to do.

Since leaving school three years earlier, she had taken on more and more of the housework. Her mother, Sarah, had never fully recovered from a still-born pregnancy: twins, two years ago, when she had been close to death. Her once fresh complexion had greyed to almost the colour of her hair. Her energy had deserted her. She reminded Mary of a fading flower, the vibrancy of the bloom paling and drying to a delicate crispness. She was forty-one years old.

Mary had assumed the heavier domestic work, labour-intensive, repetitive, essential. With no running water and the unhealthy environment, everything was laborious, grinding, exhausting. Sarah's 'I'll just sit down for two minutes,' had become her recognition, though not admission, of failing health.

Albert, Mary's father, was hardworking, but all miners lacked the security of regular wages. They were at the mercy of the Company's managers. Thankfully, Mary's older sisters were all working, contributing much-needed financial assistance. Betty now worked at Denaby Co-op, Gertie was still a factory worker at Kilner's Providence works and Ivy had just started at the newly opened Powder Works. She was getting used to the teasing when she returned home about the dust that covered her skin and clothing. Bob, now a sensible nine-year-old, needed less of Mary's attention, giving her more time for all the chores.

It was while wiping down dusty surfaces in the scullery and living room that Mary and Sarah heard crying outside. The back door opened, and Mary smelled Bob before she saw him, the stench even competing with the reeking middens. His tears fell onto his slime-stained clothes. His matted hair was spiked with grass stalks.

'What on Earth?' Sarah breathed, with gaping eyes as another figure emerged.

It was Jim, none too sweet-smelling himself, his face sombre. He was holding Rex, the puppy that Bob had always wanted. The little boy rushed to his mother and sister, attempting to relate the awful event in anguished, blurted words. He could not be comforted, but gradually he quietened to rhythmic sobs. He told them what had happened.

That night, Mary thought back to Jim's part in the incident. The look in his eyes, especially when stating Tommy Prince's involvement, was something she recognised and understood.

The conflict between Jim and Tommy was long-standing, from childhood through to recent events. Tommy was a troublemaker and caused even more upset when crossed.

Mary knew he had regarded her in an amorous way. Tommy's eyes gleamed and his mouth danced when he spoke to her, confidence making him blunt and personal. She knew many girls found him attractive, but not her. His arrogant, callous attitude chafed her sensitive, caring nature.

'Prince by name and Prince by nature,' he would boast. She could never like him, but she worried she could be to blame for the day's events. Tommy Prince harboured grudges, and got revenge one way or another.

Sarah had nagged Albert as soon as he returned from work.

'It's not right that our Bob's bullied, he could have drowned! He's heartbroken over that puppy, too. Get your coat on and go round to sort it out with that Prince lad,' she grumbled.

Albert refused. He felt Sarah over-protected Bob. 'The lad's got to fight his own battles and toughen up or he'll get picked on even more,' he reasoned.

The real reason for his reluctance to tackle the Prince family was left unspoken. Tommy's father was a senior deputy at the pit, a status which afforded him considerable power and influence. He was an awkward man, direct but temperamental. If he took a dislike to someone, he bore a grudge. That could impact on work opportunities as he had the authority to decide and allocate work to miners he preferred.

Albert was annoyed with his own subservience, but times were hard. He would have to swallow his pride.

'I'll go round myself then,' Sarah retaliated, exasperated, and still worried about the effects on Bob's health.

Only Mary's protestations that more harm than good would be done, and Albert's stern look, stopped her.

Chapter 15
August 1889

Bob could not face burying Rex; he was still so shocked and saddened to lose his beloved pet. He had begged his parents for a puppy, and even though it meant another mouth to feed, they had reluctantly agreed. Bob bestowed all the love and loyalty within himself onto the animal, feeling true friendship towards the puppy, empathising with its needs and weaknesses.

Mary gently stroked Bob's hunched shoulders.

'Jim says he'll go with me to bury Rex. Is that alright? How about Bluebell Woods?'

Bob had nodded, looking up to give her a weak smile. His brimming eyes brought a lump to her throat.

The sun, a glowing orange sphere, was close to dipping beneath the horizon, but the warmth of the day still lingered, caressing the evening air. Jim had just shovelled the soil back into place. They looked down at the small mound of earth within the shade of a glorious oak tree, in full summer foliage. Neither knew what to say next; both felt jumbled emotions.

'Thanks, Jim,' Mary whispered. 'Thanks for everything you've done, helping Bob, maybe even saving his life, and now for doing this.'

Jim nodded awkwardly, a flush spreading across his cheeks. Mary was close enough to see damp wisps of dark hair clinging to his glistening forehead, his dark lashes, thick and curved. She turned to look at a clump of wildflowers almost hidden in the tall grass.

'I'll just pick a few flowers to take back,' she murmured.

Jim watched the curve of her back, the squareness of her shoulders as she stooped to pick a selection of poppies, moon daisies and rosebay willow herb.

'You like flowers, too, then', Jim stated rather than asked.

'They brighten up the place.' She smiled ruefully. 'Though they don't last long.'

The terraced houses in Denaby had been built so densely packed that no space had been allocated for gardens or trees. No grass or flowers softened the regimented lines of houses. Brick, dust, earth and cinders spread and sprawled to create barren, harsh surroundings for the miners and their families. No thought had been given by the Company bosses to the aesthetic requirements of the homes. Surely, brick boxes with windows and doors would suffice?

'At least it's a splash of colour,' Mary smiled.

'Nobody should have to live like we do!' Jim surprised her with the sudden passionate tone of his voice. 'Why can't we have gardens and trees, beauty and nature? Why should we have darkness down the pit and drabness up above?'

Mary moved closer to study his expression. 'That's just what I think,' she breathed.

Jim gently touched the flowers she was holding. Mary felt his hand brush hers. The sensation was branded in her memory. The scent of the blooms mingled with his earthy, masculine odour as he lowered his head to tenderly place his lips on hers. Their first kiss. Mary felt the rush of love for him that was to remain always. Jim knew she was the only woman he would ever want.

Chapter 16
September 1889

Mary's workload felt lightened by the joyous feelings of love and happiness that coursed through her. Fire grates were emptied, floors swept, and clothes washed and dried, almost without conscious effort. Her thoughts bubbled, her heart raced, she had limitless energy. Plans and dreams of what might be jostled with her need to concentrate on reality and jobs to be done. Her sisters teased her, her parents watched her. Bob openly stated his feelings,

'I like Jim and I'm glad you're courting!'

Reaching into her apron pocket, Mary brought out a small wooden object and studied it intently. Her forefinger traced the perimeter of the heart-shaped base, then lifted to feel the raised shapes of opened, slightly curling petals. It was a beautifully carved wooden rose. Jim had made it for her. The memory of how he gave it to her was imprinted on her mind in vivid detail.

A few weeks after that first kiss, it was her seventeenth birthday. They had gone for a walk along Denaby Lane into the older, rural village of Denaby. It was an Indian summer, a warm September evening, ideal for a stroll. Mary had escaped domestic duties for once, and luckily Jim was on morning shifts. She felt proud and happy to be walking by his side.

They turned off the lane down into fields where clumps of scarlet poppies peeped from ripened corn stalks. Jim had picked a stalk with its feathery head and tickled her nose with it. Their laughter mingled with the tuneful singing of darting birds. They zig-zagged to a bordering copse, edged by an old stone wall. Rosebay willowherb flowers stood tall, their wispy, white trailing heads heralding the approaching autumn.

'Happy Birthday, Mary,' Jim murmured, cupping her tiny hands in his. 'I've made this for you.'

She watched him reach into his jacket pocket and take out a small wooden object, which he handed to her.

'This flower will never die – it'll last a lifetime.'

They had not planned what followed. To Mary, that moment had encapsulated pure joy in her life. The warm stillness and musky smell of nature enveloped them. The feel of moist lips and murmuring breath – all these overwhelmed any reserve or conscious decision. Their love was the essence of their lives, something new and wonderful. They both abandoned themselves to it.

Chapter 17
1889

Mary's sister, Betty, married at the age of twenty-three, just as she was giving up hope of finding a "suitable" man. As the first-born child in the family, she had always assumed an air of superiority, even within their humble conditions and surroundings. She had an expectation of being first with everything, and a reluctance to do the messier jobs in life.

Even Sarah and Albert regarded her differently to their other children, although perhaps not consciously. Thus, she was referred to as 'our posh Betty', though not to her face.

Betty lived in the same poor environment, but her perceived higher status produced subtle differences. She was the first to wear a new dress or pair of boots; she was always on 'first sitting' for meals, seated in the good chair when her father was not there. First, also, to have 'pressing jobs' to do when dishes needed washing or floors required sweeping.

By comparison, Mary, as the youngest girl, was the last to acquire things, even expected to have reduced aspirations. She was just 'our Mary'.

From this was born her love of daydreaming. She could quickly and easily slip into wishful thoughts of warmth, comfort and time for consideration of life's nicer aspects beyond the menial and starkly basic. This escapism aided her quiet acceptance of her status within the family.

Despite all this, Mary loved her family and worked hard for them. She respected Betty's aspirational hopes for a better future as well as her desire to 'better oneself in life'.

This wish had been greatly enhanced when Betty started work at the Co-op. She revelled in the delights of bagging flour, packeting tea and patting butter into neatly wrapped blocks. Such a job provided her with a feeling of almost innate power and control. It nurtured her self-esteem beautifully. Albert and Sarah looked on proudly.

The pinnacle of Betty's delight was in the meeting, and subsequent courting, with Arthur. He was a miner, but not from Denaby or its nearby villages. He was an Elsecar lad, who worked at Earl Fitzwilliam's pit, and lived in a pit house built by the Fitzwilliam estate. Denaby folk had heard about the better working and housing conditions provided by Wentworth's Earl Fitzwilliam, even though the jobs were essentially the same.

To Betty's mind, Arthur represented her saviour, viewing him as being on a higher social level than the local men she knew. The thought of possibly living in Elsecar, with Arthur as her husband, satisfied her longing to rise in the world.

Arthur was a quiet, practical man who liked peace and harmony, an ordered life. His parents had recently died, only weeks apart, both succumbing to influenza. As it was not the Fitzwilliam estate's policy to evict miners, he was able to stay in the family home, unlike in Denaby where no such sympathetic treatment was afforded to bereaved relatives by the Company bosses.

Arthur felt it was the perfect time to start a new life with Betty; they complemented each other perfectly in their aspirations for a better standard of life, even though Betty had to leave her beloved job at the Co-op.

Betty moved to Elsecar after the wedding, delighted to have such a prestigious home. Mary and her sisters, Gertie and Ivy, visited Betty's home, producing a mixture of wistful envy and sincere shock due to how different the Elsecar pit houses were compared to theirs.

The short rows of stone houses were fronted by small gardens, neatly walled from the road, each with its own gate. The paving stones and colourful flowers immediately made the girls realise why Betty had a seemingly permanently close-lipped, upturned grin. Hers was a proper home.

'Of course, we have our own ashpit and back garden,' she would frequently remind people. 'And even a pig sty!' she usually added gleefully.

'Oh aye, so's we, but our pig sty's on the inside!' scoffed Gertie under her breath.

The proper conveniences attached to every six houses were kept perfectly clean, with doors that locked.

'Not so much need to have a good singing voice while you use them then, like us,' whispered Ivy.

How they would love not to have the rank smells and constant flies and dust that their middens produced. The extra rent for that – and a garden – would be gladly paid.

Inside was just as desirable. The four rooms and pantry were neat and clean. No damp crept up the walls, no cockroaches scurried when disturbed by light.

The range gleamed from the black leading that Arthur performed weekly, he considered it a man's job to get it black bright. The clean floors and open windows felt strange to the sisters, no dust flying under doors, no flies and stench through the open windows. The kitchen even had a space for cooking and washing utensils to be neatly arranged. Heads were shaken in disbelief and longing for such an ordered existence. Mary's mouth suppressed a giggle as she recalled Betty's words when she recently visited the family home in Denaby.

'I always say if your hearth and sink are tidy, then your house is, too,' Betty had confidently pronounced.

Sarah and her children's gazes had swept around their crowded, cramped mess, inwardly cringing. But posh Betty was too lost in her own joy and contentment to notice the resigned looks of her family.

PART THREE

Chapter 18
January 1890

Mary was in denial. It couldn't be. She felt her thickening waist and rounding stomach. Maybe it was a bit more "puppy fat". But she had counted the number of missed months of being "unwell", as her mother called it, and she had counted four. Even though pregnancy was not discussed openly, births and deaths were common events in the community, even in their own homes. Accidents and diseases abounded.

Houses were too small and money too lacking to afford discreet privacy at such momentous times. Children were quickly exposed to the sounds and "messiness" of childbirth, hearing the wailings of labour and the sight of bloodied bedding. Death was likewise clearly overt, bodies and coffins evident in homes, awaiting funerals.

Mary's early childhood memory of the first dead person she could remember seeing was still clear in her mind. She had been 'calling' for her friend, Bridie. She had stepped into the living room of the Flannagans' house, but was unprepared for the sight of the coffin propped up against a wall, squeezed into the only available space in the room.

In it lay Bridie's grandmother, Maria. Mary's snatched gaze at the dead face both surprised and revulsed her. The mouth was slightly open, as if in suspended surprise, the flesh of the cheeks had fallen sideways, producing sharp angles previously absent in life. A shadow of pain still lingered around the face, visible even in the murky light of the blinded room. Mary had shuddered and run outside into the warm light, into the land of the living.

Mary's thoughts now returned to her predicament. She had managed to cover up any suspicious signs of her condition so far, wearing a folded pinny over her stomach and tucking a shawl into the waistband of her skirt. Her frequent bouts of vomiting were, so far, undetected in the cinder piles outside.

However, she imagined she saw a new expression on her mother's face from time to time, a narrowing of her staring eyes, which tracked Mary's movements and actions with a deeper scrutiny. Other members of the family seemed too preoccupied to notice subtle changes in her, but she felt a heavy weight of impending doom, an inevitability of the future conflict around the corner. Her father's probable reaction struck terror into her.

She sighed deeply, in turmoil. She loved Jim; she knew he was the man that she wanted above any other, but she regretted the implications that her condition would enforce on their lives.

If truth be known, she felt regret that circumstances would dictate their future paths in life. Would they have to abandon any thoughts of "bettering themselves"? Would their lives inevitably follow those of their struggling families? She had better relinquish any fanciful dreams and aspirations and resign herself to harsh reality. In other words, she had made her bed and now she must lie in it.

It was almost a relief when her mother finally confronted her. Mary was washing herself in the tiny scullery. Sarah walked in, unexpectedly, and immediately noted the bared, swollen breasts and the rise of her belly above the lowered skirt waistband. Their eyes locked for a moment before Mary hastily looked away, covering herself with a frayed square of towelling.

'I knew it!' declared Sarah. 'You've gone and got yourself into trouble! Oh, my God, how could you, Mary?'

There was no reply, Mary was struck dumb. Her lowered head and the droop of her shoulders told Sarah everything. They might be a poor, lowly family, with next to nothing, but there was still the intense shame attached to an unmarried seventeen-year-old girl being pregnant.

'I take it Jim is the father,' sighed Sarah.

'Of course it's Jim's, but he doesn't know yet.'

'Well, just you wait until your father tells him.'

Albert returned from his day shift at half-past two. As usual, he washed his hands and arms up to the rolled-up shirt sleeves above his elbows, then sat at the table to eat his meal. He still wore his blackened work clothes.

He preferred not to speak until he had eaten, as if realigning his mind and body from heat, cramped conditions and darkness, to the relative comfort of light and space. Hewing coal was back-breaking work.

Sarah would soon clean his scarred, dirt-engrained back with sweeping arcs, deft in their familiarity. Not all miners allowed this, believing that cleaning reduced strength, but Albert was not one of them.

Mary hovered outside in the cold, undecided in her actions, waiting for the trouble to start. She was glad her brother and sisters were not at home to witness the confrontation. Sarah would tell Albert calmly, as she knew all too well what his reaction would be.

He was a man of steady, almost ritualistic nature. Jobs had to be done in a certain way; mining had taught him that. Life had to be lived in a measured, calculated way; mining had also taught him that. It was as if a fuse was slowly, steadily smouldering, but every so often, it would ignite into frustrated temper and exasperated anger.

Being the youngest of ten children had taught him patience, but also an inclination to indignant, almost violent outbursts when his emotions were roused. Sarah had experienced that side of his nature many times. She knew he would be livid with Mary, and angry with Jim, but there would, later, also be sorrow and keenly felt disappointment for his daughter's situation. Sarah knew she had to steer him through this. Her body may be frail, but her mind was strong.

The raised voices heralded the news that Albert had been told. He came striding into the small backyard, oblivious of the bitter cold wind that scuttled up and down the middens. He stopped, inches away from his shivering daughter. She raised her eyes and focused on his grim, set mouth, his flushed, thread-veined cheeks and pale grey eyes, edged with long-accumulated coal dust.

'You fool, you bloody fool!' he spat out.

He lifted his rough, calloused hand. It hovered close to Mary's face. She burst into tears, fear and shame weakening her so greatly that she doubled over.

Sarah rushed between them, ashen faced. She steered Mary back into the house, throwing a beseeching look over her shoulder towards Albert.

He paced up and down, considering what to do. His mind made up, he strode purposefully onto the lane that led along the backs of the terraced houses. He wore no cap or coat, but he didn't feel the cold.

Within ten minutes, Albert returned. Jim was one step behind him, cap in hand, his demeanour sombre. They entered the house. Mary could hardly meet his gaze, but his look softened when he saw her worried expression. Sarah looked on, ready to step in if necessary. Albert's rage rekindled as he broke the poignant silence.

'Don't think you're going to wriggle out of this one, lad! You got her into this mess, now you can get her out of it!'

'I've got no intention of not taking responsibility,' Jim stated quietly, 'I love Mary. Of course I'll stand by her.'

'You better had, by God,' rasped Albert.

He threw his daughter a searing look, hunched into his work jacket and opened the door.

Sarah watched as he slammed the back door behind him, then glanced from Jim to Mary, sympathy replacing her initial anger.

'He'll calm down after he's had a few pints, but stay out of his way,' Sarah advised them both.

Outside, as Jim was leaving, he gathered Mary in his arms and murmured reassuring words.

'I love you, Mary. Don't worry. I want to take care of you and our baby. Why didn't you tell me?'

'I couldn't believe it myself, but I don't want you to think you're trapped. I know you wanted more out of life than working down the pit and living here. I've brought shame on the family too…' Her words trailed off, replaced by sobs.

'Shh, shh,' Jim soothed. 'I've never wanted anyone else. I'll never leave you. I don't mind where I work or where we live, as long as I'm with you.'

Mary smiled through her tears, hope and relief replacing trepidation when contemplating the future. She still dreaded the reaction of her sisters, though, especially posh Betty.

Chapter 19
June 1890

Mary eased herself slowly into a standing position, then raked the ashes vigorously, ready to bank up the fire with slack for the night. Her pregnancy was nearly at an end, and she longed to see their baby.

They had married as soon as it could be arranged, early in the new year. It was a quiet wedding, partly through lack of money, but mainly not to highlight their circumstances. Mary was grateful that her sisters and friends had received the news with quiet benevolence, although not without surprise and regret for her situation. Mary suspected that her mother's involvement had influenced their reactions.

'Families have to stick together through thick and thin,' was her mantra. 'And there's always plenty of that!'

Her father had calmed down enough to let her stay until the wedding, but hurt and disappointment still lingered. Bob was the only one openly delighted, naïve in his comprehension of events.

'Jim'll be like my brother, then!' he cheered.

Mary had worn a decent dress and hat for the wedding, kindly donated by Betty, who, almost unexpectedly, showed genuine kindness and sympathy towards her youngest sister.

'You'll look a picture in those,' she assured, gently squeezing Mary's shoulders, her smile reinforcing confirmation. Ivy and Gertie had clubbed together meagre savings to provide a pretty shawl, made by a friend, and a brand-new pair of shoes, something Mary could never remember having before.

Sarah had passed on her mother's wedding ring, often pawned in times of dire need. Mary had cried when she received her Grandma Annie's ring, as she knew how much it meant to her mother.

'It's your turn to look after it now, love,' she murmured, briskly patting Mary's hands to detract from her emotional state. Her daughter smiled a tearful thank you, choked by her own emotions, as well as relief at their kindness and understanding.

The newly married couple lived at Dick's house. This new arrangement felt strange to each of them. Mary found a house with only three people living in it very unusual, so used to having constant company.

She was still familiarising herself with being a married woman, and a soon-to-be mother. The changes in her life were significant, but her overwhelming love for Jim bathed her in a wonderful glow of contentment. The house certainly needed a good "fettling" though, so she was kept busy.

Jim was also adapting to these new circumstances. Mary's presence felt as though a shining warmth had pervaded the house. Although minimal and humble, it was now a home, filled with a homeliness previously lacking.

He felt that his life had new dimensions. Mary's love provided him with new-found ambitions, a sense that a massive void was now replete with contentment.

He remembered how beautiful Mary had looked on their wedding day. She had radiated love and happiness, as well as looking so pretty. He felt so proud to be marrying her. He was thankful, too, that Aunt Hilda and Uncle Edmund had provided him with a good suit and new shoes.

Dick had accepted Mary into his home and life in a benevolent, approving way. Having a woman in the house had initially awoken painful memories, but he liked this sensible, hardworking girl, although he never voiced his feelings.

He could see the love that the couple shared. Dick was so pleased for his son. He'd always had guilty feelings about how Jim's life had been affected by his lack of a mother, although he was eternally grateful to Hilda and Edmund for their love and support through the years. He even allowed himself feelings of excitement at the prospect of becoming a grandfather, rekindling long-lost emotions of tenderness and belonging.

The rattle of the back door broke into Mary's reverie. She turned, expecting to see Dick, back home from his afternoon shift. Instead, she saw Jim, cap in hand, hesitating.

'There's been an accident, a roof fall. Mi dad's been killed.'

He then broke down and sobbed in Mary's arms.

Jim was surprised how deeply his father's death affected him. He felt such a keen loss, even with all the comforting support from Mary. He realised just how deep the bonds between father and son had been, even though they had remained largely unexpressed.

The saddest thing was that Dick would never know his grandchild. At the age of forty-five, he had been active, hardworking, but unlucky. Accidents underground were frequent, especially falls of coal and stone.

All the coal was "got" by hand at Denaby pit; no machinery aided the getting of the precious commodity. It was hewn by miners with picks, shovels and hard labour. The very nature of the work was rife with danger. Jim had witnessed falls, and considered himself lucky to have escaped injury or death. Dick had not been so fortunate.

Jim had been walking towards the cage, ready to take his turn to descend for his night shift, when Jack, the overman, had called to him.

'Wait here, lad. I need to talk to you.'

Jim moved aside to allow the other men to line up, looking at Jack to try to glean any information from his expression.

'There's been an accident, a fall. Two men dead. I'm sorry, lad, but your dad's one of them.'

Jim felt as if he'd received a hammer blow. He sucked up a sudden intake of breath, staring at Jack's sober features.

'Oh, God,' Jim gasped. 'Who else?'

'Mick O'Leary,' Jack told him sadly.

'But he's so young!' Jim exclaimed.

'Aye, lad. Twenty-seven, married with three kids.'

'What happened?' Jim's voice was ragged.

'Dick was hewing a section, and a prop must have given way. A really heavy fall, stone as well as coal. Mick was filling. It must have been instant for them both.'

Jim had been taken to the colliery office. The bodies had been placed in a corner of the room, side by side. A sack cloth completely covered Mick's body, while just Dick's face was visible above a heavy blanket. Jim could only guess at the state of their injuries, so he nodded agreement when Jack warned him not to touch the coverings.

Dick's face was blackened and smeared but hardly bloodied. Jim gazed down, scrutinising his features. It was his father, yet his face already looked so different. Life had been literally drained from him, only the shell remained. Jim inwardly said silent goodbyes, gently touching the dust-streaked hair.

'You get off home, lad. We'll look after him till you can get him home tomorrow.'

Jim nodded. 'Thanks', he added, gruffly.

He was about to leave when wailing cries filled the air. He recognised Beth O'Leary, now widow of Mick, as she stepped into the room. Two women were either side, supporting her. They, too, were sobbing. Mick's wife, mother and sister were overcome with grief.

Jim was glad of the darkness as he walked home to Mary. It hid his falling tears.

* * *

The inquests into the deaths were held two days later in The Reresby Arms. The coroner recorded verdicts of *Accidental Death* rather than any hint of blame or neglect on the Company's part.

Jim looked at his weeping Aunt Hilda, arm in arm with Uncle Edmund. They had accompanied him to the inquests. They shared his grief, but they all had to be resigned to yet two more fatalities at the pit. Many more would inevitably follow.

More blood on the coal.

Chapter 20
June 1890

After Dick's death, Jim experienced a variety of emotions so intense and extreme, that he was left in a daze. Regret, anger, sadness, each took their turn to engulf him. This stirring of emotions unsettled his usual calm composure, leaving him feeling vulnerable rather than strong.

It pained Mary to see him so upset; she was melancholy too. She looked forward to the birth of their baby, to feel happiness and renewed hope and enthusiasm for the future.

* * *

The baby was born two days after Dick's funeral. Sarah and Ivy had been visiting Mary to help with chores. It was midsummer, the light nights providing a welcome, comforting ambience. The first, sudden spasms of pain surprised Mary, but she felt strong, capable. It was Sarah who was worried.

'I'll be fine, Mam,' Mary reassured her. 'Jim will be home in a few hours.'

'We're not leaving you on your own,' Sarah retorted. 'We'll get things ready for you.'

It was fortunate that they stayed as Mary's waters broke not long afterwards and the contractions quickly became more frequent. Her gasps and groans accelerated so rapidly that Sarah told Ivy to run round to Nellie MacArthur's to ask for help.

'I know she's probably had her fill of gin by now, but she's the nearest thing to a midwife we've got,' Sarah whispered to Ivy.

Nellie arrived fifteen minutes later. Her wiry, salt-and-pepper hair had started off as a bun earlier in the day, but was now like a halo around her freckled forehead and flushed cheeks. Few teeth had lasted her sixty-one years, but her tongue continually prodded lumps and bumps in her mouth, as if searching for them. Her

Scottish accent provided her with a loud, resounding voice which was both comforting and alarming.

'There, there. You'll be fine. You just save your strength for that baby,' Nellie ordered as Mary's shrieks escalated.

Though Nellie's actions could be almost rough, she emanated a stoical, practical control of the situation. Her love of gin blurred her dilemma of being the abortionist as well as the midwife in the village.

Water, rags and brown paper assembled, Mary abandoned herself to the contractions and Nellie's instructions. They both sweated and reddened as the evening progressed. Sarah and Ivy looked on, worried but excited.

Finally, one last push and one last scream resulted in the baby's birth. Mary lay still, exhausted but elated. The complaining cry of her daughter flooded her with relief. Jim would be so proud and relieved.

'Well done! You did it, good girl!' Nellie praised. Sarah and Ivy wept with joy.

'You're a grandma now,' Ivy whispered to her mum.

'And you're an auntie,' Sarah replied.

The women gazed at the newborn baby.

'Has she got a name?' Nellie boomed, wiping and washing where it was necessary at the same time.

Mary cradled the baby tenderly.

'Rose,' Mary whispered. 'We chose Rose.'

Jim returned home, excitement jostling with concern. Ivy had met him as he left the pit, eagerly informing him of the good news. They had practically run back to the house. Jim was suddenly overcome with emotion as he stood, panting, in the kitchen. Sarah smiled and gently steered him to the stairs.

'A daughter, Jim. She's beautiful. I'm so happy for you both,' and then Sarah's tears began to fall.

'I'm just being silly,' she said, embarrassed to show such emotion in front of Jim and Ivy.

Jim took her hand and squeezed it gently. He understood just how she was feeling.

'It's a special day for you,' he grinned. 'This is your first grandchild.'

Sarah smiled her appreciation; Ivy hugged her mother.

Jim slowly climbed the steep stairs to the bedroom, fearful of making a noise.

Mary lay with the baby in her arms, gazing in wonder at the tiny features, the lustrous skin, the wispy promise of dark hair, just like her father's. She sensed his presence and smiled her welcome.

'This is your daughter, Jim,' she whispered. 'Say hello to baby Rose.'

Jim stepped closer, his loving gaze moving from wife to daughter.

'She's beautiful,' he murmured. 'Just like her mother'. His look of pure love stayed with her always.

Chapter 21
September 1890

The three men walked, and occasionally stumbled along Doncaster Road, heading to The Pig at Denaby. Gossip and anecdotes, loud and often blasphemous, were exchanged as they left Mexborough behind. The lengthy, light nights of early September had enabled them to have a "good drink" in their favoured pubs, The Montagu Arms, The Bull's Head and The Ferryboat Inn.

Tommy Prince, Eli Shaw and Percy Naylor were all used to long "sessions". They worked hard as miners, played hard as drinkers and were well-known for their loud, brash behaviour. The local landlords knew their reputations, but they were good spenders, so were largely tolerated.

Jim and Walter crossed the road from the pit to The Pig, glad to have finished their afternoon shifts. Darkness was closing in.

'We'll just get a couple of pints in before closing time,' Jim said as he opened the pub door.

'Good, I'm parched,' Walter replied.

The taproom was busy, full of workers enjoying slaking their thirst before going home.

Amos Lowe greeted them. He was a popular, affable landlord, but he stood no nonsense. He knew how to run his business and handle awkward customers. He understood the temperaments of the local men, strong and hard, who sometimes allowed alcohol to affect their judgement and behaviour. Most of them could handle their drink, but some could not, and they often caused trouble. He pitied their wives, waiting for money already spent.

Jim had only recently started calling for a drink after work. Rose was three months old now, and Mary had persuaded Jim to enjoy a drink with Walter. She was fit and well now. He worked hard and deserved time to relax with friends. Jim was touched that Mary was so caring and understanding.

He and Walter were downing their second pint with relish when the door opened. Tommy swaggered in, followed by Percy and Eli, all obviously inebriated, but ready for more beer. Mr Lowe served them, looking from under his bushy eyebrows to gauge their degree of intoxication.

'Just made it for the last pint, lads,' he stated, sliding their tankards towards them. 'Time, gentlemen please!' he shouted and rang the bell. The men were too busy drinking to answer.

Jim and Walter had seen the trio enter, unwilling to have their friendly relaxation interrupted. They turned away; they always avoided Tommy Prince and his cronies, not wanting any trouble. Fortunately, they were all working in different districts on the coal face, and often on different shifts, so there had been no further confrontations.

Walter still remembered Tommy's reaction when he lost the fight, and Jim still remembered what Tommy had done to Bob and the puppy. Neither wanted dealings with him.

'Ready?' Jim asked Walter, placing his empty tankard on the bar. Walter nodded and swallowed his last mouthful. They were about to join the steady stream of men heading for the door when they heard Mr Lowe's raised voice.

'I said no more drinks tonight. I've called time. It's time to go home,' he cautioned, leaning forwards, looking fixedly at Tommy.

'Aw, come on Amos, just one more round for us,' he wheedled.

'No, on your way, Prince. Drinking time's over for today', was the brusque reply.

'I said, another round before we go!' Tommy slurred. He swayed and slammed his hand on the bar. Other customers stopped, watching and listening.

'On your way!' Mr Lowe commanded. 'You three have had enough.'

'Make me go,' Tommy hissed, jabbing at the landlord's chest. Percy and Eli watched but remained silent and still. Jim and Walter had watched too, and tried to intervene.

'Come on now, Tommy, listen to Mr Lowe. You've overstepped the mark,' Jim reasoned in a measured tone.

Tommy reacted by shoving his face in front of Jim's.

'Do you mean like you overstepped the mark with Mary? It took more than kisses to make that babby, and before the wedding too!' he rasped, spittle flying. These jealous, callous taunts enraged Jim. He was just about to launch himself on Tommy when Walter stepped between them.

'Shut your mouth, Prince. That's enough!' he yelled, grabbing Tommy's arm. But Tommy's taunts continued, this time directed at Walter.

'Young girls can't get enough of it these days. You ask your Ellen, she knows all about it. I know she does,' he sniggered.

Murmured gasps rippled around the onlookers. Walter's eyes narrowed and fixed on Tommy's smirking face.

'You're a fuckin' liar, Prince. Nowt but a liar!' he retaliated.

'You just ask that sister of yours, then tell me I'm a liar,' Tommy jibed.

As Walter squared up for a fight, Amos Lowe sprang into action.

'You two stay here,' he ordered Jim and Walter. 'I said out, and I mean out, now!' he shouted, frogmarching Tommy to the door.

A hefty shove resulted in Tommy staggering into the night. Eli and Percy sneered and scowled to save face, but followed without resistance. The three of them jeered and hooted to the starry sky, happy to display their apparent indifference and derision.

Jim and Walter were the last to leave the pub. Amos had not wanted the trouble to escalate outside; he hoped the men would have calmed down before they left.

'Take no notice of Prince,' Jim reasoned with Walter. 'He'll say anything when he's drunk. He's a nasty piece of work, all right, a real troublemaker,' he added.

Walter's distant gaze and grim expression informed Jim that his advice would not be heeded. Neither of them knew the strife that would follow.

Chapter 22
September 1890

Walter made his way home, his thoughts in turmoil. Prince's accusations about his sister had made him agitated and confused. Part of him resolved that Prince was a coarse, vulgar loudmouth, willing to say anything about anybody, but a niggling doubt in Walter's mind would not be suppressed.

Even though this suspicion made him feel disloyal, he knew Ellen's personality and nature may have led her into vulnerable situations. She was a hardworking girl, and being the eldest daughter still in the family home, she had to be. Yet Walter also recognised her lack of confidence and low self-esteem. He had shared the same weaknesses for many years until maturity – and boxing – had changed his outlook.

He had never really felt comfortable and wanted in his family, but he had always felt the closest bonds with Ellen, both in age and nature. The first-born child in the Smith family was Harriet, yet Walter felt he hardly knew his eldest sister. She had worked in service, then married, and had not lived in the family home for more than seven years.

Gilbert, his elder brother, was also a remote figure in Walter's reckoning. He had never been a loving child; he shared his father's nature. Both Alf and Gilbert were hardworking miners, but they were similarly dour, interested only in limited things and few people. Their plodding, self-centred outlook on life revealed a lack of ambition and imagination. Each was quite happy in his own company, others were not needed or particularly wanted.

But Walter had respect and admiration for his mother, Peggy. As he had matured, he had better understood and recognised her resilience. She was the strength within the family, despite receiving little recognition and scant rewards for her constant diligence and loyalty. She was an undemonstrative woman, married to an undemonstrative man. Walter could well understand his own dispassionate feelings, yet he did want to care for his family.

His four younger sisters had appeared in a steady succession. Ellen, Ada and Beatie were close in age and had always been a little clique, sharing things and providing each other with friendship and camaraderie. His youngest sister, Alice, was nine years younger than him, the 'baby' of the family. Walter still felt the odd one out in many ways, but his protective instinct had been aroused when Ellen was slighted. He wanted to know the truth.

* * *

The following morning, after the confrontation in The Pig, was the first opportunity to broach the subject with Ellen. He waited until he could speak to her alone, having to interrupt her floor-washing to gain her full attention.

'Has Mary said anything to you about Tommy Prince recently?' he began.

Ellen looked up from where she was kneeling and dropped back onto her heels. Sweat glistened on her nose and above her upper lip, tendrils of loose hair wafted and brushed her cheeks. Scrubbing floors was hard work, even for a fifteen-year-old. She was already flushed with all her exertion, but her colour deepened. It was a spontaneous response, uncontrollable.

'Mary told me he made a crude remark to her when she was expecting, something about only just married and already "showing",' Ellen replied, trying to sound nonchalant. She leaned forward and dipped her scrubbing brush into the bucket of water.

'Hang on a minute, I need to ask you something.' Walter spoke gently, choosing his words carefully. 'Have you been going out with any boys – are you courting anybody?'

Ellen's eyes widened, but she averted her gaze. She continued to scrub the dusty floor.

'Well, have you been out with any boys?' he repeated.

'What do you mean? No, I haven't been out with anybody,' she protested, her voice louder than intended. She looked up at Walter, her face set, but then her lip trembled.

'I'm asking you because somebody was saying things about you last night, insulting things that aren't nice,' he continued.

'Who's said things about me?' she cried, her composure crumbling. 'Do, do you mean it was T-tommy P-prince?' she stammered.

The look on Walter's face answered her question.

'What did he say?' she cried.

'That you like being with boys, and you might have done things with them,' he spoke slowly.

Ellen flung down the brush and stood up.

'He's no right saying such things!' she retorted, leaning forward to reinforce her words.

'Ellen, I need to know. If he's telling lies, he'll wish he hadn't when I'm finished with him. Tell me.'

Walter's words, his searching look as he grasped her shoulders, all had the effect of breaking a dam on her emotions.

'We met Tommy at The Pig and we went for a walk to Vinah's pond,' she murmured. 'But Ada, Beatie and Alice were there too!' she continued, searching for her words.

'Did anything happen there?' Walter questioned.

Ellen was silent, still searching for her words.

'What happened there?' Walter repeated.

'When the other girls went home, we went for another walk, and... and... he kissed me,' she stuttered.

Walter felt alarm rising within himself.

'He just kissed you?' he demanded, his voice loudening.

'No, he... he... he just wouldn't stop!' she finally screamed.

'Are you telling me what I think you're telling me?'

Ellen gave an imperceptible nod, then lowered her head. She saw the scum in the dirty water. That's what she felt like, scum.

'He just wouldn't stop. He pushed me down onto the ground, he... he started feeling up my skirt. His hands were everywhere. I kept saying no, stop, but he wouldn't.'

Walter listened in horror, blistering anger building inside.

'He... he got on top of me. I tried to shove him off, but he was too heavy. Then he...' Her words faded.

'Then he raped you.' Walter spat out the words.

She nodded, shocked to hear the word 'raped', but finally admitting to herself that she had been raped.

'Yes, he raped me,' she whispered. 'Then he laughed, and told me it had to stay a secret. Then he walked away... he left... he was whistling,' she finished, exhausted.

Walter felt a rush of blind anger and indignation, then concern for Ellen.

'Why didn't you say something? Who knows about this?' he asked gently.

'Just Mam,' she replied, her shoulders sagging. 'I knew you'd go mad if you knew. I didn't want you to get into trouble. Please don't tell anyone or do anything!'

He took her hands in his, not trusting himself to speak. All Walter knew was that he would have to punish Prince.

Ellen's frightened reaction was to rush to her mother, to warn her that Walter knew that Tommy had attacked her. Peggy's immediate response was alarm, and fear that there would be big trouble if the whole truth was revealed.

'Does he know you were pregnant and got rid of it?' Peggy asked her anxious daughter.

'No, and I don't want him or anybody else to know! Please don't tell him, Mam!' she begged. 'I just want to forget about it all!'

* * *

Walter subdued his anger and tried a calm confrontation with his mother. He had the sense to do it in private.

'You should have told me,' he stated. 'You should have told me.'

'She was just so scared and humiliated, son,' Peggy tried to explain. 'And she didn't want you to do anything silly and get into trouble. The lass has suffered enough, and she was just getting over it. I can't understand why Prince let it slip in the first place – she's only a girl, and he said it had to be a secret.'

'It was the booze talking, as usual,' Walter said. 'But in this case, I'm glad it was. I'm glad I know.'

The tone in his voice made Peggy look up in alarm.

'You're not going to do anything stupid, are you? I know what he did was very wrong, but I just don't want any trouble, for you or Ellen,' she added, almost in tears.

'Leave things to me, Mam. I'll sort it out. There'll be no more trouble.'

Chapter 23
September 1890

Jim looked uncomfortable. He didn't know what to say. Walter's penetrating stare unnerved him; his silence perturbed him.

'I just can't do it, Walt,' Jim broke the silence, 'it's not right.'

'It wasn't right what Prince did to our Ellen, I thought you'd understand. I thought you'd want to help me,' Walter interjected.

The two men peered closely at each other, as though searching for common ground, for an acknowledgement of their friendship.

'I know what he did to your Ellen was wrong,' Jim sighed. 'But beating him up till he's half senseless would be wrong too,' he reasoned. He felt guilty that he had refused to help his best friend.

'Why don't you go to the police?' Jim asked.

Walter shook his head.

'Mi Mam and our Ellen don't want everyone to know – they don't want any trouble.'

'You'll get yourself into trouble, Walt,' Jim warned.

'There'll be no more trouble,' was Walter's decisive retort. 'But I'll remember you didn't want to help me,' he threw back scornfully at Jim.

'Don't be like that, Walt.' Jim tried to take his arm, but Walter shrugged him off and turned away.

'I'll do it mi fuckin' sen, then,' was the derisive reply.

* * *

Tommy Prince turned the corner from Doncaster Road and walked up Tickhill Street. It was dark, chilly and pouring with rain. The weather had suddenly turned; autumn had definitely arrived, although he was oblivious of the uncomfortable conditions. The alcohol he had consumed had warmed his insides and numbed him on the outside. Amos Lowe had barred him from The Pig for the last two weeks, but he was now able to get his fill there again.

The new outside gas lamps cast shadowy shapes on the shiny cobbled street, but the dim lights didn't prevent him from lurching and falling heavily. He lay on the cold, wet ground, rain splashing onto his upturned face. He didn't see the figure looming over him at first. He blinked to focus through his drunken stupor.

The dark ginnel had aided Walter. It had been easy to prod the long metal bar from its shadows, easy to trip up the drunken Tommy. He stood over him in the quiet, deserted street.

'You bastard. You fuckin' bastard,' he rasped.

Tommy's puzzled gaze cleared. He recognised the face, and the voice.

'Walter Smith… what you doing?' he slurred.

'What am I doing? I'm letting you know your "little secret" is out. You raped a fifteen-year-old girl. You raped my sister,' he hissed.

Tommy's reply took Walter by surprise.

'Yeah, I had her. First time for her. I enjoyed it.'

He tried to roll over and stand up, but Walter pushed him back down and knelt on the sprawled body. He grasped the metal bar in both hands and positioned the jagged end over Tommy's face. Rain dripped from one face to the other. The single, forceful thrust tore at skin, flesh and bone as it scored its mark from eye to chin.

Tommy didn't feel any pain at first, such was his drunkenness.

'You touch my sister again and I'll fuckin' kill you.'

Tommy's face suddenly registered pain. He lifted his heavy arm, and allowed his fingers to locate the throbbing sting on his face. His bleary eyes stared at the pink fluid that coated his fingers, as blood mingled with the rain.

'This is our secret,' Walter mocked. 'Tell anyone and the police will know what you did to our Ellen.' He then kicked Tommy between the legs, hard.

'That'll slow you down a bit,' Walter laughed. 'Watch your step next time – these cobbles are slippy, you might fall again.'

Walter walked away, whistling. Prince's good looks wouldn't be so good anymore.

Chapter 24
April 1891

Bridie watched Rose as she grasped the chair and pulled herself to a standing position. The infant swayed on chubby legs, regained her balance, and managed two faltering steps before falling down again. She didn't cry, however, but just grinned at the women.

'It's a good job I've put this extra rug down, she'd be covered in bruises before she manages to walk!' Mary exclaimed, gazing fondly at her daughter. 'She's doing well, though, she's only ten months old. She doesn't seem to be interested in crawling, just walking,' she added, proudly.

Bridie looked on, smiling as a response, but offering little conversation. Mary was pleased to have her unexpected visitor, it was a while since she had seen Bridie, but she was also sad to see that her long-time friend still seemed aloof, detached, almost uncaring.

But she understood why. Poor Bridie had witnessed a tragic event, and was still finding it difficult to overcome the shock. Mary felt the same, such was the tragedy.

* * *

The Flannagan household was still cramped and crowded.

'Sure, we're bursting at the seams!' Hannah retorted. Bridie did not share her mother's genial acceptance of their living conditions, nor her father's good-natured stoicism about their situation.

'We get by,' Willie reasoned. 'At least we have a roof over our heads, though we could do with more space,' he added with ironic understatement.

Bridie shared the house with her parents, five brothers and two sisters. Willie also insisted on having lodgers stay from time to time. He still remembered how it felt when he and his family had arrived in Liverpool after leaving Ireland. They had no home, no jobs, but had to rely on help from others for food and lodgings.

He felt for the young men who travelled to Denaby in search of work and lodgings. They needed lodgings; the family needed their money, so a steady stream passed through the Flannagan household.

For Bridie, the introduction of strange men into their home had been completely unwelcome, catastrophic. The unusual sleeping arrangements and close intimacy of their living conditions had resulted in furtive, unwanted advances. She had not told anyone about the frightening incidents. At first, she had not really understood what they did, then, later, she was ashamed. She felt she could not divulge anything to anybody, she kept it all inside. But the abuse produced a developing rancour that festered and damaged her.

As the eldest daughter, Bridie's help was needed more and more in the home. Her father and four of her brothers were all miners, all on various shifts. This meant that Hannah and Bridie were cooking, cleaning and working all hours to look after their menfolk. The only benefit from their being on different shifts was increased space in the house and the ability to rotate beds for sleeping. It was very tiring for the women to sustain such long, demanding hours of work.

There were also three younger children to look after. Seamus was eleven, Eliza nine and the new baby, Martha, only two months old.

Hannah had suffered three miscarriages and a stillbirth in the last nine years since Eliza was born. She had thought her childbearing days were over. 'Sure, my body's telling me it needs a rest,' she had concluded to Willie. 'Maybe no more babies for us.'

She was wrong, and very surprised, when she gave birth to baby Martha at the age of forty-three. Her body was still recovering from the birth. Her first-born, Paddy, was twenty-one. She could feel the difference between this one and her earlier births. She felt her age.

Bridie had helped Hannah even more during her pregnancy and after the birth. She saw how Hannah struggled to cope with everything, especially the demands of a new baby at her age, and so she had assumed responsibility for more and more of the chores, as well as helping to look after the baby. Hannah's usual cheerful enjoyment of life had been dulled, and this disturbed Bridie.

The fateful day had begun like many others. The new year had brought bitterly cold weather, cutting winds and penetrating frosts. Bridie and Hannah had left warm beds to start the early morning jobs that needed to be done to look after their men. Willie had thrown on his work clothes, trying to ease his shivering.

Hannah had placed his drink of hot tea on the table, along with a thick hunk of bread spread with dripping. He did not like to eat a bigger breakfast as a full stomach affected his ability to work properly. Kneeling, bending and hewing in cramped, awkward positions was gut-wrenching work. He preferred to take plenty of 'snap' to sustain his energy through his shift.

It was more bread and dripping and more tea that Hannah placed in his snap tin and flask. Things didn't taste the same deep down in the hot mine, butter was rancid, and meat had a sour flavour, so bread and dripping had to suffice. He opened the back door and braced himself against the icy blasts that swirled up and down the lane.

Bridie tended the fire, building it up from its overnight smoulder into a glowing blaze. The lads were due back home from their night shifts shortly, hot food and water would be required. Paddy and the two younger children were still asleep upstairs, the baby lay on a chair near the fire, quietly grizzling. Bridie broke the silence.

'Why don't you go back to bed with the baby, Mammy? Isn't her feed due?'

'If you can manage, love, I think I will,' Hannah agreed thankfully.

Dermot, Martin and Michael arrived home, glad of the blazing fire and hot porridge that awaited them. After a brief wash, they climbed the stairs, ready to lay down on the mattress squeezed into part of the back bedroom. Paddy grumbled as they disturbed his sleep; he could lie in as he was on the afternoon shift. He turned over, pushing at the thin curtain that divided the room. Bridie's mattress lay behind the curtain.

Seamus, Eliza and the baby shared the front bedroom with their mother. A wave of fatigue swept over Bridie, she felt almost nauseous. It was still too early for Seamus and Eliza to get up for school.

She hesitated, undecided whether to stay in the living room or lie down on her mattress for a while. As she crept upstairs, gentle snores and deepening breaths could already be heard. The mattress felt welcoming. She relaxed her body into it and quickly fell asleep.

* * *

The shrieking penetrated Bridie's semi-consciousness, at first mingling into her dreams, then rousing her with its increasing volume and intensity.

Seamus ran into the bedroom, screaming.

'Come quick! Our Liza's on fire!'

Paddy leapt out of bed, half-asleep, and almost fell down the stairs. Bridie's breath deserted her momentarily, stunning her into shocked stillness, then she ran after Paddy. Downstairs, the sights and sounds that met her would haunt her forever.

Liza's nightdress was ablaze. Flames climbed upwards, engulfing and extending over the little girl's body. Blood-curdling screams reverberated around the room.

Paddy grabbed the hearth rug and wrapped the child in its heavy folds. He patted and rolled until the flames subsided. He could hardly bear to look at his poor little sister. She had become still, shallow breaths escaping her open mouth. The rug was carefully spread open. Terrible injuries were already evident.

'Quick, run round to Dr Clark's!' Paddy ordered Seamus. The young boy, white faced and trembling, nodded agreement. He thrust his bare feet into a pair of nearby boots and ran outside into the freezing darkness.

Hannah and the boys appeared moments later, unable to comprehend what they saw. An acrid odour permeated the room. Then Hannah started. Her wailing moans changed into uncontrollable sobbing, so intense that she doubled over, rocking and swaying in her despair.

'Is she dead? Is she dead?' she gasped, at last. They all looked at each other unsure, in shocked disbelief, then their sobs joined their mother's.

* * *

Dr Clark arrived shortly afterwards. He looked up, grim-faced, from where he knelt beside Eliza. He shook his head sadly.

'She has deep, extensive burns to her feet, legs and upper body. She is still alive, but I have to warn you that she will probably not survive. The shock after such burning is overwhelming and very serious. She needs to go to the Doncaster Infirmary as soon as possible.'

The journey to hospital was not necessary. Eliza died two hours later. Willie had been sent for and he arrived home just before his daughter stirred, took several rasping breaths, then exhaled slowly and finally. The family wept together, bitter tears of shock and despair. Their lovely Liza lay shrouded in a blanket, still, unmoving, as if asleep, but she was dead.

Dr Clark certified her death and offered his condolences. He informed them that there would be an inquest into the circumstances of her death. He picked up his bag and added,

'I'll inform the undertaker. He'll be here shortly.' Such was his shock and grief, Paddy only just started to feel his own injuries. His hands and arms were already blistering.

* * *

The whole community mourned little Liza. Neighbours, friends and workmates visited the family, shocked and saddened at the awful accident. The Flannagan family experienced a whole gamut of emotions. Grief and sorrow flooded their lives, guilt and remorse, also. They struggled to comprehend what had happened, fearful that they were to blame, that it could have been prevented. Seamus had tearfully explained:

'When I woke up, our Liza wasn't there. I got up and was going down the stairs when I heard her screaming. She was in the living room and her nightie was on fire, all the front of it was in flames. She shouted to me, 'I didn't mean to be naughty, I stood on the fender to reach the mantel!' I didn't know what to do, so I ran upstairs to get you'.

Hannah and Bridie both felt they were to blame.

'I should have stayed up and fed the baby downstairs,' was Hannah's repeated anguished cry. 'Then my Liza would still be here'.

Bridie's feelings of guilt were even greater than her mother's. She blamed herself. If she hadn't gone to lie down, the accident wouldn't have happened. It was her fault. Neither woman could be consoled, so severe was their torment.

* * *

The inquest concluded with the verdict of *Accidental Death*, but not before harsh criticism was delivered by the coroner. He had presided over the inquests into five children's deaths within the last two years, all by burning, all in Denaby.

The reason for his annoyance and condemnation was that, in every case, there had been no fixed fireguard. He had become exasperated that such a basic safety item wasn't considered to be sufficiently important.

'A fireguard costs only one shilling!' he had declared.

Seamus's evidence had been taken into consideration and Paddy and Bridie were questioned at the inquest. Bridie had stated:

'There was no fireguard in place at the time of the accident – I'd moved it to tend the fire. I was on my own downstairs when I went up to bed – I didn't know Eliza would be downstairs on her own,' she finished tearfully.

'*Accidental Death*,' the coroner stated stonily.

Bridie felt such guilt and heartache afterwards that she found it hard to carry on with normal life. She felt she should be punished.

Chapter 25
Late Summer 1891

Bridie realised she could no longer live with her family in that house. The painful memories crowded her mind, invaded her senses, preventing her from enjoying even the simplest of things. In the seven months since Liza's death, she had tried to reason her thoughts, accept what had happened, assuage her guilty feelings. But she could not.

Her head swam with flashbacks that sprang up, dazing her. She could still feel the rough hands that groped and explored her little-girl's body, making her cry in the night. She could still see the dead baby abandoned in the sack. She could still hear the screams of her burning sister, still smell her scorched skin and flesh.

Images of the consuming flames interrupted her vision, dizzying her. The taste of remorse and futility sullied her mouth. Friends and family tried to help her, but she sensed their fading enthusiasm to support her. They, too, were sad and bewildered.

But they did not fully comprehend the depths of her hopelessness, did not understand her feelings of worthlessness.

* * *

Eli Shaw had started smiling at Bridie in a special way. She frequently found him waiting at the end of her street, or hovering near the backs of the houses, looking nonchalantly from under the peak of his cap, whistling a tune up into the air.

They had known each other since school, even though he was two years older than her. But she had never really noticed him until recently. He was a close friend of Tommy Prince, so he had always faded into his shadow, and gained a bad reputation through association.

Nods and smiles developed into banter and flirtatious conversations. This was a new feeling for Bridie; she had never really allowed herself to react to men in this way before.

Part of her liked how this new behaviour lifted her gloom, allowing her to feel more normal, more optimistic. Part of her also recognised this was a possible way of escape. She needed new things, new places to replace the bad experiences. She set her cap at him.

Eli was a tall, thin man, wiry and strong. His curly black hair gave him added height, and his almost-black eyes afforded him a searing stare. His pale skin hinted at prolonged periods without sun and light, either hewing underground, or time spent inside, often drinking in pubs. His bristly, dark moustache broke up his pallid complexion, but Bridie had especially noticed, and liked, his smile, the way it suffused his face with a look of mischievous amusement.

He had been reticent in the past where women were concerned. He was a man's man, happy to live his life in a male environment. His miner's job provided close, almost tribal bonds with his mates.

They worked together, relying on each other in their shared difficult conditions. Banter and joking helped lighten their mood. He was often teased about his tall, skinny frame, which was not readily suited to underground work.

'Tha's a long streak o' piss all rate, Eli,' they joked, seeing the contortions of his body to fit and function in the restrictive, tight spaces.

'Tha's only jealous,' was his standard reply.

Bridie knew the Shaw family was rough and tough, even by Denaby's standards. They were hard drinkers, even some of the women. The local pub landlords all knew the Shaws. Their drunken, disorderly conduct often required the attendance of the police to quieten matters. But Bridie's desire to further the relationship with Eli outweighed any doubt about his suitability as a husband.

Eli, likewise, had surprised himself with his developing feelings for Bridie. Her chestnut-gold hair and smattering of freckles aroused his latent eagerness for a woman's company. Her husky, Irish accent attracted his interest and attention. It was almost exotic.

His mother, Bessie, was not overly feminine or maternal, the result of her own upbringing within a large, belligerent family, and also her marriage to Fred, a big, brute of a man, prone to vicious mood swings when irritated. Eli and his brothers and sisters had learned at an early age to avoid confrontations with either parent; it was easier to adopt the culture of self-preservation.

To the surprised bewilderment of family and friends, Bridie and Eli began 'courting'. Others doubted their compatibility, but at twenty-one and nineteen, they were old enough to decide for themselves.

Mary's reaction was a mixture of surprise, hopefulness and worry. She just prayed her friend's life would be happier from now on.

Chapter 26
Spring 1892

Mary rocked the infant in her arms, humming softly. Rose's eyelids drooped, gradually succumbing to sleep. She gazed at the dark hair that waved and curled as it thickened, and her rosebud lips, now parted in sleep.

She was such a good baby, contented and cheerful, a smile always ready to blossom, outstretched fingers happy to touch and be touched.

Everyone loved her. Sarah and Albert doted on their first grandchild. They loved the way Rose would kiss and cuddle them, chubby arms wrapped around their necks, wet kisses on their faces. Even Albert showed his softer side in this new relationship. Betty, Gertie, Ivy and Bob – they, too, wanted their turn to hug and play with her.

Jim adored his baby daughter; he had never felt so protective and devoted. This was his daughter, his wife, his family. He belonged. Mary had seen the sadness in his eyes gradually fade as his life became centred around herself and Rose. Dick's death was not forgotten, rather accepted. Deep feelings were deposited and cherished.

Mary laid down the sleeping infant, then stroked her rounded stomach. Their second child was due in a few months' time, another summer baby, two years apart. This time she had been able to enjoy the news that she was pregnant. Her family shared her delight, pleased at the way she and Jim had matured to become proud parents and a contented couple, despite their youth and testing circumstances.

There had been quite a few changes during the past two years. They had moved to a different house, a new one, midway between Denaby and Conisbrough.

The Company was still building lots of new houses, some for the ever-increasing number of migrants recruited to work at Denaby pit, but also some for the proposed new pit only a mile away. This new pit, Cadeby Colliery, was going to be a sister pit, run by the same Company, alongside the River Don at Conisbrough.

Sinking operations had started there two years previously, but problem after problem had caused delays. It was a difficult, hazardous job to try to reach the 'Barnsley' bed of coal. Deeper and deeper they had sunk, meeting challenge after challenge, from endless water, and the lay of the land. It was much deeper than Denaby pit, a "hot" pit as the miners called it.

'All the time and money they've spent on it, it had better be a good 'un,' was the general opinion of the miners.

Mary and Jim were pleased to have a new house, although they knew that the standard of building had hardly improved since the first ones built twenty years earlier. The same density of buildings meant terraced houses still had too few rooms, minimal facilities and no running water. However, Jim and Mary were content to have their own home, where happiness overcame lots of external hardships.

Jim was thankful that he had managed regular work over the years, and he had just progressed to being a proper "collier", able to do piecework, able to negotiate a rate of pay with the Company. He had his own small group of labourers that he paid in the production of the agreed amount of tonnage.

The problem was, there were endless disagreements between bosses and workers concerning pay or employment rules, which resulted in frequent strikes or lockouts when the Company stopped them working. The price of coal also fluctuated greatly because of external influences, so the Company was often ruthless in its dealings with the workers.

Only a year after Jim had started working, there had been a six-month conflict, resulting in great bitterness and hardship. He remembered his father discussing with him how clever the Company had been in the way they had hoodwinked the workers.

'They said they wanted to change the pay structure and terms of employment,' Dick had stated. 'But yon buggers really wanted to do us out of twenty-five percent of our wages.' He emphasised his anger by banging his hand on every spoken syllable.

Jim remembered how two weeks' notices were given to every single employee at Denaby pit; even he'd got one as a thirteen-year-old lad. The intention was to force agreement and threaten evictions.

'All that time we didn't work, all that money lost, and they still won in the end,' Jim spoke ruefully.

'Aye, but at least we put up a fight,' Dick reasoned. Jim had listened to lots of miners at that time, realising the growing resentment that was building at the trickery of the bosses.

'They brought all of the pit ponies up and organised an auction to sell them as they said there'd been a drop in demand for coal and the horses weren't needed,' one old miner recounted. 'Then, bugger me, it was all a sham! Hosses were never really sold. Just a pretence to twist our arms into agreeing to new pay!' he retorted.

'Aye, and they brought in all those workers from Staffordshire, told them they were recruiting for a new pit, and it was our jobs they were taking!' exclaimed his mate.

'Some did refuse to take our jobs when they found out.'

'Aye, but a lot stayed and took our jobs, and houses,' was the scornful reply.

Jim and Dick had also realised that they would need the power of a union to fight their cause. People could only strike for a limited time, ultimately overcome by hunger and destitution.

There were a few small, district "Associations" that had helped them in the past, but it was dawning on the miners that unanimity would create more power. Trade Unions had been legal for over a decade, but it was still difficult to organise picketing and strikes because of other laws.

Jim had come to the conclusion that, for now, he just wanted regular work and regular money to look after his family.

He was thrilled that Mary was pregnant again – maybe he would soon have a son. His thoughts strayed to his father again. How he wished Dick had lived to enjoy his grandchildren. He was also sad that Walter avoided him as much as possible, barely speaking unless necessary. He'd heard that Walter had married a girl from Conisbrough. Jim missed the banter and camaraderie he used to share with his friend.

Chapter 27
Spring 1892

Mary was still very close to her family, even though she no longer lived with them. She tried to help her mother as much as she could, although pregnancy limited her strength and energy.

Sarah's pleasure at being a grandmother seemed to have invigorated her. She was still quite frail physically, but her outlook on life seemed much more positive. She counted her blessings that she had a loving, supportive family. That fact gave her strength and happiness.

Her delight was further enhanced when Betty announced to them all that she was expecting a baby. Since marrying Arthur three years earlier, she had longed for a baby, but each month, those hopes were dashed. She and Arthur didn't openly discuss it, instead, each privately absorbed their own disappointment, rationalising and compartmentalising it. Arthur's outlook on life was:

'What shall be, shall be. Some things can't be rushed.'

Betty's attitude was less stoical, less patient. She was used to organising, being proactive, but she knew Arthur was right. When she realised that she was pregnant, she was thrilled.

Arthur had smiled and nodded. 'I told you. I knew one day it would 'appen.'

Betty wallowed in the joy of her condition, luxuriating in the delight of achieving a long-held ambition.

'Our Betty will be organising everything from top to bottom,' Sarah had chuckled, smiling at Albert.

He nodded, knowingly.

'Those knitting needles won't stop till she's got a drawer full of things,' he added.

Sarah and Albert shared contented looks. They hoped all their children would be settled and safe in the future.

Mary had differing relationships with each of her sisters. Betty's confident, assured nature had always impressed her. She respected Betty almost as a mother figure and was so pleased to hear the news of her pregnancy. She knew this fitted her aspirations; she would be fulfilled. Mary smiled to herself, she knew Betty would be a good mother, but wondered about the possible high standards the child would need to meet to please her!

Gertie and Ivy each had strong personalities, yet very different natures. Gertie had always been very independent and strong-willed. She insisted on doing things for herself, dismissing help unless it was absolutely necessary. She was practical, good with her hands, competent at cooking, sewing and mending things.

At times, her strong will manifested itself as stubbornness, and others learned to leave her alone. Fortunately, her sense of humour and playful jesting often softened her obstinacy, producing harmony once more. Mary felt that Gertie could always be relied upon in times of trouble. She would always be dependable. Sarah had so often reflected:

'Gertie, you're so like your father.'

Her daughter responded with a grin and a chuckle.

She had met Charlie Talbot at Kilner's Glassworks where they both worked, and they soon began 'courting'. His looks and personality immediately attracted her.

He literally stood out from the crowd. His thick, wavy hair was a deep copper colour, as were the brows and lashes that framed his bright blue eyes. She had stared at his white teeth; never before had she seen such perfect teeth, and she saw them frequently as he was a joker, laughing and cheerful, even though working conditions were demanding.

The glass blowers had to suffer stifling heat from the furnaces, especially hard in summer, but Charlie's happy and determined nature impressed her. They were not dissimilar; they shared a lot of characteristics.

Charlie had noticed Gertie, too. Escaping brown curls skimmed her square jaw, grey-green eyes contrasted with her olive skin. She had her father's colouring, unlike her other sisters.

Her slim, petite frame belied her strength and capability. Charlie had watched her climbing ladders in the warehouse, washing bottles and packing jars and phials. He especially liked her cheerful chatting and joking with the other women. Her smiling, friendly personality attracted many friends and admirers.

He had first spoken to her just after their bosses, the Kilner brothers, had announced that the Glassworks had been awarded a prestigious medal in London.

Kilner's Providence glass products were considered some of the best in the country. People were wanting more and more of them, from beer and water bottles, pharmaceutical phials, to storage jars. Business was booming. There was even a railway line alongside the factory, where goods were loaded on trucks that travelled directly to a London warehouse. Gertie and Charlie had chatted about this to each other.

'Just think, these jars and bottles travel all the way from Denaby to London King's Cross, then they're exported all over the world,' Gertie had mused.

'Hope people know how much hard work it takes to make them all,' Charlie replied. A shadow crossed his face momentarily, as he thought about an accident only the week before. His mate, Eddie, had been burnt when he was working near the furnace. Luckily, it wasn't too bad, but he'd be off work a while.

Gertie smiled reassuringly. 'I'm glad Eddie's on the mend. He was lucky to have the doctor see to him so quickly,' she added.

Charlie's bright blue eyes shone, his white teeth flashed. Each was smitten with the other.

Ivy was two years older than Mary, but seemed younger in many ways. She was exceptionally pretty with blonde, wavy hair that, when released, cascaded over her shoulders like floating clouds. Her large, pale grey eyes perfectly suited the shape and dimensions of her face. She looked angelic. She reminded Sarah of her own mother, Annie. She, too, had been beautiful, with the same lovely hair and eyes.

'Your Ivy's such a beautiful baby,' people had remarked.

'She takes after her Grandma,' Sarah had replied.

As she grew up, Ivy's prettiness intensified, giving her a delicate, almost fragile appearance. She had a naivety and vulnerability about her that made others want to protect her. Even as a young woman, that child-like quality remained and Mary, too, felt protective towards her.

Ivy wasn't vain, however. She just took for granted that she had always been blessed with attractive features, and that others loved and protected her.

At times, she used this to her own advantage, wheedling her way out of trouble, coaxing her way into favour, just by using her persuasive attributes. Even Albert could be swayed into submitting to her, by a coy smile or a shedding of tears.

Sarah understood her daughter's strategies better, however, and would rein in Ivy's crafty manipulation when necessary. She had always been a very loving child, both towards her parents and siblings, happy to be liked and loved.

She had worked at Kilner's when she first left school, but she had not liked it there. She knew young girls and women didn't have much choice of employment where she lived, but she was adamant that she didn't want to work in service and live in an employer's home. She didn't want to leave her family.

The Glassworks was noisy, hot and strenuous, all of which sapped her strength and well-being, but she had put up with it. She admired others who coped with it, like Gertie, but she was glad when the Powder Works opened in Denaby.

Lots of girls and women wanted a job at The Flameless Explosives Company, and Ivy was delighted when she managed to secure employment there.

'First time this explosives powder's going to be made in England, and they've picked Denaby!' was the excited gossip amongst the villagers.

'Aye, powder's for blasting work in the pits,' informed another.

'There's talk that they want women to work there as they've got a more delicate touch when handling explosives,' volunteered another, much to the merriment of all who heard.

Ivy had explained how workers had to change into specially provided woollen clothes at the beginning of every shift, although a fine film of dust settled on their skin and hair. She liked it there, working with other women, in a quieter environment. It was good pay, too.

She had always had plenty of male admirers, such was her beauty, but so far, she had not met a man she liked enough to court or marry. She was quite happy to stay with her family for now.

Chapter 28
July 1892

Mary sat down, trying to find a comfortable position to rest her heavy body. She knew the birth would be very soon and she would be glad when it happened. The pregnancy had become difficult in the past couple of months, and this surprised and alarmed her. She had felt fine earlier on, then the problems had started. Swollen legs, aching joints and breathlessness had drained her energy and sapped her strength.

The living room was stiflingly hot. The fire burnt brightly; it was needed for cooking and heating water, but outside was just as hot. The prolonged heatwave that they were experiencing depleted everyone's vitality. Everyone was suffering, and the lack of water in Denaby and Conisbrough made the heat doubly hard to bear. Everyone was complaining, water was needed for so many things, yet there was a shortage. Mary's neighbours had kindly brought her water, as they knew her condition, but there was never enough.

The miners were sweating in the deep, "hot" Denaby pit, where temperatures had soared, then they sweated when they came up to searing sun and breezeless air.

Jim had always told her how exhausting the heat was underground, but she now better understood and appreciated the difficult conditions as the heatwave continued. She had renewed respect for the miners.

'I don't know how you do it,' she told him, 'I don't even feel like moving, let alone shovel coal for hours on end.' He had made her laugh, though, relating some of the antics of his fellow colliers.

'When they're ready to start hewing, off come the clothes, just their pants left on, it's so hot.' He grinned. 'Some of the older men wear women's bloomers.'

'Why?' Mary asked, puzzled.

'They say they're easier to take off, wring out the sweat and put back on, better than woollen ones,' he explained. 'Bert Williams says his missus is always complaining she can never find any to wear herself!'

Mary smiled to herself as she remembered this, shuffling in the chair, trying to ease her aches and feel some cool. She had tried leaving the back door open, but the flies and stench from the middens outside had made that impractical. Even opening a window created the same problems.

It was a good job the night soil men were due that evening with their horses and carts. There was a whole week's waste and refuse in the ditches that needed clearing. It would take some shovelling to empty them.

'There's no water to flush them either,' the villagers grumbled.

'They deserve a medal for what they do,' they agreed.

Mary could hear children playing in the "backs" despite the dust and flies. It was the only space they had, and the middens were only yards away. No wonder so many children contracted infections and diseases; some of them even dying.

Few parents escaped the heartache of seeing their babies and infants suffering from illnesses. Dirty water and untreated sewage caused diseases such as typhoid, dysentery and diarrhoea, but they were commonplace in Denaby. People worried about their children's health but felt helpless. Apart from complaining to the Company, what could they do? She remembered how, as a young girl, she had suffered with countless eye infections, and Bob had frequent chest infections. She sighed, trying to push away the worrying thoughts about their unhealthy environment.

It felt strange to be alone in the house. Jim was at work and Rose was with Sarah and Ivy. They had insisted that she needed to rest. Drowsiness washed over her; she felt her eyelids droop and her body relax. She drifted off to sleep.

Later that same evening, she gave birth. Jim had returned from his morning shift to find Mary asleep in the chair. He had been worried about her more and more recently, and he just wanted the baby to be born safely, and Mary to regain her strength and vitality.

She had felt the first contractions later that evening. They squeezed and pushed and pulled her insides, catching her breath with their increasing length and ferocity. Jim had asked a neighbour to go and fetch Nellie MacArthur, not wanting to leave Mary alone.

Such was the speed of the labour, Mary was in the final stages when Nellie arrived an hour later, flushed crimson and perspiring profusely.

The baby was born a few minutes later. It was a boy, healthy and of a good weight. His long body and lusty cries promised hopefully he would be a sturdy, strapping lad.

The air was hot and still. The scraping of the nightsoil men's shovels cut through the sultry silence of the darkening night. Jim and Mary gazed at their son, John, and smiled thankfully.

Chapter 29
July 1892

Bridie and Eli did not have a very long courting period. They were both keen to marry and have their own home. Each was relieved to be moving out of their own family home.

Eli did not have a romanticised view of marriage; he was too practical, too straight-thinking. If he wanted something, he would get it, if he needed something he would sort it. Bridie's way of thinking was less direct, less rational, but they both agreed that living together in their own home was preferable to what they already had.

Bridie had assured her mother that she would still help her with the work. She knew Hannah was still grieving for Liza, still struggling to cope with infant Martha. In some ways, Bridie felt guilty leaving behind her brothers and baby sister, but she knew this was the right time for a new beginning.

* * *

The slap on the face had stung not only her face but also her pride. Bridie glared at Eli, his almost-black eyes glazed over, abandoning their focus. He swayed and stumbled until the chair was reached. Within seconds he was asleep, breathing in with sucking rasps, breathing out with harsh pants.

His mouth was open, saliva dribbling from each side. The bristly moustache covered his top lip completely. His curly hair splayed out at varying angles, his long legs folded and wrapped as though struggling for space. Bridie stood gazing at him and her heart sank.

In the beginning, she had been almost happy. They had married in a simple ceremony with little fuss and sense of occasion, which had suited them both. Neither enjoyed being the centre of attention.

Eli had asked the Company for one of the new houses and they had felt fortunate to be granted one. Basic items of old furniture had been gathered, mainly donated by kind neighbours and friends wanting to help the newly married couple. Bridie had felt proud, almost special, to have a husband and a new house. She had felt optimistic about the future.

Eli was a good worker. His robust, direct nature was suited to hard graft; he liked to get the job done and earn his money. He was intolerant of laziness, short-tempered with idlers who shirked their duties. He was a collier through and through. But his downfall was drinking and gambling.

At first, they had accommodated each other's ways, adopting the typical roles of husband and wife. He worked down the pit and earned a wage; she worked at home but with no pay.

Eli had been used to paying his mother a nominal sum for his "board", enjoying the rest of his money for his own pleasures. Bridie had been used to her menfolk earning money, providing the essential items. Both were unprepared for providing things for themselves. Bridie was completely dependent on Eli, yet he was reluctant to share.

The rent for the house was stopped from Eli's wages, so Bridie was relieved about that, but problems had increased when money for food and household items was needed. At first, Bridie had been reluctant to ask for money. She saw the irritated looks flit across his face when the divvying up of his wages was mentioned. He resented being asked; she resented being so beholden to him. The arguments started.

Bridie felt betrayed. She was trying to be a good wife, but Eli had a very different viewpoint. He still wanted to spend money on drinking, gambling, going out with his mates. He wasn't prepared to give up those pleasures just because he was married. Bridie was hurt that he would not compromise, would not even listen to her.

Resentment slowly built. Things about Eli that she had previously found endearing now irritated her. She rarely saw the mischievous smile light up his face. She even found his size annoying – he seemed to fill up and overwhelm any space that he was in. But the drinking was the worst problem. He was regularly drunk, unwilling to accept new responsibilities as a married man.

Bridie was crestfallen. She had hoped that she would matter to him. She found it difficult to show him affection when she considered him to be so inconsiderate and unfair. Then she realised that she was pregnant.

* * *

Mary was delighted when Bridie and Eli moved into the same block of houses as her; only a few doors separated their homes. They had been neighbours as children and were now neighbours as married women.

Bridie had shown renewed interest in life, her lovely Irish voice excitedly recounting the generosity of family and friends.

'Sure, they'd give us the coats off their backs if we let them,' she had smiled, touched by their kindness.

'Everyone needs help sometimes,' was Mary's wise reply. 'Nobody's got very much, but giving and sharing makes everyone feel better.'

Mary had watched and listened to Bridie very carefully during the first few months of her marriage. She knew about Eli's nature and personality, frequently making her feel relief that she had such a loving, caring husband as Jim. She wished Bridie received similar love and support from Eli. But certain comments had alerted her suspicion, certain looks that darted across her face had reinforced her scepticism.

'Eli's not one for staying in,' she had sighed. 'He's out now with Tommy and Percy, they're gaming cards, but he won't say where.'

'They've already been fined for gambling on cards and cockfighting,' Mary retorted. 'Jim told me.'

'He says it's his money and he can do what he wants with it,' was Bridie's derisory reply.

Everyone knew about Tommy Prince's fall and injuries. He'd been left with scarring to his face and some eye damage. He could still work, but he'd given up the boxing. He now released his energy on more drinking at the pubs and increased illegal gambling. As Eli had always been within his clan, he, too, had become involved in the shadier exploits in life. Mary could well understand Bridie's bitterness.

Bridie had visited Mary immediately after John's birth. She had kissed and cuddled the baby, fussed over Mary, but the light had gone from her eyes, her smiles were forced, almost insincere.

As she leaned over to place baby John back into Mary's arms, the bruises on her face became clearly noticeable.

'What's happened to your face?' Mary asked, with concern in her voice.

'Oh, I bumped into the door in the dark,' was the airy reply. 'Anyway,' she continued. 'I've got something to tell you… I'm expecting.'

'Oh, Bridie, that's wonderful news,' Mary began, but Bridie stared at her and burst into tears.

Chapter 30
Christmas 1892

The icy-cold December winds rushed along the lanes, whooshing and whirring between the rows of houses, rattling loose windows and knocking on doors. Mary was visiting her mother, pleased to sit and talk as she nursed baby John.

She watched the intent look on Rose's face as she concentrated on copying her grandmother. They both pushed and pulled at the balls of dough, kneading it until it was stretchy and malleable. Rose had discovered that the flour would puff and billow if she blew hard enough. She giggled as the fine powder clouded in the air then descended.

'You'll soon be white all over, Little Miss Rose,' Sarah laughed.

Mary thought her mother looked thinner, but seemed stronger in health than before. Grandchildren had certainly reinvigorated her. As well as Rose and John, Sarah and Albert had a new granddaughter. Betty and Arthur had recently become proud parents of Clarissa Maud, names carefully chosen. Betty had decided on Clarissa as she liked its refined sound, and Maud after Countess Fitzwilliam. Arthur had winked at everyone as the names were announced.

'Most likely she'll be known as Clarrie,' he stated.

The baby had been brought to Denaby to be shown off to friends and neighbours, as well as the family. Betty had glowed with pride as the white, lacy swaddling blanket was carefully opened to reveal the sleeping baby, warm and sweet-smelling. Reddish-brown lashes curved above her rosy cheeks, and auburn hair, fine and silky, complimented her creamy skin. Betty's contemplative gaze as she studied her daughter illustrated her complete pride and joy.

'She's a little treasure, all right,' was Arthur's fond comment.

'She is that,' Grandad Albert agreed.

'How's Bridie and the baby?' Sarah asked, shaping the balls of dough into breadcakes. She took Rose's finger and prodded a dint into each one. The infant produced more giggling.

'They're all right, but Bridie is still in bed and the doctor is visiting the baby most days,' Mary replied.

Bridie had given birth to a boy, Benjamin, on Christmas Eve, but there had been many problems.

Mary remembered how Bridie had cried when she told her she was pregnant. Gentle questioning had revealed that Eli was still drinking heavily, and had sometimes become aggressive towards her when drunk.

'He just changes when he's drunk,' she explained sadly. 'He gets irritated by the least little thing. I try to keep calm and not nag him, but I can't always keep my mouth shut…' Her words faded away.

'Look, it's not right that he hits you, especially now you're expecting,' Mary had retorted. 'You should tell your dad or Paddy – they'd sort him out.'

She wrapped her arms around Bridie.

'I'm all right. I don't want anyone else to know. It's probably as much my fault as Eli's,' was her quiet reply. Mary studied her face, smiling reassuringly.

'You know you've always got me, Bridie. Remember that.'

* * *

The pregnancy had progressed well, and Eli had shown interest in the news of a baby for them. He agreed to give her regular money each week, but he regarded the whole matter as women's business, something for Bridie to sort out and cope with.

His drinking had continued, so Bridie was not happy, but at least things had calmed down between them, though there was little affection.

Bridie felt her first twinges of pain early one morning. Eli had left for his morning shift, but without speaking. She was amazed how he managed to get up and get off to work, considering the state he had been in the previous night.

The rituals of rising, dressing, eating and drinking seemed to be reinforced when carried out in silence. Neither needed to speak, but Bridie was hurt by his lack of interest in her condition. He had looked and nodded to her before opening the back door, but it was closed without a word.

It was the day before Christmas Eve. She had expected the birth to be a few weeks ago. Lethargy and increased weight had slowed her movements, so relief was her first emotion with the onset of the contractions. She just wanted it all to be over.

As the morning progressed, so did the contractions, steadily becoming more frequent and intense. Her mother had been calling round with Martha the past few days, hoping the birth was imminent. She had missed having Bridie's help recently, but she was eager to hold her first grandchild. That morning, Hannah was immediately concerned when she saw her daughter. Bridie's skin was pallid, her eyes dull, her lips pale. Each contraction doubled her over, stifled her breath.

'We need to get you to bed, I don't think you've got long now,' Hannah pronounced, smiling reassuringly. But she was wrong.

Nellie, the midwife, had been sent for. She had arrived in the afternoon, coming straight from another birth in a nearby street.

'These babies all want to be born for Christmas!' she had proclaimed.

Hannah stayed with Bridie, pleased that a neighbour was looking after Martha. Eli had returned from work, but only stayed long enough to wash and eat before he left. 'I'll be back later on, so babby should be here by then,' was his explanation.

Nellie and Hannah watched Bridie endure hours of intense contractions. She tossed and screamed when the pain coursed through her body and panted with relief at the few minutes' respite before the next wave arrived. But there was little progress, and even Nellie showed concern. She spread her brown-freckled fingers over

Bridie's stomach, gently manipulating the tight skin, using her experience to assess the situation. She noted the exhaustion on Bridie's face, now glistening with mingled sweat and tears in the flickering candlelight.

'Come on, my wee girl, you can do it,' Nellie coaxed.

'Come on, Bridie love, push!' encouraged her mother.

The long, piercing scream roused Eli from sleep. He was slumped downstairs. It was the early hours of the morning. Upstairs, Nellie was busy. The baby's head had been born, but the body had not followed. Poor Bridie shrieked in agony, but the baby's shoulder was stuck. Nellie wheezed and panted, her tongue dampening her dry lips, as she manipulated the baby. She knew time was of the essence.

'Push, push, Bridie, push!' Hannah managed to shout, aghast at the situation.

The combination of pushing and pulling finally resulted in success. The baby was out, but he did not cry. Nellie scooped fluid from his nose and mouth, then rubbed his body briskly with a cloth to stimulate breathing. Bridie's panting was the only sound until a feeble cry eventually puffed from the baby's mouth.

'Oh, thank the Lord,' Hannah exclaimed as she watched Nellie tending to Bridie. The midwife had carried out the immediate duties necessary, but she had seen that there were problems with the baby boy.

'I think we need the doctor to see this wee bairn,' she spoke in a quiet but firm voice.

Bridie and Hannah stared as Nellie unwrapped the baby from its cloth blanket. They saw that his legs and feet were set at a curious angle to his body, shrivelled and malformed. One of his hands was also deformed.

'Oh, my poor baby!' Bridie cried, shock and exhaustion overwhelming her.

Hannah felt hot tears stream from her tired eyes. Disappointment radiated throughout her entire body.

'Welcome to the world, my darling wee grandson.' She managed to sob.

* * *

Bridie stared at her baby son's face, searching for reassurance. Swaddled in his blanket, he looked like a normal, healthy baby, but there was fear and deep sadness in her heart. He had managed to breathe regularly since the difficult birth, and he had even taken a little breast milk after careful positioning and coaxing.

But she was feeling a myriad of emotions. Exhaustion, disappointment and pity jostled with guilt, anxiety and envy. She had wanted to succeed in giving birth, to be a good mother, to have a healthy child, but she had none of those things.

Her own mother had shown immediate, overwhelming love for the baby, kissing and cradling him with infinite tenderness and compassion, while she, his own mother, had been reticent to show such feelings. Was it her fault that he had not been born more easily? Was it her fault that he did not have a perfect body? Would there be long-term problems because he had not breathed more quickly?

'The doctor will come and speak with you,' Nellie explained.

'Sure, you're worn out, love,' her mother soothed. 'Get some rest, then you'll feel better. You've had a hard time.'

Bridie had turned her face away and allowed her tears to flow.

Eli had hovered at the bedroom door looking thinner and taller than ever. His eyes met hers. Those almost-black eyes scanned her and the baby in fleeting glances. She wanted him to hold her, comfort her, console her. But he did not. She had loosened the baby's blanket so he could see his son. He stared but said nothing.

'He's breathing all right now, and he's even managed to take a little milk,' she whispered, attempting to give confidence and reassurance to them both.

'He has such a bonny face, too,' she added, trying to smile. Eli listened to her words while his eyes registered the child.

'I'm off to work then. Last shift before Christmas.'

Then he left. In that moment Bridie experienced a rush of love for her son. She knew he needed her love and devotion. Eli's indifferent attitude worried and saddened her. She hoped he could share his feelings one day. But she felt she was being punished yet again.

Chapter 31
June 1893

Bridie smiled at Mary, but her eyes reflected dulled sorrow. It was six months since the traumatic birth, but she was still struggling to come to terms with the situation. The labour had ravaged her body, ripping and tearing, but it had slowly healed. Her emotions, however, were in chaotic conflict.

Lots of people had offered help and support: family friends, neighbours and especially Mary and Dr Clark. Mary had visited her friend almost every day, either helping with practical tasks or just listening and talking to her.

The first time Mary had visited Bridie after the birth had been demanding for them both. Mary had tried to conceal her shock and sadness when told of baby Ben's problems, and Bridie had steeled herself to be strong and accepting of the situation. But both knew each other too well and, in the end, they had cried in each other's arms.

'He's a beautiful baby, with a beautiful mother,' Mary said through her tears. Bridie listened.

'I love him,' she replied. 'But I wish he was all right. What will his life be like? I feel so sorry for him. It's all my fault.' Bridie cried bitter tears, overcome by uncertainty and hopelessness.

'No, it's not your fault! We'll all help you to take care of him.' Mary encouraged her, but she knew Bridie. She knew she would need lots of support to lift herself out of her gloom.

The practical routine of looking after a new baby had helped Bridie to assume her maternal role. Feeding, washing and caring for Ben had roused her from her initial apathy. She felt genuine love for her son.

Eli still seemed indifferent, however. He looked at Ben, but did not kiss or cuddle him. His almost-black eyes followed Bridie as she cared for him, but they showed a resigned disinterest.

PART FOUR

Chapter 32
1893

Denaby was changing dramatically. Hundreds of new colliery houses had been rapidly built by the Company, swallowing up more and more of the surrounding open countryside, all in anticipation of the expected need to accommodate thousands of employees who were required to work at the new Cadeby Colliery.

Coal had finally been reached, nearly four years after sinking operations had begun. The lengthy period and huge expense had worried the Company, fearful that the whole project could have been a "white elephant". Much relief was felt when the Barnsley Bed of coal was reached, but at a depth of seven hundred and fifty yards, much deeper than had been expected. The local miners had strong opinions about the new pit.

'Denaby pit's four hundred and fifty yards deep, and that's deep enough for some, so God knows what it'll be like working at Cadeby.'

'Aye, deepest mine in South Yorkshire.'

'It's got to be hot and gassy.'

'Plenty o' work for a long time, though.'

Denaby pit already employed one thousand five hundred men and boys, and the bosses estimated three thousand more would be needed to work at Cadeby pit.

'I can remember when there were only two hundred people living round here thirty years ago, and most of them were in Old Denaby,' recounted one of the older residents. 'Now there's over a thousand pit houses and must be near enough three thousand people living 'ere.'

Many of the changes had been instigated by Mr William Henry Chambers, managing director of the newly named Denaby Main and Cadeby Colliery Company. He was the driving force behind developing Denaby Main, the colliery village. He was known as the "King of Denaby".

He had moved to Denaby in 1882 when he was appointed manager of Denaby Main pit. Coming from a family of colliery managers, he had gained his mining engineer knowledge by working at a variety of pits from an early age. The necessary qualifications had been obtained through extensive study and course work.

Denaby pit was developing the Barnsley seam, and there were frequent "gob" fires, fed by gasses released from the layers of coal and rock. Mr Chambers had to deal with the many dangerous fires and became regarded as an eminent authority on the subject in the mining industry.

'Chambers can be a stubborn bugger when he's dealing with the men and disputes, but tha's got to hand it to him, he knows his stuff when it comes to working mines,' was a commonly shared opinion amongst the miners.

As time passed, Mr Chambers became embroiled in many conflicts and disputes, but he also devoted a great amount of his personal time to developing Denaby Main, the small village named after the pit. Houses were built, Cadeby Colliery was developed, as well as shops and schools to service the community.

Mr Chambers sat on many committees, including the Rural District and Parish councils, hospital and school boards, the Co-operative Society and the popular cricket club. It was a "Company" village, built, owned and run by the colliery bosses. The "King of Denaby" ruled for many years.

Chapter 33
1893

The children of Denaby had been watching every day as their new school was being built on Rossington Street. It grew bigger and bigger. They couldn't believe it was for them and that they would soon be moving into it. Their present, smaller school, at the bottom of Rossington Street, was only ten years old, but it was already too small for the hundreds of children in Denaby Main.

The two pits in the village had brought in lots of people and their families. A few of the children could remember the very first school, behind Denaby pit. The infants were still there but would soon be moving to the smaller Rossington Street school, as soon as the older children moved to the brand new one.

Three of the older pupils stood together, looking up at the impressive building. They were Bob, Mary's brother; Seamus, Bridie's brother and Walter's sister, Alice.

'It's a pity we'll only have a short time here,' Alice remarked. 'It's so much bigger than our old school!'

'I suppose so, but I want to start work as soon as I can,' Seamus explained. 'I want to earn some money.'

'Me too,' Bob agreed.

The thirteen-year-old children shielded their eyes from the sun with flattened hands as their gazes travelled upwards.

'It's massive!' Seamus cried.

'I like the tower part best,' Bob decided. 'And that bit on the top,' he added.

'Miss Stacey said it's called a cupola,' Alice reminded them, 'it's like a dome. It's got a huge hall too – it's going to be the biggest village hall in England!'

'All those red bricks to build it came from Ashfield Brickworks, you know, in Conisbrough, at the bottom of Clifton Hill, onto

Sheffield Road. My uncle works there. He told me,' Seamus said proudly.

'Well, it's going to be a school church, so it's got to be big,' Alice continued. 'It's like two buildings in one.'

'Mr Chambers said we can all go and look inside it next week,' Bob declared.

The children smiled and nodded agreement. They were all looking forward to that.

* * *

Miss Stacey organised the excited school children into double lines that snaked through the classrooms.

'Stand quietly with your partners, then we'll walk up the street to see inside the new school,' she announced. 'Mr Chambers has kindly granted you permission to see what a splendid new building the Company has provided for you. You are very lucky children,' Pride and excitement was displayed in her ringing voice.

'Please, Miss,' Seamus raised his hand. 'Is it true that it's got the biggest village hall in England? My dad said he'd read that in the *Times*.'

'Possibly and probably,' replied the teacher. 'This is a colliery school like no other. It is a school church of outstanding proportions, costing between four and five thousand pounds to build.'

A few boys whistled their astonishment at that fact, quietened only by Miss Stacey's famous glaring stare.

'Alice and Bob, lead us out, please,' she commanded.

The bubbling, restrained whispers from the children conveyed their excitement and curiosity.

* * *

'Ooohs!' and 'Aaahs!' rebounded along the lines of school children as they stepped into the entrance of their new school. They peered at the tower surmounted by a cupola, and noticed the shiny, red bricks, as well as the stone dressings.

'It's all so fancy,' someone called out.

'Now, children, we are walking into the central hall. This is a very special room.' Miss Stacey's voice echoed in the huge space.

The floor was paved with wooden blocks, and the walls were plastered, with lower panelling of varnished pitch pine. The arched ceiling was also pine, lit by a huge skylight that swept almost from one end of the hall to the other. There were also extra lights on both sides of the sloping roof. Classrooms led off from both sides of the hall.

'I'd just like to run round and round in here, it's so big!' one child declared.

'The Company decided that it was not only a new school that the village needed,' Miss Stacey explained. 'But also a church, and this building is intended to meet the requirements of both. During the week, it will be used as a school, and on Sundays, as a church. At that far end of the hall is a chancel, a space with an altar, also a moveable pulpit and a reading desk. Revolving shutters will close off the chancel area in the week, then, when raised, this becomes a church.'

The children listened carefully, in awe of their surroundings. They were excited about moving into their new school church. They couldn't wait to tell their families about it.

* * *

'All that space made me want to jump and run and dance,' Alice had laughed as she chatted to her parents.

'Chambers has certainly spent some brass on it,' her father, Alf, declared.

'It'll be nice for you to finish your schooldays there,' her mother, Peggy, agreed.

Bob had described the school to Sarah and Albert.

'There's so much space, it's huge!'

'So's the size of the classes – I don't envy those teachers,' Sarah retorted.

'Better than the old school behind the pit, that's for sure,' Albert concluded.

Willie and Hannah listened as Seamus told them about the school visit.

'It's got a tower, a cupola, a chancel and lots of classrooms. Best bit was the hall – it's the biggest one you've ever seen!'

'Our Liza would have liked it,' Hannah whispered, a sob catching in her throat. They all nodded slowly, their lips sealed, for fear of what they might say.

Chapter 34
1893-1894

Mary's life had settled into a happy routine. Rose and John were healthy and thriving, which was no mean feat in their unhealthy environment. Water was still often in short supply, which made it hard work for the women to try and maintain hygienic surroundings for their families.

Many of the women threatened to tackle Mr Chambers about the water situation, so dispirited about the never-ending toil of coping with the problems that lack of water produced.

The recent whooping cough epidemic had worried everyone. Schools had been closed for four weeks and, thankfully, no one had died in Denaby, although two children had died in Mexborough.

Jim had recently moved to the new Cadeby colliery. He was impressed how modern it was compared to Denaby pit. It was one of the largest pits in Yorkshire, and certainly the deepest. Thousands of men and boys were employed there, above and below ground.

Mr Chambers had installed hydraulic and mechanical equipment which assisted and enhanced the coal production rate, making Cadeby one of the most productive collieries in the north. Complex ventilation and haulage systems also boosted productivity.

The colliery surface was large and advanced. Screens separated the "hard" from the "soft" coal, and washers and coke ovens processed the different sorts of coal.

Workshops for various uses were spread around the pit shafts, as well as abundant rail tracks to assist the conveyance of the coal to various destinations. However, miners still hewed the coal by hand and pit ponies were still used to haul the filled corves.

Jim was a steady, reliable collier, fair both to his gang of labourers, and to the datallers, workers paid by the day when needed, often to build or repair roadways underground. Many of the more experienced, reliable miners had been transferred from Denaby to Cadeby.

Walter had also moved to Cadeby, but there was still a rift between the men. Jim had tried to reason with Walt, tried to regain their past bonds of trust and friendship, but to no avail.

Walter bore a hostile grudge, still smarting from what he regarded as Jim's lack of loyalty. Tommy Prince's fall and injuries were well-known in the community, but Jim felt the weight of responsibility, knowing that Walt had carried out the assault. Jim had mixed feelings about it all, but he had told no one else about this secret, not even his wife.

Mary heard that Walter had married a Conisbrough girl, Esther, and that they had been living with her parents on Ivanhoe Road in Conisbrough. They had one child, a boy named Joseph, and they had recently moved into a new pit house near Cadeby pit.

All this information had been gained from Walter's sisters, Ellen, Beatie and Ada, who were still friends with Mary. They had all questioned why the two men were not as close as before, but Jim had just shrugged his shoulders and pretended to explain the reason.

'He's married and a father now. He wants to spend his time with them rather than me,' he had smiled. 'I think Esther was the first woman he'd ever been serious about. I can understand that.' He placed a tender kiss on Mary's lips.

She smiled, returning his kiss, still thrilled that Jim was her husband. She counted her blessings in life. Happiness blurred the hardships. So many people were not as fortunate, eventually ground down by oppressive situations and relationships. Not everyone was strong enough to cope. She still worried about Bridie.

* * *

Rossington Street school church had opened and it quickly became an important building for the whole community. The children loved their new classrooms and especially the large hall. Class sizes were big, but the light, spacious rooms felt so much more welcoming than those in the earlier schools.

The infants had moved from the first colliery school into the smaller Rossington Street school, which especially pleased the newly formed Salvation Army Corps. They rented part of the old school from the Company and began using it for their meetings, as well as a venue for tea parties and money-raising events for the poor and needy in Denaby.

The new school was used on Sundays for church meetings and worship, as well as Sunday school classes. The older St. Chad's church was also attended by some worshippers. It was next to The Reresby Arms on Doncaster Road. The Wesleyans had already built Epworth Hall, a few years earlier, in Rossington Street, on land donated by Andrew Montagu esquire, and a Methodist Chapel was being built on Doncaster Road.

'Only a Catholic Church is needed,' was the fervent opinion of the many Catholic miners in Denaby.

'We have to travel to Doncaster or Wath-upon-Dearne for our masses. We really want our own church here in Denaby.'

There were so many miners from Ireland in Denaby that it was known locally as 'Little Ireland'. The Company had decided to appoint a Roman Catholic priest. He was provided with a house to live in, and the use of part of the old colliery school as a temporary church.

'This priest is energetic and enthusiastic,' Mr Chambers had reported to the Company. 'He'll calm and control the Irish miners until enough funds are raised to build their own Catholic church.' The Company agreed with the "King of Denaby".

* * *

The large hall in the new school had become very popular for musical events. Concerts, orchestral, and choral performances were held regularly in the spacious venue, attracting audiences of enthusiastic music lovers from Sheffield and surrounding towns. The Company was happy to promote the classical music, hoping it would reflect a refined reputation for the village, although not many of the local people attended. The hall was described in local newspapers as:

A spacious and magnificent building, whose acoustic properties carry the volume of tone produced by singers and orchestras, with telling effect.

The school soon became known as "The Large Hall" as it was used so much for community events.

Bob only attended the new school for a few months, as he left when he reached his fourteenth birthday. Although still small for his age, he had become stronger in health during the last few years. His mother was surprised and relieved at his sturdiness and improved constitution. She remembered the many chest infections he had suffered as a sickly child.

'It must be all that goose grease you slathered on me that worked!' Bob teased, grinning at Sarah.

'I don't care what it was as long as you're well!' she retorted. 'These houses certainly don't help!'

Bob had often been teased by the other children about his short stature, but he had retaliated good-naturedly:

'They don't make diamonds as big as bricks!' His jaunty, determined voice had subdued the taunts, gaining him friendly acceptance with his peers.

Sarah and Albert had never wanted him to work down the pit, so concerned had they been for his health.

'Your chest and breathing will never cope,' Albert reiterated many times, hoping to convince his son. 'As well as it being damned hard work,' he added.

Bob had remained determined and stubborn, however. 'I want to be a pony driver, or even maybe a horse keeper one day,' he had affirmed repeatedly. 'I know I can do it. I want to work with the animals.'

His parents pursed their lips and sighed.

'We'll just have to wait and see,' his mother soothed, tactfully.

'No way are you goin' down t' pit!' Albert had declared, 'You'll 'ave to find another job!'

* * *

Bob left school at Christmas and started work at Denaby pit in the new year.

'I'll be all right, I'm stronger than I look, and this is one job where it's better if you're small!' he explained to his family, winking and grinning. His parents and sisters looked on, partly anxious for their Bob, but also with admiration for his quiet determination.

'I'm sure you'll be a really good pony driver,' his sister Gertie said.

'Maybe even a horse keeper one day, if I know our Bob!' Ivy said, giving him a friendly cuff.

Mary and Betty had smiled at their brother, proudly.

'I can't believe our Bob's going to be a worker soon,' Sarah said, shaking her head.

'It'll certainly make him grow up fast!' Albert had said, though not without a hint of pride that his lad was so strong-willed and resolute.

Chapter 35
June 1894

Sarah watched her son and husband leave the house. They were on the morning shift. The warmer, lighter mornings of June made their walk to work much more pleasant than the previous weeks of cold, wet weather. Bob had been working for six months and the family could already see changes in him.

'My word, Bob, you're shooting up,' Mary had declared. 'I think you've grown a good few inches since you've been working!'

'You're certainly filling out,' Gertie informed him, noticing the changing details of her brother's body and features.

Bob's face showed signs of growing adulthood. The thin, soft curves of boyhood were developing into angled contours of manhood. His defined chin was sprouting whiskers, his eyebrows had thickened and darkened to a coppery shade. He could feel the difference in himself, even after such a short time.

School life already seemed distant; he could feel the reality of adult life. This realisation affected him deeply. He recognised the strength of character in the hardworking men and women of his community. He truly felt that he was no longer a child, physically or mentally.

Bob had felt an assault on his senses when he first started work at the pit. The sights and sounds of a working colliery had appeared exaggerated, magnified, much greater than his expectation. Noises and changing views had swirled around him, as if in a maelstrom. He had braced himself to confront and adapt to the harsh, raw surroundings of coal, rock, metal and darkness.

The changing atmospheres, from cold, wet and dank, to hot, humid to dusty, enveloped the workers, as if changing their moods with pressing, controlling hands. Smells were stark and pronounced, of the earth, of toiling men and animals. Even the taste of food and drink was noticeably altered, as if the underground world had continued to manipulate the men in its grasp. Bob had reeled at first, but he had coped.

The new experiences eddied in Bob's consciousness, revolving and spiralling until his mind made sense of them. A growing appreciation of the complexities of mining had been kindled, along with a pronounced admiration for its hardworking employees. He had, in the past, asked his father to describe what it was like working down the mine, but Albert had not much enlarged on his stock reply:

'It's damned hard work.'

Bob had grown close to Jim, the older brother he'd never had, and turned to him for information and conversation about his work as a collier. They had often walked the fields and woods together, sharing their love of nature, sharing ideas and opinions.

Jim had answered him truthfully about his work, stating the many difficult aspects of working underground, the back-breaking toil, the dangers, the monotonous drudgery, the lack of light and sun. He had also patted Bob's back, adding:

'But that's how we earn our money, lad – that's what we do to put food on the table. We are a special breed of worker.'

Bob had listened intently, churning over Jim's remarks.

'Do you think I'll belong to the same special breed, because I want to be a pony driver?'

Jim had smiled.

'Get ready to find it hard at first,' he replied. You'll soon know if you can cope with being a pit worker.'

* * *

Bob's first few weeks were spent working on the pit top. Many of the miners knew him as 'Albert's lad', and greeted him with friendly, good-humoured banter, as well as down-to-earth remarks.

'Na then, Bob, tha's mebbe ont' small side but thi dad says tha can work as hard as t' next lad, and tha's stubborn enough to prove it,' was one of them.

'Little 'uns are just as good as big 'uns, if not better down t' pit,' was another.

Bob's first responsibility was as a lamp boy. The lamp room was near the pit shaft, which loomed and towered over the adjacent sheds. He peered at the rows of safety lamps arranged on shelves around the room.

The lamp keeper, Enoch Jones, had slowly and clearly explained to him what his duties would be, and had impressed upon him the importance of being a careful, conscientious worker.

'Every man comes here before and after every shift. Every man knows his own number, and that number is on his check and the same number is on his lamp. He gives you his check and you give him his lamp at the beginning of his shift, then he returns the lamp, and you return his check at the end of his shift.'

Bob nodded, his eyes wide, his sense of responsibility boosting his self-esteem.

'Those lamps over there are what the night-shift men have left. They have to be cleaned and ready for their next shift,' Enoch continued. 'So tha'd better get started, lad.'

As Bob cleaned the lamps, he gazed at the lines of hooks on which the numbered discs were hanging. Each check belonged to a miner, deep below them. They could be quickly tallied in times of need or emergency, giving important personal information about the workforce underground.

'Come on, lad, get cleaning.' Enoch's order interrupted Bob's thoughts. 'We haven't got all day'.

'Yes sir,' Bob replied, polishing and dusting with renewed vigour. He was still looking forward to going down the pit though, still hoping to work with the horses.

Chapter 36
Autumn 1894

Bob's next job was underground as a coupler. That first day, he had descended in the cage along with his father and other miners, many of them quiet and still groggy with sleep.

It was six o'clock on a cold, wet morning. They had left the damp darkness outside and were clanking down the shaft, deeper and deeper. Albert's sidelong glances at his son provided him with little evidence of Bob's reactions. The boy was silent, cap pulled down, body rigid, transfixed by a tumult of feelings. He was thrilled that he was at last going to experience life underground, yet nervous and anxious about his ability to prove his worth.

The men around him appeared so calm, so at ease; they knew what was coming. Past experience rendered them resigned but competent. Each had a job, a status, each had expectations of what was needed from them. Bob had tried to reassure himself, had told himself that one day he would be as relaxed as they were; that it would become second nature to drop to the deep, dark depths of the terrain.

The cage jolted to a stop; the onsetter opened the doors. The miners headed along the roadways, walking with confident steps. Their boots and clogs struck the uneven ground, producing echoing, staggered thuds in the dimly lit tunnelled spaces. The last of the night-shift men passed by, on their way to the cage for their ascent to the pit top and home.

Albert nodded to Bob.

'Head down there, son, and you'll come to the flats. One of the pony drivers will tell you what to do.'

With that, Albert nodded again, mustered up a brief smile and then continued his walk to the coal face.

Bob watched as his father walked away. He steered himself towards the flats, the collection point for the tubs of coal. He stumbled walking on the bumpy surface of the roadway. He now had to learn how to be a coupler.

As Bob worked underground that first day, the shadowy tunnels had felt eerily constrictive, yet almost intimate, as if wrapping around the men and animals with both a protective but clear-cut statement. The creaks and groans from straining props seemed to speak a language:

Respect your environment, beware, be prepared.

There was a steady flow, back and forth, of full and empty corves travelling along the rails, pulled by the resolute ponies. The iron tubs were connected by coupling chains to form a set, or train. The heavy chains linked the metal tubs, and Bob marvelled that a pony could pull three full corves.

He was shown how to do the coupling by an experienced pony driver, a big, thick-set lad with a resonant voice and booming laugh, who explained the complex routine of getting the coal to the surface.

'The colliers fill the tubs at the coal face, and they're pulled to the flats. Smaller ponies have to work on the side roadways at the coal face as they're too low and narrow for the bigger horses. At the flats, the bigger ponies pull the full tubs on the main roadways to the pit bottom, ready to be taken to the surface. The empty tubs are brought back to the flats, then the smaller ponies take them on to the coal face, ready to be filled again.'

Bob listened carefully, fascinated by the quiet, working animals. They worked with their driver, or 'putter', to move the corves along the roadways, which were often on inclines or in narrow passages.

He studied the equipment the ponies wore, a leather head harness to protect the tops of their heads from low roofs, and the wooden shafts fitted to the harness, which could be quickly attached and detached from the tubs when they were changed. He patted their steaming flanks and hoped he could be a driver very soon.

135

* * *

Bob's wish was realised not long afterwards. He had, at last, become a pony driver. The horse keeper, Cyrus Hinds, had agreed that the boy could be trained as a driver. He explained, in great detail, the requirements when choosing a pony for a long working life underground.

'First, the pony needs to have the right temperament. It has to be even-tempered. Lively horses can cause injuries and accidents, but nervous and timid horses are no good either – it takes too long and too much money to break them in. The Company buy and pay for the upkeep of the horses – they want strong, healthy animals, so choosing the right ones in the first place is really important. They want intelligent horses that can be trained to do the job and obey commands,' he stated in a concise, measured tone.

'Next, ponies have to get used to being handled and harnessed. They need to be strong to pull heavy weights, and hardy enough to work in dark, noisy conditions, and for long hours. They have to be small enough to work in low, narrow roadways, and be able to turn in small spaces. Not easy to find all these things in a pony, lad,' Cyrus concluded. 'But colliers earn money by getting the maximum coal in the minimum time, and that's one thing the Company agrees about with them. So the ponies have to be right and looked after.'

Bob absorbed all the information, and incidents soon occurred which affected his understanding of the relationship between pony and driver.

Cyrus Hinds had been the horse keeper at Denaby pit for a number of years. His dedication to the job was well-known and admired by all. He was strict but fair with the pony drivers, and resolute in his belief that the horses should be handled and looked after with as much kindness and compassion as possible within their challenging working environment. He was responsible for their stabling and well-being. He would not tolerate cruelty or ill-treatment.

Most of the drivers had close relationships with their ponies.; affection and trust grown from working together in long shifts, often in the dark, sometimes with only each other for companionship.

Bob quickly noticed the strong bonds between the men and horses, and the experienced drivers readily shared the quirks and idiosyncrasies of their individual animals, each pony a character in its own way.

Kruger, Percy's pony, loved tobacco. Percy would chew it and dangle it from his mouth, to be rasped away by Kruger's eager tongue. Patch was a feisty one, and always hungry. Snap had to be removed from pockets and hung high if it was to survive until mealtimes. His handler, Fred, insisted that Patch had once chomped his way through a set of false teeth left in one alluring coat pocket. Pride, the oldest pony, was the most stubborn, refusing to work a minute more when meal-times were due. However, once replenished, he was also the strongest and most dedicated hauler.

Bob had been shown how to work as a pony driver by a few different men, and he slowly grew in confidence as he practised leading the ponies along the various roadways. He quickly appreciated the intelligence and stoical nature of the horses, almost as if they were teaching him. He was applying all the rules as his experience grew.

'Never walk in front of the pony, don't ride on the pony's back, and don't ride in an empty tub,' he had been told.

'Walk between the pony and the first tub, or ride on the chains between the pony and the first tub,' they ordered. 'And mind you bend down when the roof drops low, or your back will be torn to shreds.'

Although Bob was conscientious, he had witnessed incidents where rough treatment and cruelty had occurred. It was often the younger drivers, only thirteen or fourteen years old, who ill-treated the horses, and mostly out of ignorance or short tempers. One driver had kicked a pony hard, with his clogs on, which resulted in injuries to the horse's legs, and the loss of four shifts for the pony.

'He wouldn't pull quick enough,' was the boy's excuse. He was summoned to a meeting by the Company and accused of cruelty. He received a fine of thirty shillings.

Another driver had attached four full tubs instead of the usual three, and when the pony had refused to pull them, he had kicked and injured it. He was fined twenty shillings, plus costs of fifteen shillings and sixpence.

The worst incident of cruelty was when a driver hit a pony with a metal bar, causing it severe leg injuries, the pony needing a month off to recover.

'I was in a bad temper,' was the indifferent excuse. He received twenty-one days imprisonment.

Bob was also shocked at the many injuries received by the horses and drivers. The ponies' legs often got caught in the rails, or were knocked by the heavy corves. Some of the injuries were so severe that the horses had to be put down immediately to stop their suffering. Cyrus had warned Bob that, one day, he might witness one of these killings.

'We put a heavy cap on the horse's head. It's got eye protectors and a hole in the middle. A metal spike is put into the hole and driven down into its skull. The horse dies instantly – it's put out of its pain.'

A shiver ran down Bob's spine as he listened to Cyrus. He hated to think of such a death, even though he knew it was the humane thing to do.

'Lads get injured too, mind you,' Cyrus continued. 'And it's usually when they don't stick to the rules or aren't concentrating.'

Bob nodded, remembering Harry Martin's recent accident. Harry had started as a pony driver only a few weeks before Bob. He had suffered a badly broken arm when it was caught between two of the corves.

'I must have slipped on the rails, it all happened so fast,' he later explained.

'It's a good job Harry was taken to Mexborough Cottage hospital on Bank Street,' Bob said to Cyrus.

'It is, lad, saved his arm, they did. With luck he'll be able to work again. Mind you, he'll maybe watch where he's walking next time,' the horse keeper remarked, the grim line of his mouth parallel to his black moustache.

* * *

After only a few months, Bob was given his own pony, Ginger. He was five years old, with one year's work experience. His previous driver had moved away, and Cyrus decided that Bob and Ginger would make a good working team. He stated the good points about Ginger, the characteristics that made him suitable for mine work.

'Ginger's only eleven hands high, but he's heavy-bodied and heavy-limbed, with plenty of bone and substance. Aye, and when he hauls, he's low-headed and sure-footed. He's just right for all those narrow, low passages.'

Bob gazed at the pony, almost in disbelief that he was being trusted as his handler and driver. He patted Ginger, feeling a close bond already. He knew drivers had to work their horses hard, that was required in the job, but he also knew that trust and respect would enhance their days working together.

He soon learned how to clean Ginger's stable, to make sure the water and food was in sufficient supply, and how to clean and check the pony's body. All this was carried out under the watchful eye of Cyrus Hinds.

Chapter 37
1894-1895

Mary and Jim enjoyed their married life, especially watching their children grow. Rose was as loving as ever and although only five years old, she had already developed an open, affectionate personality that endeared her to friends and family. She had readily accepted and cared for her brother, John, and was very close to the little three-year-old boy.

Mary and Jim would often watch them playing together, noting their fond but different natures. Rose happily chatted and acted in a demonstrative, tactile way, whereas John was quieter, self-contained, focused. Mary could certainly see traits of Jim, her father Albert, and Dick, all rolled together in her son's personality, but she was proud of both her children, as was Jim. Rose had already started infant school at Rossington Street, which she loved, just as her mother had always enjoyed school life.

Sarah and Albert thrived on seeing their grandchildren develop and mature. It added another dimension to their lives. They felt fortunate that their children and grandchildren were happy and healthy, as so many other families could not say the same. They were especially pleased that Bob was managing working at the pit. He had matured and strengthened since leaving school, something they had not thought possible when he had been a sickly, weak child.

He loved working with the horses; he loved the feeling that he had proved everyone wrong, and had achieved his ambition.

Betty and Arthur visited frequently, wanting daughter Clarrie to be part of the whole family. Betty still counted her blessings that she had her Arthur, Clarissa and her Elsecar home, but she also felt close bonds to Denaby and her family.

She doted on her daughter, still thrilled to be a mother. She often thought about her dreams and ambitions for her little girl.

'Bettering oneself' was still a prominent feature in her outlook on life.

'Just think, Arthur, one day our Clarissa might be able to work at the "Big House" for the Earl and Countess. Just think...' she would often remark to her husband with a far-away look in her eye and a satisfied smile on her lips. Arthur always smiled and nodded.

'Aye, just think – that would be summat,' he confirmed.

* * *

Mary's sister, Gertie, had recently married Charlie, her long-term fiancé. She was twenty-six years old, a year younger than Charlie. Sarah and Albert had been surprised that the couple had not married earlier, but Gertie had been adamant about the timing. She had been determined to carry on working at Kilner's, hoping to save up some money.

Then they heard the exciting news that their bosses, the Kilner brothers, had decided to build over seventy new houses in Denaby for their workers.

There were to be five streets of the new houses, each with a name connected to the Kilner family. John Street, William Street and George Street were named after the three brothers, and Thornhill Street and Lees Terrace were named after Thornhill Lees, the West Yorkshire village where the family had originally lived and worked.

Gertie and Charlie had been so excited to think that they might have a chance of getting one of the new houses. Their eyes shone and hearts raced as they discussed the prospect, and they were overjoyed to be told they could have Number One George Street, which was near to completion.

'We can get married now!' Charlie had announced, his broad grin showing gleaming teeth, his blue eyes flashing with happy anticipation.

'Oh, I'm so happy, Charlie,' Gertie had replied, thrilled at the thoughts of being Charlie's wife, and of having a brand-new house of their own.

* * *

The couple were married one week after receiving the keys to their new home. It was a quiet wedding, with just family and a few friends as money was scarce.

Gertie and Charlie had eyes only for each other, so the day was very special to them. Charlie's family was small, just his parents and one younger sister, but they loved Gertie as one of their own. Sarah and Albert had felt pride and admiration for the young couple, pleased that they were so happy together and that they had a good start to their married life.

Gertie had shown Sarah, Mary and Ivy the new house just before the wedding.

'All the new houses are the same,' she had explained, 'but I like this one as it's right onto Doncaster Road, and not far from your houses,' she beamed.

'And only a short walk to Kilner's,' added Mary.

'This is the living room and through there is the scullery,' Gertie pointed out as they walked through the downstairs.

'Oh, and there's a coal cellar, and another cellar next to it with a cold slab.'

Mary and Sarah nodded approvingly.

'How many bedrooms?' asked Ivy, taking in the surroundings.

'Three!' Gertie announced proudly.

'Three? My, you are lucky,' Mary agreed. 'Not many houses have three.'

'There's just the one toilet in our own little back yard, too,' Gertie continued.

'You'll soon be as posh as our Betty!' Ivy and Mary chorused together coincidentally, falling into a fit of giggles.

'Nothing wrong with trying to be a bit posh,' Sarah mused with a satisfied sigh.

Charlie and Gertie moved into their new home in the 'Glasshouse buildings' as they had quickly become named by the locals, and began married life with love and optimism for a happy future together.

* * *

Ivy was still working at the Powder Works, and still living with her parents and brother Bob. She helped her mother with as much of the housework as she could, although with Betty, Mary and Gertie now married and in their own homes, the house was less crowded, less busy.

During the six years she had worked at the Flameless Explosives Works, the workforce had increased as the business grew. The company had been granted a government permit to manufacture 'Securite', which was claimed, had special properties that superseded gunpowder or the other materials used for blasting operations in mines.

The regulations in force at the Works were to be: 'of the most stringent character, although only the remotest danger is to be feared and a catastrophe can only be brought about by the most gross carelessness', according to the company's dictates. The workforce was only too pleased to have well-paid jobs, and even social facilities, such as a garden and a bowling green.

Jobs at the Powder Works were much sought after, and although the majority of the workers were women and girls, there were also men who maintained the equipment and machines.

A new man had recently started working there, and Ivy had immediately noticed him. She had almost been aware of his presence before she had seen him.

She had been standing at her workstation, one of the many in lines throughout the factory, when he walked by. She saw a tall, broad-shouldered man with a fresh complexion, something most young men lacked, especially the miners that she knew. He was clean-shaven, no moustache as was fashionable, with a thick, quiff of light brown hair. His soft-spoken voice hinted at a more southern accent, unusual to her ears.

He progressed up and down the lines of workers, discussing any faults or problems with the equipment being used. Ivy noticed the way the women had looked at him, their eyes inquisitive, yet shy beneath lowered lashes.

As he neared Ivy's workstation, she experienced an almost magnetic draw towards him, as if an invisible aura surrounded him. Her breathless, involuntary reaction had been something new to her.

'Everything all right here?' he asked.

Ivy turned to meet his gaze, and their eyes met, hers large, pale-grey, dewy, his a warm brown, with bright amber flecks. There had been an apparent casualness in the focused stare, yet both had scrutinised and recorded each other. She had lodged a handsome, virile man, he had registered a beautiful, exquisite woman.

'Yes, everything's all right, thanks,' Ivy replied, her Yorkshire accent sounding flat and drab compared to his, she thought. He smiled in reply, hesitated a moment, then added:

'I'm new here, as you probably know. My name's Frank, Frank Chapman. Let me know if you need me for anything.'

Ivy smiled, certain he could hear her beating heart.

'I'm Ivy Cooper. Yes, I'll let you know.'

They held each other's gaze for a moment, before Frank moved on, then each of them was left with their own thoughts to mull over and digest.

Chapter 38
1895

'Bloody hell, has it got gold and diamond fittings in it?' Jim exclaimed. He was reading the article in the *Mexborough and Swinton Times* about the new commercial hotel that had recently opened in Denaby.

'It's cost the Company fifteen thousand pounds to have it built and furnished,' Jim continued, shaking his head in disbelief.

Mary nodded her agreement. 'No expense spared, I've heard,' she stated.

'I'll see for myself when I go there,' Jim added. 'Mr Chambers is going to use the dining room there for our Denaby and Cadeby Cricket Club meetings from now on.'

'He's not daft, then,' Mary laughed. 'The managing director of the Company uses the brand new Denaby Main Hotel for the cricket club that he's also chairman of!'

'He did organise and develop the building,' conceded Jim. 'You've got to hand it to him – yet another Company-owned-and-run community building,' he added.

'I reckon it's going to be very popular round here,' Mary agreed.

'If last week's anything to go by, I think you're right,' Jim said. 'Packed out every day.'

* * *

Ellen made one of her regular visits to Mary's home the following day. The young women remained firm friends, even though their lives were very different.

Although only one year older than Ellen, Mary felt almost matriarchal, being married with two children aged five and three. Ellen was still living with her parents and siblings, although it still felt strange without Walter living there.

In the six years since the traumatic events in her life, Ellen had struggled to overcome feelings of guilt and lack of self-worth, but her job had been her saviour. She had started working at the Denaby Co-op a few years earlier, in the Post Office.

The formality and responsibility of her job gradually subdued her self-doubt and boosted her self-confidence. She slowly blossomed, like a flower opening up to sun and rain.

The uniform of a smart, white blouse tucked into a long, black skirt immediately allowed her to adopt an official, almost ceremonial persona. She felt that the role of assistant Post Mistress bestowed on her the ability to be detached yet valued by others.

She carried out transactions of money orders and Savings Bank business for the Rotherham postal district with accuracy and precision. She even prided herself in sending telegraphs, a facility only recently available at the Post Office.

She had managed to avoid close contact with Tommy Prince since that awful time. Subconsciously, she would scan the streets or places where she walked, fearful of a sudden confrontation with him. This permanently cautious behaviour had resulted in her being introverted, happy to enjoy the company of family and close friends, but unwilling to take on new challenges and experiences with others.

She had been unable to escape close contact with Tommy on one occasion, however. She had been working in the back stockroom of the Post Office, checking supplies, and had stepped out to see him at the counter, waiting to be served.

Her first instinct had been to retreat, but pride, or resilience, had shunned that reaction. Instead, she had raised her eyes sufficiently to see the pink scar marking his features, though not to meet his eyes. With a detached formality, she had served the stamps that he requested.

'Thank you very much, Miss. And a very good day to you,' were his mocking words as he walked away, whistling.

She had then trembled and shook, inhaling deep, ragged breaths to calm herself. She was proud that she had not reacted to his calculated stare and superior smirk.

* * *

Ellen made a fuss of John when she arrived, as she always did. He gave her his usual brief smile and prolonged stare, then returned his attention to his toys, scattered on the colourful peg rug that Sarah had made for them during long winter nights.

Jim had lovingly made him a variety of wooden objects to play with. John watched his father intently as his knife blade fashioned the pieces of wood into cubes and cuboids of varying sizes. The little boy had patiently waited while the blocks were smoothed and polished, all rough edges and splinters planed and whittled away.

Then it was Jim's turn to study the little boy. He loved to watch John's focused concentration as he handled and placed the blocks to make interesting towers and bridges, his fingers gaining deftness as they stacked and balanced the objects.

When they inevitably fell and crashed to the floor, Jim admired his son's resolute acceptance, his brief sigh, then his next attempt to create an acceptable building. Jim saw an inkling of the boy's future character, determined and tenacious.

The conversation between Ellen and Mary soon turned to the new Denaby Main Hotel.

'Our Ada and Beatie couldn't believe their luck getting jobs there, so many people want to work there,' Ellen beamed. 'I know they're only chambermaids, but it's so exciting for them to work in such a grand place – and in Denaby!'

'Tell me all about it, then,' Mary happily replied.

'Well, Mr Gibbs, the landlord, gave the new staff a guided tour, and this is how the girls described it,' Ellen began. 'The entrance hall is really elaborate, with a mosaic-tiled floor, wood-panelled walls shone up 'til you could nearly see yourself in them, and a lovely stained-glass chandelier with matching lamps, so everything glows, they said. On one side there's a bar parlour with leather seats, and our Ada said she'd never seen such a big table running down the room, just like in country mansions, she imagines. Oh, and Beatie said there's hat-pegs on all the walls. On the other side, there's a tap-room and a dram-shop all finished to a much higher standard than most pubs. The bar's fitted with the latest appliances, so drinks can be served quickly and easily.'

'What's upstairs then?' Mary enquired, her eyes shining as she tried to visualise the building from Ellen's words.

'Well, there's a dining room that can easily seat one hundred and fifty people, and when it's used as a club room or for public meetings, three hundred folk can be accommodated,' Ellen explained.

'How do they get the food upstairs, surely not up lots of steps?' interrupted Mary.

'Oh, there's a lift from the kitchen up to the dining room for the food to be carried in,' Ellen continued.

'There are bedrooms for up to ten travellers, and a commercial salon that's like a quiet room upstairs, where the travellers can sit, rather than the downstairs public lounge. Our Ada and Beatie couldn't get over the bathroom, though. It's got a big fancy bath, with a huge cistern over it that holds two thousand gallons of water, Mr Gibbs made a special point of telling everyone about that, so the whole household can draw a supply of water from it.'

'Eeeh, just fancy!' shrieked Mary. 'All that water – and inside! What about the servants, where do they stay?'

'Well, local staff like our Ada and Beatie will still live at home, but there are some servants' quarters on the third floor for people who live further away.'

'Well I never,' Mary breathed. 'It sounds really posh.'

'The outsides are just as good. There's a yard and stables, a saddle room as well as corn bins and a fodder store for the horses. There's even another cistern over the stables that holds one thousand five-hundred gallons of water for the outside supply,' Ellen stated with a flourish.

'Those horses will be better looked after than us, then!' Mary exclaimed.

'The drinkers will be, too,' Ellen replied. 'There are cellars for beer, wines and spirits, with lots of stock and a wide choice.'

'Denaby folks will be supping to their hearts' content, then,' Mary quipped.

'Only if they have enough money,' Ellen replied with a rueful smile.

Chapter 39
1895-1896

Bridie and Eli had fallen into an estranged relationship. They lived in the same house, slept in the same bed, ate at the same table, but their behaviour and conversation was limited, lacking in companionship, devoid of closeness.

They each found themselves looking, contemplating, deliberating instead of conversing, sharing and communicating. Any words spoken were brief, informative, necessary. Rarely was there any genuine interest or affection shown. Each stuck to the practicalities of life.

This had not created a supportive, united approach in their treatment towards their disabled son. Bridie still harboured guilty feelings about Ben's problems. She had felt a failure as a mother from the moment he was born. The continuous, eroding remorse conflicted with her craving to experience affectionate, maternal feelings, to relish a happy mother and son bond.

Eli would look at Ben as if he was a visiting stranger, not as a father whose help and support were needed. Bridie would watch this, feeling the resentment towards Eli grow day by day as her sadness increased accordingly.

Had they been able to communicate, she would have confessed her guilty feelings, and he would have revealed his inability to be overtly loving and tactile towards his son. He just did not know how to be demonstrative and caring; how to express his repressed emotions.

Therefore, he sadly withdrew from his wife and son, and remained on safer ground by being detached and unresponsive. He would leave it to others to succour his child; he did not know how to show such compassion. The lure of hewing coal and downing pints was much more easily dealt with. Even when Ben learned to say 'Dada', Eli had just looked away to hide his emotions.

Bridie cared for Ben with an almost obsessive vehemence. She kept him clean and well-nourished, and gave him instant attention when required. Her whole life revolved around his needs.

Ben's deformed limbs were obvious, but she had accepted those problems. He could move around in a fashion, shuffling with difficulty as his legs and feet were like unwanted attachments to his body, weak and malformed, appendages that had to be towed. Yet he persisted, scrabbling around on the floor between the table, chairs and sofa as best he could. Despite all this, he was a happy, smiling child, good-natured and amiable.

It was Bridie's constant scrutiny of Ben, always inspecting and evaluating the various aspects of his development, that tormented her, yet she could not control it. She knew he could hear and react to sound, she knew he could see and track movement of people and objects, but she feared that he had not developed mentally and socially as he should have. It was even more difficult for Bridie, as she was surrounded by other people's children who were of a similar age to Ben.

Mary's son, John and Betty's daughter, Clarrie, were all nearly four years old, the same as Ben. Even her own sister, Martha, was only five, yet the differences between Ben and the other children were glaringly obvious.

Bridie had always tried to encourage Ben to talk, repeating key words slowly and clearly, yet his vocabulary was sparse. She found consolation in the fact that he would say 'Ma-ma' and 'Da-da', but usually his preference was to point to things, or stare if asked a question. His favourite response was clapping his hands and grinning a toothy, salivary smile.

The other children had a wide variety of vocabulary, speaking in sentences, questioning their environment or verbalising their experiences. Bridie's continual comparisons only succeeded in reinforcing the fact that Ben had some kind of mental impairment as well as physical disabilities, something that the medical profession had discussed with Eli and herself.

Eli shuffled in his seat, extending and withdrawing his long legs, a habit of his that Bridie had often noticed, which confirmed his unease or disquiet. He had averted his almost-black eyes from the doctor's face as he explained Ben's probable disabilities, as though, literally, not wanting to face up to the problems.

Bridie listened and briefly nodded, allowing silent tears to fall. She worried for her son's future, for his quality of life: times were hard enough without extra difficulties. The knot of despair in her stomach was forever present, the melancholy in her mind forever forceful.

Chapter 40
1896

Bob developed a close, almost intuitive relationship with his pony, Ginger. Each respected the other, sensing and allowing for certain times when a drink or a short rest was required, not losing patience with any hold-ups. Bob soon recognised Ginger's intelligence and stoicism, his willingness to toil and his tolerance of the harsh working conditions that both man and animal had to endure.

Ginger often showed flashes of his mischievous character. He would gently nudge and nuzzle Bob if there was any food being eaten, continuing until some treat or titbit was shared. Bob would laugh and note the tossing of the head and the sparkle in the eye of his equine friend.

'Here, have a bit of this cheese I've brought you,' Bob offered. Ginger's tongue would gently fold around the food, then a hoof was knocked against the ground, as if to say thanks.

'Have those mice and insects been stealing your food again?' Bob enquired, patting and stroking the horse's neck. Cyrus had been trying to sort the problem of vermin being brought down along with the horses' food and straw for their bedding.

'I keep telling Cyrus we could do with some cats down here to get rid of the mice,' he added. Bob had seen how Ginger had to snort away the cockroaches before he could eat his oats or hay.

In particular, Bob was sensitive and attentive to any reluctance that Ginger might show when working. If he hesitated or unexpectedly stopped, Bob would inspect the rails for any obstacles, or check the points that allowed the crossing over of tubs from one rail to the other. Ponies' hooves were shod, but could still get stuck or knocked in the rails.

Sometimes, ponies sensed or heard danger, creaking props or straining sprags. Many lives had been saved in the past by heeding the horses' warnings.

1896 had become the worst year for fatalities at Denaby Main pit, with seven miners killed. The most recent one was especially significant to Bob as it was George Tuffrey, a long-time close friend and almost kindred spirit. They were of a similar personality: quiet, sensible lads to the casual observer, but both possessing strong, determined natures.

George was one year younger than Bob, but they had gone through childhood and school life as firm friends. Both had been afflicted with poor health as young children, and both were of small, slight stature, which were additional bonds to their friendship. Yet both had overcome problems to realise their joint wishes to become pony drivers.

When Bob started work, George would readily listen to his friend's relaying of information and anecdotes about working with the horses. Then, when George had also started at the pit, they had eagerly shared their thoughts and experiences. But all that ended abruptly.

George had been working as a driver for eight months, but in a different area of the pit, and on different shifts to Bob. Then, George was moved to the same area and the same shift as Bob, so the lads were pleased.

During that first week in the new district, George had been learning the new routes and inclines of the roadways and passages, familiarising himself with the awkward places where access suddenly narrowed or was especially low. He knew the importance of following rules and always concentrating, as danger was ever-present. Shortcuts could not be taken, as injury or death could result. Yet, on that fateful day, George had not remembered or carried out the good practice.

Bob and Ginger were working nearby, hauling three full corves from the coalface to the flats, when a loud, crashing noise reverberated along the passage, soon followed by urgent shouts and cries. Bob steered Ginger into a siding, where they could safely halt.

He had listened intently, a panicky foreboding washing over him. Sam Schofield, the day deputy, hurried past Bob.

'Stay where you are, lad, 'til I tell you!' he shouted.

Bob was later to find out what had happened from Joe Bailey, another pony driver.

'I was going up the passage with a train of full corves when I saw George coming down with two empty ones, but they were on the wrong road. George was in front of them – he was trying to stop them, but he wasn't big enough or strong enough, they just crashed into the full tubs. George was jammed between them – he was very badly injured but conscious.' Joe's voice broke, but he sighed and resumed.

'He can't have put the lockers on the tubs, or they wouldn't have run away like they did.'

'But George knows to put lockers on to act as brakes!' Bob exclaimed.

'I know, Bob, but there were no lockers on those tubs,' replied Joe quietly. 'When the deputy arrived at the scene, George managed to tell him that the lockers must have broken. But we couldn't find any lockers there, broken or unbroken.'

Bob had been shocked to hear what had happened, and even more surprised to hear that no lockers had been used. He couldn't understand why George had not followed the rule of using them to act as brakes and to turn the points on the rails.

George had been taken to Montagu Cottage hospital. Bob had visited him, an experience he found very stressful, but something he felt he had to do. He knew George had been questioned again about the lockers, and that the poor lad had started crying and admitted he had been careless. He survived for seven days, but then succumbed to his terrible injuries.

The day after his death, an inquest was held at the George and Dragon Inn at Mexborough. As well as the Coroner, Mr Chambers was present on behalf of the Company, and an Inspector of Mines also watched the inquiry.

George's father gave evidence and confirmed that George had been working at the colliery for eight months. But he also stated that, in his opinion, the accident would not have happened if iron lockers had been supplied to his son instead of wooden ones. He later admitted, on cross-examination, that he was an experienced collier of eleven years' connection with the pit, and he had frequently seen both wooden and iron lockers lying about.

Sam Schofield had confirmed that there had been seven lockers if George had wanted them, three iron ones and four wooden ones, but he did not think George had used any lockers on the tubs. Joe Bailey also confirmed that there were always lockers to use, both iron and wooden ones, and stated he did not mind which he used. He agreed with Sam Schofield that he did not think the empty corves were locked with either a wooden or iron locker, so George could not stop the corves and turn the points as he should have done.

The coroner returned the verdict of *Accidental Death*. But he also added: 'The poor lad seemed to have contributed to his own death with his carelessness.'

Bob reached the verdict that his best friend, a fifteen-year-old lad, was dead due to a brief lapse of concentration. The sadness was to stay with him throughout his life, such had been the strength of their friendship.

Chapter 41
1896

Denaby and Cadeby pits continued to produce impressive amounts of coal, often leading the productivity lists of tonnage extracted, even though there were many competing South Yorkshire pits. Development within the village also continued, with an increasing number of houses and other buildings.

The Catholics in Denaby were especially pleased that their new church was going to be built. In 1896, the Montagu family had gifted an acre of land in Denaby where St. Alban's Roman Catholic Church could be built and opened for worshippers.

Father Thomas Kavanagh had succeeded in fundraising the necessary four thousand pounds for the build. His enthusiasm and determination had been widely admired and appreciated. Attending Mass would be much easier for the Catholic population, as the Church was to be in the heart of the village, so long journeys to Doncaster or Wath would no longer be required.

The Denaby Main Hotel had been immediately successful.

'It was so packed today that Mr Gibbs had to close the front doors for a while, and landlords don't usually do that!' Beatie and Ada had informed the rest of the family.

Father Alf, and brother Gilbert, had looked up, met eyes and shared a lengthy stare at this information.

'I'm not surprised it's allus full, fine pint o'beer there – you'll not get a better glass o' John Smith's anywhere!' Alf had declared with confidence.

'You should know if anyone does, amount you've drunk in t' past,' Peggy interjected, giving him a sidelong glance and a hearty sniff into the air as if to prove her point.

'I tried a glass o' Bentley's 'Timothy' beer there last night,' Gilbert said, licking his lips at the very thought of it. 'Better than mi usual Worthington's,' he decided, pursing his lips and nodding his head as if to confirm it.

The female members of the family, Peggy, Ellen, Beatie, Ada and Alice looked at each other, rolled their eyes and shook their heads.

Men and their beers was their common thought. 'I wish they'd show as much interest in helping with jobs round t' house,' Peggy hissed to her daughters.

Such had been the popularity of the hotel, with its beer trade and commercial accommodation, that only a few months after opening, Mr Chambers had sought consent to extend the plans both to the building and the outside area. He had stated to the solicitor and magistrates at Doncaster that the Company had originally thought that the proposed accommodation and lounge areas would be amply sufficient to meet the requirements of the neighbourhood.

However, since it had opened, there was no doubt that they were totally inadequate to cope with the trade of the district. He, therefore, was seeking permission to build a concert room and a billiard room to the side of the building, and to construct a building to the rear of the hotel, where beer that was to be consumed off the premises could be sold. Extra stabling was also needed outside.

'No wonder it's always full, they've just built four hundred and seventy new houses at the back of it!' was the common opinion of the Denaby residents.

The magistrates and the solicitor had granted consent, and the building work and alterations were to be swiftly carried out.

The hotel was only a short walk from the new Cadeby pit, and it was soon decided that it would be a very convenient and popular place for the miners from both pits to receive their pay, instead of from the pit offices.

It soon become the custom that miners picked up their wages from the hotel bar area on Saturdays. Some of the first miners to try out the new routine swore to other doubting folk that a drum was beaten to signal that the wages were ready for collection, and that was why the hotel had become known locally as "The Drum".

Mr Gibbs, the landlord, soon decided that the bar would be closed at five pm for a short while every Saturday evening to persuade the men who were reluctant to stop drinking and go home, to leave and take money home to their wives and families.

'Don't sup it all away before your wife gets some of it for food and the house,' was his reasoning to protesters.

'Eeh, there's allus summat to pawn on Monday,' was the nonchalant reply of some uncaring husbands.

Isaac Gibbs had been carefully chosen by the Company to manage The Drum. He had a great deal of experience as a landlord from previous inns and public houses, but more especially, he had a reputation for really understanding his customers. He knew how to deal with people of varying characteristics, and how to be decisive and professional when handling possible volatile situations.

He also had an understanding with the local policemen, and they respected his judgement when dealing with disputes or drunkenness. This was fortunate, as arguments frequently led to confrontations or even brawls when too much alcohol had been consumed.

Isaac often noted the irony of the circumstances, that the miners earned their money by working for the Company, but they then paid it back in rent money for Company-owned houses, money paid for food in Company-owned shops, and money in the Company-owned public house for beer.

If they broke the law, some were arrested by police, who were managed by the Company, and their fines were paid back to the Company. Isaac thought that some of the Denaby men seemed to be locked into the grinding pattern of earning and having it taken from them as if on a treadmill.

* * *

Another significant development had been proposed in Denaby at that time. Water was to be supplied to the houses. For years, the residents had complained about the lack of water and its availability. Women and children had the drudgery of collecting the water that was so necessary for all domestic chores, compounding their workload.

It was the determination of a group of women, representatives for all the residents, which brought about the agreed change. Four Denaby women had decided that they would ask for a meeting with Mr Chambers to explain the intolerable situation. They had impressed upon him the acute need to have water supplied to the houses. It was a basic, essential requirement that would greatly help everyone.

Their request was listened to and granted by Mr Chambers. It was agreed that a reservoir would be built on the top of the Crags, which would be supplied by water pumped from the nearby Cadeby colliery. There would be an open tank, which would have to be cleaned out at intervals, but the Denaby folk were overjoyed that water would be supplied to their houses, piped from the reservoir.

'We don't know what those four women said to Mr Chambers, but the "King of Denaby" listened and promised to do something about it!' was the overwhelming opinion of the residents, especially the wives and children.

'Let's hope it won't take too long to get that water – our coppers are allus full o' mucky work clothes!' was the heartfelt desire of the long-suffering women of Denaby.

Chapter 42
1896-1897

Mary's life was physically demanding, busy, but largely happy. She knew she was like other Denaby women in the way they had continuous work in a harsh, unpredictable environment, but she still felt blessed with her family.

She and Jim were closer than ever. A look or a smile could convey more than words. A touch of their hands could evoke memories of tender, passionate intimacy. She still treasured the wooden rose that Jim had made for her. It sat on their bedroom shelf, a visible symbol of their lasting, shared love and devotion. Rose had often handled it, gently feeling its contours.

'It's a flower, a rose,' Mary explained to her daughter. 'Daddy made it for me, he knows how much I like flowers.'

'I'm Rose too!' the little girl declared gleefully, clapping her hands in delight.

'Yes, you're our special Rose,' Mary smiled, sharing a hug and a kiss with their precious daughter.

The one main heartache in their lives was that they had lost a baby when Mary miscarried the previous year, six months into her pregnancy. She had been thrilled to find out she was pregnant, as more than three years had passed since John's birth. It had been an unexpected shock when she had miscarried, almost taking it for granted that all would progress well.

'It's all that lifting heavy water jugs and heaving buckets of coal!' Sarah had asserted, wiping tears from her eyes. Mary had nodded, silent in her sorrow. She knew how common miscarriages were, such was the toll of continual backbreaking work on female bodies.

Jim had tried to console her, murmuring words of comfort, but he had brushed away his own tears and had felt deep sadness when alone with his thoughts.

Mary had not been the only one to experience miscarriage. Gertie had suffered a similar fate. She and Charlie had been so excited when they had shared the news of the pregnancy with family and friends. Charlie had laughed and joked even more, as if happiness bubbled inside him and could not be contained. He whistled merry tunes and beamed his gleaming smiles; such was his delight. Gertie had observed his happiness, bathing her in pleasure and contentment. She had the man she so loved, a home of their own and a supportive family.

For a few months, she was blissfully happy, then her miscarriage had snatched away her feeling of fulfilment. The disappointment of losing the baby had felt like a hammer blow, affecting her deeply. Her usual practical, independent optimistic nature completely deserted her. She had cried and cried, sadness flooding and overwhelming her, bitter disappointment crushing her.

She turned to Charlie, literally leaning on him for love and support. He managed to cope with the double blows of the shock of losing the baby and the change in his wife's demeanour. He had never seen Gertie like this, so negative, so subdued, so withdrawn.

'Give her time she'll be all right, she's a sensible lass,' Sarah and Albert had advised Charlie, with heavy hearts. 'Our Gertie is made of sterner stuff than most, but she needs time.'

Gradually, over the coming months, Gertie lifted herself, slowly regaining her vitality and positive outlook on life. Charlie looked on, worried about her, but supporting her with his kindness and understanding. She eventually sighed, smiled and dared to hope that one day there would be a better outcome; one day they would have their own baby.

Yet, she always felt that she had lost a part of herself for ever. She had decided to keep that emotion private, a secret held within her heart.

Chapter 43
Autumn 1897

Tommy Prince walked along Doncaster Road, heading for the Denaby Main Hotel. He had been for a walk to Mexborough, stopping off at the Ferryboat Inn and the Montagu Arms for a few pints. He enjoyed his walking, and his drinking even more. The late autumn air had freshened his face to a rosy glow, visible despite the sooty atmosphere depositing specks of dust and grime on his skin.

He flicked his fingers across his cheek, a long-established habit since his "fall", as if hoping to feel smooth, unblemished skin, instead of the raised scar that marked a path from eye to jaw. He had become used to turning and angling his head to aid his vision, still affected by his injury.

However, he had still not become used to seeing his altered appearance. His parents had tried to reassure him that the scar was hardly noticeable, which was partly true, as the vivid red mark had calmed and faded to a delicate shade of pink. But he knew it was there. He knew he was marred.

Part of him had wanted instant revenge on Walter Smith for what he had done, but he had decided to bide his time. His was a life of working, drinking, gambling, just pleasing himself. Walter's attack was unfortunate, but his vanity had been the only thing to suffer.

He still felt superior to others. Prince by name, prince by nature. He did not want a woman for marriage, family or security. He regarded women as annoyances by and large, only really useful for meals, clean clothes and sex. He had never felt real affection for any woman, not even his mother. Yes, he would bide his time until he got his revenge.

As Tommy reached the front doors of The Drum, a voice behind him made him turn.

'Eh-up Tommy, fancy seeing you 'ere,' Eli Shaw laughed as he followed Tommy into the entrance hall.

Eli was still working at Denaby Main pit, but Tommy had moved to Cadeby pit, so they did not see each other as much.

'Nah then, Eli, what's tha been up to?' Tommy asked as they headed towards the taproom.

'I can see you've started afore me,' was Eli's reply, noticing the glaze in Tommy's eyes and the drawl in his voice.

'Just a walk and a few bevvies in Mexborough and now I'm closer to home, I can have a few more,' Tommy replied with a smug grin.

'Well, I'm stone cold sober, so I've got some catching up to do,' was Eli's brisk remark, his long legs striding to the bar.

'What's up wi' thee? It's five o'clock and you've not had a drink yet?'

'Oh, it's our lass. Bridie had t'babby this morning, so I had to see to a few things when I got home from work. Her mother's there now,' was Eli's explanation before gulping the frothy beer.

'Another kid then! What's it this time?' Tommy asked, savouring the taste of his beer with a smack of his lips.

'A lass this time,' replied Eli. 'She's a big 'un an' all.'

The two miners sat down at a table, and the talk soon turned to the prospect of playing pitch and toss the next weekend. Their discussion about gambling on the game entertained them until they had drunk their fill of beer and stumbled home.

* * *

Bridie's eyes opened and travelled around the bedroom. Her mother appeared in the doorway, her arms cradling the swaddled baby, rocking gently back and forth as she whispered to her sleeping granddaughter. She looked at Bridie who was lying on the bed, propped up by pillows.

'Ah, you're awake! Sure, you needed that sleep! How do you feel?' Hannah asked her daughter, concern evident in her hesitant words.

'Oh, I'm fine now. How's the baby?'

'She's a beautiful wee girl,' Hannah murmured, scanning the pure, luminous skin of the newborn baby. 'She's just lovely.'

Bridie felt a mixture of relief and elation rising within her. It had been a long, difficult birth. She had been petrified that the baby would get stuck, like Ben, but in the end, she had felt the welcome sensation of emptying, expelling the heavy weight that seemed to be ripping her asunder. She had been surprised when Nellie, the midwife, had announced:

'Bridie, it's a girl! You have a beautiful daughter!'

'A girl?' Bridie had queried, almost in disbelief. She had been so certain it was going to be another boy.

'It most certainly is a girl, and just look at those long legs!' Nellie declared, her smile revealing her few remaining teeth.

Bridie's shock had almost prevented her from checking that the baby was healthy and had no problems. The lusty cries reassured her that her daughter was certainly breathing well.

'Everything is fine, my love.' Nellie quickly informed Bridie. The midwife remembered Ben's difficult birth, even though it was nearly five years ago, and she had delivered many babies since then.

Bridie gazed at her daughter, so relieved that she was healthy and well.

'Black hair and long legs,' she had thought to herself, perhaps one day she would also have almost-black eyes, like her father.

* * *

Eli had arrived home from his morning shift a few hours after the birth. Hannah greeted him at the back door, eager to deliver the news.

'You have a beautiful daughter, Eli. She and Bridie are both fine.' Her Irish accent intensified in her excitement, so that Eli had to concentrate to absorb her words. He looked away and made a fuss of taking off his scarf and work jacket. Hannah had watched him, waiting for his reaction.

'Oh, rate, that's good,' were his eventual words, but Hannah did not see the light in his dark eyes or the smile curving beneath his black moustache.

He was surprised to feel pride that he had a daughter. He looked over towards Ben, who was sitting quietly in his chair, following his father and grandmother with his eyes, but saying nothing.

'I've been telling him that he has a baby sister,' Hannah smiled, stroking the little boy's hair. 'You go upstairs and see them, then you can look after Ben while I see to a few jobs that need doing,' she persuaded Eli.

He sighed and nodded briefly, unused to dealing with unfamiliar domestic duties, almost awkward in his own house, with his own son.

Eli climbed the steep stairs up to their bedroom and stood, silent, in the doorway. Bridie sensed him before she opened her eyes. His coal-streaked, sweat-stained shirt revealed arms patterned with blue scars, remnants of past scrapes and cuts, forever engrained with coal dust. His hands, long-fingered yet always slightly cupped, as if holding a shovel, or a tankard, were wiped down the sides of his trousers, as if to attempt the futile task of cleaning them.

'Are you all rate, Bridie?' he asked, his deep voice breaking the silence. She was so shocked and surprised at his words, that tears sprang to her eyes. She had stopped expecting much affection or kindness from him, yet she was secretly thrilled that he had shown interest and concern about her.

'Yes, I am now I know the baby's all right.' The words had no sooner left her lips than she suddenly burst into tears, pent-up emotions spilling from her like showers of raindrops.

Eli strode towards her, his almost-black eyes fixed on her as she sobbed out the worry and anxiety so long held within her. He held his long-fingered, cupped hand above her head, then gently patted her chestnut-gold hair. Bridie's eyes met his, and for once, he did not look away. That brief, shared connection raised hopes within her that all might not be as bad as she had thought.

Bridie opened up the shawl that swaddled their baby daughter, still sleeping beside her.

'She's got your dark hair, and she's going to be tall, just like you,' Bridie murmured, almost shy in the intimate, emotional situation. A flicker of pride flashed across Eli's face as he stared at the baby, perfect in every way.

'I like the name Maria, after my grandmother. What do you think?' Bridie had whispered.

Eli had nodded with pursed lips, which was almost a smile. For a moment, he felt the draw of affection towards his wife and child. He enjoyed the pleasant sensation of togetherness and belonging. He almost wished things could be like this all the time. He did not realise that Bridie was thinking the same.

For years she had avoided sexual advances from Eli. She still remembered the times when he had been abusive, the sting of the slaps, the bruise of the punches. That was in the early part of their marriage.

After Ben was born, the slaps and punches had stopped, but he did not realise that his indifference, his lack of affection, had caused mental abuse to Bridie. She craved his love and attention, but often rebuffed his rough, drunken advances with disdain. She felt she was worth more; she deserved better treatment. Slowly, his awkward attempts at intimacy had reduced until they became a rarity.

But Bridie remembered last Christmas being a special time, something to share with her family. It was also Ben's birthday. For once, she had felt calm and relaxed, enjoying Ben's happy smiles. She was also amazed to see the special, illuminating smiles on Eli's face, those she remembered when they were courting.

Those smiles had warmed and mellowed the tense hostility between them, so much so, that tentative, hesitant sex had been surprisingly pleasurable for them both. There was still a regretful aloofness between them, but baby Maria was the result of a happy Christmas.

PART FIVE

Chapter 44
1897 – 1898

Frank Chapman had quickly settled into his new job at the Powder Works. His friendly, open nature soon gained him friends with the other men there, and his attentive, considerate way, when dealing with the women and their problems, was also well received. The girls' eyes would follow him at any opportunity, admiring his manly physique and handsome features.

'Those eyes! He makes you feel so special when he looks at you,' was one of the comments in the excited exchange between the female workers.

'Yes, I've never seen such warm, brown eyes. I'm almost glad when I have a problem with the equipment, then I can talk to him and study his eyes!' was another comment, sending the other girls into laughing agreement.

'I like how he talks to us, like we're his equals, not talking down to us just because we're women,' was another astute comment. 'There's not many men like that!'

'Aye, he's charming all right. Trouble is, he's only got eyes for one person – and that's Ivy!' one of the girls stated. Ivy blushed and joined in with the general laughter and banter, shaking her head in mock denial, but inwardly glowing at their remarks.

She felt almost as if she was holding her breath, waiting and hoping that something would come of their new acquaintance. She thought that Frank was a very special man, capable and strong, yet kind and sensitive. Never before had she met a man with such a complete range of attributes. Their meeting had changed her outlook on life; it was the first time she could foresee a future relationship with a man, even if that meant leaving her family.

She was not disappointed, as Frank showed his interest in her from the start. At first, there were shy looks and slow smiles between them. Working within the same building had resulted in frequent opportunities for brief, shared remarks which quickly extended to prolonged conversations.

They seemed to be aware of each other even when not close by, such was the powerful intensity of their attraction. They knew that other people looked on with interested, appraising eyes, judging the progress of their relationship, sharing quick, darting looks and assured arches of eyebrows, as if they could influence and affirm a successful outcome. It didn't matter, Frank and Ivy literally had eyes only for each other.

Ivy found it fascinating to gradually gain information about each other. In good weather, they would find a quiet spot in the factory's garden, sharing conversation along with their food and drink. Ivy related incidents and anecdotes about her family. She could see Frank watching her intently as she talked.

She, too, recorded his range of facial expressions as he listened, smiling and relaxed. She grew to know his mannerisms, from the crinkling of his nose as he laughed, to his habit of regularly pushing the curls of hair from his forehead. Most of all, she was aware of his lips, full and even, moist from the flicks of his tongue. She even grew to daydream, imagining how his lips would feel on hers.

Frank had told her about his family and background. He was from Ashby-de-la-Zouch, born in 1870, the same year as Ivy. He had lived with his mother and father until his father had been killed in a mining accident, quickly followed by the death of his mother, Iris. Her death had been registered as a heart attack, but Frank told Ivy that he thought she had died of a broken heart after losing her beloved Len.

Ivy saw his brimming eyes and she felt genuine sympathy for him. He had moved to Denaby after their deaths, and now lodged with a widow and her daughter in Conisbrough.

His father had always been adamant that he did not want his only child to follow him down the mines. He wanted Frank to have an education, and so Frank had studied mechanical engineering, something that really interested him with the increasing changes in industries from manual to machine-led processes.

Frank had welcomed the move to his new job in Denaby, as he viewed the Flameless Explosives Works company as modern and progressive. Ivy had listened to his words, feeling growing admiration for his enthusiastic, ambitious outlook on life, despite the sadness of losing his parents.

Frank's admiration of Ivy also knew no bounds. He thought she was the most beautiful person he had ever met, for her nature and personality as well as her stunning looks. He felt both exhilarated yet protective in her presence, so he took care to develop their relationship cautiously, not wanting to overstep the appropriate boundaries of their friendship and attraction.

They started to see each other out of the context of the factory, firstly walking to and from work together, happy to be on their own as a couple. At weekends, and some evenings, they met to share common interests.

Frank had always played cricket in his hometown, and Ivy had been quick to introduce him to Jim, who had gladly informed him all about Denaby Main Cricket Club. They soon struck up such a friendship that Jim arranged for Frank to join the club, and it was not long before his talent was recognised.

He was chosen to play in the first team, which was in the South Yorkshire league. Mary and Ivy regularly watched the cricket matches, happy to support their men.

Football was also another sporting interest for Frank, and he soon started supporting Denaby Main Football Club, which had recently changed its name to Denaby United. The team was in the Swinton and District League so there were always plenty of local matches to watch.

Ivy and her friends also enjoyed watching the team, and there was added interest as Bridie's younger brother, Seamus, was a talented up-and-coming member of the club. Their home matches were played on the Red Rose, a piece of ground between the River

Don and the canal in Denaby, so there were always crowds of supporting locals in attendance.

The couple also shared a love of music and often attended the many orchestral and choral performances at the "Large Hall" school. Both enjoyed the cultural stimulation from such evenings, nurturing satisfaction at experiencing the more refined aspects within the community.

Ivy was thrilled to introduce Frank to her family, the first time she had ever felt like doing such a thing, as no man had previously reached her expectations. Sarah and Albert were welcoming but almost shy with this handsome, likeable man. Ivy's sisters all agreed that Frank was a lovely man; even Betty was charmed by him. They all agreed that he was the perfect man for Ivy.

Bob watched and admired the quiet-spoken, stylish man, unused to appraising a man in this way, realising he seemed different to his other Yorkshire friends.

'Eeeh, don't they make a lovely couple!' was Sarah's contented verdict to the rest of the family.

'At long last, she's found somebody. It's about time at her age,' Albert stated with a satisfied sigh before returning his attention to smoking his pipe.

* * *

Frank and Ivy's relationship developed into a serious courtship, with the blessing of everyone who knew them. Ivy was deliriously happy, stunned that Frank was as captivated by her as she was by him. She radiated her joy, making her look more dazzling than ever.

Frank would hold her hand, gaze into her pale grey eyes that shone with love, and tell her how beautiful she was. He would gently stroke her cheek, easing to one side the blonde curls that framed her face in a halo of light.

Their first kiss had literally made her breathless, she was so overcome with emotion. His soft, full mouth had found her willing lips and she had experienced utter pleasure. She no longer had to wonder or daydream about the experience, now it was real.

* * *

One year after meeting, much to the delight of friends and family, Frank and Ivy were married. Ivy had found it sad that Frank had no family to attend the wedding, but he had reassured her that it did not matter, and that he already regarded her family as his own. Nothing was going to spoil their special day.

The happy couple began married life in a rented cottage in Conisbrough, not far from the Powder Works. Ivy could continue to work there, even as a married woman. The company was modern-thinking, unlike many others.

Despite being so happy to marry Frank, Ivy shed tears at the prospect of leaving her parents and her home. They were not an overly demonstrative family, but Ivy's bond with her parents and siblings had always been innocently pronounced.

Sarah and Albert had been almost embarrassed to witness their daughter's tears, brimming and spilling from her huge eyes, as they discussed their farewells. Sarah had smiled and reassured Ivy with emotional hugs and squeezes. Even Albert's eyes had welled up as he delivered Ivy a quick, tight embrace, self-conscious in the emotionally charged situation. He tried to alleviate his bashful embarrassment by stating:

'Nay, lass! You're only moving up t' road, not to Timbuktu!'

Chapter 45
1897 – 1898

1897 was a special year not only for Frank and Ivy, but for the whole of Denaby. It was Queen Victoria's Diamond Jubilee year, when she became Britain's longest-reigning monarch.

The official Jubilee day was Sunday 20th June, but Tuesday 22nd June had been declared a Bank Holiday by the Queen for all the nations of Great Britain, as so many celebrations had been planned for that day. Those people who remembered the Golden Jubilee, ten years earlier, doubted that anything could be better.

'Nowt could be better than that day!'

'It were a sight never to be witnessed again!'

'I don't know what they might think up this time, but it'll take a lot to beat that Golden Jubilee!' were some of the comments of the Denaby folk.

* * *

Mary met Rose and John outside their school at home time.

'Mam, we're all going to get a special treats day! There's sports on the field, and Mr Pope is giving us lots of prizes! We're going to have a procession and sing Jubilee songs, and there's even a special tea for us all!' Rose delivered all these facts, hardly pausing for breath. Her eyes shone with excitement and her cheeks were flushed with anticipation.

'There's going to be a bonfire on the cricket field and a fireworks display too!' John added, skipping with delight.

'Slow down!' she laughed. 'I reckon all this is about the Queen's Jubilee. Let's go home and you can tell me all about it'.

'Oh, I forgot the Punch and Judy Show!' John added.

* * *

175

A special planning committee had met the previous month at the Denaby Main Institute to discuss how Denaby Main and Denaby Village would celebrate the Jubilee.

Mr Chambers was chairman, and prominent local dignitaries made up the committee. They all acknowledged the generous offer of Mr John Buckingham Pope, Chairman and Managing Director of Denaby and Cadeby Collieries Company Ltd., which was to pay for a fete in Denaby, with special treats for the children and old folk on Jubilee Day.

'He did the same ten years ago for the Golden Jubilee, and he wants to provide a day that the children, especially, are not likely to forget,' Mr Chambers announced.

'Hear, hear,' was murmured around the room, with satisfied nods of heads reinforcing their consensus.

They had agreed on the arrangements for the schedule of Jubilee Day in previous meetings.

'I propose a further committee be appointed to look after the organisation of the treats for the children and old folk,' Mr Chambers continued, which was carried by the committee. Six eminent ladies of the area were named to take charge.

The meeting also focused on the previously proposed building of a Cottage hospital in Denaby. It had been agreed that it was a necessity, and it had been pointed out that the Mexborough Cottage hospital had been a boon and a success in the community.

'But if a man is badly hurt at the colliery, it is too far and too dangerous to take him to Mexborough. He should be brought to a place nearby,' stated a committee member.

It was agreed by all, that Denaby deserved a hospital and nursing staff. Various opinions were given, however, on how the hospital should be financed and maintained. Mr Witty, a mine's official, stated:

'I have seen officials at the collieries and the men are in sympathy with the movement to have a hospital. I think the miners would give a subscription to maintain the hospital.'

Mr Chambers acknowledged that there had already been offers of subscriptions from prosperous gentlemen in the district. 'Let us, therefore, contact others to give subscriptions towards the cost of the building.'

The committee members were in agreement with their chairman.

* * *

Jubilee Day passed in a happy blur of activities. The fine, warm June weather increased the enjoyment of the celebrations, just as well, as most of the entertainment was outside.

Parents had done their best to ensure their children were as clean and well presented as possible. "Sunday best" clothes were worn by those lucky enough to own them.

The children assembled in the morning, ready to begin the procession through the colourfully decorated village, stopping from place to place to sing Jubilee hymns and songs. Onlookers lined the route, proud parents and grandparents waving to their offspring, wiping tears from their eyes as they witnessed such patriotic events.

After some refreshments back at school, the children moved to the gala field to begin a variety of sports. It was proudly announced that Mr Buckingham Pope had provided over three hundred prizes to be won and enjoyed, which received a round of applause from the gathered crowds.

In the afternoon, the children returned to school to have a substantial tea, a real treat that everyone thoroughly enjoyed.

Following the meal, they returned to the gala field to enjoy different kinds of entertainment. The Punch and Judy show produced wide eyes and cheerful laughter from the fascinated children, while the adults marvelled at the mountebanks from London, displaying and discussing their range of patented medicines, persuading and reassuring their audience that their potions and lotions would readily cure an amazing range of medical problems, from insomnia to "female disorders"; even "fussy" babies would benefit from their goods.

'Why would I buy those when I can get two penny-worth of laudanum from the local shop – that cures all!' laughed one of the old men in the watching crowd.

'My brother died from the laudanum habit!' a young woman called out. 'He was told it would cure his bad stomach when he was doubled-up in pain. Doctor said he ended up taking too much and poisoned himself,' she added. 'Don't take anything out of those bottles!'

Nearby people were shocked to hear her story, but they knew desperate people could easily buy laudanum. It was cheap, but some soon became addicted to it.

'The doctor told my father that laudanum's a solution of opium powder in alcohol!' another man shouted out.

'No wonder people get to like it!' guffawed a younger man who was sceptical of the stories. The mountebanks looked on, waiting to convince the next group of passers-by that it was a necessity to buy their medicines.

A ventriloquist and a clown also attracted lots of attention on the gala field with their unusual and entertaining performances.

The older people were provided with a lavish tea, served in the old Doncaster Road school building. The bonfire and fireworks display completed the festivities, leaving behind tired but happy children.

Many of the adults admitted that this Jubilee Day had surpassed even their memories of the Golden Jubilee Day. The mystique surrounding royalty had manifested itself in a wonderful day to remember, and countless times to reminisce to others about its utter enjoyment.

In darker days of hunger and poverty, these recollections would give comfort.

Chapter 46
1898

Jim was sitting in the reading room of the recently extended Denaby Main Institute. He was browsing through a few newspapers, enjoying the quiet environment.

The Institute had originally been the idea of Mr Chambers when he first came to Denaby as Manager of Denaby Main pit in 1881. He had used two adjacent houses on Annerley Street to make the club, which comprised of an entrance hall, a billiards room, a reading room, an upstairs bagatelle room, and accommodation for a caretaker. He believed that it was important for the colliers and their families to have a place for reading and recreation.

The new extension had provided an extra billiards room and a bigger reading room that was well-stocked with a library of over one thousand four hundred books. Weekly and daily newspapers were also supplied.

The members of the club paid a small subscription, and annual donations had recently started from the Denaby Main Co-operative Society, which had enabled the setting up of the library that could be used by both miners and co-operative workers. Mr Chambers was president of both establishments, and he gladly extended the use of the Institute for Parish Council meetings, committee meetings and it was also the headquarters of the Denaby Brass Band – another interest of Mr Chambers.

Jim especially liked reading the *Daily Mail* newspaper which had only become available to the masses of working-class people in the past few years. He found a saved copy of the Mail from the previous year which described Queen Victoria's Diamond Jubilee celebrations in London.

Queen Victoria's journal had provided many details and insights into those events which Jim found fascinating. He especially liked the section that described Queen Victoria's feelings about the outpouring of affection and esteem from her subjects as she toured a large area of London:

'No one ever, I believe, has met with such an ovation as was given to me, passing through those six miles of streets. The crowds were quite indescribable and their enthusiasm truly marvellous and deeply touching. The cheering was quite deafening, and every face seemed to be filled with joy.'

The Mail also informed that the celebrations had lasted a fortnight, and a garden party and state banquet at Buckingham Palace for the many royal guests, were held to mark the occasion. Memorial fountains and towers were also erected, including the Jubilee Tower in Lancashire.

Rudyard Kipling had written special poems in honour of the Queen, and Thomas Lipton had even distributed free ale and tobacco to residents in London who took part in street parties. Jim read all of this with great interest and enjoyed sharing the information with Mary and friends.

Mary had also shared her thoughts about the Institute with Jim.

'I'll look forward to going to the reading room – all those books! I'll take Rose and John, too. Wouldn't it be lovely if, one day, we were allowed to borrow some of the books, bring them home to read, then exchange them for different ones when we take them back,' she mused, wistfully.

'Yes, that would be wonderful,' Jim agreed, understanding Mary's wishful thinking. Jim also read the up-to-date weekly *Mexborough and Swinton Times*.

He especially enjoyed reading about the new Catholic Church. It stated, with great pleasure, that the new St. Alban's Roman Catholic Church in Denaby had opened to worshippers on 22nd June 1898, two years since Mr Andrew Montagu had gifted the land by Mr Andrew Montagu, and one year after the official laying of the foundation stone by the Roman Catholic Bishop of Leeds.

Father Thomas Kavanagh was praised for his enthusiasm, determination and dedication to the raising of funds for the new building.

'I should also love, one day, to have a Catholic school in Denaby,' he had announced with a twinkle in his eye.

Chapter 47
May 1898

Mary placed two mugs of steaming hot tea on the table, then sat down opposite Bridie. She watched her friend unwrap the shawl that held the sleeping baby Maria close to her chest, easing her gently into the crook of her arm.

'I bet she's quite a weight now. She's certainly a good size for an eight-month-old!' Mary laughed. Bridie nodded, looking at her daughter adoringly.

'She's always been a big baby for her age, but she's so good, even Eli says how settled she is.'

Mary was pleased that Bridie seemed much happier and more contented since Maria was born. She knew how much Ben's birth and condition had affected her, but she now seemed to have a more optimistic outlook on life, it even showed in her appearance and behaviour. She smiled and chatted, more like the girl Mary could remember.

'Ben's at his Grandma's – he loves going there and everyone loves having him,' Bridie continued. 'Since Jim and Paddy made him a new pushchair, I can't get him out of it!' she laughed.

Ben's attempts at crawling had gradually declined as he grew older and bigger. His legs could not support his body, and they were too heavy and awkward to be dragged.

Reluctantly, Bridie and Eli had to recognise that Ben would never walk, but at least he could now be pushed around.

'Yes,' Mary nodded, 'it might only be a wooden chest with handles, set on wheels, but it means he can be taken around the village and enjoy more things.'

Bridie's face held a secretive smile as she continued, 'Mind you, I'm not sure how I'm going to manage to push everyone soon.'

'Oh, you mean with Maria, as well?' Mary asked. The smile on Bridie's face now spread to a knowing grin, and Mary looked for more clues from her expression.

'You're never! ...Do you mean... you're expecting?'

Bridie nodded slowly.

'Due about September I reckon.'

'Oh my goodness, Bridie, another baby!' Mary shouted in surprise, jumping up with a scrape of her chair.

The sudden noises resulted in baby Maria stirring, opening her eyes, then smiling up at her mother. Bridie gazed into her dark eyes and stroked her silky black hair.

'Hello, my wee sweetheart. Sure, you must be hungry. Mammy will feed you now,' she crooned lovingly to her daughter.

Mary looked on, delighted to see Bridie so happy, and with only a fleeting twinge of envy. She so wished she was pregnant too.

Chapter 48
June 1898

The young woman wiped away the sweat dotted along her freckled nose and forehead. She was wishing she had worn her lighter coat rather than her woollen one, which felt too heavy and warm in the late morning, summer sunshine.

The train journey had been uncomfortable in the stuffy, airless carriage; she needed to stretch out and feel the breeze. She stood on the platform at Conisbrough railway station, narrowing her eyes against the puthering steam as the train departed. She needed to get her bearings in the unfamiliar surroundings.

The nearby Cadeby pit came into view as the steam dispersed. Its headgear jutted into the overhanging smog, as if searching for clean air and blue sky.

She climbed the steps from the platform, onto the bridge, then onto the road, turning right towards the signposted village of Denaby Main. The valise she was carrying felt awkward as she strode out.

She noted the smoky atmosphere, so many chimneys belching out sooty streams of billowing fumes. Her vision was fogged until she reached a large building, The Denaby Main Hotel.

Before entering, she quickly brushed at her cheeks, hoping to wipe away any dusty deposits, then patted down the grey felt hat that rested on her auburn hair that was loosely caught back into the nape of her neck. Stray strands of wafting hair were smoothed to the sides, revealing more of her strikingly pretty face.

Her stomach churned, partly through hunger, but mostly with nervous apprehension. The confusion of bitterness, sadness and determination halted her progress momentarily. Everything felt surreal, unreal and bizarre, but she knew it was something she had to do.

She stepped inside the hotel's entrance hall. Despite her nervousness, she gazed around, impressed by its glowing richness, noticing the mosaic floor, the shiny wood-panelled walls and the beautiful stained-glass chandelier.

'Excuse me, miss. Can I help you?'

A young girl's voice cut into her reverie. The woman smiled at the hotel maid and put down her valise.

'I hope so. I'm looking for someone who, I'm told, lives and works around here – a man called Frank Chapman.'

'Sorry miss, I've only just started working here, but Mr Gibbs, the landlord, is in the bar parlour. You should ask him – he knows lots of people.'

The woman nodded and smiled her thanks.

'That way, miss,' the maid pointed, before running up the elaborate staircase.

The bar parlour was almost empty, but some noise could be heard from the nearby tap room.

'That's the miners coming to collect their wages. Same every Saturday morning,' Isaac Gibbs stated, breaking off wiping down the bar to speak to the young woman hovering in the doorway.

'Mr Gibbs?' she asked.

'That's me,' he smiled.

'I wonder if you could help me, please. Do you know Frank Chapman? I've been told he lives near here.'

'Yes, I know Frank, he works at the Powder Works.'

'Yes, that's him. Do you know where he lives? I have some news for him about his mother,' she continued.

Mr Gibbs studied her flushed but very pretty face. He knew he hadn't seen her before, but he felt obliged to help her.

'Yes, he lives in an old stone cottage next to The Station Hotel, just across from Conisbrough Railway Station. It's the house with the green shutters – you can't miss it.'

'Oh, thank you. That's very helpful,' she replied, then added, 'I may need a room overnight if you have one available.'

'Yes, we have a room. What name is it?' Mr Gibbs enquired.
'Chapman. Florrie Chapman,' was her reply.

* * *

Florrie brushed away the breadcrumbs from her coat. The food had helped ease her churning stomach, but the turmoil of emotions still rendered her unsettled, almost breathless.

She sat on a low, stone wall, not far from the railway station, trying to will herself to go through with the confrontation. For more than two years, her feelings had see-sawed from anger to despair, from bitterness to heartache. She had fluctuated from pungent resentment to exasperated remorse. Sorrowful regret pervaded her life.

They had been so happy, so in love. The treasured memories momentarily softened her mouth into almost a smile. Frank had swept her off her feet, literally, when they had accidentally collided when navigating icy pathways. She had fallen heavily; Frank had helped her stand, apologising profusely, concerned that she was all right. This first, chance meeting had led to a swift romance. She had been struck by his masculine charm, he had been struck by her unpretentious beauty. Each was completely content with the other, joyous in their shared love and devotion.

She realised her innocent naivety, however, when she became pregnant. Both had been shocked, but gladly married when a wedding was hastily arranged. Their married life began, full of hopes and dreams for a happy future.

Florrie's smile suddenly faded as unhappy memories forged their way into her recollections... They could hardly wait for their baby to arrive. But in the end, he was born too early. Florrie heaved and pushed, fearing the worst.

'It's too soon, it's too soon!' she wailed, grasping comforting hands.

As usual, these memories caused Florrie to stifle the sobs caught in her throat. As she sat on the stone wall, with the rushing of the trains and Cadeby pit behind her, she blinked back the threatening tears. But she could not suppress the images that replayed over and over in her mind.

Her poor baby, her poor, longed-for baby. He had struggled and fought for life. He had waved little stick arms and legs as if to help his heaving chest suck in more air. His mouth had made whimpering gurgles, trying to find the freedom of breathing and living. But, in the end, his flailing limbs had stilled. His gasps had gradually subsided into quiet, gentle sighs.

They had kissed their baby son goodbye before even saying hello.

Grief had made her descend into a deep, all-consuming depression, with boundaries that no one could penetrate. Nothing and no one could give her solace, not even Frank, her beloved Frank. She realised later, how much things changed because of her depression.

In the beginning, Frank had been understanding and accepting. He tried his best to comfort her, to coax her back into life. But she rejected his sympathy and compassion, throwing off his comforting arms, spurning his loving kisses, bristling at any of his attempts to show tender support.

She even became irritated by everything he said and did, finding fault with petty details, preferring to remain aloof and alone in her misery. She then found comfort in gin, spending money she did not have, racking up debt they could not afford, becoming a crazed, bitter woman who did not care. The arguments became more vicious, more personal.

One day, she woke from her drunken stupor to discover that Frank had gone. He had left with a few of his possessions, but without trace. He did not even tell his recently widowed mother that he was going.

For over two years, there was no communication between wife and husband or mother and son. Then, out of the blue, his mother had received a letter.

Chapter 49
June 1898

A smoky haze hovered in the taproom where a raucous din rose and dipped, interspersed with boisterous laughter. The men were always in good spirits on Saturdays; pay day.

Good natured banter passed from table to table. The ale loosened tongues and promoted profanities as bodies and minds relaxed. Two days of being "above" rather than "below" was always a welcomed, pleasurable feeling for the pit men, a respite before the next week's toil.

Mr Gibbs and his staff understood and appreciated this masculine, virile behaviour. They knew the close bonds between a lot of the men, working together, drinking together, relying on each other in hard times.

It was a camaraderie that helped them cope with the many struggles in their lives. Mr Gibbs, however, always kept a watchful eye on his customers, ensuring that the boundaries of accepted behaviour were not overstepped, hopefully nipping in the bud any possible trouble or aggression. He was an experienced landlord as well as a sensible, decent man.

Frank Chapman stepped into the taproom, nodding acknowledgements to some of the men as he approached the bar.

'Pint of bitter, please, Isaac,' Frank requested to the landlord.

'A pint coming up, Frank. Oh, there was a young woman in here not long ago asking for you.'

'Oh aye, hope she was good-looking,' Frank joked as he paid for the beer.

'As pretty as they come, all right. Wanted to know where you live.'

'Did she say who she was?' Frank looked up sharply.

'Florrie Chapman's her name,' Mr Gibbs replied.

Frank's hand jerked slightly, spilling some of his beer. He stared at Mr Gibbs briefly before saying, 'Oh… my sister. What's she doing here?'

'Said she has some news about your mother. I told her where you live so she might be there now. Hope your Ivy's in.'

Mr Gibbs turned to serve another customer and was surprised to see Frank walking out, his beer untouched.

Chapter 50
June 1898

Florrie left the stone wall seat, still thinking about that letter from out of the blue, a letter from Frank. His mother, Iris, had been overjoyed to receive his letter, even though deep hurt had ruled her life since he left. First, she had lost her beloved husband Len, then Frank had left without a word. She had tried to rationalise how he could do such a thing to her, especially at such a sad time.

She had swayed between loathing and longing for Frank, eventually reasoning that he must have been so unhappy and desperate, that he had acted completely out of character in order to withstand the stress and pressures within his life.

His letter contained a mixture of factual information and heartfelt apologies. He informed her that he was working at the Powder Works in Denaby, and lived nearby in Conisbrough. He had settled into the community and made friends, but he felt such regret at how he had left and not been in touch. He knew it was unforgivable, but he realised that he had to make a break from Florrie, he could not stand how they were living anymore.

Only now did he feel it was the right time to contact home, but he insisted that he did not want Florrie to know anything about the letter or his whereabouts. He felt it was for the best.

Iris's tears had wet the paper as she read his words. Her resentment disappeared, replaced by joy that he was safe and sound. But she thought that Florrie should be told the truth, that she was a good person, like a daughter.

Against Frank's wishes, Iris told Florrie the contents of the letter. She had been surprised but delighted to hear about Frank. Her anger and bitterness faded, now she would have the chance to find him and tell him how much she had changed. What had happened was all her fault. She still loved him and wanted him back. She forgave him for everything.

Florrie's walk slowed as she saw the Station Hotel further along the road. The sun had finally broken through the smoky haze. She could feel the strength of its rays on her face. Once again, she wiped her moist skin, stepping ahead slowly. She felt irrevocably drawn forwards, yet her mind resisted, fearful of the possible outcome.

She finally broke the stalemate of her emotional tussle by striding purposefully towards the pub, scanning its nearby houses. Her mind was made up, there was no going back. She reached the pub and immediately spotted the old stone cottage, complete with its green shutters.

Mr Gibs had been right when he'd said, 'You can't miss it'. The sturdy door was old but freshly painted in green to match the shutters. *Someone cares about this house*, she thought to herself.

She placed her valise on the ground, knuckled up her right hand, and knocked firmly against the green, wooden surface. A few moments later, the door was opened by a young woman, very pretty, with blonde hair and large, grey eyes.

'Can I help you?' Ivy asked Florrie. Florrie noticed the perspiration and sooty smudges along the woman's face, thinking she must be in the middle of cleaning.

'Sorry to disturb you, but I'm looking for Frank Chapman. I've been told he lives here.' Ivy nodded. 'Yes, he does, but he's not in at the moment. Who should I say called?'

'Tell him Florrie, Florrie Chapman, his wife.'

'Oh, I think you've got the wrong house and the wrong Frank Chapman. I'm his wife. I'm Ivy Chapman.'

'Frank wrote his mother a letter saying he lives here,' Florrie stated calmly, yet her mind was reeling.

'Then you have got the wrong Frank Chapman. His mother's dead. He has no family back where he lived,' Ivy retorted, staring hard at Florrie.

'Do you mean in Ashby-de-la-Zouch? His father's dead but his mother's very much alive. So am I, his wife. His mother hadn't heard from him these past few years, until last week. Neither had I, but now I've come looking for him.' Florrie spoke slowly and firmly as if to increase the truth of her words, but fears and doubts were mounting inside her.

Ivy's face wilted, her brow furrowed, her stomach churned.

'I think you'd better come in,' Ivy finally whispered. Her voice was hollow and remote. She suddenly sensed that trouble was looming and would erupt.

The two women stood in the small living room, momentarily bereft of words. Their eyes met, and Ivy was the first to look away. She pushed away the mop and bucket that she'd been using and sat down heavily on the chair. She felt robbed of energy.

'You might as well sit down.' She gestured to Florrie. 'I think you might have a lot to tell me.'

Florrie studied Ivy, noting the tears that brimmed in her large, grey eyes. She was surprised to feel pity for her rather than anger, she looked so vulnerable. She sat down, still finding her words. She, too, felt shocked and weakened. They should be ranting and arguing but they were not.

'You say you are his wife, but you can't be – he's already married to me,' Florrie began. 'Frank married me nearly four years ago. We fell head over heels in love from the day we met.'

Ivy listened, almost in a daze, realising that Florrie's story was the same as her own. 'We were so happy, even though the wedding had to be hasty, if you know what I mean,' Florrie continued.

'You have children with Frank?' Ivy exclaimed, visibly pained, her face flinching with every spoken word.

Florrie looked down at her clenched hands. Her auburn hair spiralled around her face. She tried to control her ragged breathing.

'We had a baby, a boy...' Florrie's monotone voice faded away with a sigh. 'But he died a few minutes after he was born. He was born too early...'

Ivy's penetrating gaze spurred her into continuing.

'I just fell apart. I couldn't cope with the grief. I couldn't cope with anything. I changed into a different person...' Florrie's words again drifted to a halt. 'In the end, Frank left. I suppose he didn't want me anymore. It was all my fault. Mind you, I've cursed him many a time for just leaving without a trace. His mother too.'

'I can't believe Frank could do such a thing. I thought he was a such a kind, caring man...' Ivy's voice broke. 'I trusted him...' Her tears flowed freely as she faced the awful truth.

Florrie leaned forward, her eyes holding Ivy's tearful gaze. 'You do realise you can't be married to him. Frank is a bigamist.'

Chapter 51
June 1898

Frank left The Drum in a daze, his mind in turmoil. Florrie was here, in Denaby. Thoughts tumbled and turned in his head, making him dizzy with panic and confusion.

He should never have contacted his mother, but he had wanted to assuage his guilt after treating her so badly, especially when she was grieving for his father. He felt foolish; he should have known that she would tell Florrie; she must have. Now he was caught in a dilemma.

He pounded the streets, noticing little, then turned up towards the Crags. He needed time to think, but he knew he probably had little time to do anything.

Part of him wanted to flee, to just run away from all this mess, to leave everything and everyone behind him. It was all his doing; the lies and deceit had escalated until there was no going back. But the fact was, he truly loved Ivy, so much so that all sense had left him.

He knew he should not have married her; it was wrong, but she had wanted him, and he had wanted her. His guilty feelings about lying to her had been overwhelmed by his desire to marry her.

He sat on jutting rocks, partway up the rugged Crag. His elevated position afforded him a panoramic view over Denaby. Despite the pockets of cloudy smog, he could easily see Cadeby pit, Kilner's Glass Works and Conisbrough Castle.

The endless rows of pit houses made a gridwork pattern on the landscape, like toy houses assembled to play with. His narrowed eyes picked out The Station Hotel, with his cottage alongside it. His heart pounded and his breathing quickened as he imagined a possible scenario taking place in there.

A stab of hope spiked his panic. Maybe Florrie had not found his house, maybe she changed her mind about finding him; maybe she had already decided to return home. Most of all, maybe she had not discovered he had married Ivy, and Ivy had been spared the pain of finding out that Florrie was his wife.

He ran his fingers through his hair, backwards and forwards as if trying to contain and order his untamed thoughts. What he had done was bigamy. He was a bigamist. He would go to prison.

These unequivocal admissions finally shocked him into facing reality. He wanted to flee, but he had to go home and find out what was happening. He walked down the Crags, his face grim, his mouth set.

He stood outside his cottage. Nerves had rendered him motionless. He flicked his tongue to moisten dry lips and swallowed hard.

'See you've got a visitor, Frank. Such a bonny lass, she's been in there a while now.'

His neighbour's comments punctured his lengthy pause. He glanced at old Mrs Brown who smiled her toothy grin, inviting more conversation.

Without speaking, he opened his front door and stepped inside.

The two women were sitting across from each other. Both looked up at him, neither spoke. Frank sighed deeply and blinked several times, as if trying to wipe away the sight before his eyes. An eerie silence possessed the room. Then it was broken.

'Frank, how could you? How could you?' was Ivy's primeval wail. He had never heard her make such a sound.

'Ivy, Ivy, I'm so sorry, I'm so sorry!' Frank began, striding towards her.

'Don't touch me, don't you dare touch me!' she warned, recoiling from him. 'All those lies, all the deceit about your family. I was such a fool. I thought you loved me!' she sobbed.

'But I do love you, that's why I couldn't tell you I was already married!' Frank insisted, suddenly aware that Florrie was watching, listening.

'Don't mind me, Frank. Then again, you haven't minded me for the past few years, have you? You didn't even mind your own mother! That's unforgivable!' she spat out. 'What you've done to me and Ivy is also unforgivable.'

Frank looked at her with sad eyes and a blank expression. Ivy was shocked at the change in his appearance. His handsome, masculine features seemed reduced, his sturdy physique shrunken, wiped away by feeble hesitation and a growing acceptance of the inevitable consequences of his actions.

'To think I came here looking for you to tell you I wanted you back, that I forgave you for leaving me like you did. I was going to apologise to you! All this time I've been blaming myself,' Florrie carried on, resentment in her eyes and voice. 'I thought I still loved you, but I don't. You're weak, Frank, and selfish.' Florrie's words ended in suppressed sobs.

Ivy stood up slowly, as if summoning up strength. She glared at Frank. 'You know all this will have to come out, don't you? Everyone will know you're a bigamist and that our marriage is just a sham. And you know what that means – prison!'

Ivy paused, as if running out of resilience, but she continued.

'I'm going to the police tomorrow to tell them everything. I want you to get your things and go, now. I mean I want you to leave Denaby for good, and it's no good going back to Ashby, that's the first place the police will look. Just go. I never want to see you again!'

Frank stared at her. She looked so fragile and vulnerable, but her words were decisive. He believed her.

'I agree with Ivy!' Florrie screamed. 'Get your things and disappear, you're good at that. In the end, the two women you've hurt most are giving you a chance to get away. That's more than you deserve, but it's what we've decided. Just fuck off!'

Florrie stomped into the kitchen, hiding her tears. Frank turned to Ivy, his voice pleading with her to understand.

'I'm so sorry, Ivy, that I've hurt you like this, but I do love you, that's the honest truth. I'll always love you. Please forgive me!'

His words almost made her relent and go to him, but she did not. The pain in her heart was just too great. They stared at each other for a moment, then Frank turned and went upstairs.

Florrie saw Ivy's shoulders shaking, silently weeping, stunned by shock and regret. She felt pity for the young woman, but there were no words to speak, everything was too raw, too emotional. Instead, the two women clasped hands briefly and nodded a sad acceptance of the situation.

Frank left by the back door without a word. He carried one small suitcase and a heavy coat, but his heart was heavier. The two women sat in silence for a while, as if absorbing the reality of the situation. Finally, Florrie picked up her valise, patted down her felt hat and said her farewells.

'I'm going now, Ivy. There's a train due soon. I'm going home. I think we've done the right thing. I hope we can both get over it. Take care of yourself.'

They nodded a sad goodbye and shared one last meaningful gaze before Florrie let herself out. She could hear Ivy's sobs as she closed the old green door behind her. Old Mrs Brown waved to her.

'Nice day, isn't it!' she called to Florrie, and watched as the young woman lowered her head and quickly walked away.

Chapter 52
June – July 1898

Ivy lay on the bed and closed her eyes. She allowed her thoughts to drift back over the last few weeks. Since that awful day when her life had changed completely, she had been in a daze.

Her world felt shattered, broken into tiny pieces that could never be mended. She had cried and cried, heartbroken that her life would not be as she had hoped and wanted, crestfallen that Frank, the only man that she had ever truly wanted and loved, had proven to be a liar, a fraud and a criminal.

The day that Frank had gone was the worst of her life. After he and Florrie had left, she sat alone in the cottage, numbed into inaction, shocked as her brain absorbed the reality of her predicament. Waves of despair and apprehension washed over her, eroding what little confidence she had left to face up to her situation. She wanted to hide, but she knew she could not.

The following day, she sought the comfort of her parents. Their Sunday morning tasks were abruptly forgotten as she rushed into their house, falling into their arms, unable to speak coherently at first amid choking sobs. As she thought back to their tender concern and loving embraces, tears welled up again.

'Ivy, love, whatever is the matter?' Sarah asked, stroking her daughter's blonde hair, fearful of the answer she might get.

Ivy's memories of the following few hours were indistinct, with only jumbled recollections as she told them everything.

'He was already married! I don't believe it, never! His wife came here, to Denaby, to your house?' Sarah exclaimed, incredulous when she heard Ivy's words.

'A bigamist! Where is he now? I'll fuckin' kill him!' was Albert's savage retort.

Bob had looked on, shocked to see and hear poor Ivy in such a state. He had run round to Mary's and Gertie's homes, delivering the unbelievable news to them.

Ivy could recall the tender hugs and kisses from her sisters, their shocked expressions revealing alarm and concern. Kind words were volleyed around the room:

'You're not to blame for any of this.'

'None of this is your fault.'

'Hold your head high, you've nothing to be ashamed about.'

'We'll look after you, everyone knows you're a good lass.'

Albert fumed, however. 'You should've gone to t' police straightaway. He didn't deserve a chance to run away again!'

Sarah and Mary accompanied her to the police station later that afternoon. She steeled herself to report Frank, even though some reluctance had started to develop in her thinking.

'It's something you have to do, Ivy love,' Mary coaxed gently. 'Things need to be sorted so you can plan for the future.'

Ivy looked from one family member to another.

'What future? I have no future!' she declared, in tears.

'You're bound to feel like that now, but of course you have a future!' Gertie exclaimed. 'You have all of us to help you. You'll get through this.'

Police Constable Midgely listened carefully to Ivy's outpouring. She gave as much information as she could, her words faltering as she explained everything. She was so thankful to have the support of her mother and sister; she needed it to help her endure the awful task.

Constable Midgely was kind but professional, only allowing a raise of his winged eyebrows to show his surprise.

He knew bigamy was a fairly common crime; people moved from place to place, often with no ties and no one to check any wrongdoings. He also knew that it was easier to become a bigamist than to get a divorce. But it was still a shocking crime in Denaby.

He assured Ivy and her family that he would write his report and issue it to his colleagues in Ashby-de-la-Zouch, where the original marriage had taken place. He would attend to all other necessary formalities, and he would inform them of any other future requirements. He then took off his spectacles, looked kindly at Ivy and said:

'You've done the right thing reporting this, Ivy. We'll see to it now.'

* * *

Ivy recalled the utter fatigue and emptiness she had experienced after speaking to the police. Back at her parents' house, she had fallen into a brief but deep sleep, completely spent.

Sarah gazed down at her beautiful daughter, remembering her as a child, noting her remarkable resemblance to Annie, her own mother. Sarah wept for her daughter's broken dreams.

Albert placed his hands on her shoulders.

'Nay, lass, she'll be all right. We'll look after her,' he murmured gruffly.

* * *

Ivy's next challenge had been going to work, knowing she had to explain Frank's absence and face other people's reactions. She was dreading it, but just wanted to get it over with.

The Monday morning had started as usual, with greetings from colleagues as they put on their work clothes.

She was at her workstation when Bill, the supervisor, came over to speak to her.

'I'm looking for Frank, Ivy. Do you know where he is?'

A fierce defiance suddenly surfaced within her. She determined that she would be candid, plain-spoken.

'I don't know where he is, Bill, because he's gone, left here,' she began. Bill had frowned, puzzled at her words.

'He's gone? Do you mean he's left his job here?'

Ivy had looked him straight in the eye, her chin raised.

'Left his job, left Denaby, left me. Turns out he already had a wife when he married me – she came here looking for him the other day. She didn't know he'd married me, she hadn't seen or heard from him in over two years. He took off before the police got him.'

Ivy's words were spoken with an attempt at bravado, but she then lowered her eyes to conceal her pain. Bill looked stunned, and still perplexed.

'Do you mean he's...?'

'Yes, Bill,' she interrupted. 'Frank's on the run. He's a bigamist.'

The rest of that day had been a blur of snatched stares and sympathetic smiles from other workers. The news had shocked them, but they were kind, offering understanding comments and tactful assertions of their loyalty and support.

* * *

Ivy opened her eyes and halted her recollections. Her mother kept telling her that time was a great healer, and she would get over it. Ivy hoped she was right because her pain felt just as raw and wounding as before.

The only comforting thing for her was that she had returned to live with her parents and brother Bob. She no longer lived in the old stone cottage with the green shutters, next door to old Mrs Brown. That life was gone.

Chapter 53
August 1898

'Are there any more sandwiches, Mam?' John called to Mary. She grinned at him, shaking her head in mock surprise.

'More sandwiches? I don't know where you put everything! You never stop eating, and you're allus hungry!'

'He's a growin' lad,' Rose stated, copying her Grandma Sarah's often repeated words. Mary looked at Sarah and they both laughed. Rose was only eight, but had an adult's sense of humour.

They were enjoying a picnic in Old Denaby. It was quiet and peaceful, a treat while it was still warm and balmy, almost the end of the school holidays.

Sarah and Mary watched the children playing tag, shrieking and laughing in their enjoyment. Six-year-old John was already as tall as Rose. *It must be all the food he eats*, Mary thought to herself, smiling. She and Jim were so proud of their children, so thankful that they were happy and healthy.

Sarah watched Mary, seeing her deep in thought, but almost wistful in her reverie. She decided to broach a sensitive subject.

'Our Betty was sayin' the other day that her and Arthur don't think there'll be any more children for them. She said Arthur would've loved a son, a brother for Clarrie, but they're just thankful to have one healthy child. She said they really feel for Gertie and Charlie, though, knowing how much they want a baby.'

Mary nodded.

'Gertie covers it up well though,' she said to Sarah. Sarah gazed at her daughter, choosing her words carefully.

'Perhaps you'll be expectin' again, one day.'

Mary sighed, giving her mother a rueful smile.

'Hopefully one day, and one day soon,' she murmured.

'How's Bridie? I haven't seen her for a few weeks,' Sarah asked, changing the subject.

'She's eight months pregnant – she thinks – and enormous! I wouldn't be surprised if it's twins!' Mary laughed.

Chapter 54
31st August 1898

Bridie heaved herself up from the living room chair. She had sat down to rest her swollen legs, but Maria was crying, awoken from her afternoon nap by the repetitive banging noise.

Ben was in his chair, his eyes sweeping around the room, but saying nothing. He had recently begun the habit of banging urgently on the side of his chair, then chuckling to himself. Bridie wiped the drools of saliva from his chin.

'No, Ben, no. Quiet please, for Mammy.' She attempted patience in her voice, but she was tired and miserable. Her stomach was huge, her body ached, making even the simplest of tasks difficult. Everyone told her she must be having twins; even Nellie the midwife had passed sensitive hands over her straining belly and surmised:

'You're going to have your hands full with all your babies.'

At first, she had been pleased about her pregnancy, feeling a renewed optimism about married life with Eli. They were now much more tolerant of each other, and baby Maria had rekindled strong maternal feelings within her. She had been able to shift to the back of her mind all the demons of guilt and sadness that previously dominated her moods.

But this long, arduous pregnancy had depleted her expectations, as well as her energy. She was also realising, more and more, how gullible Eli was. He got himself into trouble without even recognising possible dangers. He was so easily led, especially if Tommy Prince was involved.

Only a few weeks ago, she had been exasperated with him when he and Prince had to appear at Doncaster Magistrates Court. The case had been reported in the *Mexborough and Swinton Times*, which she had found embarrassing, but Eli had merely grinned and shrugged his shoulders.

'I got off wi' it, not Tommy, mind you, but we 'ad a laugh about it.'

The case was concerning an incident at The Drum, between Mr Gibbs and Tommy Prince, together with Eli in tow. 'A Lively Time at The Denaby Main Hotel' had been the title of the report in the newspaper. Bridie had been scathing about that.

'Why can't you just go out and have a drink without getting "lively" and causing trouble?' she had asked Eli.

He produced his illuminating grin, like a mischievous child, and, once again, shrugged his shoulders.

'Trust it to be with Tommy Prince!' she raged. 'Don't you realise he's always trouble?'

'He's a mate,' Eli stated simply. Bridie flounced off in exasperation.

The newspaper report had described how Tommy Prince had visited The Drum one Saturday afternoon, after having already been drinking in a few Mexborough pubs. He had started to sing loudly, and at length, in the taproom, much to the consternation of the barman, who asked him to be quiet.

Eli joined Tommy at that point, ready for his first pint of the day. When Tommy carried on his singing, he was again warned by the barman, who asked him to be quiet or he would have to leave for being disorderly. The two men had laughed, Tommy stating he would only be quiet if the landlord, Mr Gibbs, asked him to.

Mr Gibbs decided both men were drunk and disorderly and asked them to leave. Both proclaimed their innocence, refusing to quit the pub.

'I'm not even drunk!' Eli retorted.

'And I'm doing no harm singin',' Tommy had drawled. Mr Gibbs made the decision to manhandle Tommy to the front door, whereupon Tommy had pushed the landlord.

'You're too fat to fight!' Tommy had scoffed.

'Oh, I am, am I?' Isaac Gibbs had replied, hitting Tommy forcefully in the face.

Tommy Prince summoned Isaac Gibbs for assaulting him, whilst Mr Gibbs issued summonses charging Tommy Prince and Eli Shaw for being disorderly and refusing to quit the hotel, and also Prince for assault at the same time.

The outcome of the case was that the case against Mr Gibbs was dismissed, also the summons against Eli Shaw. Tommy Prince was ordered to pay a ten-shilling fine and costs of twenty-four shillings for refusing to quit.

Eli had later chuckled when telling Bridie.

'Tommy's punch on the nose meant he missed a shift at work, an' all… an expensive "lively" bit of singing!'

* * *

Bridie's recollections were suddenly interrupted by a sharp pressure pain. She felt the warm fluid falling between her legs, gathering in a pool on the kitchen floor.

Her young sister, Martha, was playing with Ben and Maria in the living room.

'Martha, run back home and tell Mammy that my waters have broken,' Bridie called out to the little girl.

Hannah returned quickly with Martha to find Bridie grimacing with the contraction pains.

'Martha, run round to Nellie MacArthur's, quick. You know where she lives, don't you?' Hannah asked.

'Yes, Mammy, I'll be as quick as I can.'

Hannah saw the fear in Bridie's eyes.

'Sure you'll be fine, my love. It's better to get all this over with,' she assured her daughter.

Bridie nodded as she gasped at the building contractions.

* * *

On the last day of August, 1898, Bridie gave birth to twin boys. At times, she had doubted that the pain would ever stop, but she had clenched her teeth and clung on to her mother as the labour progressed, and finally culminated, in the deliveries of two small but healthy sons.

Nellie sweated and strained along with Bridie, until the old lady's face was scarlet with effort.

'Two wee boys, a bit on the small side, but breathing and crying!' she announced triumphantly to Hannah and Bridie.

Martha peeped around the bedroom door, wide-eyed and shy.

'Are you all right, Bridie?' she whispered to her big sister. Bridie summoned up a weak smile and nodded.

'Yes, my love. Two more nephews for you, Auntie Martha.' Martha's face crumpled into a smile moistened by tears. Hannah looked on proudly.

'Wait till we tell Eli and your dad and brothers,' she declared excitedly. 'Sure, they'll be made up to have the boys!'

* * *

Eli shuffled into the bedroom and peered at Bridie. She was sleeping, her chestnut-gold hair fanned along her pillow. A warmth seeped into his body, pride and love, although he could not readily identify the sensations.

His large, cupped hand stroked the chestnut-gold hair and his features suffused into a glorious grin. Bridie opened her eyes and smiled back. She remembered why she had married him, and promised herself that she would try to understand him more. He wasn't perfect, but then neither was she.

'Two more sons for you,' she whispered.

Eli nodded and walked around the bed to peer at the two babies. They had identical faces, both with their mother's chestnut-gold coloured hair.

'We'll have to think of two names, then,' he stated.

'We'll have to have two of everything for them,' Bridie smiled. 'Four children, Eli. Nellie says I'm going to have my hands full of babies.'

Eli stared, as if only just realising his responsibilities. Part of him was unsure of changing his self-centred ways, but he was surprised to feel the desire to help Bridie. His brain pondered what he could do.

PART SIX

Chapter 55
1899

Denaby and Cadeby pits continued to flourish, producing record tonnages of coal, outshining many other South Yorkshire pits. Work was plentiful and regular for the miners, but, unfortunately, so were the accidents and fatalities. So common were injuries and deaths, that they became a fact of life for the families of Denaby and Cadeby miners.

Women lived in constant fear that their husbands and sons would be the next victims while executing their highly dangerous jobs. The returning footsteps of their menfolk at the end of a shift would always produce relieved sighs and silent thanksgivings. The men knew all too well the acute hazards of their daily work, but they had to compartmentalise their fears and continue earning.

Over the years, there had been many consultations between masters and men regarding stoppage of work when there was a serious accident or a fatality. It had always been the miners' instinct to down tools and leave work when such incidents occurred, as well as being a mark of respect, but this was fiercely contested by management.

A death was not always considered a good enough reason to stop work. Money and time could not always accommodate such sentiment. Gradually, a compromise had been reached and a written contract was drawn up, listing exactly when stopping work would be acceptable. But there were occasions when the contract was contested because of unusual circumstances, and this conflict created passionate responses from the hardworking miners.

* * *

The morning shift had arrived at Cadeby pit, and the men were swiftly plunged underground, exchanging sleepy nods and

'Mornings' with the night shift men as they assembled outside the cage, ready for their ascent and home.

Two of the lads were Seamus Flannagan and his friend Tobias Green, both pony drivers and both eighteen years old. They headed towards their working district, their clogs striking and rapping against the hard, uneven floor.

Seamus carried his snap tin containing the sandwiches made for him by his mother, Hannah, who insisted on getting up early to see him off, even though he urged her not to. Since Liza's death seven years earlier, his mother had been extra protective of her children, including him, her youngest son.

'Sure, I'll see you off like I do with all my menfolk,' she always repeated with a determined nod of the head.

Tobias turned onto the jenny, a side roadway, while Seamus continued on the main gate, heading for the stables.

An hour or so later, Seamus was hauling back some empty corves, when a reverberating clank ran along the tunnelled walls. It was not the usual sounds of coupling and uncoupling, or wheels grinding on rails. He decided to investigate.

The sight that met his eyes shocked and repulsed him. Toby Green lay crushed between corves. He made no sound, his body still, crumpled and distorted by terrible injuries. Seamus extricated his friend as gently as he could, barely able to look at the gruesome wounds.

Shouts and clanging boots pierced his disoriented stupor. Men were gathering at the site of the accident, including his brother, Paddy, and Jim, yelling comments to each other:

'It's Toby Green, in't it?'

'Poor bugger, he's only a lad.'

'Is he unconscious or dead?'

'Don't think there's much hope by the look of those injuries.'

Paddy and Jim spoke gently to Seamus,

'You get off home, lad. You're in shock after seeing that. We'll see to him.'

Seamus nodded, still dazed, but had to retch and vomit onto the black, gritty ground before he made his way back to the cage and up to light and life.

Tobias had been taken to Mexborough Cottage hospital. Everyone was surprised to hear that he had been still alive when he first arrived, but he had died two hours later from his injuries.

Seamus was surprised and upset when he heard that the Denaby and Cadeby Colliery Company had brought a case against him for damages of five shillings for wrongly absenting himself from his work. Seamus had to appear before magistrates, who accepted his defence that he had left work in the bona fide belief that a fatal accident had occurred.

It was in the written contract between men and management that, if an accident occurred in the mine and the person died, any workman was entitled to leave the pit for the rest of the shift. However, an argument arose questioning whether death must occur in the mine, or whether, if death ensued elsewhere, a worker could legally absent himself from work.

The Yorkshire Miners' Association asked to appeal Seamus's case, stating the conditions of the contract were unclear. In the end, the appeal case was dismissed, but it was recommended that men and management should meet, and put in writing, whether it was really meant that the death from accident must occur in the mine. The Yorkshire Miners' Association intimated through Counsel that they were prepared to meet the employers amicably to elucidate conditions.

'Our Seamus still had to pay five shillings damages though,' the Flannagan family grumbled. 'But thank the Lord, we still have our Seamus with us, alive, unlike Toby's poor family. They've lost their wee boy for ever.'

* * *

Walter Smith waited by the cage along with other miners, all keen to get home after their shift. Coal dust, caked hard with sweat, covered their skin and clothes. The whites of their eyes contrasted to their blackened faces.

'Thank God it's Friday – pay day tomorrow,' one of the older miners stated, his voice flat and weary.

'No more pay days for the two poor buggers killed here last week,' another man retorted. 'First Toby Green crushed, then George Hibbard buried under a fall, one eighteen and t'other sixty-eight.'

A brief silence fell between the men, as if their thoughts stifled communication.

'I feel sorry for Willie Flannagan's lad, Seamus. Poor lad saw his mate mangled, then he ended up in trouble wi' t' gaffers and had to pay five shillings damages for leaving work!' another man declared.

'Bloody ridiculous, that was. Death by accident is death by accident – it shouldn't matter where or when he dies,' called out another miner.

'I don't think it was ridiculous,' Walter interrupted. 'Company were right when they said it was a written agreement that men could only leave work if there was a fatality there.'

The men snorted and guffawed in disgust.

'Bloody hell, Walter! Whose side are you on? Don't tell us you're agreeing wi' t' gaffers!'

'I'm on mi own side,' Walter stated calmly. 'I make mi own way in life. I don't need a Union to speak up for mi.'

'Tha's on yer own there then, Walter Smith,' one man retorted. 'One day you might want t' Union's help.'

Walter sneered and stepped into the cage.

I'm mi own man, he thought to himself. *I'll look after miself and mi family.*

Chapter 56
November 1899

'I like lookin' at all the books here!' Rose declared, shuffling into a comfortable position on her chair.

'I like lookin' at pictures, and it's nice and warm in here,' John agreed.

Mary and Jim smiled at their children.

'Well, you've certainly got lots of choice here,' Mary retorted. 'Even though a lot of books are a bit hard for you.'

They had all discarded coats and hats before sitting in the reading room at the Denaby Main Institute. It was warm and cosy compared to the wet and windy weather outside.

Jim and Mary often visited the 'Stute' and encouraged Rose and John to enjoy handling the literature there. As well as daily, weekly and monthly newspapers and magazines, there was a good library of books.

'I'm so glad Rose and John enjoy their books,' Mary often remarked to Jim.

'They take after their mother,' he would reply.

'Look at that elephant, it's massive!' John exclaimed, pointing at a picture. 'I wish I could see one, a real one!'

'We'll have to take you to Blackpool Tower one day. The Tower circus has lots of animals, they even do tricks!' Jim replied. 'They live in stables and pens deep beneath the circus ring, and I read t'other day in t' *Daily Mail* that the horses and elephants are often taken for a mornin' walk along the beach. That must turn a few heads! It's only been open for five years, but the Tower gets thousands of visitors, it's so popular.'

'Aw, can we go Dad?' John pleaded.

'If we save up enough pennies for the annual outing,' Mary interrupted. 'The other year there were three full trains of folks from round 'ere on a day trip to Blackpool.'

'I'll get saving mi pennies, then,' John agreed.

'Miss Jones says Blackpool Tower was copied from the Eiffel Tower in Paris,' Rose said, looking up from a copy of her favourite story, Johanna Spyri's *Heidi*.

'Your teacher is right,' Mary agreed. 'The Eiffel Tower was built five years before Blackpool Tower, and it's twice as tall.'

'But it has no elephants and clowns in it, like Blackpool Tower,' interrupted Jim. 'And I think it's magic that Blackpool Tower Circus can change its arena into an artificial lake in less than a minute!'

The children shrieked with delight.

'I definitely think we'd better get saving those pennies!' Mary declared, smiling and winking at her husband.

* * *

There was a special reason for their visit to the reading room this time. Mary and Jim wanted to see, with their own eyes, the magazine article written about Denaby Main that had caused great controversy, both locally and nationally.

'Here's the periodical we want, the November issue of *The Christian Budget*,' Mary announced. 'Let's read why they think Denaby Main is "The Worst Village in England", and "A Hell on Earth",' she added sarcastically.

As they read the article, they could hardly retain their anger and irritation.

'How unfair and how exaggerated!' Mary cried.

Jim's mouth set as he read the biased report. He regarded the subjective view of the author very unfair.

'*The Christian Budget* sent a "Special Commissioner" to describe Denaby,' Jim began, scathingly. 'Who only stayed a few hours and listened to a few people's hearsay, yet he decides to write in such a biased way. He wrote that nearly all the men and most of the women devote their high wages to betting and gambling, that religion is forgotten, homelife is shattered, immorality and intemperance are rife, wives are sold like cattle, and children are neglected.'

Jim shook his head in exasperation.

'We're not all like that, and no worse than a lot of other villages!' declared Mary. 'What about the honest, hardworking people who fight for a better life for themselves and their families?'

'It was even worse when the *Mexborough and Swinton Times* decided to reprint the articles,' Jim stated, grimly. 'That really did set the cat among the pigeons.'

* * *

The women tightened their shawls and shuffled from side to side in their attempts to keep warm. The biting November wind stung chapped hands and billowed even the heaviest of skirts.

The queue for the water was longer than usual, annoying already harassed wives and daughters. The only thing that alleviated their weariness and irritation was the shared conversation, and the main topic was the article written about Denaby Main. Comments bounced between them, indignation and anger rising as they shared information and opinions.

'I couldn't believe it when the *Times* printed a copy of that "Worst Village in England" article. It was a right kick in the teeth for us, as if they believed everything that the Commissioner wrote!' one woman declared.

'I know, but have you seen this week's *Times*? A man, he calls himself J.F., has written to the Editor to complain. Right indignant he is, says 'Denaby Main – Certainly Not the Worst Village in England!' He's very clever because he argues the point about everything that the first article claimed were the true facts, and he gives proof that most were lies!'

'But Denaby is a hard place to live and work in, and some folks are guilty of wrongdoings,' an old lady insisted.

'I know some are, but not everyone!' interrupted another. 'And no worse than lots of other places.'

A shout came from the queue.

'It said most men and women drink and gamble away the money that's meant for food and the house. I'm lucky to get cups o' tea, let alone tots o' gin! And I've never gambled in mi life, I need all the money I can get!'

A ripple of laughter and agreement passed around the group.

'What I can't understand is, it said we don't clean our kids or houses – does he think we spend hours queuing for water just for fun? It makes my blood boil!' one exasperated young woman retorted.

'Well said, love. We may be poor, but we don't all neglect our kids!'

'And another thing, it said Denaby has no church-goers or Sunday School. J.F. points out that a new Catholic church has opened, a new Protestant church is being built and there's already Wesleyan and Methodist chapels.'

'And don't forget the Sally Army and the Sunday School at the Large Hall, love,' chipped in another.

'He called us thriftless, but he didn't bother to find out that we save at the 'Penny Bank' and pay into the Friendly Societies for our annual outings,' contributed another.

'My Billy's learning the violin at school,' one lady proudly announced.

'My Emma's learning piano,' chorused another.

'Not to mention the dances and concerts at the Large Hall. Does that sound like Hell on Earth?'

'That Commissioner had better not show his face round 'ere, or he might find other things he doesn't like!'

'Well said, love. We stick together and look after our own!'

* * *

The group of men relaxed in The Drum, enjoying their ale. Bitter comments proclaimed their indignation at *The Christian Budget's* accusation that Denaby was the worst village in England.

'That Commissioner – and he's no Christian – wrote Denaby should be a paradise – lots of work, well paid and beautiful surroundings,' Paddy Flannagan scoffed.

'Think he must have had sore eyes, like he criticised our children for having, when he looked around, as he wasn't seeing straight!' his father, Willie sneered. 'He'll not have open middens and God knows what germs flying around outside his house!'

'Aye, and he'll not shovel coal eight hours a day like us, then complain when we have a drink,' Dermot Flannagan insisted.

'He said we had 'St. Monday', a day off work every week because of the drink,' their friend added. 'I'd like to hear what my missus would say if I had Mondays off!'

Willie smiled, a twinkle in his eye.

'He said most couples don't bother getting married, but just live together. Now that could be one thing I'd like to be true,' he quipped, winking at his sons.

* * *

Mr Chambers sat in his office, a deep frown etched into his features. He was discussing *the Christian Budget's* article with Mr Witty, manager of Cadeby pit, Mr Williamson, a Doncaster engineer and Councillor Dixon, a member of the Denaby Main Parish Council.

'This is outrageous!' declared Mr Chambers. 'These accusations are exaggerated, biased and downright lies!' His voice rose in pitch and volume as the gross unfairness of the article increasingly angered him.

'Little literature in Denaby Main – did he not see the Institute with its wonderful library – mostly provided by Messrs. W.H. Smith and Son Ltd of London?'

'Immorality and no close bonds between the residents?' Councillor Dixon contributed to the condemnation. 'Does he not know of the well-supported football and cricket teams, and the recreation ground for the children?'

'Yes, and the technical and evening classes for the older youths,' added Mr Williamson. 'With a view to qualifying for important positions such as under-managers or managers?'

'I have personally founded and supported the St. John Ambulance Corps here,' continued Mr Chambers. 'The miners have gained invaluable knowledge which could save lives in times of accidents and emergencies. Many of the men wear their medals proudly on their watch chains. Does all this sound like a shattered home life within a "Hell on Earth" community?' Mr Chambers concluded with a rap of his hand on his desk.

Mr Witty nodded, in agreement with his colleagues' disdain.

'Gentlemen, there are also indications that the Colliery Company is being blamed for the supposed description of the village, that it has caused the conditions he so outrageously depicted. In short, it is libel to suggest that the Company has created such an immoral, intemperate community.'

The other men stared at Mr Witty. There was a sudden scrape of chair legs as Mr Chambers stood up abruptly.

'We'll have to see what Mr Buckingham Pope has to say about all this!' proclaimed the "King of Denaby", this time slapping his desk with both hands.

Chapter 57
March 1900

Ivy peered into the small hand mirror, turning her head slowly to see the various angles of her face. The mirror had a cracked surface, but she could see her reflection sufficiently well to feel pleased with her appearance.

Even though her thirtieth birthday was only weeks away, she still had the flawless, luminous skin, the beautiful pale grey eyes and the mass of blonde, wavy hair that had always made her strikingly attractive. She felt that her appearance was like a layer of armour, disguising her true inner emotional state. She feared that, one day, that layer would peel away, revealing the scars inflicted on her bruised ego and diminished self-esteem.

It was almost two years since Frank had gone, leaving her shattered, cracked like the old mirror she now handled. At first, she had felt hopeless and helpless, so profound had been the shock that her beloved Frank had lied to her, duped her, left her. Her family had protected her, encouraged her and nurtured her spirits, all done lovingly and willingly.

Now, much to her surprise and secret relief, hope was quietly evolving within her. She had met someone, a man she liked and hoped she could trust. She needed to believe in herself again, and in others.

The man was Sam Baker, a butcher who worked in his uncle Edward's long-established butcher's shop on Doncaster Road, not far from The Drum. Sam's father, Robert, and his uncle Ed were brothers, who had set up shops in Conisbrough and Denaby.

Sam had always worked in his father's Conisbrough shop until a few months ago. His move to Denaby was due to several factors. His Uncle Ed had four daughters and one son, but his lad, Ernest, had been struck down by a wasting disease. Ed had watched his only son grow thinner and weaker, until he died at the age of thirty.

Sam had readily agreed to help his uncle with the shop, but there was an even more compelling reason why he craved a change of environment.

His wife, Emelia, had died giving birth two years previously. Sam had lost his beloved wife and his only child, a boy, on the same dreadful day. He had felt grief that cut into his heart and soul. He had endured months of regretful mourning, as if waiting for some sign of solace, some sign that he could rejoin the world, mentally and emotionally.

Sam had continued working throughout, reluctant to drown in his sorrow. He decided his move to Denaby would be beneficial for everyone.

Ivy first saw Sam when she visited the shop on an errand for her mother. Sarah had a heavy cold and Ivy insisted on her staying inside until she was feeling better.

'I'm quite capable of choosing and buying a joint of beef, Mam,' Ivy had teased. It was a standing joke within the family that Sarah always liked to go to the butcher's herself. She loved looking at the cuts of meat hanging on hooks along the walls or laid on the slab. She loved having the money to buy meat.

'Eeh, that's a lovely piece of beef,' was her highest accolade. 'Now then, Ivy love, choose a nice piece of beef, about two pounds should be big enough, and mind there's no sinew on it, or it's going back. That nice new butcher seems very pleasant. He's a big help to Mr Baker. Such a shame about his lad.'

'Yes, mother. Now you sit down by the fire, it's freezing outside.'

'You're a good girl,' Sarah sighed as she sat down and snuggled into the blanket draped around her shoulders.

Ivy glanced up at the sign above the butcher's shop: 'E. Baker the butcher and son. English beef and pork butchers'. She noted that Mr Baker had not changed it since the death of his son, and probably would not. She understood how he must feel.

She entered the shop, glad to escape the gusty, wintry winds and closed the door against them. The man was serving a little boy, but he looked up as she walked towards the counter, nodding with a widening smile.

'Now then, young man, what can I get you?' he said to the boy, wiping his hands down the white apron tied around his body.

'Half a pound o' ram, please.'

'I'm afraid I haven't got any ram today,' Sam replied, winking at Ivy.

'Well mi mam said you 'ad!' the lad retorted.

'Aah, yes, you mean half a pound of ham!' Sam smiled. 'I'll get you some.'

Ivy looked at the boy's puzzled face and chuckled to herself. Sam handed over the wrapped meat, took the money, then produced a dish of sweets from under the counter.

'Would you like a bull's eye? A mint humbug I mean, not a *real* bull's eye!'

'Ta,' the boy answered and promptly filled his mouth with the unexpected treat.

'One happy little boy,' Ivy laughed as they watched him running along the street.

'Now, Miss, what can I get you?'

'I'd like a piece of beef weighing about two pounds, please,' Ivy began, glancing around the joints. 'And I've been told to ask for one without –'

'Sinew?' interrupted Sam, grinning. 'I'll find you a nice one – with definitely no sinew!'

Ivy felt her face flush. 'My mother's orders,' she confessed, also smiling.

'Your mother's not Mrs Cooper, is she?' Sam asked.

Ivy blushed again. 'That's right. She's at home with a cold so she's entrusted me with buying the meat. I'm Ivy Cooper.'

'Sam Baker,' he replied, 'Sam Baker the butcher. It always gets a smile – I only need a candlestick maker!' They smiled as their eyes met. She noted his grey eyes, his fair hair, his kind voice.

'I think this joint should suit your mother,' he continued, waiting for her nod of approval.

'If I don't bring it back, you'll know you were right,' she laughed.

'I believe I noticed you at the concert last week at the Large Hall?' Sam remarked as he wrapped the meat.

'Yes, I was there. I really enjoyed it,' she replied.

'Maybe I'll see you at the next one,' Sam said, this time flushing the same shade of red as his hands.

'Maybe you will,' she smiled. 'Good day, Mr Baker the butcher.'

* * *

'Do you mean you saw the man stealing the meat?' Ivy asked her sister Gertie, who was only too willing to recount the recent incident.

'Plain as day,' she replied. 'I was just outside Baker's window and as I looked inside, I saw the man pick up a joint off the side slab and put it in his coat pocket. He didn't run out, but just carried on queuing, waiting to be served.'

'Didn't Mr Baker or the new butcher see him do it?'

'No. Mr Baker was in the back and the new butcher was wrapping meat,' Gertie explained.

'So what did you do?' Ivy asked.

'Well, the new butcher…'

'Sam's his name, Sam Baker, he told me last week,' Ivy interrupted.

'Sam, then, asked the man if he was ready to be served and he asked for four links of sausage, so I said, 'I think he's already served himself,' and I told them what he'd done.'

'Gertie! You never did! What did the man say?'

'Denied it, denied it flat. He got quite abusive, so Sam came round the counter and made him empty his pockets. Things were getting nasty, so I was glad Mr Baker spotted Constable Midgley walking past. He soon sorted things. Heard the man's only recently come here to work, he's from Wolverhampton. He got ten days in prison with hard labour. I can't stand liars and thieves!' Gertie exclaimed.

* * *

'I'll go to the butcher's for you,' Ivy persuaded her mother. 'It's no trouble.'

Sarah studied her daughter's face. She had recently noticed a subtle change in Ivy's countenance, a calm composure with underlying knowing looks and expressions. She imagined she saw a new spark of light in her eyes and a new spring in her step. Sarah hoped her daughter was emerging from her personal ordeal.

'Yes, all right, I'll have a sit down while you go,' she said, noticing the smile hovering around Ivy's mouth.

'I'll remember to ask for no sinew,' Ivy laughed as she reached for her shawl.

* * *

Sam greeted Ivy with a pleased look and a big smile as she entered the shop. She felt her heart quicken.

'Hello, Ivy. What can I get for you?'

'The usual, please, Sam, same as last week. My mother was really pleased with the quality of the beef, she told me to tell you.'

'Only best quality meat sold here, dear,' old Mr Baker declared as he stepped in from the back room. 'Your Gertie was a good lass t'other day,' he continued. 'Caught that thief red-handed, and she weren't afraid to speak up,' he added with a firm nod of his head.

'Yes, she told me all about it,' Ivy smiled. 'That's our Gertie – always speaks her mind.'

Sam threw Ivy a questioning look.

'Yes, Gertie's my sister,' Ivy said. She was rewarded with a beaming, thoughtful smile from Sam. Her mind and pulse raced. Uncle Ed looked over the top of his spectacles at them. For once, he felt gladdened.

Chapter 58
Spring 1900

The Spring sunshine ushered thoughts of warmth, new life and the pleasant anticipation of longer, lighter days to the people of Denaby. But these things were of no importance to Bridie. The new century had brought her nothing but a sullen depression, feelings of apathy and overwhelming fatigue. Worst of all, the new year had confirmed that she was again pregnant. She felt no pleasure at this news, more a mounting despair.

After the birth of the twins, she never seemed to have enough time, energy or desire to be active and organised. Other people had offered her help and support: her mother, friend Mary and sister, little Martha, regularly ran errands and carried out necessary chores.

Even Eli obliged by carrying out more domestic duties after a fashion, but her spirits never lifted. It was as if she was in a fog, struggling to find brightness and clarity. Moreover, she felt guilt, from her memories, and now from her inability to cope properly.

The twin boys, Edward and William, were thriving, but she almost resented all the time she spent feeding and cleaning them; the repetition of chores was constant and relentless. Very rarely were both children settled at the same time, straining her patience and affection.

'Let me take the boys for a while, you get some rest,' Mary kept offering, but usually Bridie stubbornly refused.

'I can manage, thanks, Mary. Sure, you've enough to do without seeing to me!'

'But I want to help, I love having the boys,' Mary insisted.

Occasionally Bridie would concede.

'Well, maybe for an hour then.'

Sleep was repelled by guilty feelings; she wasn't spending enough time with Ben, and she even felt she was neglecting Maria, her lovely wee Maria. She tried to reason that she would soon feel better, able to cope. But she felt as if she was falling into a deep, dark, frightening hole.

Chapter 59
May 1900

The first year of the new century had heralded many new incidents and events in Denaby, some good, some bad.

The new church was almost finished, and the Protestant worshippers were informed that Denaby Main All Saints Parish Church would soon be opened and consecrated by the Most Reverend, the Lord Archbishop of York.

'We'll soon be leaving St. Chad's Church, then,' the churchgoers announced. 'It'll be strange, but wonderful, to have such a big, new church.'

'Aye, we just want to get all our lads back safe and sound from the war now. We've all been praying for that.'

The Boer War had started the previous year, in October 1899, and it had affected quite a few families in Denaby and the surrounding villages, whose sons or husbands were reservists. There was, at first, little understanding about the war.

'It all seems so far away, fighting in South Africa!' people declared.

'And fighting for what? Since gold and diamonds were discovered there – that's what for!'

'Aye, the Boers don't want the British Empire to get their hands on all that treasure, they want it for themselves.'

Some of the reservists were miners from Conisbrough and Denaby, selected for active service in the war between the British Empire and two independent Boer states, the South African Republic and Orange Free State. The British Empire's influence in South Africa was resented by these states, and bitter conflict ensued.

The Mexborough and Swinton Times regularly printed letters sent from the fighting soldiers to their families, as local people were keen to be informed about the conditions and operations carried out by the army all those miles away. Jim had a particular interest in one of his workmates, Dougie Johnson, who had been called up and given his "khaki" dress, the uniform of the British soldiers.

Jim had organised a meeting of Dougie's friends and work pals at Cadeby Colliery to give him a good send off. They all wished him 'God speed and a safe return', as well as presenting him with an inscribed gold medal. They had wanted to give him something personal, and small enough to take with him.

'It's a token of our respect, Dougie,' they had told him. 'And it can be a constant reminder of all your pit mates.'

Another Denaby man fighting in the war was John Dunne, a sergeant in the St. John Ambulance Brigade. His letters to his parents in Denaby told of his work there, looking after three wards in the camp and seeing to all the dressings of the surgical patients. He marvelled at how the soldiers travelled over the hills and mountains, and how many had survived the bitter sieges, the Boers being well-equipped with guns. He described the surroundings of the camp as barren, but had seen many small plantations and pretty sights when travelling around the country. He especially noticed the wide variety of fruit growing there.

One of the reservists was already on his way home, invalided out because of his poor health and injuries. Corporal James Collins, a former employee at Cadeby Colliery, was an orderly to Lord Kitchener. He described in his letters home how they had to fight for long hours with hardly any food or water for the men or the horses.

They had managed to relieve villages, and were treated well by the grateful residents there. They had thankfully eaten the food provided for them, although they had not realised their meal was cooked mule.

As they pressed on, they were forced to drink water from the river where bodies of Boers, cattle and horses floated. That was why so many soldiers became victims of dysentery and enteric fever, and he had also suffered a bullet through his shin. He informed his parents that he would be sailing home from Cape Town on board the *Umbria* and was looking forward to being home soon.

Jim was pleased and relieved to be regularly informed by Dougie Johnson's parents that he was very tired, but healthy and in good spirits.

'Let's hope that gold medal brings you continued good fortune,' Jim muttered to his distant friend.

Chapter 60
May 1900

The magazine article that labelled Denaby Main as the "worst village in England" had angered many people, including residents, workers and management. Their resentment was compounded by the many different newspapers that had republished the original report, as if strengthening and validating its condemnation of the village.

Mr Chambers had been unhappy at the way the article suggested that the Company was to blame for all the supposed faults within the community, but one man was even more outraged by the unfair portrayal of Denaby, and that was the Chairman of the Company, Mr John Buckingham Pope.

One newspaper, the *Eastern Morning and Hull News*, had sought to link him, personally and directly, to the conditions described in the village. Mr Buckingham Pope regarded this as libel and decided on a court case, 'Pope v *Eastern Morning and Hull News*', for alleged libel published in their newspaper in November 1899.

The Mexborough and Swinton Times reported on the court case in May 1900, much to the interest of both local readers and Yorkshire readers further afield.

'A Libel on Denaby Village' made for entertaining reading.

Mr Buckingham Pope was seeking to recover damages of three thousand pounds for the alleged libel, but the newspaper considered ten guineas as sufficient to satisfy damages. They admitted the publication, and that the matter was libel, but they maintained it was published without malice or gross negligence, and that they had offered an apology.

However, in the ensuing case, it was stated that Mr Buckingham Pope was chairman not only of the Denaby Main and Cadeby Main Colliery Company, but also of the South Yorkshire railway, which operated between the collieries and the Hull and Barnsley railway system.

Issues had previously arisen between the managements of the two railways, with litigation still ongoing. Nine months previously, the *Eastern Morning News* had to pay Mr Buckingham Pope damages because of their libel while reporting the litigation. When *the Christian Budget* article appeared, they had seized the opportunity to republish it, as well as adding their own libellous comments:

'Mr Buckingham Pope might devote some of his leisure time spent in the task of instructing the Hull and Barnsley Railway Company in the way it should be run, to the more pressing work of promoting reforms nearer home.'

These scathing comments, together with a full recount of the original report, incensed Mr Pope. He considered it libel to print a gross misdescription of the village, to infer that the Colliery Company was responsible for conditions there and that it was a personal attack on himself, whose name had been unnecessarily dragged in, as further evidence of his responsibility for the damning conditions.

During the summing up for the jury, the Judge alluded to the fact that the Colliery Company had built churches, schools, institutes and many other advantages in the mining village.

He also alluded to the fact that revenge, over previous damages paid by the newspaper to Mr Pope, may have played a part. It was a question of damages, and whether the jury thought ten guineas was enough.

After only five minutes deliberation, the jury found a verdict for Mr Pope, deciding on damages of a hundred pounds.

'Mr Pope got one o'er those buggers,' was the general, satisfied opinion of many Denaby folk.

Chapter 61
June 1900

Sam and Ivy were strolling through the hamlet of Old Denaby. It was a glorious summer's afternoon, with warm sunshine, a refreshing breeze and a blue sky dotted with fluffy white clouds, something not readily seen in the polluted atmosphere that hung over Denaby Main.

'It's so nice to see blue sky! It makes you feel free. I hate all the soot and smoke we usually have, it feels like it's choking your lungs!' Ivy exclaimed.

'I agree,' Sam said. 'Sunday afternoon walks are a treat when the weather's like this.' He smiled at Ivy, thinking, once again, how beautiful she was.

They had walked out together more and more as their acquaintance had strengthened, happy to share opinions and each other's company.

Not long after their first meeting, they had both attended a concert at Rossington Street School, almost bumping into each other as they entered the Large Hall.

Sam had asked if he might sit next to her, and she had smiled her agreement. They had looked at each other shyly, hesitating at first, each waiting for the other to speak, then they had both spoken at the same time.

Their laughter seemed to break the ice, and they chatted, enjoying their close proximity. Sam glanced at Ivy's profile: the straight nose, the glowing skin, the blonde waves peeping from under her hat. She made sidelong glances at him, his square jaw, broad shoulders and straight, fair hair. They relaxed, sat back and enjoyed the concert.

The Denaby Main Orchestral Society was performing a benefit concert for Denaby United Football Club. The object was to raise funds for the club which had recently incurred a large expense of one hundred and fifty-five pounds for the fitting of fencing and barriers to their playing field, the recreation football ground behind The Pig.

The team was very popular, especially as it was leading Division One in the Hatchard Cup, not having suffered one defeat that season. They had been in possession of the large, handsome Silver Cup, as champions of the South Yorkshire League for three consecutive seasons, and supporting crowds enjoyed seeing the Cup on display at matches.

The concert had been widely anticipated and, with the demand for tickets, hoped to realise a considerable sum for the club.

The large audience had thoroughly enjoyed the performances of the orchestra and singers. The conductor of the thirty-five strong orchestra was Mr Soar. His daughter, Gertrude, performed solo and in a duet, her soprano voice being much admired, along with Mr Foxton, a tenor, who sang in a high key, but with much ease. Mr Soar's son, Tom, performed a solo on his oboe to great applause.

Miss Soar had ended the concert with a 'Goodbye' song so tuneful and so enjoyed that she agreed to do an encore.

Ivy's mind strayed to the times she and Frank had attended concerts, but she was determined to push away those thoughts. That was in the past. During one round of particularly enthusiastic applause, her hands touched Sam's. They turned to look at each other, each intensely aware of their nearness. They smiled in a moment of brief intimacy, before returning to their hearty clapping.

In more recent conversations, both Ivy and Sam had felt comfortable enough with each other to discuss their own personal ordeals. Ivy listened to Sam as he talked about Emilia, his wife of five years before she had died.

He recounted how happy they had been, especially when she found out she was expecting. They had waited a long time for a baby, but then everything was cruelly snatched away. The complications in the long, painful labour resulted in both mother and baby dying. Sam had lost his beloved wife and never had a chance to know his son. Ivy wiped the tears from his cheeks as he shared such personal feelings, her own eyes brimming as she witnessed this big, strong man showing such emotion. She felt a close bond with him; she identified with him in her understanding of pain and loss, although death had made these feelings even harsher for Sam.

She had gradually trusted him more and more, until she confided in him her true feelings about what had happened between her and Frank. Sam had admitted he had heard rumours about Frank being a bigamist, but he had listened quietly as she explained her feelings about it all. He hoped she was ready to believe in herself and others again.

Now, as they enjoyed their Sunday stroll together, Sam decided it was time to divulge his true feelings for Ivy. They headed towards the ferry that would carry them to Mexborough, stopping beneath a huge oak tree not far from the river.

Sam placed his hands on Ivy's shoulders, looking intently into her beautiful eyes. She looked up at him, not afraid to show her happiness.

'Ivy, I love you. I want to know if there's a chance that you might feel the same way. I want to know if we have a future together.'

'I feel we are kindred spirits, Sam. I never thought I could love, or even trust another man, but I do. You make me feel safe and wanted. I love you, Sam.'

He gently gathered her in his arms, and both felt joy in their hearts.

Chapter 62
July 1900

Mary looked down at the sleeping baby, then swivelled her gaze to Bridie who lay in bed, still, and staring absently into the distance.

'She's so beautiful, Bridie!' Mary exclaimed. 'And she's the spit of you!'

Bridie blinked, as if returning her thoughts to present reality. She gave an imperceptible nod, followed by a weak smile, as though even minimal movements were beyond her strength or desire.

'Has she got a name yet? Can I pick her up for a cuddle?' Mary asked, trying to fill the bleak silence and promote warmth and enthusiasm into such a special occasion. This was the first time she had seen Bridie and Eli's newborn baby.

'Louisa – she's called Louisa after my other grandmammy,' was Bridie's quiet reply as she turned to look at her daughter. She wanted to feel joyful that she had just given birth to a healthy, beautiful baby but fatigue and apathy stifled that emotion. Her deep sigh helped to stem the rising panic that threatened to overwhelm her. *Five children. How would she cope with five children?*

She allowed her eyelids to droop, as if blocking out her predicament. She so wanted to feel strong and capable like lots of other women that she knew, to be robust and enthusiastic enough to cope with all her responsibilities. But the more she yearned for those attributes, the more they eluded her. She watched Mary cradling little Louisa and she felt envious. Why couldn't she be strong and loving like her? *Where was Eli?* He hadn't even seen his new daughter yet.

'Here, go to your mammy.' Mary smiled as she handed the baby to Bridie. Bridie stared at Louisa, but she could not smile.

PART SEVEN

Chapter 63
January 1901

Sarah and Albert smiled at each other, enjoying the warmth from the blazing fire and also an inner warmth from their shared happiness and contentment.

The house seemed quiet and peaceful after all the recent festivities and celebrations. Sarah was becoming frailer as she aged, but Albert still saw her as the same beautiful woman he had married, his love disregarding any fading looks or ageing body. She was his Sarah, although he seldom expressed those feelings in words.

'What a lovely Christmas this has been, Albert,' she sighed.

'It has been, lass,' Albert agreed, puffing on his pipe.

'I can't believe how things have turned out so well for Ivy,' Sarah said. 'I never thought she'd be this happy.'

'Let's just hope they have a happy future together,' Albert replied, not wanting to tempt fate.

Ivy and Sam had married a few days before Christmas. Neither of them had seen any point in waiting any longer. They loved and trusted each other, both overjoyed to have found happiness again.

They were both thirty, so the sooner they were married, the better. At first, Sarah, Albert and the rest of the family were unsure if it was wise to act so quickly, but their fears were quelled when they saw how happy they were.

Ivy was now Mrs Baker and lived with Sam above the butcher's shop. They determined to enjoy life together.

Another cause for celebrations was that Gertie and Charlie were expecting a baby. They had announced the news on Christmas Eve.

'We saved it as a special Christmas present for you all,' Gertie beamed as she told the family.

'Well, you've done that all right,' Albert had declared. He had stood up, squeezed his daughter's shoulders and shaken Charlie's hand vigorously before turning away and blowing his nose noisily.

'Oh, Gertie, love!' Sarah had cried out. 'That's wonderful news!'

Everyone had tears in their eyes. Everyone hoped that this time, things would go well for the couple.

* * *

'Queen Victoria, dead. I still can't believe it!'

Mary's shocked statement caused her visitors to show their mutual disbelief with slow, silent nods of their heads. Gertie, Ivy and friend Ellen were sitting in Mary's living room, enjoying cups of tea and discussing the news that had recently surprised and stunned the country.

'Sixty-three years as queen – that's longer than most folks live to round here,' Ivy said. 'Not many people are old enough to remember King William before her.'

'That's true enough,' Ellen agreed. 'Her reign was the longest in British history.'

'Wonder how long King Edward's reign will last,' Mary said.

'Well, not as long as his mother's, that's for sure!' Gertie retorted. 'He's nearly sixty years old already!'

'He's waited all that time to be king,' Mary mused.

'Aye, he should be a good 'un, then,' Gertie asserted. 'Papers say he's very popular, a bit of a Jack-the-lad with the ladies though.'

'Gertie! You can't talk about the king like that!' Mary exclaimed.

'I'm only saying what's in the newspapers,' Gertie replied, feigning innocence.

'Time will tell what kind of king he'll be, then,' Ivy concluded. They all agreed.

* * *

Everyone followed the news of Queen Victoria's death and funeral with great interest. Such an exceptional event produced many printed pages in local, national and international newspapers. She had been the ruling monarch of Great Britain, as well as the British Empire, for so long.

It was reported that Queen Victoria died on 22nd January 1901, at Osborne House on the Isle of Wight, aged eighty-one. The cause of death was cerebral haemorrhage, a kind of stroke. She had been growing weaker for several years before her death, and used a wheelchair due to rheumatism. Her eyesight was also clouded by cataracts.

She had left clear instructions relating to the service and ceremony that she wanted at her funeral. Although she had dressed in black after the death of her beloved Albert, she dictated that she wanted a white funeral. As a soldier's daughter and head of the army, she wanted a procession and a funeral in full military service, so her coffin would be carried on a gun carriage, navy and army officers would be in the procession and there would be no public lying-in-state, where the people could visit the coffin and pay their respects.

Before being placed in her coffin, she wished to be dressed in a white gown with her wedding veil and other family mementoes.

Her final journey began on 2nd February 1901, when her body was carried by sea from the Isle of Wight to Hampshire, then by train to Victoria Station, London. A procession began from Victoria to Paddington Station, where the streets on the funeral route were crowded with spectators.

From Paddington, a train conveyed the coffin to Windsor, where it was placed in the Castle's St. George's Chapel.

On 4th February, the coffin was carried to Frogmore Mausoleum, which had been built for Albert upon his death. Queen Victoria had written the words carved above the mausoleum's door:

'Farewell most beloved. Here at length, I shall rest with thee, with thee in Christ I shall rise again.'

As Victoria's subjects read this, there was a unanimous feeling that this was truly the end of an era like no other. Change was in the air.

Chapter 64
July 1901

The expectant crowd filled the platform at Conisbrough railway station. The balmy, evening air encouraged chatter and banter. Excitement rippled around. People were waiting to welcome back Boer War hero, Dougie Johnson, now Corporal Johnson, who had been invalided home.

One group of people there included Jim and Mary, together with Rose and John, and Charlie and Gertie with their one-month-old daughter.

Most eyes in the crowd scanned the distance, seeking the arrival of the train from Doncaster which, hopefully, carried the returning soldier. Gertie's eyes, however, seldom left her daughter's face. Disbelieving joy still washed through her; she felt so blessed to have their baby, Annie.

As she adjusted the swaddling blanket with delicate, protective fingers, she remembered how happy everyone was with the longed-for, safe arrival of the baby, particularly Sarah, who had breathed a sigh of relief. Her delight was increased when Charlie and Gertie told her that they had named their daughter Annie, after her great-grandmother. Sarah's tearful smile rewarded the whole family with love and respect.

'It's here!' A voice shouted as the puffing train came into view. Decorative flags fluttered in the summer breeze like gentle breaths. Cheering voices mingled with the hissing steam. Then the Denaby brass band struck up a vibrant tune.

Even the men in the crowd had moist eyes as they watched Dougie step from the train and fall into the arms of his loving parents. Jim strained his neck to see his old friend.

Dougie looked thin, which was hardly surprising as he had endured seven weeks in hospital with malaria and jaundice, before sailing from Durban to Southampton, then travelling by train back home.

Dougie was lifted onto the shoulders of celebrating friends, who hailed him a 'conquering hero'. Both fatigue and relief were etched across the soldier's face, but he managed shy waves and bashful grins as he was carried to The Drum.

Jim managed to shake his hand, saying: 'Welcome home, Dougie,' simply but sincerely.

'Thanks Jim,' Dougie replied, as he reached into his top pocket. 'I believe this brought me good luck.' The inscribed medal had been carried thousands of miles, but it remained intact. Jim smiled and nodded.

'You take care of yourself now, Dougie. You deserve a rest after everything you've been through.'

Dougie nodded and smiled as he was swept away by another group of well-wishers. Jim was so pleased his mate was safe and sound, but he was worried that there was an outbreak of typhoid in Conisbrough.

The stinking water of the River Don was unbearable in the eighty-five-degree Fahrenheit heat of the past week. Everyone would have to take care, disease was rife.

Chapter 65
August 1901

'Oh, no, Jim! You don't think you'll be going on strike, do you?' Mary exclaimed, wiping wet hands down her pinny. Her heart sank at such a prospect.

'It's looking that way. The last two meetings we've had at The Station Hotel and The Masons Arms at Mexborough have both been well attended. The men are getting more and more angry. It depends if there's a two-thirds majority next time we vote.'

'But the dispute's between Denaby pit men and the Company, not Cadeby!' Mary insisted.

'It's all about the bag muck at Denaby, but plenty of men from both pits are willing to support the men it affects. It's just not fair, and the gaffers refuse point blank to even discuss things, let alone do anything about it.'

Jim thought back to his early days of mining at Denaby pit. The Barnsley bed had layers of coal separated by a layer of earth, sometimes soft and dusty, sometimes hard and more like rock. This "muck" was between the top layer of coal called the "day bed" and the lower layer of coal called the "bags" and was soon known as "bag muck".

It hadn't been a problem at first, as it was only about eight inches thick and was easily extracted and used for packing walls to support the roof, or for making roadways. However, as the Barnsley seam advanced, it became thicker and thicker and harder to extract.

Jim had listened to men who were involved in this increasingly difficult and time-consuming section of the coal face and could well understand their mounting anger and frustration.

'It's bloody ridiculous! Bag muck's three foot thick in some places, and you need a hammer and wedges to get it out! Time's money – we get paid for coal, not bloody muck!'

Jim knew that the Company and men had negotiated a contract price of one shilling and four and a half pence per ton of coal, the extra half-penny being paid for the removal of bag muck. But that was in 1890.

Conditions were very different now and the men sincerely believed they needed more payment for the extra time and labour necessary to hew the coal. Mr Chambers, unfortunately, thought otherwise.

* * *

September 1901

'That's it then. No strike action,' Albert stated, his lips pressed into a dour line. Mary and Sarah looked at each other, as if reading each other's thoughts. They both felt relief and quiet contentment at this news.

The men, Albert, Jim and Bob, seemed to share very different emotions, however.

'I bloody knew it!' Albert continued. 'I knew we wouldn't get the majority vote. I can't understand why so many voted against strike action. Don't they realise it's the only way to get anywhere with these damn gaffers?'

Jim nodded his agreement. The two pits had balloted for strike action but had failed to get the required two-thirds majority. The local Denaby Association had advised their support, but many workers were still reluctant to strike.

'Some men voted against it, and lads under the age of eighteen weren't even allowed to vote!' Bob said, his voice ringing with the same exasperation as his father's.

'Things are only going to get worse. This bag muck problem will only fester, you mark my words!' Albert concluded, banging his cap on the table, sitting down and reaching for his pipe.

Mary and Sarah cast furtive glances at their menfolk but said nothing. They knew when to be quiet. At least there was a temporary respite. No woman wanted a strike.

Chapter 66
February 1902

Albert was right. Things did get worse. Bitterness and annoyance festered. The hundred and fifty Denaby miners, who were directly affected by the bag muck problem, became increasingly frustrated.

The Denaby Lodge Association, supported by the more powerful Yorkshire Miners' Association, decided to challenge the Company's decision to refuse any increase in remuneration. They awaited the court case at Doncaster County Courts.

During that wait, some of the affected miners refused to remove the bag muck, but the Company decided to harden their attitude.

* * *

March 1902

The colliers sat at the big table in The Drum. They were discussing the recent unfolding events in the dispute. Emotions were rising, bad language was flowing.

'Some men's wages are down by ten fuckin' shillings! From twenty-eight shillings a week to less than eighteen! Ten bob! It's scandalous!'

'Chambers is a ruthless old bugger. He's brought in other men to teck out t'bag muck and paid 'em wi' money deducted from t'other men's bloody wages!'

'Ar lass didn't believe me when I said I was ten bob down last week. Accused me o' drinkin' and gamblin' it away! I slapped t'money down on t' table and told her she'd 'ave to teck a fuckin' cut an' all. Bloody gaffers have taken it, not t' landlords and bookies!'

'Y.M.A. are involved with all this now, so we might get somewhere with this 'ere court case.'

* * *

April 1902

Their optimism was misplaced. The judge ruled in favour of the Denaby and Cadeby Collieries Company, not the men. Judge Masterman stated that he had to judge by the existing rules. There was an agreed contract between men and management regarding the removal of bag muck.

However, he also stated that he felt it was the right time for another price list to be agreed, given that the muck was getting thicker. The Y.M.A. agreed and were willing to discuss this with management, but the Company would not go to arbitration. They would not budge.

* * *

May 1902

The mounting tension in the mining community was so palpable that it could almost be tasted. People were ill at ease, uncomfortable with the ever-threatening prospect of a strike.

Everyone could well remember the extra, all-encompassing hardships that past strikes and disputes had brought. The women watched their men and listened to their words, while looming foreboding gripped their insides. The constant volleying of arguments, disagreements and controversies was like a rising river ready to burst its banks. Strike action seemed to be advancing. Dread would soon become reality.

There were, however, little chinks of light to relieve the gloom. At last, water had begun to be piped to the houses from the reservoir. The supply of water was more plentiful and more easily accessible, a great boon to the beleaguered Denaby residents.

'Hallelujah! It's about bloody time!' was the heartfelt reaction of everyone.

Another reason for relief was that the Boer War had ended. The treaty of Vereeniging had been signed at the end of May. The British had crushed the Boer resistance and hostilities had ended. The treaty recognised the British administration over the Orange Free State and the South African Republic, ending their independence. Lord Kitchener had used ruthless tactics to overcome Boer resistance, but the British soldiers would soon be returning home.

'We'll be able to welcome back our old mates soon,' the Denaby lads said.

'Aye, and we can tell 'em Denaby United's just been promoted. They're in t' Midland League nah!'

Chapter 67
June 1902

The men stood shoulder to shoulder, their faces sombre, their looks attentive. More than three thousand men and boys from Denaby and Cadeby pits were gathered outside The Reresby Arms. The mass meeting was to decide, once and for all, whether strike action was to be taken. Their patience had run out.

The Conisbrough and Denaby unions' officials stood at the front on a makeshift stage, delivering their varying opinions and suggestions. They wanted to fully inform the men, who listened carefully, their expressions revealing where their own personal alliances and allegiances lay.

'We've allus been dissatisfied with the amount listed for removing bag muck! It's allus been too little for the amount of work involved! We've been underpaid for years! No other South Yorkshire miners work for nowt! Strike action is the only way to force management to negotiate a fair price!'

This official's speech had prompted a rousing reaction. Heads were nodded, hands were clapped, and supportive comments shouted.

'Tha's rate! They've been robbin' us for years!'

'It's time things changed!'

Some of the older men pursed their lips and shook their heads, still reluctant to give their whole-hearted agreement. Another official offered a more cautious viewpoint.

'Think very carefully about all this. I know you're angry and frustrated, but many of you know all about the implications of strike action. It's not just us – it's our families and homes we have to think about. It'll be a long, hard slog and you know how bloody stubborn and ruthless Chambers and t' Company can be! Maybe one last attempt to negotiate would be better.'

In the end, the overwhelming opinion of the men was that strike action was necessary. Over three thousand men and boys from both pits would down tools in support of the one hundred and fifty affected Denaby miners. Strike action would begin on the last day of June. They had to go home and tell their wives and mothers now.

* * *

2nd July 1902

A strange atmosphere descended on Denaby. The women had been told. Silent tears had been wiped away by shaking hands. Families would still need food, clothing and coal for cooking and heating, but those all required money.

Few people had any spare resources. Life was lived week to week, hand to mouth; money was eked out to last until the next pay day or visit to the pawn shop. The future was unknown, insecure, but most Denaby women had learnt to be resilient. They could not change the circumstances so they would have to adapt. They hoped the dispute would soon be resolved; they prayed that they would be strong and hardy enough to cope and survive.

Things got off to a bad start, however, when miners were told there could be no immediate strike pay from the Yorkshire Miners' Association. They had come out contrary to the rules. They had not given proper notice to the Company.

The Y.M.A. recommended that the men go back to work for the required fourteen days' notice, then strike, which was carried by a 97% in favour vote. Once again, the Company thought otherwise.

* * *

The Denaby and Cadeby Collieries Company refused to allow the men to work unless they signed a new contract of service. Few wanted to. That first day, groups of miners stood outside both pits, unsure of what to do.

'We can't get strike pay from t' Union 'til we work two weeks' notice, but gaffers won't let us work unless we sign up for their new contract! What are we supposed to bloody do?'

The Y.M.A. suggested that they report for work every day to cover the fourteen days' notice, and the miners agreed to that.

* * *

7th July 1902

Unfortunately, the management disagreed, and responded by summonsing a group of about twenty men for breach of contract. The court case was to be held later in July at the Doncaster Courts. Mr Chambers and his management wanted significant damages, and they were in no mood to relent.

* * *

9th July 1902

A meeting of the Mexborough and District Trades Council was held to discuss the plight of the Denaby miners. The resulting resolution would prove to be very important.

'Three thousand men and boys out of work. We will pledge our support. Mexborough folk want to help as much as they are able. We must organise ourselves to raise money and provide food to help them and their families.'

Collection cards were distributed to give valid credentials to the people asking for donations. Word had spread far afield about the dispute, and newspapers had reported, in great detail, the facts leading up to the strike. Unions and tradespeople, throughout Yorkshire and beyond, followed the events with interest. The resulting widespread generosity and support would prove to be, literally, a lifeline for the Denaby miners and their families.

* * *

19th July 1902

The Company won the court case and were awarded damages of £6 per man. This was a blow to the miners and the Union, but attitudes were hardened even more. Anger and resentment grew, galvanizing the men into stubborn contempt for their employers. It was fervently hoped that strike pay would soon be able to be awarded by the Y.M.A. Everyone was feeling the effects of weeks without pay.

* * *

26th July 1902

'Thank the Lord! Strike pay at last!'

The old miner's relief was shared by all the men attending the Union meeting.

'Ar lass telled me not to bother coming home if there was no strike pay!' another disgruntled miner said.

'It won't be as much as normal wages, but owt is better than nowt!' This remark was the opinion of many. They had been told details of the weekly strike pay they could expect from union funds. A father and elder sons in a family would each receive nine shillings, younger sons four shillings and sixpence and each child one shilling.

Big families with only one breadwinner would need "nipsey" money, collected in addition to strike pay. The worst-off would be a family with only one breadwinner, who was not a member of the Y.M.A. They would have to rely on charity alone.

'Thank God I'm in t' union!' miners muttered to themselves. 'God help them who's not!'

Chapter 68
Early August 1902

'I can't believe how much support we're getting! Local people and folks from across the country are collecting and donating everything from money to food and clothing!'

Jim was visiting his Aunt Hilda and Uncle Edmund, enjoying the food and drink he'd been given.

'You're right, lad,' Edmund agreed. 'I heard even Grimsby fishermen are sending regular donations of food and money.'

'Miners from nearby pits are giving parts of their wages, too. They might not have much, but they're willing to help fellow union members,' Hilda added.

'It said in *The Times* that eight thousand loaves were distributed in Denaby last week. Now that *is* generous!' Edmund retorted.

'I bet you're glad you're not a miner,' Jim said.

'I am that, lad. Born and bred in Old Denaby, always happy to work in t' quarries,' he replied.

'Well, you know you can always rely on us to help you and Mary and the bairns,' Hilda said, squeezing Jim's hand and giving him a crinkly smile.

'I know,' Jim nodded. 'Let's hope things get sorted before too long.'

* * *

The women lined the road to Denaby and Cadeby pits. They howled and brayed at the miners who pushed through the crowds, trying to gain entrance to the pits. Each day they ran the gauntlet of the jeering women. Pans were rattled and whistles blown in a cacophony of noise, parallel to the rising derision of the angry women. But some shrill, screeching remarks rose above the din.

'Black legs! You're nowt but blacklegs!'

'Call yerselves men, scabs more like!'

'My menfolk aren't earning like you, they're stickin' together like t' union asked them to!'

'My kids are goin' to t' soup kitchens for their dinners – are yours?'

The miners looked down, kept their mouths shut and strode on purposefully. One of them was Eli Shaw. He saw nothing wrong with still working. He wasn't even a member of the union. He just wanted to work and earn money.

Bridie was always moaning they'd never got enough. She was torn, undecided. All the Flannagan men were striking and they didn't like the fact that she was married to a blackleg. But she could not stop Eli even if she wanted to. She knew Tommy Prince was still working at Cadeby Pit. His father disagreed with the strike too, but he was more like management. Whatever Tommy did, Eli followed suit, she knew that.

* * *

'I never thought Walter would end up a blackleg!' Mary's anguished tone made Jim look up sharply.

'He said he wouldn't join the union. You know how stubborn he can be. I can't understand him, neither can Peggy and Alf,' Jim answered quietly.

'It can't be easy for them knowing their son's a scab. I feel for them,' Mary said.

'This bloody strike is going to break up families, I can see it!'

Mary was surprised and shocked at this unfamiliar despondency from Jim. It felt like a warning.

* * *

19th August 1902

Still the strike dragged on. The Company had summonsed a further ninety-four miners for breach of contract, but the men would not give in. They had lost many weeks' wages; the Company had lost thousands of pounds in coal sales.

But there was stalemate between men and management until, on 19th August, the Company finally lost patience. They closed both pits. No one could work, even if they wanted to. This marked a decisive stage in the dispute. Mr Chambers gave the order to bring up the horses. Only a small group of miners would be allowed to carry this out. No one knew how prolonged the strike would be.

Chapter 69
August 1902

An acrid smell of fear and excitement emanated from the pit ponies as they were shoved and herded nearer the upcage. Their heavy, low-set limbs pounded angrily, creating undulations of clattering echoes. Nostrils snorted puffing air as their memories awakened. The full-bodied, sure-footed creatures were now using their bone and substance to resist rather than comply. Spittle and sweat flew as shouts struggled to be heard.

'These three 'ave had their shoes off. Get 'em up! Right, Bob lad, your turn, get Ginger in!' ordered Cyrus Hinds, the horse keeper.

Bob looked at the cage, newly fitted with wooden doors like two boxes, then swivelled his gaze to Ginger, his long-time pony, his long-time companion. He hoped their shared trust would help them now.

Soothing words ricocheted and evaporated as he steered the straining animal into the box. Ginger's wild eyes knowingly heralded the prospect of a terrifying journey up to light and space. He could remember from before. One final push, and Bob jumped out of the cage at the last moment, just as it lifted. Though shoeless, the pony's echoing kicks thundered above him, lessening only gradually as the ascent progressed.

Bob knew the extended strike necessitated the bringing up of the horses, but he also remembered the upheaval it always caused. Injuries and violence often resulted from the sudden change in surroundings and conditions.

The miners called it a form of "madness" once the ponies had sudden freedom and brightness. They had to be backed out of the cage into the surrounding fields. Handlers jumped out of their way as a blindness overtook them. The change from prolonged darkness and gloom to dazzling brightness and light was stark. Many ponies suffered this blindness for a long period.

Bob's eyes travelled across the large, grassy field, tracking for Ginger. He felt great relief that his pony had managed the journey up and into the field without injury. He wanted Ginger to see daylight and breathe fresh air, but he knew the experience would unsettle him for months.

Bob had mixed feelings. Which was crueller, to deny Ginger a taste of freedom, or to allow it and then have to return him to the gruelling labour in the earth's black depths?

All the ponies had bucked and screamed, kicked and fought with untethered power as they first experienced light, freedom and space. They wanted to exhaust their excitement and confusion brought on by the release from close control and stifling darkness. Bob watched the exhausted ponies, easily picking out Ginger.

The ponies had slowed their frenzied movements, adjusting to the strange environment of sun and space, as though relaxing their minds and muscles. Stamping and head tossing continued, sweat steaming and air wisping around them. Bob knew that they would soon sort themselves out and create a 'pecking order' of status within the group.

Forced inhibitions on behaviour would soon loosen to allow natural, wild responses. Many would soon be reluctant to respond to their names, even when called by their handlers. Acceptance and obeyance to human dictates would be plucked and blown away, like dead leaves, kicked and strewn. Wind, rain, sun, grass and unrestrained movement would soothe and cleanse their unnatural, girded servility. The true temperaments of each pony would emerge and flourish.

Bob just hoped that the trust, respect and affection between himself and Ginger would survive and continue. He left the field, hoping that he, too, would have more settled emotions in the days to come. It depended on how long the strike would last.

*   *   *

September 1902

The lack of money was becoming increasingly serious for the majority of miners. In the fourteenth week of the strike, many families were feeling desperate. The cost of food was high, and Mr Chambers had forbidden any credit for the striking miners and their families at the many Company-owned and run shops in Denaby.

People were hungry. Soup kitchens at The Plant and The Park Hotel at Mexborough, and at The Station Hotel, Conisbrough were gratefully attended, and the many donations of food from nearby communities were thankfully accepted. But hunger was never far away.

At the beginning of the strike, many men and boys had felt a certain freedom. Long walks could be taken in the warm, summer weather. Time could be spent with dogs and pigeons. Allotments could be tended to gain precious produce of fruit and vegetables. Wild fruit and mushrooms could be foraged to augment meals. Some even took to doing odd jobs in nearby villages for coppers, holding a horse, cleaning bicycles, weeding gardens or running errands.

But as the strike wore on, many became aimless, frustrated, bad-tempered. Precious money was spent in pubs to drown sorrows. Wives complained bitterly.

Coal became scarce. The miners were used to their "free" monthly ton of coal, which, they argued, was really part of their wages. Some coal could be scavenged from tips, but most was bought in small quantities, and at inflated prices, from local hawkers.

Most of all, relationships were strained. The women were unused to their menfolk being in the house so much; they were literally in each other's way in the cramped houses. Tempers flared. No one liked the lack of money, no one liked being hungry, no one liked to feel guilty at not providing for their children. Most of all, no one liked the total insecurity of their situation. But they would not give in.

September brought applied pressure from the Company. They were hell-bent on forcing the miners back to work. Most of them lived in tied houses, Company built, Company-owned and rented by the Company.

Each miner was sent a letter by the Denaby Main and Cadeby Collieries Company stating: 'Unless all rent owed was paid by 15th November, the miner and his family would be evicted.' Still most men refused to give in.

* * *

October 1902

There was an oppressive atmosphere hanging over Denaby. The weather was cooling, the daylight hours shortening and the morale of the families gradually dipping.

They had already endured seventeen weeks on strike, with no end in sight. Conditions were rapidly deteriorating. Many items had already been sold or pawned to raise a little money, but food, clothes and footwear always needed to be replaced.

Meals were basic, reduced, insufficient. Stomachs groaned as much as voices; health was significantly affected. The constant threat of evictions gnawed into people's strength and determination.

Some families had fled Denaby, so distressing and hopeless was their situation, but many could not. They simply did not have the means or the will to move elsewhere.

Wives and children resorted to begging. Each day, groups of women held children's hands and tugged them relentlessly as they trudged to nearby villages, sometimes nine miles a day. Money, food, clothes, boots – they would take anything offered. Winter was advancing and despair mounting.

* * *

Mary was trying to stay positive and supportive, but, like all the women, she craved more security, yearned for less hardships and worry. Jim saw her reduced vitality and diminished spirits and wished he could change things.

He knew she was always saying how fortunate they were compared to many others. They had support from other members of their family, Aunt Hilda and Uncle Edmund, Betty and Arthur, Charlie and Gertie, and Ivy and Sam.

They all helped them, as well as Sarah, Albert and brother Bob, as much as they could. Working people were glad to give food and coal, as well as time and moral support.

What Jim did not yet know was that Mary was pregnant.

Chapter 70
December 1902

'There's Ginger, Uncle Bob!' John shouted as he watched the pit ponies nibbling grass in their fenced field. Bob smiled at his nephew. The boy also had a fondness for horses.

'He looks well, they all do,' Bob replied, casting an experienced eye over the herd of ponies. 'They've calmed down now in their new surroundings. Mind you, they should have, they've been here nearly four months!'

Bob visited the field daily, sometimes alone, often with John or Rose. The miners and their families felt a connection, even affection, for their equine work companions. There were always clusters of watchful folk assessing and admiring the ponies and their antics.

A "pecking order" had been established, just as Bob had predicted, and there seemed to be a settled, accepted hierarchy within the herd.

Ginger was not the most dominant pony, but neither was he the most submissive. He knew when to move away from the more dominant horses and was intelligent enough not to display aggressive behaviour. He knew how to use body language to communicate and fit into the herd. They were all males, an unnatural factor within wild herds. Mares were rarely, if ever, trained as pit ponies.

'Call Ginger, Uncle Bob! See if he'll come over!'

Bob knew what would probably happen, but he called out:

'Here, Ginger! Come here, boy!'

As usual, for the past few weeks, Ginger stopped munching grass momentarily, looked towards Bob, but did not come over to him.

In some ways, Bob was hurt by this, but he knew it was Ginger's natural way of living within the herd. He was glad his pony seemed calm and settled. He just hoped their old relationship could be reestablished when they returned to work underground. After previous periods "above", the old trust and companionship had eventually returned. He trusted it would be the same again.

* * *

Nearing Christmas, the strike was in its twenty-fifth week, and conditions had further deteriorated. On 13th December, the Company had applied to the Courts for the eviction orders of seven hundred-and-fifty miners and their families. Thankfully, they had been adjourned for two weeks so that evictions would not take place in Christmas week.

More miners had left their homes, doing 'moonlight flits', leaving unpaid rents, but avoiding the shame and stress of eviction. Windows in those houses had been boarded up, adding to the depressing dejection that hovered over the Denaby streets.

There was little food in the houses, and there was less food to forage in the winter months. Some people were existing on bread and lard. Anything and everything that could be sold or pawned had been relinquished by some families – furniture, sheets, blankets, even footwear. Some children had to stay away from school because they had no shoes or boots. The severe lack of coal meant cooking and heating was restricted, many families pooling resources and sharing the same fire to cook.

The increased daily expeditions marked the desperation of the people. Any "nipsey" money gained was welcomed but insufficient.

Then the Y.M.A. warned the miners that strike pay may have to stop. The Company had filed a suit, months ago, against the Y.M.A., stating that, in their opinion, the strike had never been official.

No proper ballot had been carried out and no required notice had been given. The miners could not return to work to give notice after they had already started strike proceedings. This meant, they argued, that the strike was unofficial, and no strike pay should be given. It was taking months for the case to go through, but the Y.M.A. feared the judge would favour the management and damages would bankrupt the union.

As if this wasn't bad enough, another significant factor was coming to the fore. This concerned the Taff Vale judgement. In 1901, a suit was brought by the Taff Vale Railway Company against the Railway Union, the A.S.R.S., The Amalgamated Society of Railway Servants, in Wales. The Railway Company had not agreed with its employees striking to gain union recognition and higher wages, especially when picketing had violated the Conspiracy and Protection of Property Act of 1875.

The A.S.R.S. had argued that, because it was neither a corporation nor an individual, it could not be held liable. Judgement went against the union and was even upheld in the House of Lords. This verdict, in effect, eliminated striking as a weapon of organised labour for all Trade Unions. Moreover, the courts held that a union could be sued for damages caused by the action of its officials in industrial disputes.

The Denaby strike was the first test case since the 1901 judgement. The Denaby and Cadeby Main Collieries Company brought an action against the Yorkshire Miners' Association for damages of £150,000 in respect of losses incurred during the strike.

'We'll be fuckin' done for if Buckingham Pope wins this one,' was the shared Denaby miners' opinion.

* * *

Christmas Week 1902

No one was looking forward to Christmas. People were suffering untold hardships. Craving bellies and nagging despair outstripped any kind of festive anticipation or enjoyment. Hunger, cold and dejection swirled around, like grasping fingers, squeezing and pinching at minds and bodies. The miners and their families were trying to remain resilient, but the prospect of no strike pay and evictions overshadowed everyone's thoughts.

Mary sighed deeply as she looked around her home. Her rising melancholy had created a battle within herself. She was still thrilled to be expecting but was saddened that the circumstances were so depressing.

She had felt such elation when she'd realised she was pregnant. Ten long years had passed since John's birth. At first, she had been disbelieving but was delighted with the unexpected news. She remembered the look on Jim's face when she had told him. He had squeezed her shoulders and stared into her unblinking gaze, as if trying to gain extra understanding from her amazed expression.

'Oh, Mary!' he had managed to say. 'My darling Mary!' His tears glistened as he kissed her gently. They were still looking forward to the birth of their baby, but felt heartache that the increasing austerity and worry in their lives had diminished their ability to fully enjoy such a long-awaited event.

Mary sniffed and dabbed away her tears. She knew she had to stay as strong and as optimistic as she could, but it was not easy. Nothing was easy, but they had managed before and they would manage again, she told herself. She felt a fluttering kick inside her rounding belly, and she managed to smile through her tears.

* * *

The pine trestle tables and benches ran the full length of the Methodist school room in Mexborough.

The Reverend Jesse Wilson, the minister of Mexborough Primitive Methodist Chapel, cast an eye over the assortment of food spread out on the many plates and dishes that filled each table. He silently thanked the generous folk of Mexborough, who had responded to the letter he had sent to all his parishioners.

'We need to feed a good meal to between 500 and 1,000 children during Christmas week – and their parents if there are sufficient funds. Any donations of money or provisions would be most gratefully accepted,' the letter had read.

He had not expected such overwhelming generosity, but it had pleased his heart and soul. He still remembered hunger and hardships from the days when he was a miner's child.

The directors of the local football clubs had given permission for collections at their grounds, and the visiting spectators had been generous in their donations. Many local ladies had volunteered to organise the children's meals. They knew how needy and destitute the miners and their families were after six months on strike.

The excited chatter indicated the arrival of the large group of children. Parents had tried their best, but Reverend Wilson and his helpers were shocked to see the state of the clothing and footwear of the children. Jackets and dresses were threadbare, trousers stitched and patched to hold tatters together. Boots and shoes had gaping soles and open toes.

A hushed reverence replaced chatter as the children filed into the schoolroom. They stared at the food overflowing from plate to plate. Eyes widened in pale, pinched faces. They were quickly shown to places on benches, but their eyes could not leave the abundance of food.

'There are buns and sweets and even oranges for you!' the serving ladies announced to the quiet children.

The Reverend Wilson and his helpers were surprised, and humbled, when, almost without exception, the children asked for plain bread first. That would fill their hungry bellies. Jesse Wilson closed his eyes and prayed, 'Lord, help me to help them.'

Chapter 71
5th January 1903

Albert stared at the letter that had just been delivered. Varying expressions flicked across his face as he read its contents. Sarah watched him, anxiously fiddling with her apron.

'What is it? What does it say?' she whispered.

'It's what we've been expecting. It's an ejectment warrant. The police are coming to turn us out tomorrow.' Albert's voice betrayed a mixture of anger, resentment and defeat.

The threat of eviction had been hanging over them for months, but this was the stark reality of their situation. Tomorrow was the day the Company was getting their house back.

'I'm buggered if I'll be thrown out wi' crowds watchin'. We're leaving today!'

'Oh, Albert!' Sarah cried. 'I know I've complained about this house many a time, but at least it was a roof over our heads! All these years we've been here, and now we'll have nothin'!' Her words ended in choking sobs.

'Nay, lass. Don't take on like this. We'll be all right. We're lucky Ivy and Sam have said we can move in wi' them if needs be, our Bob too. Some folks have no family round here to help 'em. God knows what they'll do.' Albert's words were both soothing and alarming. Soon, people and their possessions would be out on the streets. They would have to fend for themselves.

'I'm off to our Ivy's,' Albert said, reaching for his jacket. 'Sam said he'd sort out a cart or a dray when we needed one.'

'Oh, Albert,' Sarah repeated. She sat down to gather her thoughts and settle her emotions. 'This damned strike!' she muttered to herself through stiff lips.

* * *

'That's that, then.' Sarah's voice was flat, dulled and resigned as she looked around the bare rooms of her house. Mary looked at her mother, unsure of what to say. Ivy and Gertie looked at Mary. Nobody knew what to say. They had spent the afternoon at their parents' house, helping to pack up their few remaining belongings. The men folk had loaded up a cart with the bigger items, and Sam and Albert had taken them to Mexborough to be stored in a barn.

'Thank God Mexborough tradesmen have offered to lend us their carts and drays,' Albert had declared earlier. 'And sorted out places to store all these things.'

The flickering candlelight cast an eerie atmosphere in the empty house. The dying embers fell into the grate. The air was cold and damp.

'Just left with these few things, then,' Sarah continued, looking at the small pile of clothes and a few household items. She was on the brink of tears.

Mary saw how the worry and hardship over the past months had taken its toll on her mother. Sarah was fifty-four and had been fragile for a long time, but she had somehow shrivelled and wilted in recent months. Her hair was snow white, her skin like faded parchment.

Mary had recognised similar ageing in many other Denaby women, herself included. The strike was draining them, even if they did not admit it. Jim insisted she was as beautiful as ever, but Mary could see the increased lines and wrinkles on her face.

'It won't be for long, Mam, then you'll be able to come back,' Mary tried to reassure her mother.

'Not if Chambers decides to bring in new workers!' Sarah retorted. 'He'll promise them our houses!'

'The men will have to go back to work soon, it can't go on for much longer,' Gertie reasoned. She was so glad Charlie worked at Kilner's, even though business had been slack lately and some workers were on part time.

'You're more than welcome to stay with us, Mam,' Ivy said, slipping her arm through her mother's. Mary and Gertie held their mother's hands. Sarah gazed at her daughters and sighed a deep breath.

'You're all such good lasses,' she said. But she still wept.

* * *

The Company had notified the miners that they would soon be evicted forcibly. Rents had not been paid for months and the houses were needed for new workers, soon to be recruited. Ordinary notices had been disregarded by the tenants, so ejectment warrants had been obtained.

The Company had put the warrants into the hands of the police to execute. Many houses were already empty, but more than seven hundred still needed to be emptied of people and possessions. Evictions were to start on 6th January, with one hundred planned to be cleared on that first day. Those occupants had been given notice by the police the previous day.

The warrants entitled the police to clear the houses up to a period of one month from the date stated, between the hours of 9.00am and 4.00pm, except on Sundays. Keys and possession of the houses would be given back to the Company.

Even miners who were willing to work again had no money to pay rent owed, and no power to overturn the ejectment warrants. Eviction was inevitable. The police had been well-informed of their duties, even though many felt a reluctancy to carry out the harsh tasks. The people of Denaby would soon witness events that were reported nationally to disbelieving readers.

* * *

6th January 1903

The biting wind rushed along the Denaby streets. Daylight struggled to penetrate the winter morning's gloom. The atmosphere was hushed, expectant, almost silent, despite the many gathered groups of people who waited and watched. Shawls and scarves were pulled tighter, feet were gently stamped from side to side, anything to warm their cold, stiff bodies.

Mary and Jim linked arms, huddling together for warmth, their breaths clouding and dissipating into the freezing air. Jim had tried to dissuade Mary from coming with him. She was seven months pregnant and not as robust as she used to be, but she had insisted.

'I need to watch these evictions. It'll be our turn soon. I need to see with my own eyes what the Company is willing to do to break us,' she had reasoned, her voice bitter, her words confrontational. She noticed the expressions of the people assembled nearby, tired faces that showed pride jostling with despair, stolid determination disguising fear. She felt the same as them.

A buzz of whispers travelled along the lines of onlookers.

'They're coming, police have arrived!'

'Bloody hell, there must be near enough two hundred of 'em!'

'Aye, and some on horses an' all!'

The police force appeared from all quarters of the surrounding streets. The crowds watched and listened as orders were shouted out.

Superintendent Blake from Doncaster split the officers into two groups. One group carried on marching in unison towards streets at the Conisbrough end of Denaby, while the second group remained on the streets near to Denaby pit.

Mary and Jim watched as each end of the first street to be evicted was guarded by mounted officers. Next to them were about a dozen officers on foot, almost filling the width of the roadway.

'It's clear they expected trouble,' Jim said, 'but I don't think there'll be any. What's the point? We've suffered enough these past

273

months without adding on any more trouble. It's the Company at fault, not us, and we want other people's support for us to carry on.'

Mary nodded her agreement as she watched the police constables knocking on the doors of the first few houses. The large crowds of people stood on tiptoes and craned necks to view the proceedings, but only a few were allowed within the cordon. A steady stream of carts and drays churned through the muddy roadways, ready to move possessions from the streets to awaiting out-houses and sheds in Mexborough. The doors of the houses were opened, and the police were allowed in without any resistance or disorder.

Two of the first men to be evicted were miners' officials who lived in the same street. Bert Harrison was chairman of the Cadeby branch, and his brother, Ernie, was a committee man. Neither acted with any kind of resistance or insults, instead behaving with dignified respect and even an attempt at humour. They had pre-packed small things into parcels and even offered to help the police carry them outside onto the street, but the police declined their assistance, saying it was their duty to fulfil the work, not the occupants.

Soon the streets were filled with furniture and other household possessions that some had managed to keep during the strike. Out came chairs and tables, sofas, fenders, clocks and bedsteads, bedding and mattresses, all in piles on the cold, damp streets. The police constables climbed ladders to lift out items through upstairs windows, passing them down carefully, handling them with a respectful sense of responsibility.

There was no bitterness from the police, and the miners put them to no unnecessary trouble. Outwardly, the miners displayed calm, but they felt other emotions inside. They recognised that the police were simply fulfilling their duty and were showing their silent sympathy in the manner they conducted the evictions.

Women and children could not always conceal their emotions though, so upsetting were the sights. The young children viewed the proceedings with wide, tearstained eyes and confusion. They could not understand why all their things, including their favourite toys, were being taken out of the only homes many of them had ever known. Mothers took hold of their children's hands.

'Come along with Mammy,' they said. 'The big men with helmets on have to put our things outside.'

The women tried to be brave, but any kind, sympathetic words from others produced unchecked tears. But they were determined to be equally as resolved as their menfolk 'to see this thing through.' The eviction of a home and family was a hard thing to bear.

* * *

As the day wore on, the police passed from street to street, emptying houses and locking doors after them. Items piled on the ground were quickly removed, stacked high on carts and drays that snaked through the streets. Some of the belongings were taken to friends' houses in Conisbrough or Mexborough; most was taken to any available storage place. People wanted to help the miners in any way they could.

Pressmen, artists and photographers scrutinised the events taking place before their very eyes, sketching pictures, capturing images and jotting down notes in preparation for their reports, soon to be displayed in local and national newspapers. They recorded scenes so pitiful and harsh that readers' beliefs would be challenged.

The weather had deteriorated, becoming even colder, with flurries of snow dancing in the freezing wind that snatched at breaths and grazed bare skin. The evicted people stood outside, shivering in their ragged, threadbare clothing and inadequate footwear.

The lucky ones had managed to seek refuge with family or friends, even though accommodation was scarce and overcrowding common in almost every local home. Some were taken in by people awaiting eviction. They knew they had to stick together and help each other in any way possible.

Some, however, wore haunted expressions as they realised they were homeless, with nowhere to go. Even the police were in tears as they witnessed the plight of those people, especially the children, who cried from hunger, cold and fear.

One homeless family attracted special interest and sympathy as they wandered the streets. The father walked in front, his wife followed, carrying a baby and holding the hand of a toddler, helping him to walk. Behind were eight other children, the eldest about thirteen years old. All twelve of them looked dazed and miserable as they leaned into the bitter wind.

The Reverend Jesse Wilson was one spectator who saw their bleak outlook. It was fortunate for them that he decided to step in to give support and succour to the desperate Denaby miners and their families who had nothing but their solidarity and stolidity.

* * *

By the end of the first day, almost one hundred houses had been emptied and nearly one thousand people evicted. Somehow, everyone had managed to find some kind of refuge. Mexborough people had offered stables, haylofts, wash houses and even kitchen floors to the homeless.

Conisbrough folk had squeezed smaller families into already overcrowded homes. Reverend Wilson had taken the homeless family of twelve into the vestry of his Methodist Chapel, much to the parents' relief and the children's wonder. He had also opened up the schoolroom within the Chapel to accommodate the homeless.

Tents and poles were ready to be assembled in nearby fields as a last resort, but none was needed that first day. Meanwhile, occupants of the next streets to be evicted had been issued with notices by the police.

Mary's house and Bridie's house were two of these planned for eviction. They waited for the new day to dawn and the loss of their homes with heavy hearts and suspended thoughts.

Chapter 72
7th January 1903

'I'm cold, Mam,' John complained. The room's air was frigid. No fire burned brightly, no comforting warmth radiated from glowing coals. The embers had died and turned to ashes. The lack of fire felt strange, as if the house had lost its personality.

Mary sighed as she looked at her children. She felt saddened and despondent, but she was trying to sound optimistic for their sakes.

'We'll be going to your Aunt Gertie and Uncle Charlie's later. They'll have a lovely big fire for us, and some hot food, I bet.'

Rose turned her attention to her brother, hands on hips.

'Mam told us there wouldn't be a fire today. No point using coal if we're going,' she chided.

Despite her melancholy mood, Mary smiled to herself. Rose had a realistic, pragmatic attitude, making her mother realise more and more how sensible and mature the twelve-year-old was. She had helped in the assembling and packing up of their possessions, delegating jobs to her brother and supervising his activities.

Mary was proud and grateful that she could rely on her daughter so much. Rose had noticed her mother's increased weariness and despondency as the strike, and her pregnancy progressed.

John pursed his lips but stopped complaining. He hated how the strike had affected everything. He didn't want to leave the house; he didn't want to see everyone so unhappy. He felt the seeds of resentment beginning to grow. He promised himself that he would not suffer the whims of the rich and powerful when he was older. He would fight for a better, fairer life. He shivered and watched his breath clouding in the icy air.

The back door opened, admitting a draught of freezing air, as well as Jim and Gertie. Their flushed faces shone, polished by the chafing cold. Snow had fallen overnight, whitening the muddy streets and roadways. A hard frost gripped everything it touched.

'The police are just arriving,' Jim announced. 'It won't be long before they'll be knocking on doors.'

Mary stared at him, unsure of how to control her emotions in front of the children. Gertie saw her sister's turmoil and quickly took charge of the situation.

'Now then, you two.' She smiled at Rose and John. 'You're coming with me now. I've tea and porridge waiting for you. You'll be able to eat your breakfasts and even get to school on time!'

'But I don't want to leave you,' Rose began, looking at her parents imploringly. 'I want to stay and help you.'

'Now then, we'll be all right, your mother and me. We'll see to everything here. Your Auntie Gertie's right, you two go and get fed and warmed up, then you can go to school as normal.'

'But it's not normal!' John wailed. 'We're being thrown out of our house today!'

'Hush, son,' Mary soothed. 'Do as your father says. We'll be all right, and remember to go back to Auntie Gertie's house at home time!' she teased, trying to lighten her children's moods.

Rose and John slowly nodded their agreement, but both had glistening eyes.

'Race you there!' John called out to his sister, not wanting to show his tears.

'Don't worry, there's enough porridge for both of you!' Gertie laughed. She looked at Mary and Jim, and smiled with a reassuring nod. They smiled back but did not speak.

* * *

The knock on the door made Mary jump, even though she had been expecting it. The police had worked their way along the street. It was their house next. Jim opened the front door and stepped to one side as two constables entered.

'Thank you, Sir. We'll be as quick as we can,' one of them stated.

'It's all ready for you,' Mary said, standing up from her chair. 'We'll help you to carry things out.'

The policeman noted that she was heavily pregnant and quickly informed her that they would manage everything.

'Why don't you go to Gertie's now?' Jim muttered to Mary, 'I'll see to everything. I don't want you upsetting yourself, love.'

She shook her head and bit into her lip. She had promised herself that she would not cry. She felt defiant but resigned. The strike had robbed them of money, food, security, and now a home. Yet pride and perseverance fed her soul. People believed in solidarity at all costs, but, as she watched her possessions being taken outside onto the snow-covered street, a voice in her head asked: *At what cost?*

* * *

The house had been emptied in less than half an hour. The police had lifted heavy items with care, placing them outside with thoughtful attention. As the last items were brought out, the constable turned to Jim and met his gaze.

'We've finished now, sir. We just have to lock up. Thank you for your cooperation,' he added.

Jim nodded a brief but courteous reply, then turned his attention to the horse and cart waiting to transport their things to storage. He wondered when they would be able to use them again. He and Mary were so grateful that Gertie and Charlie had offered to share their home with them, but he hated the feeling of being without his own home. He sighed and began stacking items on the cart.

Mary looked on, mixed emotions jumbling in her mind. She felt relief that they had somewhere to stay, but such sadness that she no longer had a home of her own. She reasoned to herself that she still possessed the most precious and important things to her: Jim, her devoted husband, Rose and John, her beloved children, and her parents and family, who were so loving and generous.

She touched her wedding ring, her Grandma Annie's wedding ring that Sarah had passed onto her. So often she had been tempted to sell or pawn it when desperate for money, but she had not, she could not.

Her baby's gentle kicks within her growing belly gave her comfort and hope for happier times. She heard children playing in the nearby school yard and she experienced optimism for the future, despite it being such a bleak day.

'Mary!' a voice called, breaking into her thoughts. It was Bridie, standing outside with some of her children. Her house was soon to be emptied and locked up. Mary straightened her shoulders and strode over to help her friend.

The cold air buffeted Bridie's skirt and whipped loose tendrils of hair around her face. Two-year-old Louisa was folded across her chest, resting in the crook of her arm. Bridie's other arm clasped her twin boys against her legs. The children were subdued, quiet and pale.

'Are you alright?' Mary asked, concern for Bridie and her children overriding her own feelings. She stared at Bridie, surprised and shocked to see how old she looked in the harsh winter light. Her once luminous skin now had a greyish tinge, her once shiny, thick hair was brittle and faded. It was as if moisture and a healthy bloom had been sucked out of her, leaving a dried, desiccated façade. She widened her pale, cracked lips to produce a hesitant smile and raised her drooping eyelids to reveal tired, bloodshot eyes.

'Sure, I'm fine,' she replied, but her voice was thin and faint, as if it was an effort to speak.

'Go back inside,' Mary ordered, alarm making her words sound brusque rather than coaxing. Bridie turned, as if in a daze, and led the children back inside the house. The all-pervading atmosphere of dank chill cut like a knife, penetrating and numbing flesh and bones.

It was colder inside than outside. No fire had warmed the air for many days. No hot food had probably been eaten for many days either. Guilt permeated Mary; how could she have not realised how bad things were for Bridie?

They walked through to the living room. It was completely bare except for one chair, a few piles of items on the floor and Ben's chair. Everything else downstairs had been sold or pawned. Upstairs had only a few mattresses and blankets remaining. Mary looked at Eli who was sitting on the solitary chair, his long legs tucked underneath, his eyes closed. Faint snores puffed from his open mouth.

Little Maria was on his lap, shivering in her thin dress, her bare feet gently rubbing together, trying to find some comforting warmth. Ben was silent in his chair. Only his eyes moved as he languished in the cold.

'Oh Bridie, my love!' was all Mary could say.

'We have nowhere to go,' was all Bridie could say.

* * *

It did not take long to empty Bridie and Eli's house, as so few possessions remained. Mary stayed with her friend, trying to comfort and support her as the task was being carried out. Bridie stood and watched, clutching her children as if she feared they would be taken too. Eli looked on in silence, looking taller and thinner than ever. His unruly hair, ragged moustache and dirt-stained clothes made him a pitiable figure.

Being unable to work for the past six months had affected him in many ways. He had not known how to fill the hours. There was no labouring to structure his day, and no money to allow his drinking and gambling. He missed the banter and camaraderie of his workmates. He was unused to being in the house so much, surrounded by children and with the annoyance of domestic duties being continuously carried out around him. His natural reserve deepened into a sullen withdrawal from Bridie and the children, which only increased the friction between husband and wife.

Bridie's inherent propensity for melancholy and depression was fed by the array of circumstances in her life. Her husband was on strike, though he did not want to be. He was earning no money, and as he was not a member of the union, was not entitled to any strike pay. She had five children, all dependent on her for care and sustenance.

The prolonged strike had made this virtually impossible. Just when she needed more support and understanding from Eli, she saw him withdraw into an infuriating detachment from the reality of their situation. She found this weak and unreasonable. The old feelings of resentment and disappointment returned, making everything even harder to bear. She felt her energy and spirits slowly descend into a fatalistic, resigned forlornness. Worst of all, she felt alone.

Her family had tried to help as much as they could, but they were all in similar dire situations. There was resentment towards Eli for continuing to work at the beginning of the strike, but support was still offered to Bridie and the children.

Bridie's mother, Hannah, was particularly distressed and upset that Eli had caused a rift within the family. She felt dual, conflicting allegiances. Bridie and the children were close to her heart, yet the rest of the family baulked at the actions of Eli, unable to understand his reluctance to be a union member, and aggrieved that he did not support his fellow workers. The eviction notices had brought matters to a head.

The Flannagan household had fewer members than before. Michael, Seamus and Martha still lived with their parents, but Bridie's older brothers, Paddy, Martin and Dermot, were married and living in rented accommodation in Mexborough. This was fortunate, as they readily agreed to squeeze in family members when the ejectment orders were served.

'What about our Bridie and the wee bairns?' Hannah had asked.

'I'm sure they'll find accommodation somewhere,' Willie had assured her. But they did not. Eli had refrained from organising anything. He was so used to Bridie sorting things out, she always did. But he did not realise the depths of her depression and the physical toll on her body. They had existed on charity for so long, but it had not been enough to sustain health and peace of mind.

On the day their house was taken away, emptied and locked, the Shaw family found themselves on the street with nowhere to go.

Jim returned to find Mary also on the street, talking to the Reverend Jesse Wilson. Nearby, the Shaw family stood in a huddle, dejected as the icy wind cuffed their bodies. Ben banged his hand on his chair, as if to revive them into action.

'Oh, thank you, Reverend!' Mary cried, near to tears. 'Thankyou!' She stepped towards Bridie and Eli. 'Reverend Wilson is taking you to his Chapel. You can stay there with the other families,' she announced.

Eli's almost-black eyes raised to meet her own and she saw a flicker of hope in them. Bridie's face contorted as she struggled to hold back her tears.

'Thank you, Mary,' she whispered, 'I'll never forget this. Sure, you are a true friend.'

The two women hugged each other before they parted. Mary watched Jesse Wilson shepherding them into a cart, with kind words and caring hands. They would ride to his chapel. They would have food, warmth and compassion.

Mary and Jim turned, heading towards their new home at Gertie's. They didn't speak, they just held each other's hands and walked into the stinging wind. The wooden rose was stored safely in Mary's apron pocket. It gave her comfort.

Chapter 73
9th January 1903

The evictions continued, until the last house was emptied and locked by noon on Friday 9th January, much earlier than had been expected. Most of the policemen left that day, relieved that their undesirable duties were over. Many had privately expressed the opinion that it had been the most unpleasant work they had ever undertaken.

Witnessing the pitiful plight of so many people, especially the children, had been a heartrending experience. A few policemen remained, in anticipation of possible future trouble, but doors were locked, windows boarded up and the streets were eerily deserted.

Many families had been unable to find any kind of lodgings, even the most basic or unsuitable, such was the severe lack of accommodation in the area.

Some of the older miners could remember the similar plight of two hundred miners and their families in the 1885 strike. They, too, had been evicted by the Company, but were unable to find other lodgings as Denaby was in the midst of an outbreak of smallpox. People in nearby homes and villages were sadly reluctant to take in people for fear of the contagious disease spreading.

Now, tents were the only refuges available. They had been erected by the local authority in fields on the outskirts of Denaby. Snow, rain and bitter cold rendered the canvas shelters most unsuitable for the occupants, but they had no option but suffer the inhumane conditions. People near and far could hardly believe that men, women and children were forced to tolerate such an appalling environment, but they came to see the forlorn sights for themselves, and both local and national newspapers reported their circumstances in vivid detail.

* * *

14th January 1903

A week after the evictions started, the striking miners were dealt a devastating blow. The London judge who was deliberating on the court case of the Company against the Yorkshire Miners' Association, ruled that the strike was illegal, unofficial and that strike pay should cease. The news was delivered at a union meeting, in a field next to Denaby pit. The thousands of assembled miners had walked from their temporary lodgings, anxious to find out more about the unwelcome verdict.

The union officials explained how serious this legal defeat was. It would result in the union having to withdraw pay to the men. The miners had varying opinions and reactions to the news. Some felt increased defiance and determination to carry on striking, but many experienced the first crumbling of resolve, and the growing probability that defeat would have to be conceded.

Strike pay, even though much less than wages, had enabled them to survive and continue to fight, but without strike pay, continued resistance seemed a hopeless quest.

Members of the Strike Committee gave rousing speeches, imploring the men to carry on the fight, encouraging them to stick to their principles after so much hardship. But the seeds of doubt were already sown. Even the Union men were hinting at capitulation. The prospect of defeat was already being contemplated.

'They've taken our jobs, our houses, now they want to fuckin' starve us!' agreed the men and boys, with sinking hearts and declining spirits.

* * *

15th January 1903

The newspapers continued to report the circumstances of the evicted miners and their families. People travelled to see the fields where tents had been erected, staring disbelievingly at the terrible conditions being endured by the unfortunate people who lived there.

Some were marquee tents, some were smaller bell tents, but all were situated in open, unforgiving environments, at the mercy of whatever weather occurred. The ground was either crisped rock hard by severe frosts, or a muddy quagmire after downpours of icy, slicing rain. The marquee tents had inside fires, but the bell tents were too small, requiring outside fires that produced stinging smoke when spluttering in the fanning, gusty winds. Much living was outside, either trying to get warmth from the inadequate fire, or waiting for menfolk to return from their expeditions for any donated food or money.

Once again, the Reverend Jesse Wilson felt the need to step in to give much needed help and compassion, both to the tent-dwellers and the other striking miners scattered around in temporary homes. He had not appreciated the sightseers gaping at the "concentration camps", as if they were some kind of free spectacle, but he was pleased with the generosity of people from far and wide who had been deeply moved by the events and conditions suffered by the Denaby miners.

Money, provisions and sympathy flooded in, and Jesse Wilson decided to give further aid by organising and distributing this welcome largesse. On Tuesdays, he gave away hundreds of parcels of food, each valued at 1 shilling and 7 pence. Each parcel consisted of:

Half a stone of flour – 8½d
1d of barm (yeast)
One quarter of tea – 6d
2lbs of sugar – 3½d

On Fridays, Jesse Wilson distributed fish that had been donated. The hungry, if not starving, miners were grateful for any kind of help, such was their desperate need.

The people living in Reverend Wilson's Chapel gave thanks for such charity, and realised how fortunate they were to have a man of Jesse's nature and stature guiding them through such difficult circumstances.

They had somewhere to sleep, albeit on mattresses on the floor, and warmth and the ability to cook. Jesse had "tortoise" stoves in the Chapel and school rooms. The children living there had been curious and fascinated by the cast iron stoves which had a tortoise shape and the motto 'slow but sure' imprinted on the front.

Reverend Wilson had explained to them that the stoves had the best efficiency, they burned so slowly that they extracted the maximum amount of heat from the fuel. They were 'slow but sure', just like a tortoise. The adults had just been grateful for their comforting warmth and the ability to cook on them.

* * *

16th January 1903

The news spread like wildfire. The Company announced it was planning to reopen both pits, Denaby and Cadeby, the following week. Contract workers were being brought in from other areas.

A new workforce was being recruited, with the promise of jobs and accommodation in the vacant houses. Hundreds of men and boys would be needed for both pits, but once a full quota had been attained, the striking miners would have no jobs or houses to return to, even when the strike was over. This turn of the screw by the Company was intended to hasten the end of the strike, and to succeed in negating any bargaining power of the miners.

Men would only be able to sign on for work at the old rate of pay and under the same working terms. In effect, they were being made to capitulate.

Some miners acted swiftly, signing on immediately, willing to work on any terms. These were mainly non-Union people and miners who had never agreed with the strike. Eli Shaw, Tommy Prince and Walter Smith were three of the first to gain their old jobs back, together with the promise of accommodation. They were unbothered by any expected intimidation from others. They were desperate for work, desperate for money, at any cost.

Privately, some of the other striking miners were thinking similar thoughts. Only their feelings of loyalty and solidarity affected their wavering decisiveness. They were beginning to see the hopelessness of their situation. Strike pay would soon cease, "nipsey" money would be reduced, and their future jobs and houses possibly permanently threatened.

Even the union were on the verge of recommending the return to work, especially as the action being brought by the Company against the Y.M.A. for damages of £150,000 for losses incurred during the strike, was impending.

Yet still, many miners refused to give in. They were relying on "nipsey" money granted each week, and any poaching that could provide much-needed food. Fathers and sons scoured the surrounding fields and woods for anything that could be poached and eaten. Their wives and mothers listened to their defiant words. 'We'll continue the fight. We'll not give in.'

* * *

22nd January 1903

The Company stuck to their words. Denaby and Cadeby pits were opened. Mounted police escorted the contract workers and the old workers who had signed on, as they advanced towards the pits' gates. Striking miners and their families lined their routes, but only used their words as weapons. The workers heard the jeers and taunts of the affronted miners who were carrying on the struggle, but they ignored them. There were no scuffles, no fights, no violence, but the strikers made their feelings clear.

'Blacklegs! Scabs! Teckin' ar jobs after all we've been through! It'll all be for nowt!'

* * *

But as January wore on, the number of old hands signing on gradually increased. First it was a trickle of mainly older men, exhausted and too weary to battle on any longer. Then, as realisation sank in, more and more men decided to sign on, too disillusioned to summon up more energy to prevent defeat. Mass meetings were regularly convened, where the strike committee tried to bolster flagging spirits and doubting minds. But the tide was slowly turning.

* * *

February 1903

After the evictions, national interest in the striking miners of Denaby gradually dipped, especially as the Union was recommending a return to work. Donations began to decrease, reducing "nipsey" money just when it was needed even more. A steady stream of miners decided to sign on, but still a hardcore of over a thousand men vowed to carry on fighting. They could not contemplate defeat.

Local newspapers continued to report on the unfolding events of the strike, including the shocking news that there was another outbreak of smallpox, this time amongst the people living in the tents put up on Sparrow Barracks, an open area opposite The Miners Arms pub in Mexborough.

The overcrowding and unsanitary conditions there had resulted in the highly contagious disease spreading rapidly among the residents and helpers who visited the site. The airborne disease was transmitted through face-to-face exposure with an infected person, or with their personal clothing or bedding. Soon, the early symptoms of fever, headache and severe fatigue progressed to a rash of flat spots that became raised bumps of fluid-filled blisters. Contagion lasted until all the blisters had scabbed over and fallen away from the skin. Sadly, ten people died, including four young children.

Some of the surviving infected people suffered severe scarring, and one even blindness, but they were thankful for their lives. They knew, however, that their endurance had been tested to the limit. They did not know how much more they could stand.

* * *

The reporters mingled with the crowds of striking miners and their families as they jostled for space on the platform at Conisbrough railway station. They were all gathered to see the trains arriving regularly from Doncaster, filled with the new workforce brought in by the Company.

Police on foot guarded the men as they spilled from the trains, mounted police escorted them through the village to the pit gates. The new labour force had readily agreed to work for the Company, but they had to push their way through the cordons of heckling people and withstand the imploring taunting and bullying from the fervent crowds, surging and screaming as their collieries' banners were proudly raised.

As flurries of dazzling, white snowflakes settled on caps and shawls, the reporters noted the impassioned faces of the men and women, and their frenzied words, whipped up by annoyance and consternation. They realised these people were fighting for their pride and future survival. The reporters understood the striking miners and their families were confronting the terrifying possibility that they would lose everything.

* * *

12th March 1903

It was becoming more and more apparent to the strikers that they would not have the opportunity to return to work unless a decision was soon made to discontinue the struggle. Over six hundred men, old and new hands, had already signed on at the two pits, and soon work would be at full swing at the rate jobs were being taken.

Those willing to admit defeat justified their decision by stating the hopelessness of the struggle now that the Yorkshire Miners' Association had officially pronounced against it. After nearly nine months on strike, most people were penniless. Even wives and mothers were imploring them to give up the fight. They had had enough.

* * *

22nd March 1903

After nearly forty weeks on strike, the miners capitulated. They had to. Only a minority had wanted to carry on, the majority had not. But they all realised the strike had been a disaster. They had gained nothing and lost everything. The Company had been left in a strong position, with a new workforce, many of them non-union men, and many of the old workforce disillusioned and heavily in debt.

'All this for nowt!'
'Gaffers have won again!'
'Aye, but one day we'll fuckin' win!'
The birth of the Labour Party was not far away.

Chapter 74
23rd March 1903

Jim squeezed Mary's hand, relief and joy coursing through his body. What a momentous day Monday 23rd March 1903 had turned out to be.

After all the misery and hardships of recent months, his emotions felt unfamiliar, but very welcome and desired. His beaming smile invigorated Mary's weary body. She, too, smiled, partly closing her eyes as if in stunned disbelief. The situation felt almost dream-like. She couldn't believe she had finally given birth to a beautiful healthy baby, a girl who was the image of Rose.

The labour had been long and hard, with Sarah and Gertie comforting her as best they could. Mary had, at times, doubted that she could progress and succeed in giving birth.

It was the new midwife, Aggie White, a Sheffield lass now living in Denaby, who had guided and encouraged her through the difficult, painful procedure.

Mary noted the differences of this birth compared to her others. She had definitely found everything harder, feeling more weakened and exhausted, as if her body was complaining about the assault on muscles and energy. She also felt sincere gratitude towards Aggie, who had taken over as village midwife. Nellie MacArthur had died suddenly, alone in her front room, a few months earlier.

'Oh, Jim, I'm so glad it's all over and everything's all right!' Mary cried, tears spilling down her flushed cheeks. Even in the shadowy candlelight, Jim could see her utter relief and fatigue. He had always known that she was a strong woman, but he also acknowledged how the strike had depleted her, mentally and physically.

'Mary, don't cry, love. Things will be much better from now on. You'll soon feel stronger, and we may have our own house soon,' he added with a slow, meaningful smile. Mary looked up sharply, gazing deep into his eyes.

'You mean...?' she started.

'Yes, love. I've signed back on at Cadeby – should be starting work in a few days' time. We've also been promised a house...' Jim added, only stopping when Mary burst into noisy, sobbing tears. It was as if a dam had burst, and all the hurt and worry of recent times was flooding out.

'These are happy tears, Jim,' she eventually managed to say. He nodded and held her hands once more. They both looked over to their sleeping daughter and silently counted their blessings. Baby Violet was cocooned in their protective love and joy.

* * *

May 1903

Although the strike had ended two months earlier, problems and difficulties still existed in Denaby. Not everyone was able to return to the security of a job and a house. Many of the striking old hands had managed to regain work at either Denaby or Cadeby pit, but not all of them, as their jobs had either been filled by blacklegs, brought in by the Company, or necessary repair work at the pits had to be carried out before they could be taken on again.

The Company had also been ruthless in its dealings with the most militant strikers and their leaders, refusing to take back more than five hundred previous workers. These men were even blacklisted at other local pits.

Accommodation was also insufficient, as many of the empty houses had been allocated to the newly recruited workforce. The Company refused to turn them out and give preference to the old, previous tenants. Tents were still being used by many people as they waited for any possible lodgings.

Police still patrolled the Denaby streets in order to quell any trouble between old and new workers, and union and non-union men. Feelings were still running high. Pride and honour had been dented in defeat.

Even within families and friends, antagonism and hostility bubbled beneath the surface. Bitterness and resentment would prove slow to diminish, so stringent and impassioned had emotions been for so long. The women had to stay quiet and bide their time, hoping their menfolk would soften and reconcile in the future. But they knew from previous experience that the men had long memories and a reluctance to understand and forgive past conflicts.

It was heartbreaking for the wives and mothers to see the bitter rifts between husbands, fathers, sons and old, long-established friends.

* * *

June 1903

Bob sighed deeply, weary at the end of his afternoon shift, but feeling pleased that life was beginning to feel calmer and more settled than before. Since the strike had ended, there had been many changes in his life, thankfully mostly for the better.

He thought back over the past few months as he walked slowly along the street, savouring the last fading light in the darkening summer sky. He welcomed the hint of a breeze that circled in the warm air. It was much appreciated after the stifling heat of the pit face.

His body was still adjusting to the return to work, and so were the horses, but work was what all the men now wanted. Debts had to be paid, and new possessions bought to replace old ones. He felt grateful that both he and his father had been taken back on at Denaby pit. His mother had cried happy tears at the news, and even more tears when they were promised a house of their own to rent.

'I don't care which street it's on as long as we have our own home again!' she had declared, her hands placed together as if in prayer.

'We can leave you in peace now,' she had announced to Ivy and Sam.

'Oh, Mam, I'm so pleased for you, but you know we haven't minded you staying with us, that's what families are for!'

Ivy's emotions overcame her as she hugged her mother and father.

'Nay, lass, we're very grateful to you, but now you'll have more space and less work with us gone,' Albert said gruffly.

'Our Bob's been useful in the shop, too,' Ivy teased her brother. 'We might make a butcher out of you one day, you never know!'

Bob grinned. 'I'll stick to mi horses,' he replied.

* * *

The Company had given the order:

'Get the horses back down,' as soon as the relevant safety and repair work had been carried out at both pits. The bosses were keen to produce as much coal as possible, quickly.

The strike had been a costly business for everyone. The union had paid out thousands of pounds in strike pay, the miners had lost thousands of pounds in wages, and it was estimated that 900,000 tons of coal had been lost by the Company. It was time for work.

Getting the horses back down had proved to be easier said than done.

Bob vividly remembered the difficulties he and the other horsemen had experienced rounding up the ponies and preparing them for the descent to the pit face.

On that March morning, the horses had been calmly moving from one area to another within the field, heads down, munching on the springy grass, quiet and content in their surroundings. For months, they had lived out in the open, adapting to the changing weather and temperatures, free to wander at their pleasure. Yet, it was as if they had a sixth sense of what was about to happen.

The horsemen approached their ponies carefully and slowly, uttering soothing words and cajoling murmurs. At first, their advances proved fruitless. The ponies backed up and side-stepped, their eyes glinting knowingly with suspicion and latent memories. The more the men advanced, the more the animals retreated, as if they were hanging on to their very last minutes of light, of space, of freedom.

Some of the ponies kicked and bucked, snorting and sweating, puffing and panting, until their frenzied energy was spent. Bob recalled how Ginger had ignored him, backing up and giving sideways glances, defiantly refusing to obey his commands. Soothing words had no power. The animals knew what was to follow and any delay to that inevitability was searched for.

Eventually, each pony was caught and harnessed. The men sweated and strained alongside the animals, such was the energy and exertion required to contain and control the horses. Each descent down the pit produced a cacophony of clattering, thunderous noises, a reverberating din of banging, striking hooves, deafening and ear-splitting. It was safe to assume that the ponies did not relish returning to the constraints of their deep, dark workplace.

Bob and the other pony drivers felt a certain sympathy and understanding, but they had no choice. The ponies were needed. They would soon be moulded into their former state of obedience and compliance. The men had to endure such requirements and so would their horses.

Bob knew from past experience that it would take time for the ponies to settle underground. They kicked and fought against having their harnesses fitted, and their newly shod hooves were pawed and clawed against the ground, as if protesting that they were strange and unfamiliar.

The worst thing in the first few weeks was their loss of weight. For months, they had fed on grass, and the return to harder food affected their bodies. Their droppings were liquid at first as they adapted to the different food. Their general condition suffered.

It pained Bob to see poor Ginger in a weak, lacklustre state. It only added to the difficulties of conforming to the harsh, restrictive environment. After three or four weeks, Bob was relieved when Ginger seemed to be responding to his care and kind words. Some of the old trust and bonds of friendship and loyalty were returning. Once again, he felt lucky to have this equine friend and companion.

As Bob reached home, he was still reminded of the day he and his parents had been given the keys to 19 Rossington Street, their new home. Sarah had been thrilled to finally move into their own home, although it was in a sorry state. The boards on the windows had been removed, but inside it was dirty and forlorn. Scratched doors, stained walls and dusty surfaces greeted them. It was in a much worse state than their old house, but Sarah hid her disappointment, insisting everything would look much better after a good "fettle".

'I'll get the lasses in to help me,' she decided.

'We'll get our stuff from Mexborough, then it'll look more like home,' Albert suggested gently. Sarah smiled and nodded.

Bob had to admit that the house was looking much cleaner and more comfortable now. The fettling had greatly improved the feel of the house, together with a roaring fire.

But there was also another factor that made him like and appreciate their new home. A family had recently moved in next door. There was a father, a mother and five daughters of varying ages, and Bob had immediately noticed one of them.

She was small, petite in build, with a tiny waist and long, curly, auburn hair that refused to stay pinned up. It seemed to dance around her shoulders as she walked, the curls pirouetting with her every movement. He had watched her sweeping and cleaning outside, noting her brisk, energetic way of doing things that belied her delicate stature. He felt tall compared to her, a feeling that he had rarely experienced. He had taken to finding excuses to be outside, on the off chance that she would be there. He vividly remembered the first time she had looked up and met his eyes as they walked along the "backs". She smiled shyly, but gave him a direct look.

'Hello, my name's Winnie Marshall. What's yours?' Her pale, yellow-green eyes held his gaze.

'Bob, Bob Cooper,' he managed to say before blushing a hot shade of red.

'Hello, Bob,' she said, simply.

'Hello, Winnie,' he replied. Never before had he experienced such a thrill of excitement when talking to a woman, but he was helpless to feel otherwise.

He knew the family had moved to Denaby from Doncaster a few months before the strike began and had lived in a pit house before being evicted. Wilf Marshall, Winnie's father, had signed back on at Cadeby pit and had been given their new house on Rossington Street. Bob said silent thankyous for his good fortune in living next door to Winnie.

Since then, Bob and Winnie had shared furtive glances and wide smiles that lit up their faces. He felt as if he was holding his breath until the next time he could see her and talk to her.

Suddenly, his life felt different, exciting and optimistic. He dared not believe that she might feel the same, but he hoped fervently that she did.

At the age of twenty-two, he felt that his life was ready to move on, to change from being the youngest sibling in his household, to having his own family. He could hardly believe he was thinking like this, but he knew from the moment he saw Winnie that she was the one he wanted to share his life with.

* * *

July 1903

Mary and Jim were gradually settling into their new home, 55 Cliff View. The many changes over the past few months had been challenging for them both. Jim had to adapt to working shifts again, and to the hard graft that his job entailed.

Luckily, Mary felt, they had still been living with Gertie and Charlie for the first few weeks after the birth, which gave her time to adapt to her new duties. Baby Violet was content and sweet-natured, but Mary had still been grateful that Gertie had assumed all the housework, cooking and childminding tasks.

When the keys to Cliff View had finally been handed over, Mary had found the new and extra demands on both her time and energy quite tiring and draining. She was still thrilled that her wish for another child had been fulfilled, but it had given her new insight into how Bridie must have felt, coping with all the demands of her family.

Jim was just thankful that mother and baby were both well and thriving, and tried to help out whenever he could. Rose had been a godsend to Mary. At thirteen years of age, she seemed to be on the cusp of womanhood.

Mary could well remember how she had felt at that age. Rose was such a sensible, practical girl, willingly helping her mother with both the housework and looking after Violet. Mary and Jim felt at times that they were experiencing life thirteen years ago, so similar was Violet to Rose in looks and nature. John had initially stated that he would have liked a baby brother, but admitted that Violet was 'all right'.

One week after moving into Cliff View, there had been two particular events that both surprised and unsettled Mary and Jim. The first one was when a family was seen moving into the house only a few doors away from them. That family was Walter Smith, his wife Esther and their son Joseph.

There had been mixed feelings about this news. Jim felt uncomfortable with the situation, knowing how Walt had shunned their friendship and held a grudge for so long, but also the fact that he had made no secret of his scathing attitude to unions and strikes, which Jim feared would bode hostility, even trouble, in the future.

Mary had a more optimistic view, hoping that Jim and Walter might eventually resume their old friendship, but she recognised how raw and sensitive many people still were after bitter defeat.

'Let's just see how things pan out,' Jim calmly stated to Mary. She realised time and tact would be required before anything was resolved.

The second surprising event was that Bridie and Eli were also given a home on Cliff View, barely a dozen houses from Jim and Mary.

'I can't believe we've ended up near neighbours yet again!' Mary had declared. She was pleased but she knew others may not be. Eli was another miner who followed his own wishes, often with disregard for others. *At least I'm close enough to Bridie to be a good friend and neighbour*, was Mary's consoling thought. She still remembered her friend's frequent bouts of sadness and depression, and worried that she would not always be able to overcome them.

PART EIGHT

Chapter 75
January 1904

The new year was very welcome after the long, hard year of 1903 and all it had brought to the folk of Denaby. There seemed to be a raised sense of optimism, even though changes and adaptations were still required.

Nine months after the end of the strike, people were gradually coping with the resulting outcomes of the struggle and their defeat. Many miners had new homes, in different streets, with different neighbours. Some had left the area when they were refused employment by the Company. It was like shifting sand; people had to settle and survive wherever they could.

Productivity of coal was booming again, feeding the voracious appetite of industries, railways and domestic homes. Coal was essential; it provided the necessary fuel for the country to live and breathe power, as well as wealth for the colliery owners.

The miners worked hard, and the pay reflected this, but many men were still disillusioned that they had no sway or bargaining power when it came to terms and conditions of work. The reduced number of union men employed at Denaby and Cadeby would dilute any future strength when in conflict with the bosses.

There was, however, the growing instinct that the power and influence of unions would only come about with their unison. Provincial conflict would need to become national; power, as well as safety, in numbers. The problem was how to bring about this solidarity of varying unions.

With work and lodgings more settled, the men's interests and attention could be turned to more rest and recreation. They could spare money for hobbies, for visits to the pub, for relaxed conversations once again. Interest in the wider world could be discussed, opinions delivered and shared on items reported in newspapers. The men could share banter and put the world to rights.

* * *

Groups of men sat around the big tables in the taproom at The Drum. It was Saturday, pay day, spirits were high and the volume of noise even higher. Muscles were relaxed and tongues loosened by the ale supped and enjoyed. Banter flew around the room, mostly good-natured. The men relished their days off. It was as if their minds and thoughts could take preference to their muscles and sinews.

One of the tables was occupied by Jim, Albert, Charlie and Sam. They were enjoying their beer and conversation.

'Where's Bob?' Jim asked Albert. 'I thought he was coming for a drink.'

Albert smiled and raised both eyebrows. 'He's otherwise occupied. He always is since he met that lass next door. He's right sweet on her.'

The other men nodded and smiled.

'Sounds like he's smitten,' Charlie said, showing his white, shiny teeth in a cheeky grin.

'Good for him,' Jim agreed. 'She seems like a nice lass.'

'We'll just have to wait and see what comes of it,' Albert stated in his usual pragmatic way. He puffed on his pipe and stared absently, as if he could visualise the future.

'I've been reading about that new Ford Motor Company in the Mail,' Sam said. 'What do you think about this new idea? Henry Ford's joined forces with some of his business mates in America, and they want to produce cheaper cars for a wider public, they say.'

'Not just for rich bastards, then,' Albert stated dourly. 'Only ever seen one motor car and that was when we were visiting our Betty in Elsecar. It was Earl Fitzwilliam himself in it – he wasn't driving, mind. Some chap in a uniform was doing that.'

'I've been reading about it, too,' Jim said. 'And about the new Motor Cars Act that came into force last week, on the first of January.'

'What's that all about, then?' Charlie asked.

'Well,' Jim continued. 'From now on, every car has to have a vehicle registration number displayed on it. Council where you live issues them. Every driver has to have a driving licence – cost five shillings from t' Council, no test required. You have to be at least seventeen years old, though. Best bit is that the speed limit's been raised to twenty miles per hour. You can get done for reckless driving though now.'

'Can you imagine seeing loads o' cars in Denaby?' Charlie laughed.

'Only if t' gaffers up our wages!' Jim retorted.

'Can't see motor cars taking off, miself,' Albert said with a shake of his head, still puffing his pipe and gazing into the future.

'Talking about taking off,' Sam said, 'did you hear about those brothers in America, the Wright brothers, Orville and Wilbur? Aviation pioneers they are. The Mail said they've invented a machine that flies! Did the world's first controlled, sustained flight of a powered 'heavier than air' aircraft. No balloons attached either, like t' others before. It has a motor and a pair of wings to support it in t' air.'

The other men frowned and shook their heads in disbelief.

'Never!' Charlie said. 'Heavier than air?' How do you work that one out?'

Sam nodded, as if to prove his words, adding, 'Last month the aircraft travelled at sixty-eight miles per hour. and was in the air for fifty-nine seconds with Orville Wright inside it, and it went eight hundred and fifty-two foot!'

'Bloody hell!' Jim gasped. 'I can't believe that!'

'Huh!' Albert guffawed. 'That's summat else that'll never catch on. Eight hundred and fifty-two foot? I can spit further than that!'

Chapter 76
March 1904

The weather was icily crisp and cold, but Mary's living room was warm and cosy. The women were sitting at the table, sipping their mugs of tea, enjoying chatting to each other.

Gertie watched her three-year-old daughter, Annie, playing with her rag doll on the fireside rug. Mary held one-year-old Violet on her lap, occasionally smoothing the baby's dark hair into gentle waves, or stroking her soft, rosy cheeks.

Ivy idly stroked the rounding contour of her stomach from time to time, still overjoyed that she was finally pregnant after three years of marriage. Sam was equally thrilled, but Ivy knew he had moments of fear and apprehension, after all, he had lost his first wife and baby during childbirth.

Ivy had frequently cupped his face in her hands, kissed his lips and reassured him that all would be well, but she secretly worried, and prayed that, at the age of thirty-four, she could give him their longed-for child.

Ellen occupied the other chair. At the age of thirty, she was still unmarried, still living with her parents, brother Gilbert and youngest sister, Alice, but she did not seem to mind her life as a single woman. She still enjoyed her job as post mistress at the Co-op.

She was proud to have a job that interested her and stretched her mind, proud to earn a living independently. Ellen was happy to meet the ever-changing requirements that her job entailed as the new, modern-day innovations dictated. They fed her intellect and satisfied her aspirations.

In some ways she regretted that she had no husband and no children, but, secretly, she was contented that she had no man to master her. She could please herself.

'How's your Ada and Beatie?' Mary asked her. 'We haven't seen much of them since they stopped working at The Drum.'

'Oh, they're both fine, thanks. It's nice that they live close to each other in Mexborough – they can help each other out with the children,' Ellen replied.

'It still seems strange that they met and married brothers,' Gertie laughed. 'Now they're both Mrs Taylor!'

'Aye, and they both had boys first then girls second,' Ivy joined in. 'I wonder what mine will be?'

'You'll find out soon enough,' Mary smiled at her sister. 'And you'll make a lovely mother.' She turned to Ellen. 'And you're a lovely daughter, sister and aunt. You're always helping your family with something.' Mary patted her friend's hands, sincere in her praise.

Ellen smiled. It pleased her to be able to help her family, but she still felt passionate about her independence and self-sufficiency. She saw the lot of many of the women around Denaby, and noted their required and expected subservience. She did not envy them, nor their status. She was her own woman, as much as she was allowed to be.

That thought reminded her of the newspaper article she had recently read. It had both interested and excited her. It stated that a Mrs Emmeline Pankhurst and two of her daughters had founded and formed the W.P.S.U., the Women's Political and Social Union, in October 1903. Its purpose was to gain votes for women.

The campaign for women's suffrage had been ongoing since the 1870s, but it had met with little success in its attempts to persuade an overwhelmingly male establishment to agree to what they wanted. This resulted in the recognition that a more militant wing of the suffrage movement was required. Mrs Pankhurst held meetings at her own home in Manchester, stating, 'Women, we must do the work ourselves.' The W.P.S.U. would be open to women only, and it would have no party affiliation. Its motto would be 'Deeds not words.'

Ellen had felt an immediate connection to the concept that women, as well as men, should be enfranchised. There should be more equality in many areas of life. She decided to share this with her friends.

'I've been reading about the Women's Political and Social Union, led by Mrs Emmeline Pankhurst. Have you heard about this?'

The others looked at her and nodded.

'Yes, votes for women, isn't it? I can't see that happening in my lifetime!' Gertie declared.

Ellen licked her lips and rested her chin on her hand. 'Why not? We're as good as men! We'll have to see what Mrs Pankhurst can do!'

The other women looked at Ellen's determined face and heard her impassioned words, but they could only try to understand her point of view. They admired her sentiments but could not identify with her attitude. It felt too radical and progressive for Denaby women. What would their husbands say?

Chapter 77
July 1904

Sam closed his eyes and exhaled a deep, shuddering sigh. He shook his head slowly, as if clearing his thoughts, then experienced a surge of relief mixed with delight. He was a father, he had a son, Ivy was all right.

He felt as if his prayers had been answered. He looked down at Ivy's beautiful face as she slept, her alabaster skin still flushed from all the straining and labouring she had endured. Her blonde hair covered the pillow in a profusion of delicate waves. He felt such love for her.

His eyes travelled to the baby, his son, who was asleep, with only occasional faint murmurings breaking the silence. His golden hair and lashes gleamed in the rays of sunlight that beamed through the bedroom window. His lips puckered fractionally as he breathed. Ivy opened her eyes, the huge grey eyes that so enhanced her face, and were so expressive.

'Sam,' she murmured, looking up at him. 'A boy – our son.'

Sam gathered her hands in his and kissed them.

'Yes, our son, I can hardly believe it! Thank you, Ivy.'

He blinked rapidly to stifle the tears that threatened to fall. They both stared at their baby boy, basking in their utter happiness.

'Do you still want to call him Albert?' Sam asked.

'I thought Albert Samuel,' Ivy replied.

'Albert Samuel it is, then,' Sam agreed happily. He thought momentarily of the son he had lost without ever knowing. He was safely tucked away in his heart forever, but he thanked God for baby Albert.

* * *

'Albert Samuel, eh?' Albert said slowly, making a fuss of filling his pipe with tobacco.

Sarah looked over at Sam and Ivy and smiled a silent thank you. The new grandparents were visiting Sam and Ivy for their first glimpse of the baby.

'Fancy, your new grandson's named after you!' Sarah said, staring at her husband for his reaction.

'I'd better be a good grandad then, eh?' he replied.

Ivy smiled at her father.

'You *are* a good grandad, and a good father,' she insisted.

'I'll try mi best, lass, I'll try mi best.' They saw his dewy eyes and heard the catch in his voice.

Albert finally got his pipe lit and puffed away contentedly.

* * *

September 1904

The summer had been long and hot, with endless glorious sunshine that had succeeded in penetrating the pall of smoke that shrouded Denaby. Warm breezes and sunlit, balmy air had encouraged folks to take frequent walks into the surrounding countryside.

The woods boasted trees laden with their ripening fruits and abundant foliage; the fields displayed rippling stalks of golden corn. The River Don and nearby canal glinted as the sun's rays hit patches of clear surface, though the stench still hovered around them.

During the summer months, Bob and Winnie had become better acquainted. Brief meetings had lengthened to long, slow ambling at their leisure. The weather afforded them many opportunities for such strolls and wanderings, and they looked forward to spending any spare time together.

Conversation was plentiful and easy. Bob was frequently surprised at his ability to chat so readily with Winnie, something he had always found difficult before with other people. She seemed to release his long-contained thoughts and opinions in the way that she listened to him quietly and attentively.

He had been surprised to learn that she was twenty-one years old, only two years younger than him. She was so slight and dainty that he had thought she was a bit younger, but he was also impressed with her forthright, firmly held opinions and convictions. She may be small, but she was strong and determined. He realised they shared those characteristics.

Winnie showed great interest in Bob's family and work. He told her about his sisters and their families, and related many facts and incidents about his job. She had told him about her family, about the fact that her mother had died when she contracted scarlet fever, when Winnie, the first-born, was only four years old, but her father had remarried soon after and there were four more girls in the family. Winnie told Bob that she had really missed her mother but had always liked and loved Clara, her stepmother, so she had accepted the situation readily.

The family had previously lived in a small, rural hamlet near Doncaster, her father, Wilfred, only recently becoming a mine worker, so she was eager to listen and learn about the mining culture and community. She had admitted, ruefully, that it had not been the best of starts when the strike and evictions coincided with their move to Denaby, but she had a positive attitude to their new life.

September was bringing change. Daylight hours were reducing, heat was decreasing, but Bob and Winnie also recognised their desire for change. They no longer wanted to spend brief periods together, they no longer wanted to live apart, they wanted to be together, always.

One late September afternoon, they had been strolling through Denaby woods, "Bluebell Woods" as they were known.

Bob held Winnie's hand, smiling as he gazed into her yellow-green eyes. He felt strong and protective whenever he was with her. She had been asking about the ponies again, always fascinated to hear his accounts of the animals and their work. He had made her laugh when he described how the ponies would show their individual idiosyncrasies, stealing "snap" from the miners' mouths or chewing tobacco.

He also told her about something he had read in the *Mexborough and Swinton Times* the previous week. A young mine worker, a pony driver from Wentworth, had been awarded the Fitzwilliam Medal for Kindness by Countess Maud Fitzwilliam. She was the president of the Association for the Prevention of Cruelty to Pit Ponies, and had heard about a brave act at Elsecar pit, owned by the Fitzwilliam family.

A fall of coal had resulted in a group of miners being trapped. The young lad had refused to escape with the others through a narrow crack, deciding to stay with his pony until they could both be rescued. This act of bravery was rewarded with a rare medal to reflect also his kindness to animals.

When Bob finished recounting all this to Winnie, he realised she was staring at him intently, looking deep into his eyes. Her face softened with emotion. He noticed the tumble of auburn curls resting on her shoulders. His arms encircled her tiny waist, and he drew her gently closer.

'Winnie, I love you. Will you marry me?'

She nodded and lifted her face to his. Her kiss was the answer he had always hoped for.

* * *

December 1904

Sarah and Albert were delighted to hear the news that Bob and Winnie were to marry, especially Sarah. She was so pleased for her son. All her life she had worried about him, firstly because of his poor health as a boy, but also because she feared he might never find someone he could really relate to.

He was such a sensible, caring, gentle lad, but sometimes too insular. Winnie seemed the perfect woman for him, and they soon embraced her into the family.

'It's like having another lass,' Albert had said fondly. He, too, was happy for Bob's obvious contentment.

The wedding was on Christmas Eve, a simple affair enjoyed by everyone, a welcome celebration of love and happiness, the perfect antidote to the stress and misery of the strike and the evictions. Winnie moved in with Bob after the wedding, joking and laughing that she hadn't got far to travel seeing as she was only next door! The Marshall family viewed Bob in a similar light, like the son they had never had.

'I just can't get over our Bob being married!' Sarah frequently repeated. 'And she's such a lovely lass an' all!'

'Well he is, so you can stop worrying about him now,' Albert told her gently, patting her shoulder fondly. 'Winnie will be able to help you, too.'

'He'll always be my lad, though,' she thought to herself.

'Let's hope things stay nice and settled in future, and no more bloody strikes! I could do wi' some peace and quiet,' Albert stated with feeling.

Chapter 78
July 1905

Life in Denaby had settled back into a quieter, calmer phase. More than two years now since the end of the strike, the residents had become accustomed to their new homes, and in some cases, a new workplace at one of the pits. More miners had been moved from Denaby to Cadeby pit as the volume of coal production there increased.

Most people had been able to pay off some outstanding debts, even establishing some feeling of security by eking out money from payday to payday. The ability to have food, warmth and a roof over their heads was still very relevant and appreciated. No one wanted the misery of past times again.

The miners had to overcome any lingering hostile feelings towards the management, their need to work and earn money superseding any personal sentiments. Pride had to be swallowed, and resentment contained; there was no luxury of choice. The Company stood firm in their control of the mines.

Production, profit and power enabled them to dictate to the workers, any sentiment ignored. Yet the Company still showed enthusiasm and generosity in their willingness to improve and augment the facilities in Denaby.

Almost a decade earlier, it had been decided by the Company that a cottage hospital was needed in Denaby. The Mexborough Cottage Hospital on Bank Street had proved to be invaluable to the local community, especially in the treatment of work accidents. Mr Chambers and his planning committee had agreed that Denaby also needed a hospital.

Eventually, Mr J.S. Fullerton, a local landowner, had donated one acre of land as a site for the hospital and paid the cost of £3,000 for its building. He laid the first foundation stone in October 1904, and the hospital opened on 8th July 1905. It was set in beautiful, well-kept grounds, not far from both Denaby and Cadeby pits, a great advantage when immediate treatment was needed. The time saved in transportation to the hospital could also save lives.

The opening ceremony, presided over by Mr Chambers, was attended by crowds of people. They were eager to see both the building and Mr Buckingham Pope, who was to officially open the hospital. Many people knew he was the Chairman of the collieries, but few had seen him or heard him speak.

Both men gave stirring speeches from the dais. They commended the generosity of Mr Fullerton for donating the land and paying for the construction work; also the excellent standard of contractor's work, thanking Mr Wortley, whose firm had supervised all the building aspects.

The exterior of the building was traditional and unostentatious, but the interior was furnished in the most up-to-date style and wanting for nothing.

Mr Buckingham Pope stated that the hospital had been built to serve the mining population of the area and would treat workmen and their wives and children. There was a main ward with ten beds, and two smaller wards for women and children, each with three beds.

The two nurses employed at the hospital had a dining room which also served as their office. There was a small operating theatre, an outpatients' department, as well as laundry and kitchen facilities. There was also a Board Room where the committee would hold their weekly meetings.

The Board of Management was composed of officials from the local collieries and the workmen's representatives. The colliery doctors, from Denaby, Conisbrough and Mexborough, would be the honorary medical staff.

Both Mr Chambers and Mr Buckingham Pope said that it was a credit to the workforce that they had agreed to maintain the hospital through subscriptions, as it was not a charitable institution. The question of maintenance had been decided some time ago at a mass meeting of the workforce. They had decided to consent to a levy of one penny per week per man and half a penny per week per boy, which, it was estimated, would bring in about £900 per annum. This would assure the upkeep of the hospital and help fund other neighbouring institutions.

The hospital was the culmination of many years' planning and organisation and could be added to the list of other buildings and amenities provided by the Company in Denaby. The residents of Denaby were indeed fortunate to be so well served.

To rousing applause, Mr Buckingham Pope used the key to open the hospital officially. He also graciously accepted a miniature golden replica key as a memento of the occasion.

'What with the new Montagu Hospital opening on Adwick Road in Mexborough a few months ago, now this one here, let's hope they're not kept busy with lots of accidents down t' pits!' was the fervent wish of many Denaby folk who knew all too well the risks and dangers of working down the mines. At least they had a hospital to pick up the pieces.

* * *

The man was deep in thought as he travelled on the train. Fields, trees, houses, they all flashed by without him seeing anything. He knew it was foolish of him to make this journey, but he felt compelled. He had to see her and possibly speak to her again. She had been in his thoughts for the past seven years, but he had refrained from trying to make contact, until now.

He moistened his dry lips with a flick of his tongue and pushed the quiff of hair up from his forehead. He was sweating, partly because of the heat and partly from mounting nerves.

The nearer he travelled towards Conisbrough, the more he sweated. He knew he had done wrong, he knew he had hurt her terribly, but he still clung onto the vague hope that she had forgiven him and still wanted him, though he doubted that she would have those feelings.

He put on his flat cap as the train pulled into Conisbrough station, pulling the peak well down as he stepped onto the platform. He didn't want to be recognised.

The man decided to make his way to the old stone cottage nearby, and stood in the shady ginnel opposite, lurking in its shadows where the sun's rays could not reach. There was still the same old, green door, still the same green shutters, but the cottage somehow looked neglected. He wondered if she still lived there. The man waited a while but saw no one entering or leaving the house. He started to walk away towards Denaby when the green door opened, and a young woman stepped outside. He hesitated at first, but then he spoke to her.

'Excuse me, Miss, but does Ivy Cooper still live here?'

'Oh, no, not for a long time. We moved in, must be six or seven years ago. She's married to the butcher up the road, you know? Baker's. They live above the shop. Had a baby boy last year too,' she explained.

The man looked at her vacantly, in a daze, then blinked as if to rouse himself.

'Thanks, Miss,' he managed to say, then turned to walk along Doncaster Road into Denaby. The information had hit him like a sledgehammer, sucking his breath and shattering his dreams.

He tried to reason with himself. Of course she would be married and had children; it was stupid to think she could have wanted to wait for him. He only had himself to blame.

The man found himself walking into Denaby, head lowered, his hopes dashed, but when he looked up, he knew instantly it was her. She was in the distance, carrying an infant in her arms, her blonde hair gleaming in the sunshine. He quickly stepped into a recess between the nearby shops, but he could still see her. Then he heard her speak.

'Wave to your Daddy, Albert,' she said to the baby. They were standing outside the butcher's shop window, and she was helping the little boy to wave his chubby fingers.

'You be a good boy for your Mammy, now,' he heard a man's voice call out. She turned and walked along the street, chatting to her baby.

The man watched her until she was out of sight, then left the safety of the recess to head back towards the station. He felt numb, but he was glad he had seen her and heard her voice again. He knew it was the last time he would ever see or hear her again.

Chapter 79
January 1906

Mary was thankful that her life seemed to be on a more even keel than before. Stability and consistency in home life, as well as Jim's regular work, had provided her with a welcome feeling of happiness and contentment.

She often reflected on how the stress of the strike and evictions had affected her, as well as many other women. At the time, sheer determination and doggedness had propelled her through all the miseries and hardships. She had resolved to stay strong for Jim and all the family, but it was only later that she had recognised the toll that all the worry and upheaval had taken on her.

But, once again, she knew she was no different to many other women. Her pregnancy had presented her with other pressures, but she felt a certain pride in how she had coped with everything; she had stayed strong when it was necessary to do so. She had her home, her family and a quiet feeling of self-respect and fulfilment, especially now that she had Violet, her longed-for baby.

Violet was a thriving, happy little girl with a ready smile and a friendly nature. Everyone said how alike she was to Rose, both in looks and temperament. The three-year-old loved to play with other children, especially her cousin Annie, who was two years older. They would play together happily, Annie's copper-coloured hair mingling with Violet's darker locks as they carried out their "pretend" games side by side, deep in focused concentration.

They were more like sisters, which Mary and Gertie found heart-warming, especially since Gertie had failed to become pregnant again. She would have loved to have given Annie a little brother or sister. Mary felt contented with her family; she was satisfied with what she had got.

Rose had blossomed into a lovely young woman, looking and acting more maturely than her almost sixteen years.

She had left school two years previously and had been pleased to start work at the Powder Works. Jobs there were still prestigious and well paid, especially for women. Rose felt she was carrying out a responsible, worthy job, and she was pleased to be able to contribute financially to her family. She would sometimes daydream about rising through the ranks, having a career, but she knew such avenues were scarce for girls like her.

John was due to leave school in the summer and hoped to be taken on at one of the pits. Jim and Mary had tried to steer him away from naturally assuming he would become a miner, but John was practical and pragmatic. He wanted to earn money; he wanted to better his life.

Pit work was as good as any, and it was on the doorstep. He knew there was frequent conflict between management and miners, but he almost relished the thought of confrontation. Unions and their principles interested and excited him. He felt as if there would soon be a change, a new era of work relations.

John had definite views about trade disputes. He still remembered the day they had been evicted, and it still rankled with him. The inequality between rich and poor, the powerful and the insignificant, and management and labour, provided him with a resolute determination for change. Yes, he would relish the fight.

* * *

Mary's neighbours always liked to chat to little Violet whenever they saw her in the "backs" or on the street.

'What a lovely little lass your Violet is. She's a credit to you, Mary,' they would say.

Some pressed a penny into the little girl's hand, some gave her a sweet, some ruffled her hair affectionately. Mary had got to know Esther, Walter's wife, this way. The two women had exchanged smiles and nods at first, then progressed to chatting, if the weather allowed. Mary liked Esther. She was a sensible, caring person, quiet but friendly.

Esther knew that Mary was a friend of Ellen, her sister-in-law, and their conversation often revolved around her. Joseph, Esther and Walter's son, was only one year older than John and were old school friends.

Jim was pleased that the women were friendly with each other, but still regarded Walt as distant and unapproachable. The two women avoided talking about the strike and past Union differences. They did not want to rake up any past or future hostilities. It was safer to stick to women's talk.

Mary visited Bridie regularly and was heartened to see an improvement in her friend's appearance and state of mind. The new, improved surroundings and Eli's regular work had gradually revived her spirits. Mary could see traces of the 'old' Bridie that she knew and loved. Her renewed energy and positive attitude had helped her to cope with all the demands of her family, but then, more distressing incidents occurred.

Within the space of two months, Bridie lost her brother and mother. Michael had been killed in a fall of coal, with no chance of survival. One month later, Hannah had suddenly collapsed and died at home. Willie maintained that the shock of losing another child had caused it.

'She never got over losing our Liza. When our Michael died, it broke her heart. Sure enough, she died of a broken heart,' he stated sadly, the light gone from his eyes.

'Neither of them made it to the hospital,' Bridie had said forlornly. 'They both died so suddenly.'

Mary tried to comfort Bridie and her family, but everyone knew that Hannah had always been the warmth and soul of the Flannagan family. She would be sadly missed. Young Martha would now be the woman of the house, a big responsibility for the fourteen-year-old girl.

* * *

February 1906

'Why is it called H.M.S. Dreadnought?' John asked his father. They were in the reading room at the Denaby Institute. Jim was reading the detailed report in the *Daily Mail* about the recent launch by King Edward VII of the new warship in Portsmouth.

'Because it's such a deadly fighting machine that she will fear or dread nought, which means nothing,' Jim explained. 'She's special because of her fire power. She's the first all big-gun battleship, with ten twelve-inch guns. Each gun can fire half-ton shells that are over four feet tall and packed with high explosive.'

'Oh, so Dreadnought is a really good name for a battleship!' John agreed.

'The Royal Navy says it's a weapon of previously unimagined power,' Jim went on.

'This'll make the Germans sit up! It's a world beater!' John declared. 'Navy's done us proud again!'

* * *

April 1906

Newspapers were increasing their circulation by keeping their prices low enough for a mass market to afford them. Working class people could now keep up with national and international events much more readily than before.

The increased popularity of the *Daily Mail*, and the newer *Daily Mirror*, widened their knowledge and their views of distant places. Conversations could be shared, and opinions given on far-flung events and incidents. It felt as though the world was opening up to working folk.

Two such events had captured the imagination and interest of the world in recent weeks. These were a volcano eruption and an earthquake. On 5th April 1906, Mount Vesuvius had erupted, killing more than one hundred people and ejecting the most lava ever recorded from a Vesuvian eruption. It was especially devastating as the Italian authorities were preparing to hold the 1908 summer Olympics in the region, but funds would now have to be diverted to the reconstruction of the city of Naples and the surrounding areas. Another venue would have to be found elsewhere.

On 18th April 1906, the coast of Northern California was struck by a major earthquake. It devastated the city of San Francisco, killing more than three thousand people. Major fires burned for three days as gas pipes were broken and water sources interrupted. The many wooden structures fed the fires.

The residents said the only warning had been a twenty second foreshock, then the violent shaking had lasted only one minute. It had been named the Great San Francisco Earthquake due to its magnitude and destruction. Many people found it hard to comprehend such devastation.

* * *

December 1906

The men could not believe what they had been told.

'Gerraway!'

'Never!'

'Bloody hell!'

were some of the reactions expressed by the miners on being informed of the unexpected but satisfying news.

'I'm tellin' thee, it's rate. They've ruled in favour o' unions!' was the repeated announcement of the incredulous Union official.

'Company's not gunna like it, but fuck 'em!' was the general gleeful response. 'That'll be a surprise for 'em!'

The excited comments were to do with the passing of The Trades Disputes Act, whose official title was: 'An act to provide for the regulation of the Trade Unions and Trade Disputes.'

In effect, the act had overturned The Taff Vale Judgement of 1901, which the House of Lords had upheld, ruling that a trade union could be sued for damages caused by the actions of its officials in industrial disputes. The judgement had established that unions were legal corporates and, as such, their funds were liable for damages from strikes. This had caused uproar from the trade unions, as it had eliminated strikes as a weapon of organised labour.

The unions went on a campaign to secure parliamentary legislation that could reverse it. They realised representatives were needed as a voice for working men. The campaign resulted in many more affiliations to the Labour Representation Committee which had been formed in 1900. Many companies had court cases pending in their pursuit of damages from unions following strike action, including the Denaby and Cadeby Collieries Company.

More than four years later, the Taff Vale Judgement was overruled, with victory for the Unions. This had been swiftly brought about after the General Election earlier in 1906, when a massive swing to the Liberals resulted in ousting the Tory government.

The Liberal Party had a significant left-wing section who were keen for reform in industrial relations. They were willing to join forces with the first ever elected members of parliament in the newly named Labour Party. The twenty-nine Labour M.P.s pushed for swift reform.

Initially, the act was to prevent unions being held responsible for any financial losses incurred by a strike, but it became widened to include other aspects. The Liberal government also included some legal protection for peaceful picketing, the right of unions to strike, some degree of immunity to individual unionists and the initiation of collective bargaining, where working people, through unions, could negotiate contracts with employers to determine terms of employment, fair wages, hours of work and health and safety issues.

'Wait till I tell our John about all this!' Jim announced to Albert as they walked home from the meeting. 'He'll be in his element now he's working down t' pit.'

'Aye, he'll be like a pig in shit if I know our John.' Albert declared with a satisfied grin.

Chapter 80
February 1907

John had started work at Cadeby pit a week after leaving school. His first working day brought back memories to Jim as he remembered his own first day.

He and Walter had felt young and naïve, although they had tried to cover their nerves with false bravado. Jim knew how John must be feeling, but as usual, his son was calm and pragmatic. He had put on his work clothes, taken his snap tin and flask from his mother and prepared to step out into the early morning summer light, without any fuss or much conversation.

'See you later, son, and take care!' Mary said. John's response had been a minimal nod and a brief smile before closing the back door behind him. She had admired his controlled, matter-of-fact behaviour, although, as his mother, she knew he was competent at covering up any anxiety or negative thoughts.

John had taken to pit work with an attitude of quiet confidence and a willingness to graft. He first worked on the pit top, learning about the different processes of sifting and screening the coal. He had then progressed to working on the pit face as a coupler, attaching and uncoupling the heavy chains that linked the metal corves which were pulled up and down the roadways by the diligent ponies.

The darkness, noise and cramped conditions had at first felt alien and almost overwhelming to him, but he had applied his common sense and practical competence to quickly learn and adapt to his new surroundings.

He especially liked to watch and listen to the more experienced workers, absorbing and analysing their varying attitudes to the terms of work, mining conditions and the Company's management of everyone and everything to do with the colliery. It was immediately obvious to him that there were different kinds of workers, just by listening to their words and observing their working habits. The datallers, the men paid on a day-to-day basis, mainly for labouring jobs on the pit face, seemed to have a more casual approach to earning.

They did what they were instructed to do by the senior hewers, satisfied with a set wage, often only working when they chose, as long as they had sufficient money for their requirements.

The more ambitious colliers were keen to have a negotiated contract with their employers, enabling them to do piece work and have the opportunity to earn more money if they were willing to put in the required graft. He also noticed the differences between union and non-union men. John had been raised in a family sympathetic to trade unions, shaped by the opinions of union members like his father and grandfather, who believed in the strength and power of unions to better the lot of workers.

There was still tension between union and non-union men in the pits and in Denaby, especially since the recruitment of new workers by the Company at the end of the strike. The men knew they had to live and work in close proximity, but there was still latent acrimony quietly bubbling under the surface. The passing of the Trades Disputes Act had aroused and agitated subdued emotions, putting into sharper focus their distinct points of view.

* * *

March 1907

The morning shift workers had finished their duties and were waiting for the cage to take them back up. The assembled men rubbed the dust from their eyes and swiped sweat from their faces as they exchanged banter. The main topic of conversation was still the shock of The Trades Disputes Act being passed.

Not only were many of the men celebratory about the unions securing increased power and prestige, but they were also jubilant that managements had lost in their claims for damages incurred by strikes. To many, it represented a giant step forward for Trade Unionism and a bloody nose for management, all the more thrilling as it was so unexpected.

'Tha' could've knocked mi down wi' a feather when I 'eard! Who'd a thought that government would side wi' us instead o' t' gaffers!' one of the men declared, summing up the feelings of many of his workmates.

'I can't understand why so many men still don't want to join t' union!' one of the older miners shouted, unbothered if he annoyed or offended anybody with his bluntness.

'Because some of us 'ave got brains of our own!' was an angry reply. 'We've enough wi' t' gaffers tellin' us what to do wi'out Union officials an' all!'

'I just want to work, get mi money and not get involved wi' unions. Gaffers only get pissed off wi' 'em anyway!' another man called out.

One voice retaliated with an abrupt shout. It was John.

'I 'ave got a brain! I want to work an' earn an' all, but I don't want to be at t' mercy o' gaffers who only want coal, profits and power. It should be a fair day's work for a fair day's pay, and with better conditions. How many men have died working down t' pit? There's blood on t' coal, all right!'

'How would you know? You're still wet be'ind ears! You've been listening to your fatha and grandfatha too much!' a voice shouted back. It was Walter. 'Be a man and decide for yourself, not follow t' union all time!' he added. 'You're all bloody sheep!'

'I 'ave decided. I've decided only way we'll ever get a better life is through union solidarity. You're the one who's weak for not wanting to fight for better things!' John replied, eyes blazing, stung by Walter's comments.

'Why, you cheeky little bugger…' Walter began as other men guffawed.

'I think we've got a buddin' union official 'ere! Good for you, John, lad,' the older miner stated with a satisfied smile as they stepped into the cage.

* * *

Jim soon heard about the altercation between John and Walter.

'Proper little union speaker, your lad. And he's usually so quiet!' a workmate laughed.

'Not when it's owt to do wi' unions he's not,' Jim replied, keen to find out more about the exchange.

He finally heard the details from his reluctant son.

'He said what!' Jim's voice rang out as it increased in volume and irritation. John was shocked at his father's anger, so rarely did he display it. Jim was annoyed and upset at Walter's words, especially in front of others. He decided he would tackle Walter about it.

At the first opportunity he approached Walter, but now spoke calmly, though with intensity.

'If you've got summat to say about me, say it to mi face, not through my lad. What's got into you, Walt?'

Walter stared, steely-eyed, but remained silent. He did have words for his son and wife, however.

'You're to stay away from John Walker,' he ordered Joseph. 'And you're to keep away from Mary,' he told Esther. They both looked at him, surprised and saddened to hear his words.

* * *

June 1907

Mary was at Bridie's, anxious to find out how Eli was, after hearing the news that there had been a near accident at Cadeby pit.

'Is Eli all right?' Mary asked her friend.

'Oh, he's fine. You know Eli, nothing much bothers him. I think I've been more upset by it all!' she retorted. 'He's gone straight to the pub with Tommy Prince. Said they needed to settle their nerves. More like they're enjoying the day off!' she scoffed.

Mary saw the wet washing strung in front of the fire, the dusty floor that needed a good clean and smelled the acrid stench hovering in the air. Ben waved to her from the sofa, his permanent seat now that he was a hefty fourteen-year-old lad. She knew Bridie had her hands full, but was saddened at the state of the house. Bridie had a glazed look, as if unaware of her dirty surroundings.

'Oh, to be sure. The two of them will be in the pub telling the tale to anyone who'll listen,' she added scornfully.

* * *

Eli and Tommy were in The Pig surrounded by a large group of miners, interested in hearing about the event.

'That was a bloody close shave!' one of them declared. 'What happened?'

'It was just before two and we were in t' cage ready to go down. They locked it and released it and we started to go down but then it suddenly stopped part-way down, just hanging there, we were,' Eli began.

'Aye, it came to a dead stop, and we all thought we'd be dead if we were stuck or if it crashed down!' Tommy interrupted, wiping froth from his mouth.

'There were a right jolt when it stopped,' Eli continued between gulps of ale. 'Two hours we were hanging there – every bugger thought their time was up!'

'Ah, but it weren't all bad,' Tommy laughed. 'Them up top decided to send down summat to raise our spirits,' he added with a grin.

'Aye, lowered down brandy and some other drinks,' Eli guffawed, his teeth showing beneath his ragged moustache. He smiled to himself at the memory.

'Let's say we were all more relaxed about things after that! I was almost sorry when they managed to haul us back up!' Tommy roared. The other men laughed at this, but each also thought about the calamity it could have been, thirty men suspended halfway down one of the deepest mines in the country was not something they liked to consider.

'Turned out a cotter-pin connected to the winding gear had broken, and that caused it to stop,' Eli informed the others. 'All's well that ends well,' he summed up.

'Aye, Company weren't too pleased about it, but nobody was hurt, and we've got the day off!' Tommy concluded. 'Might as well have another pint to celebrate,' he said gleefully as he staggered to the bar.

* * *

August 1907

Rose walked along Denaby Lane, heading home from work. The August evening sun was still strong, even though it was almost six o'clock. She passed by the tennis courts at the end of the lane, near to the allotments, and decided that, one day, she would like to join the recently founded Denaby Main Lawn Tennis Club, another recreational association provided by the Company.

As she continued her walk, she passed by the new Rifle Club pavilion that had been officially opened only a few days earlier. She had gone along to the ceremony herself, interested to see the new building and the dignitaries there.

The pavilion had been generously provided by Mr Montagu of Melton Hall, himself keenly interested in rifle shooting. As he had been unable to attend the official opening, that duty had fallen to

Mrs Pope, wife of Captain Pope who was the nephew of Mr Buckingham Pope. Mr Chambers had hosted the opening and the warm weather, together with the lively atmosphere provided by the Denaby Main Ambulance Band, had made it an enjoyable occasion for everyone.

The Rifle club had been founded a few years earlier, with small ranges, also provided by Mr Montagu, and only a few members, but its increased popularity had resulted in a membership of over one hundred and the provision of the pavilion. Mr Chambers and Mr Witty, Cadeby pit's manager, were also very enthusiastic members of the club.

The red brick pavilion was built with windows adaptable for shooting from and was suitable to allow for winter use, so that the club's season could be extended practically all year round. As well as the club being for recreational pleasure, Mr Chambers had quipped that all the excellent shots in it would make Denaby one of the safest places in times of any trouble, at which the audience had laughed and applauded.

Rose suddenly had her thoughts interrupted by the calls and laughter of children playing nearby. The lovely weather had lured them to the nearest open spaces from their homes, and they were playing games or just rolling around on the soft, warm grass.

Older children had been told to take younger siblings to the woods or fields to enjoy the balmy air and golden light. Rose waved to some children she knew, but was then surprised to see John further on. He was talking to Joseph, both sitting in the shade of an old elm tree. She knew that Walter had told Joseph to keep away from John. It had enraged her father, unable to understand Walter's reasoning. But she also knew that the boys were old friends, with minds of their own.

'Rose,' John said, standing up and looking flustered. Joseph also stood up and looked at her intently. She stared back at him, and whenever she thought back to that moment, Rose would always remember the emotions that burned through her body.

Joseph was a year younger than her, and she had known him at school, but it was as if she was seeing him for the first time. He had always seemed young and immature to her, but he had changed so much. He had been working down the pit for nearly two years and in that time, he had changed from boy to man, even though he was only sixteen.

Time had moulded his boyhood features to produce a handsome young man. Their eyes locked and she was the first to smile. His face softened when he realised she was not hostile towards him. He studied her pretty face, flushed cheeks and warm smile. Tendrils of dark hair clung to her neck, damp with perspiration in the glow of the sun. John looked on, not realising the chemistry between them.

'I don't think it's right that we can't be friends,' John said, serious and defiant in his tone of voice.

'Neither do I,' Rose murmured. 'I won't tell on you.' She gave them a fleeting smile as she left them. She walked home with jumbled thoughts and a feeling of audacious excitement brewing.

PART NINE

Chapter 81
February 1908

The new year started well for Mary and her family. There was the welcome news that Bob and Winnie finally had a baby, a daughter called Maggie. It was especially poignant as Winnie had suffered two miscarriages previously, each one causing sadness and heartache. The midwife, Aggie, had shown concern about Winnie's physical ability to give birth, as she was so small and slender.

'You certainly don't have child-bearing hips,' she had told Winnie. 'But I've known other young women like you who have been fine.' Aggie wanted to reassure the young mother-to-be.

After a worrying pregnancy, Winnie finally delivered a small but healthy baby. There were tears of joy when their daughter cried for the first time.

'She may be small, but her lungs are strong!' Aggie announced. 'That's a proper lusty cry!'

Both Bob and Winnie's families were overjoyed for the couple, thankful for a healthy baby.

Albert grasped Sarah's shoulders when they heard the good news and clamped his lips into a wide smile as he looked into her eyes.

'That's five children and seven grandchildren we've got, and all healthy! We haven't done so bad, lass!'

Sarah nodded her happy agreement. 'We've a lot to be thankful for, Albert,' she whispered.

* * *

May 1908

Everyone was crying, their tears would not stop. Shock and grief stunned the people into silent disbelief. They did not want to believe what had happened. Albert, beloved father, grandfather and friend was dead. He had been killed in an accident at the pit where he had worked for forty years. He was sixty-one.

He had left the house that morning at half-past five, leaving Sarah with a smile and 'Ta-ra, lass,' as he had always done.

Sarah waved him off, silently sending a fleeting prayer that he would return safely, as she had always done.

At ten o'clock there was an urgent rap on the door. Ted Billups, a friend and neighbour, stood on the step, dirt-streaked, dust-covered, cap in hand, his face downcast. He lifted his gaze slowly to meet Sarah's worried look.

'Sarah, lass,' he began. 'There's been an accident down t' pit. Albert's in a bad way. They've taken him to Fullerton Hospital.'

'No! No!' Sarah cried as her knees buckled and her body swayed.

'Come on, let's get you sat down, lass,' Ted said, guiding her inside to a chair. 'Is your Bob in?' Sarah stared at him as if in a trance, her breath suspended as her thoughts computed his words.

'Upstairs, he's upstairs wi' Winnie and t' baby,' she managed to croak, spreading her shaking hands across her cheeks, as if steadying her thoughts.

Ted explained briefly to Sarah, Bob and Winnie about the accident.

'He was just moving along the face when there was a fall. A massive piece of stone and coal hit him from behind. We got him out as quick as we could and they took him to Fullerton.'

'I have to go to him!' Sarah cried, suddenly galvanised into action.

'I'll go wi Mam. Can you let Mary, Ivy and Gertie know?' Bob asked Winnie.

'I'll take Maggie next door to mi mam's then go and tell the girls,' she agreed quickly.

* * *

Albert was conscious but could not speak. He could hear quiet, muffled sobs. He could feel fingers gently stroking his hands, yet he felt removed, distant. Thankfully his pain had gone, replaced with blessed numbness and warmth. His eyes blinked slowly as they travelled from face to face of the people around his bed.

Ivy, his beautiful Ivy, bravely trying to smile through her tears. Such a lovely lass, he thought to himself. He hoped little Albert would grow up to be as sweet as her. Gertie, his loyal, reliable Gertie, a chip off the old block. She could be feisty at times but she was as straight as a die. She was blessed with little Annie.

Mary, his caring, dependable lass, Mary, always willing to help and a proud, proud mother. Bob, his lad Bob. A good husband, father and friend. He was a son to be proud of.

'Our Betty's coming to see you as soon as she can,' Sarah told him, as if reading his thoughts. Sarah, his darling Sarah, still as beautiful as the day he met her, beautiful inside and out. He had always thought himself a very lucky man to have had her as his wife and the mother of his children. His eyes now met hers for a loving, lingering look. She touched his face tenderly. It was like a cooling breeze caressing him.

'We'll soon have you, home, Albert. We'll soon have you better.' Albert heard her words as his body relaxed and surrendered to the blanket of comfort that enveloped his broken body.

* * *

They were all dazed as they stood in Sarah's house, still in shock from Albert's death. He had closed his eyes and breathed a series of deepening breaths until he breathed no more.

Sarah had not wanted to leave him. He had looked after her for the past forty-three years. How would she manage without him?

'We can bring him home before the funeral,' Bob had told her. She had nodded and slowly let go of Albert's hands, hands that bore numerous black scars, hands that had grafted to provide for his family, hands that had loved and caressed her all those years.

Betty looked around at her family. She had not managed to see her father before he died. That would always grieve her.

Ivy sat with her arms around her mother while Mary and Gertie made comforting cups of tea. Bob sat with Winnie, gazing at his sleeping daughter, which comforted him. Ivy shed fresh tears as she quietly announced that she had not been able to tell her father that she was expecting a brother or sister for little Albert. Sarah had squeezed her hand and managed to smile at the good news.

'He'll know, love,' Sarah whispered. 'He'll know.'

* * *

Two days later, there was an inquest at Fullerton Hospital. Representatives for the Company were present as witnesses gave evidence as to what they had seen before, during and after the accident.

The doctors had confirmed that death was due to a broken back and the ensuing shock and complications arising from the injury. The coroner had given the verdict of *Accidental Death*.

Sarah and the family members present had listened, with deep sadness and a forlorn resignation, to the evidence and the verdict. There was nothing they could do or say to alleviate their pain. Albert had suffered a sudden, brutal accident and an untimely death. One person there had muttered a promise under his breath.

'I'll try my best to change things, to make things safer, Grandad. Yet more blood on the coal,' John said as he dashed the tears from his eyes.

* * *

The funeral was over. Sarah had tried to stay strong, tried to comfort others, but it had been such an ordeal. She felt spent, exhausted. The house was quiet now everyone had gone home. Only Bob and Winnie were upstairs with baby Maggie.

Sarah sat down in Albert's chair and surveyed the room as if imagining she could still see Albert, expecting him to walk in any moment. She still could not believe that she would never see him again. Her eyes settled on his pipe, and she reached out for it. As she felt its smooth contours and smelled its distinctive earthy aroma, she was suddenly overwhelmed by her longing for him, her darling Albert.

Deep, painful, racking sobs rose and burst from her body as she gripped the pipe. Her Albert was gone, gone forever.

* * *

November 1908

Sarah smiled down at the newborn baby. Ivy had just given birth to a daughter, Emmie. It was so long since Sarah had felt any joy in her life that she did not recognise her delight.

'She's beautiful, Ivy,' she whispered, gripping her daughter's hand. 'She looks just like you when you were a baby.' Ivy smiled, exhausted but relieved and thrilled that, at the age of thirty-eight, she had delivered the baby safely. Sam was so proud.

'Your dad would be so happy for you,' Sarah said. Both women shed their tears, tears of happiness mixed with regret and longing.

Chapter 82
Summer 1909

Albert was sorely missed by all his family, friends and workmates.

'He were a grand chap, was Albert.'

'He stood no nonsense, but he 'ad a heart o' gold.'

'He were a grafter and a good family man.'

These remarks were honest and sincere from his mates, and gratefully received by his family.

Mary remembered how similar things had been said about her Grandad George when he died. She felt proud to be Albert's daughter. Life carried on, however. People still had to live, work and make the best of what they had.

Sarah was looked after by everyone as she struggled to adapt to life without Albert. The set of her features, the frailty of her stance and the ever-present sadness in her voice reflected her feelings of grief and depression, although she refrained from voicing those emotions.

Her grandchildren were her great source of solace. Seeing them thrive and develop brought her great comfort. Maggie and Emmie, still babies, provided her with a ready outlet for her maternal, affectionate nature.

'Babies need lots of cuddles and kisses,' she would often say, happy to share her love. Violet, Annie and little Albert were young school children, always ready to share their energy and chatter with their Grandma.

The older grandchildren were equally as loved, but she regarded them as young, independent adults now. Rose still worked at the Powder Works, John was still at Cadeby pit and Clarrie was a housemaid at 'The Big House', Earl Fitzwilliam's home, Wentworth Woodhouse. They all still admired their grandma and had close bonds with her.

Mary and her sisters and brother were heartened by Sarah's devotion to their children, but they could easily see how their father's death had affected her. For years, she had appeared frail yet had always kept an inner core of strength. Albert's death had sapped this tenacity. She was weakened and diminished in her attitude to life, but she was still the matriarchal figure in the family.

* * *

Rose often saw Joseph as he walked along the street or across the "backs". They would smile and nod a quiet greeting if they passed each other, but that was all.

She still remembered that day when she had seen him talking to John under the elm tree. She still remembered the powerful emotion she had felt, but it was as if any further development in their relationship was too complicated, not of the right time or place. It was as though they needed to bide their time, unsure of the future with the present circumstances of their families' hostilities.

Rose had become friendly with Fred, a fellow worker at the Powder Works. He had a sunny disposition, always happy and cheerful. He made her laugh and brightened her days, but she felt only a brotherly kind of affection for him. He, on the other hand, was very taken with her, and was hopeful that, one day, his serious feelings would be reciprocated.

Nevertheless, they had fun together, walking in the countryside, attending the local football matches and even playing bowls at the recently formed Denaby Bowling Club.

People's interest in sporting activities had been sparked nationwide by the Olympic Games held in London. The 1908 Games had been due to be held in Rome, but the eruption of Mount Vesuvius in 1906 had meant that money had to be diverted to the rebuilding of Naples and the surrounding area, and a new venue was needed.

London was approached as it had missed out on the original bid, and the race to prepare and organise the Games in such a short time was taken on, much to the pleasure of King Edward VII. A stadium was built in record time: ten months, by George Wimpey. It included running and cycle tracks, an open-air pool and facilities for track and field events. The stadium soon became known as "White City" because of the marble cladding used on the exhibition pavilions.

The Games ran from April to October in order to include some winter events. Over two thousand competitors from a record twenty-two nations were involved. Even though the summer was a washout, heavy rain turning the tracks and pitches into a mud bath and the pool water into a swampy, murky mess, the 1908 Olympics were a huge success and very well organised.

They were the first Games to award gold, silver and bronze medals, instead of the usual certificates. They were also the first Games in which all entrants had to compete as a member of a national team, rather than individually.

The opening ceremony was carried out by King Edward VII, and he was especially pleased that the Marathon started at Windsor Castle, as he had requested, so that his grandchildren could see the start of the race.

Great Britain headed the medal table, making the event highly enjoyable, although barely profitable. The nation enjoyed reading all about this special event. It captured their imagination and enthusiasm for sport.

* * *

Joseph had seen Rose and Fred walking out together, laughing and joking, happy in each other's company, and he had been shocked by his jealousy and hurt. He, too, could remember that day when Rose had looked at him in a different, special way, but he knew there would be hurdles to overcome due to the circumstances with their families.

His jealous feelings pushed him into defiant, stubborn retaliation. He began courting Betsy, a girl from the next street, who had always made it obvious that she would welcome any advances from him. At first, Joseph enjoyed spending time with her; having a girlfriend was novel to him, but he soon realised she was not the one for him. His true feelings lay elsewhere.

* * *

Autumn 1909

The last train from Doncaster pulled into Conisbrough station and two men stumbled onto the platform. Tommy Price and Eli Shaw had been drinking at their favourite Doncaster pubs near the market since early afternoon, and they had downed plenty of ale.

They had caught the one o' clock train from Conisbrough to Doncaster, happy that it was a Saturday, happy that they had money in their pockets and happy that it was a drinking day. They had ignored the overcast, misty, dank weather that shrouded the area.

'I'm goin' straight home, I've 'ad enough ale,' Eli began as they left the station, but was interrupted by Tommy's command.

'Come on, 'urry up, we can get t' last pint in before closing time at t' Station Hotel,' he said, already striding out, though none too steadily.

'All rate, just one last pint,' Eli conceded, keeping up with Tommy.

The pub was busy, with a smoky haze circulating in the dimly-lit room. The landlord looked at Tommy and Eli as they approached the bar; he knew them well. His furtive eyes assessed them, he could tell they'd been drinking, but he'd seen them a lot worse.

'Just made it for t' last pint, lads,' he said firmly as he slid their drinks across the bar. The men grasped their pints and were glad to sit down.

Tommy carried on telling Eli about his latest enjoyable episode with a woman, his words slurring and rising in volume as he spoke.

'Tha's telled me three times already!' Eli protested, but Tommy ignored him, enjoying repeating himself.

'I'm tellin' thee, it were her first time, she were only a young lass, she didn't know what to expect. But I gave her a rate good goin' over. Moanin' and screamin' she was, tellin' me to stop. But I were bloody enjoyin' it, I can tell you,' he drawled. 'She'll not be able to walk for a fuckin' fortnight!' Both men laughed as they drank their dregs of ale and lurched to the door.

'I'm off home, a tha comin', Tommy?' Eli said as the door closed behind them. His words were muffled in the damp, dense fog that blanketed the night. He strode out, his long legs straddling wide as he struggled to keep his balance.

'I'm goin' for a piss, I'll catch thee up!' Tommy called as he staggered into the field that led down to the River Don. He did not see or hear the man who followed him into the field, the same man who had overheard him in the pub bragging about his actions with the young girl.

Shortly afterwards, that man walked along the street. He was whistling a tune. Tommy Prince was nowhere to be seen.

* * *

The body was found face down in the water the next day by William Hare, the Denaby lock-keeper and his wife. He sent his wife to the police station and P.C. Brearley came to the scene. He recognised the dead man as Tommy Prince, son of Harry Prince, a deputy at Denaby pit.

* * *

News had soon spread that Tommy Prince was dead. It was received with varying emotions by the many people who knew him. His brash, vulgar nature and his heavy drinking led to many firm opinions on the circumstances of his death.

'He were allus a cocky bugger.'

'Nobody could tell 'im owt, he were allus rate.'

'I heard plenty o' stories about 'im where women were concerned.'

'Never knew when to stop drinkin'. It got 'im in t' end.'

'What wi' all that booze inside 'im and all that thick fog – no wonder he ended up in t' water.'

'He were allus a bloody hard worker, though, tha's got to give 'im that.'

Eli was still stunned that Tommy was dead. His brain couldn't take it in. He wore a constant, confused frown, as if slowly absorbing and sorting the facts.

Even Bridie felt sorry for him, though she was secretly relieved that her gullible husband would now not be so easily led into bother.

'Didn't I always tell you he'd only bring you trouble!' she chastised Eli. He pursed his lips and stared at her with his almost-black eyes.

'He were a good mate,' he said simply, but his tone was scornful, his look was withering. Bridie stared back at him, but, for once, she kept her mouth shut.

* * *

Mary and Jim were shocked to hear about Tommy's death. Although neither of them had ever liked him, it was still an unexpected and disturbing event.

'I feel sorry for his mam and dad,' Mary admitted. 'They worshipped him and he was their only child.'

Jim listened to her words and admired her generosity of spirit, but he could not forget the things he knew about Tommy Prince. He was glad Mary was unaware of them. They both knew he was arrogant and brazen, but not many knew about the even darker side to his nature.

He wondered how Walter and his family would react to the news of his death. Jim's frown deepened at such thoughts.

* * *

Ellen had been in the kitchen, preparing the Sunday dinner with her mother, when her sister, Alice, burst through the back door.

'You'll never guess what I've just heard! A body was found in t' River Don this morning, and they say it's Tommy Prince! Drowned himself, he were that drunk!'

'Never!' Peggy retorted. 'It'll just be gossip.'

'Well, somebody saw P.C. Brearley leavin' Harry Prince's house this morning, and Mrs Prince was takin' on so much, you could hear her screams all up t' street!' Alice continued.

Peggy looked at Ellen's face. It was blank, devoid of expression. Ellen returned her mother's penetrating stare with a look of steely contempt.

Inside, she was experiencing a flood of emotions, hatred, vengeance, bitterness, all entangled with an overwhelming surge of relief. She felt almost guilty for such feelings but, she had to admit to herself, that if Tommy Prince was dead, she would not be sorry. She would feel free to live her life again.

* * *

Walter sat in The Drum. He liked a drink on a Sunday afternoon. He could hear the men nearby talking about a body being found in the river.

'It's Tommy Prince. He either topped himself or he were blind drunk and fell in wi' all that fog,' one man said.

'More likely blind drunk if I know Tommy Prince. They say he'd been drinkin' in Donnie all day,' his mate replied.

'Harry Prince'll be gutted, and his missus heartbroken. Thought world o' their lad, they did.'

Walter listened to their words and continued supping his pint. He was looking forward to his Sunday dinner.

* * *

The inquest was held a few days later at The Reresby Arms. Witnesses gave evidence to the coroner and the jury.

Eli Shaw stated that he had last seen Tommy Prince outside The Station Hotel on Saturday night. He had said he would catch Eli up on the walk home but he never did. Eli had reached his home and presumed Tommy had reached his. He admitted that they had been drinking and were intoxicated.

The landlord of The Station Hotel stated that the two men, Eli Shaw and Tommy Prince, had arrived just before last orders and had only one pint each. They had then left the establishment, heading for home, he presumed.

The lock-keeper and his wife stated that they had found the body in the water on Sunday morning. They had immediately sent for the police and P.C. Brearley had arrived at the scene shortly after. He had recognised the deceased and had carried out all the necessary duties.

Harry Prince confirmed that he had identified the body as that of his son, Thomas Prince, aged 39, a hewer at Cadeby pit. He had last seen his son on Saturday morning. Tommy had said he was going to pick up his wages then travel to Doncaster with Eli Shaw.

The coroner returned a verdict to the effect that the deceased was found drowned while intoxicated, but there was no evidence to show whether his death had happened accidentally or not. Mrs Prince was heartbroken and cried for her beloved son.

Chapter 83
May 1910

'It's all deaths,' Jim stated sadly.

'I know, love,' Mary replied, clutching his arm. She knew how recent deaths had upset him. First, his Aunt Hilda had died, then his Uncle Edmund, only a few weeks later. Hilda had been complaining of bad headaches for a few weeks, then had collapsed one day and never regained consciousness. Jim was heartbroken. His beloved Aunt Hilda, so loving and loved, gone.

Edmund had taken her death very badly. They had been together for so long that he physically ached for her. Only three weeks after Hilda's funeral, he suffered a heart attack. He was rushed to Fullerton Hospital but died a few hours later.

'At least they're together again,' Jim had sighed. But his heart ached with his loss.

There had also been three fatalities, two at Cadeby pit and one at Denaby pit, all men well-known to Jim. The Cadeby deaths had both been from huge roof falls. The two miners were both mature men, married with large families. The Denaby pit fatality had resulted from an accident, the young seventeen-year-old lad crushed by heavy corves, injured terribly.

'So many bloody deaths, things have got to change!' Jim said in frustrated exasperation. John nodded his agreement.

'It's about time t' gaffers took more responsibility for their workers,' he said. 'They aren't bothered about health and safety or the poor sods who die. As long as coal production's not affected, they're happy!'

Jim nodded at his son's wise words. He believed John would, one day, help to improve conditions, such was his determination.

* * *

News of the king's death had been received with genuine shock and sorrow by the nation. King Edward VII died in Buckingham Palace on 6th May, 1910.

Newspapers described him as 'an immensely popular and affable sovereign and a leader of society.' After waiting for almost sixty years to become king, people were saddened that his reign had lasted barely nine years.

During that time, he had shown diplomatic skills, strengthening ties with Europe, and had been well-liked by his people. 'His effusive personality and likable character soon won over much of the British population,' another newspaper wrote.

His love of sporting activities, especially racing, yachting and game-bird shooting, led him into wider social circles. As a younger man, he had been criticised for his pursuit of indulgent pleasures and his playboy reputation, but as king, he was highly regarded and held in great affection by his subjects.

His death from a series of heart attacks, coupled with chronic bronchitis, was sudden and a great loss to the British public. Over 250,000 people filed past his coffin as it lay in state at Westminster Hall, and huge crowds lined the London streets to see the funeral procession.

It was the end of the Edwardian period. King George V became king.

* * *

June 1910

Rose knew what she had to do, but she was dreading it. In recent weeks, Fred had become more possessive, more intense about their relationship.

He had started talking as if it was inevitable that they would marry, settle down and have a family. But Rose knew she didn't want that. Fred was a decent, likable man, a good friend, but she didn't love him. She had also started to see another side to him. There were times when he sounded domineering and petulant, occasions when he quickly became short tempered. She realised it would be unfair to carry on their present relationship. She had to tell him it was over.

It was a warm Sunday afternoon. She had met Fred on Denaby Lane and they strolled along the canal towpath towards Mexborough. She was nervous. She didn't want to hurt Fred, but her mind was made up. It was only right to tell him her true feelings.

She finally plucked up courage when they paused on the towpath. She told him as gently as she could that there was no future for them together, but she did not expect his reaction. His usual jovial countenance disappeared, replaced with defiant, disbelieving looks.

'No, you don't mean that, Rose! You can't mean that! All this time I thought you wanted me, like I've always wanted you! You've made a fool out of me!' he rasped.

'Fred, I'm sorry,' Rose began, reaching out to touch his arm. 'I've never wanted to hurt you.' She stepped towards him, wanting to explain more, but he shrugged her away roughly, unbalancing her. She lost her footing and was falling dangerously close to the canal's edge. Then, she was aware of a voice shouting from a nearby group of men.

'Leave her alone!' She felt strong arms scooping her up, guiding her onto the towpath. She focused her eyes onto the man's face. It was Joseph. She began shaking as the fear and alarm of her fall permeated her body.

'I'm all right,' she began. 'It was an accident. I…I stumbled.' She turned to look at Fred. He was staring, taking in the situation. Joseph's arms still held her, concern and tenderness etched on his face. Fred narrowed his eyes and turned away.

'Goodbye, Rose,' he said over his shoulder. Then he walked away without a second look.

'I'll stay with her 'til she steadies up,' Joseph called to his friends, who were watching. They nodded and carried on walking back towards Denaby.

'It's a good job you were here, just at the right time,' Rose said, smiling at Joseph. He smiled back and nodded.

'He didn't take too kindly to me telling him things were over between us,' she continued, pausing to see Joseph's reaction to the news. His eyes widened and lit up.

'I know what you mean. Betsy was the same with me when we split up.' They looked at each other, both glad and relieved.

They walked back home together, both in a daze. Rose could still feel where his arms had held her, like imprints on her body.

Joseph still felt the searing emotion of his hands touching her body. Neither had experienced such emotions before.

Their conversation was shy, almost bashful, neither of them sure of what to say. But they both felt the magnetic attraction that drew them together. Neither doubted it, neither wanted anything else. It felt like a glorious beginning of something wonderful.

* * *

August 1910

Rose and Joseph grew closer and closer as the summer progressed. They tried to be together as much as possible, but their meetings had to be clandestine and discreet. They knew their families would inevitably find out about their relationship and would disapprove, but they did not care. They were in love.

Rose became adept at finding excuses to be out when she wasn't at work, citing meetings with work mates or attending various club activities. Joseph also became proficient in finding reasons to go out in his free time.

Only John became aware of their close friendship, but he assured them their secret was safe with him. He believed people should follow their own hearts and judgements.

The long, hot summer greatly enhanced their ability to take off into the surrounding countryside, always being careful in the village, however. They especially liked to wander the rural areas around Conisbrough, down Burcroft or along the riverbanks.

They would find a cosy, private spot to sit and talk, holding hands and sharing kisses, just happy to be together. The sweet-smelling grasses and meadow flowers decorated the fields and refreshed their souls. It was so good to be away from the factory and the mine, to feel the breeze and breathe cleaner air.

As well as the surrounding nature, they marvelled at the sight of the man-made structure recently built in the Conisbrough countryside. It was a viaduct, built over the River Don to transport minerals via a railway. It was part of a connection between the Hull and Barnsley Railway and those of the Great Northern and Great Eastern Railway.

It was an impressive feat of engineering. Rose counted the twenty-one arches, built by hundreds of men, using millions of bricks.

'No wonder it took four years to build!' Joseph said. 'It looks as big as Conisbrough Castle!'

'There were lots of accidents though and even some fatalities,' Rose said sadly. 'Those workmen certainly earned their money.'

* * *

'It'll soon be September. This good weather can't last forever,' Rose said. 'I don't know what I'll do if I can't be with you.' She touched Joseph's cheek, trailing her fingers lightly along his jaw, across his chin, up to his lips. They were in a shaded copse, snuggled together near the hamlet of Burcroft. She planted a delicate kiss on the tip of his nose and laughed when he pretended to sneeze.

They looked at each other then their laughter subsided. Joseph thought he could stare at Rose all day long, she was so beautiful. She reached up to run her fingers through his hair, enjoying such close contact.

'It's silly,' she said. 'I'm twenty years old and you're nineteen, we're old enough to know our own minds. We shouldn't have to hide and pretend how we feel about each other, just because of some past arguments between our families. I love you, Joseph. I always will.'

He folded his arms around her, hugging her with a protective tenderness.

'I love you, Rose and I always will.' His lips found hers and their kisses were deep, lingering, passionate, and this time they did not stop. They couldn't stop. They did not want to stop. Their bodies clung together, emotion and desire overwhelming them. Their breathing quickened, in tune with their bodies' ardent excitement, until they experienced exquisite emotions, a pinnacle of their love. Their breathing slowly recovered, their smiles gradually broadened.

'Rose, will you marry me?' Joseph whispered.

* * *

October 1910

Even though it was October, the weather was ideal for the formal opening, by Mr Chambers, of the new Recreation Ground and open-air swimming pool in Denaby.

The five-acre site was adjacent to the Denaby United football ground, not far from Denaby pit. The Company had leased the land to Denaby Parish Council, and the Council had provided £310 for the cost of the pool. It was in a corner of the Recreation Ground, screened off by wooden partitions.

The pool's depths ranged from three to five feet, with a diving platform erected at the deep end. Water would be provided by the

Company, pumped from Denaby pit. Mary, Bridie and Ellen were part of the crowd watching the opening ceremony, and were impressed by what they saw.

'At long last Denaby kids will have a proper playground instead of the 'backs' and the streets!' Mary retorted. 'It'll be safer and healthier!'

'That's right,' Ellen agreed, 'but I don't think it's fair that only men and boys can use the pool.'

'Maybe they'll let us women and girls use it one day a week,' Mary said sarcastically.

'That's equality for you!' Ellen tutted.

'Sure, it'll be great for the wee bairns to play here,' Bridie said, 'we'll have more room in the house then. We're going to need it.'

Mary and Ellen looked at Bridie, both with quizzical smiles. Bridie returned their looks and replied in a solemn tone.

'Yes, I'm expecting… again. I thought my body had done with babies. Four miscarriages in the last nine years. Maybe this will be the fifth…' her voice trailed to a stop.

Mary and Ellen didn't know what to say. They knew Bridie's delicate state of health. She had never fully recovered from the long strike, her body and mind weakened by the extreme hardships she had suffered, but all they could do was to offer her help and support.

'I miss my Mammy,' Bridie whispered. Mary thought she sounded just like she did when she was a child, the little girl Bridie, who had always been her friend.

* * *

Rose was thrilled when Joseph asked her to marry him. She accepted instantly, without any doubt, beaming her joy with a wide smile and glistening eyes. They felt so happy, so in love, despite the trouble between their families.

'We'll just have to tell them straight out,' Joseph said defiantly. 'Nothing's going to stop us.' Rose nodded, hoping that they would understand.

* * *

'Gettin' married! Gettin' bloody married! What are you on about?' Walter shouted, his eyes blazing.

Joseph peered at his father, shocked at his expression. Esther stood quietly, stunned by her son's announcement, and fearful of her husband's reaction.

'I told you to keep away from that family and you've been going behind my back,' Walter growled, shaking his finger as he spoke.

'Walter, let the lad speak,' Esther began, stepping towards him.

'You keep out of it!' Walter warned her. 'I'm tellin' you both, he's not marrying Jim Walker's lass, no way!'

'Don't talk about Rose like that!' Joseph retaliated. 'She's done nothing wrong to you. We love each other and intend gettin' wed! Why can't you accept that?'

'I'm t' gaffer in this house, and you'll do as I tell you!' Walter boomed.

'I'm nineteen, old enough to make my own decisions,' Joseph retorted. 'Why are you like this about Jim and his family?'

'I'm your father and I don't have to answer to you. You're not marrying Rose Walker!'

'We'll see about that!' Joseph shouted as he grabbed his coat and slammed the door behind him.

'Walter,' Esther cried. 'Whatever disagreements you and Jim Walker have had in the past, it's not right to be like this with Joseph. He loves Rose, she's a lovely lass.' Her words of reason were met with a cold stare.

'I told you to keep out of it, Esther.' She looked at him but just could not understand him. She sighed but said nothing more. Best to let him calm down, she decided. His angry outbursts were becoming more frequent. He seemed a troubled soul, different to the man she had married. Why was he like this?

* * *

Joseph walked the streets, his thoughts churning as he went over his father's reaction. He finally decided that he would go and see Rose and they could tell Mary and Jim everything. No more secrets, he determined.

Rose greeted him with shocked surprise, but agreed it would be best if they spoke to her parents together. Mary and Jim were stunned at the news, unable to take in what the young couple were telling them.

They couldn't believe that everything had been kept so secret, but also realised the probable trouble that would result from Walter's reaction to their news. When questioned by Jim, Joseph reluctantly admitted what his father had said and that he was against them getting married.

Jim was angry but not surprised. Walter bore grudges and was stubborn, unwilling to compromise or soften his attitude to things. Jim was torn. He was reluctant to rake up any more ill feeling between the two families, but he could not abandon his beloved Rose. She needed her family's support whether Jim and Mary agreed with the outcome or not. He decided he had to go and talk to Walter.

* * *

Jim knocked on the back door and Esther opened it.

'Is Walter in?' Jim asked. She shook her head.

'He's gone to t' Pig but he'll be back soon. He'll not miss his Sunday dinner,' she said wryly.

Jim looked at her for a moment before asking, 'What do you think about everything then, to do with Rose and Joseph? Were you as surprised as us?'

'Yes, but I think it's up to them. They're old enough to know best. But Walter won't listen to me.'

Jim nodded slowly. 'Thanks, Esther.' He turned and walked away.

A few minutes later, he saw Walter turning onto the lane that ran alongside the "backs". Even from a distance, Jim could see that Walter was swaying.

He must have had a good drink, he thought to himself. Walter wasn't aware of Jim until he heard his voice.

'What's wrong wi' my lass then, Walter. In't she good enough for your Joseph?'

'Leave it, Jim,' he warned. Jim heard the drawl in his voice. 'Just fuckin' leave it.'

'I want to know, in't she good enough?' Jim repeated.

'There's plenty o' women who'd want him. He could do better than somebody from the Walker family!'

'Don't you dare talk about my lass like that!' Jim shouted. 'Your lad couldn't find anyone better than our Rose!'

'You all think you're better than anybody else. You weren't fuckin' bothered about our Ellen before – you din't want to help me sort Tommy Prince out. Joseph'll marry your lass over my dead body!'

Jim stared at Walter. He saw the spittle flecked along his lips and the sway of his body on unsteady legs.

'Well, I think you know all about dead bodies, don't you Walter? You didn't see me at t' Station that night, but I saw you. I saw you follow Tommy Prince into the field down by the Don. Even in all that fog I saw you!'

Walter lunged at Jim in a mad rage, but Jim was too quick for him. His quick side-step left Walter on the floor, struggling to stand up. Jim grabbed him by his coat lapels.

'I've kept my mouth shut all this time, about how Tommy Prince had his "accident" all those years ago, and about how he ended up in the river. It's your turn now. You keep your mouth shut about Rose and Joseph. Let them do what *they* want, not what *you* want.'

'Are you bloody threatening me?' Walter spat out.

'Go and sober up, Walter. Think about what I've said. I'm sure you'll agree wi' me then.'

Walter stood up and stumbled away. Jim headed home, but his heart was heavy. He hated upset and confrontation, but sometimes it was necessary.

* * *

December 1910

Rose and Joseph were married in the last week of the year. In the end, there was no questioning the marriage as Rose had realised she was pregnant.

Walter had put up no further resistance to the wedding, but had refused to attend the special occasion at first. Another visit from Jim and a conversation about past events had persuaded him otherwise.

Esther was pleased that Walter had changed his mind about the wedding, but did not fully understand why. She was just thankful that Joseph and Rose were finally wed, although tension remained between the two families. Rose and Joseph were so looking forward to the birth of their baby.

Perhaps a grandchild would soften Walter's sullen attitude, Esther thought. She could only hope.

* * *

On the last day of the year, New Year's Eve, there was much rejoicing that a baby had been born. It was a boy, the son and heir of Earl and Countess Fitzwilliam, their fifth child.

The villagers in Wentworth were thrilled to hear that, at long last, it was a boy. As one of the villagers said, 'Well, after four lasses, you'd be celebratin' a lad, wouldn't you?'

Chapter 84
February 1911

William Henry Lawrence Peter Wentworth-Fitzwilliam was christened on 11th February, 1911. His title was Viscount Milton.

The 7th Earl and Countess Fitzwilliam already had four daughters, but had feared that the Earldom would go to another branch of the family if no son and heir was produced. Such was the joy and relief when baby Peter was born, that no expense was spared on the lavish christening.

'It were more like a coronation than a christening,' many of the Wentworth residents agreed.

It was held in the private chapel of the "Big House", the Fitzwilliams' mansion, Wentworth Woodhouse. Seven thousand official guests had been invited and the Park was opened to the public, where fifty thousand people attended the festivities.

The Earl was a landlord and employer to many people. His influence spread far and wide. Betty, Arthur and Clarrie attended the special event and afterwards eagerly related the entertainment and the formalities they had witnessed to friends and family.

'After the christening ceremony, Nurse Barwood held up the baby at one of the House's upper windows to show all the crowds,' Clarrie said.

'They say the baby was wrapped in a scarf given by William the Conqueror to the Fitzwilliam family,' Arthur added, very impressed with the historical detail.

'One hundred men were sent from London to erect the marquees for thousands of guests, and three hundred waiters were sent by the caterers, Lyons, by special trains, to serve the food and drink,' Betty related proudly.

'Whitworths from Wath-on-Dearne even made a special brew of ale for the occasion,' Arthur continued.

'The Earl's tenants presented a Cup to the Earl and Countess, and the miners' representatives presented them with a silver christening bowl,' Betty added. 'And the Earl gave wonderful thanking speeches.'

'There were bands and roundabouts and firework displays,' Clarrie described with shining eyes. 'They say it was the biggest firework display for five years. It included portraits of the Earl and Countess, Niagara Falls and a British battleship attacking and sinking the "dreadnought" of a foreign power. It were all wonderful,' Clarrie concluded.

'Don't forget they roasted an ox in the Park, for sandwiches. They were beautiful,' Betty declared.

'Aye. Only trouble, we had to pay for 'em,' Arthur chuckled.

* * *

May 1911

Mary was becoming more and more excited as the birth of Rose's baby drew closer. She couldn't believe that she would soon be a grandmother, and that Sarah would be a great-grandmother. They both expressed their passionate wish, so often, that Albert was still with them.

'He would've been so proud to be a great-grandad,' Sarah said sadly. She missed him so much.

Rose and Joseph were very happy. They had managed to get their own pit house, only a few streets away from Mary and Jim. Friends and family had clubbed together to help the couple get basic furniture and furnishings.

Esther had devoted a lot of her time to cleaning and running the house for Rose as her pregnancy progressed. She, too, was looking forward to being a grandmother. Walter preferred to stay in his own house and keep his distance.

Bridie had recently given birth to a boy, Declan. It had been such a long, difficult birth. She had feared major complications, like she had experienced with Ben, but, in the end, Declan was born small but healthy. Bridie was exhausted.

'I'm thirty-nine,' she said to Mary. 'And this has got to be my last baby. I just couldn't go through it all again.' She started weeping, completely spent.

'You'll soon feel better when you get your strength back,' Mary tried to comfort her. She knew how much Bridie missed her mother Hannah. Bridie was already not listening, remote and unresponsive.

* * *

Rose's screams could be heard throughout the house, and beyond. They were not screams of childbirth. They were screams of anguish.

Mary watched as Joseph folded his arms around his heartbroken wife and rocked her gently, back and forth. Their tears mingled as the full realisation hit them. Their baby was dead. He had been born dead. He had never breathed, never cried, never moved. He was perfectly formed, beautiful, but dead.

Aggie, the midwife, had done everything that she could, but had then gently wrapped him in a swaddling blanket and placed him in the small wooden cot at the side of the bed. Jim had lovingly made the cot for his grandchild.

They now waited for the doctor to arrive and attend to all the formalities of a stillbirth. Tears flowed freely, hurt and disappointment seared keenly.

'Why? Why?' Rose cried. 'What did I do wrong?'

Everyone tried to comfort her, but she was in despair.

Mary felt so, so sad. Sad for herself, sad for Jim and Sarah, but most of all, sad for Rose and Joseph. She leaned over to gaze at the baby. Tears dripped from her face and moistened his blanket with her sorrow. She knew she would have to be strong for everyone. She hoped she had the strength.

* * *

Summer 1911

Life in Denaby continued. Families experienced times of sadness, difficulty, worry and joy, all intermingled with other people's circumstances and affairs, like threads woven to create a tight, strong material.

People mainly looked out for each other, giving help and support where they could, and when it was needed. Families stuck together, finding happiness and security from shared moments, both small, as well as significant.

Wives supported husbands, daughters supported mothers, fathers supported sons. From these small things, bigger things grew, widening in size and importance.

The summer of 1911 brought a time of "Great Unrest" in the country. There was a new king, a government with ever-changing views, and socialism was gaining support, spreading as the workers became unwilling to accept their lot.

They did not like the terrible working conditions imposed on them; they could not tolerate the overbearing discipline at work, and wages had not kept pace with rising prices. Their money bought less than it had ten years ago.

This new mood amongst the British working class brought about such unrest that the country was rocked by national strikes. For the first time, the railway workers went on a national strike. Dockers and transport workers followed, shaking the government and upper classes to the core.

They realised how damaging sustained strikes could be. The rise of the working class, and increased power to their union representatives, could seriously affect the stability of the country.

John absorbed all this information that he read in the national newspapers and smiled.

'Didn't I tell you that solidarity would give us power?' he said to his father. 'Bloody gaffers will have to sit up and listen to us now. Tide's turning.'

Jim nodded. He was right about his son. John had always been right about what he saw in the workings of Trade Unionism. He felt proud of him, although anxious at times.

* * *

Autumn 1911

Bob still missed Ginger, his beloved pit pony. The usually steady pony had one day stumbled while hauling tubs, breaking a leg and getting a foot stuck in the points of the rails. Bob could see the animal's agony and knew what must be done, but not by him.

The horse-keeper was summoned, and he acted swiftly to humanely put down the distressed pony. Bob was left to mourn the loss of his longtime friend and work companion. The bonds between them had been long and sustained, but Bob hadn't realised their depth and strength until they were gone.

Bob had been asked if he wanted to transfer from Denaby pit to Cadeby pit, partly to start working with a new horse there, but also because his experience was required.

New major protective legislation had recently been introduced into the safeguarding of pit ponies. Many protest groups had been campaigning that the existing legislation was not sufficient for the care of the hardworking mining horses.

Even Harry Lauder, the popular Scottish singer and comedian became an outspoken advocate 'pleading the cause of the poor pit ponies' to Sir Winston Churchill, an acquaintance of his. This resulted in the Royal Commission Report of 1911, commonly known as 'The Pit Ponies' Charter', a detailed set of mandatory rules.

Bob had been given the Charter to read and digest, and he was impressed with its detailed content.

'The Pit Ponies' Charter'

1) Ponies had to be at least 4 years old before they could start working underground.
2) Every horse had to be examined at least every 12 months by a veterinary surgeon.
3) If certified permanently unfit for work, the pony had to be brought to the surface.
4) Each horse had to be housed in a stall adequate in size, and supplied with clean straw or other suitable bedding.
5) All stables had to be cleaned daily and kept in a sanitary condition.
6) The stables should be separated from the main roads, adequately lit and well ventilated.
7) Only one horse to a stall.
8) Each stall to have a drinking trough and a manger.
9) There must be one horse-keeper to every 15 horses.
10) There must be a sufficient, dust-free supply of food and water.
11) Medicines, dressings and suitable appliances for destruction must be readily available.
12) No horse should work more than two shifts in 24 hours, or three shifts in 48 hours.

Bob had decided to transfer to Cadeby pit and was keen to work on carrying out the new mandatory rules. He knew some miners still occasionally mistreated the horses, and he was determined to maintain the high standards written in the Charter. Not everyone was totally in agreement, however.

'Hosses get better looked after than us,' some men grumbled.

PART TEN

Chapter 85
January 1912

The new year had brought some very welcome news for Mary and her family. Rose was pregnant again. This hoped-for news had lifted everyone's spirits. Sarah hugged her granddaughter.

'That's wonderful news, lass,' she whispered, a sob catching in her throat. Everyone was delighted, but Mary knew Rose's real concern was that there could be problems once again with this baby. There was nothing they could do but wait, hope and pray for a healthy baby.

News of another pregnancy had not been received with such joy. Mary was astonished when Bridie informed her that she was expecting again.

'Oh, Bridie, my love!' Mary declared, not really knowing what to say. Bridie had shown little emotion, neither delight nor dismay. She seemed impassive, undemonstrative, resigned.

'I'll be forty years old. I don't think I can do it all again,' were her few words.

'You've got your Maria at home to help you with everything, and Louisa when she's not at school. They're grand lasses. And the twins are working now,' Mary tried to reassure her.

But Bridie had a sad, vacant expression, as though even the thoughts of her duties and responsibilities overwhelmed her. Mary could understand to some degree, as she also was feeling the strain of constant work and toil.

'We are forty,' she said to herself, but she did not envy Bridie's pregnancy. She promised herself that she would try to help her friend even more than before.

* * *

March 1912

The Denaby miners were feeling agitated and unsettled. The rumours of an impending strike were increasing, circulating into the hearts and minds of the colliers. This was not talk of a regional strike, however, but the growing prospect of a national strike, the first ever by mineworkers.

'I tell thi, Derbyshire and Nottinghamshire came out a few days ago. You mark my words, we'll all be out soon!'

That miner's prediction became true. On 1st March 1912, almost one million miners walked out, the most in any industry in Britain.

The aim of The Miners' Federation of Great Britain was to secure a minimum wage for all miners. The strike was nicknamed the 5's and 2's, as the Union was asking for a minimum wage of five shillings per man per day, and two shillings per boy per day.

There was no standardised minimum wage across the mining industry, and the existing complicated wage structure made it difficult for a miner to earn a fair day's pay. Earnings were based on price lists, which gave amounts per task, based on a standard ton of coal from the face, but prices differed between collieries and companies. This would be the first time that miners had combined to add significant power to their strike.

British trade was so dependent on coal, that the effects of the strike were felt immediately across the country. Transport was especially affected, causing considerable disruption to train and shipping schedules. The majority of train services had to be cancelled. The Prime Minister, Herbert Asquith, soon realised that quick, decisive action was required.

He persuaded his Liberal government to rush through the 1912 Coal Mines Act (The Minimum Wage Bill), so that the strike could be ended. After only forty days on strike, the emergency coal bill resolved the strike, and the miners voted to return to work.

Not all the Union's demands had been met, however. They did not get the 5's and 2's requested. Instead, the Minimum Wages Act stipulated that, in future, minimum wages were negotiated by local boards with a neutral chairman.

On 6th April 1912, the miners returned to work divided, many with ongoing grievances. There was still inequality between rich and poor, luxury and squalor and capital and labour.

'This is only the bloody beginning,' John said with a gleam in his eye. 'We've seen what national solidarity can achieve. We're not gunna stop now. We've got a taste for winning. Let's see what we can do in t' future.'

* * *

April 1912

The newspapers were full of the story. The Royal Mail Steamer (R.M.S.) *Titanic*, the world's largest ship, had sunk only four days into her maiden voyage from Southampton to New York City. The ship collided with an iceberg on 14th April, and sank in the North Atlantic Ocean in the early hours of 15th April.

People were incredulous that such a disaster had happened. The ship had sunk in two hours forty minutes. The twenty lifeboats had been completely inadequate. People who jumped or fell into the water had either drowned or died within minutes from "cold shock".

'One thousand five hundred people died, it beggars belief!'

'Poor buggers, they didn't stand a chance!'

* * *

May 1912

John chased the drizzle of gravy on his plate with his remaining mouthful of bread. Only when he was sure that the plate was absolutely clean, was the bread deposited into his accepting mouth.

'Thank you, Lord for the food we've had, if there had have been more, I would've been glad,' he declared, followed by a loud, forced belch.

'John!' Mary rebuked her son. 'Manners!'

He grinned at his mother.

'It's a sign of appreciation, Mam!' he mocked, still smiling.

'Think yourself lucky you've had this,' Jim chided. 'Rabbits don't catch themselves, you know.' His voice was etched with nagging criticism towards his son, but it was also mixed with his own feelings of inadequacy and trampled pride, that his family still had to go hungry at times.

Recognising the signs of possible impending friction, Mary tried diffusing tactics as she cleared the table.

'We're still gettin'' over the strike. Thank God it was only six weeks, but that's still a long time wi' no wages. I think your dad did a good job poachin' – it kept our bellies full.' Jim threw her a grateful smile, his irritation easing with her praise.

'It's havin' good neighbours an' all,' he added. 'Bill and Jack gave us taties and cabbages. Thank God for the allotments!'

John stood up abruptly, rattling the table in his frustration.

'We shouldn't have to rely on poachin' and charity from neighbours! If t' gaffers paid us a proper wage in t' first place, we wouldn't have to keep gettin' over strikes!'

Jim eyed his son with a resigned expression.

'I agree, son. I'm all for the unions, but what's use of 'em winning if we end up wi' no jobs and no houses?'

John sighed deeply and looked at his parents. He acknowledged that they were decent, honest, hardworking people, but, by God!, they'd been almost brainwashed into submission after forty years' living and working in a Company-owned village. He wanted more.

'Thank God for Lloyd George,' John retorted. 'He's got all the rich bastards, who've been exploitin' us for so long, shitting themselves with his talk of distributing wealth, and a welfare state.

It's about bloody time some of their money came down to us. Even Royalty are havin' to think about fairer conditions for the workers!'

'John!' Mary winced. 'Where have you got all this from? Talk like that's askin' for trouble! Don't you go blabbin' and makin' life harder for us!'

Both Mary and Jim grudgingly admired their son's passion and confidence, but they were old enough and experienced enough to feel uncomfortable with such open dogmatic opinions.

Their thoughts were suddenly interrupted by Violet opening the back door so quickly that she almost fell onto the table.

'You'll never guess what!' she exclaimed, her eyes wide and shining. 'King and Queen are coming!'

* * *

Violet was, indeed, correct. The King and Queen were coming. No one had believed the rumours at first, that King George V and Queen Mary were actually going to travel to South Yorkshire to see the people, the villages and the workplaces of ordinary working-class subjects. The newspapers had reported, however, that this was the wish of their Majesties.

'This'll be a first!' John declared, scathingly.

'Well, I think it's wonderful!' Violet retorted.

The King and Queen were to stay at Earl and Countess Fitzwilliam's mansion in Wentworth, a house literally fit for a king. They would be able to tour the area during their four-day visit, yet still be lavished with supreme opulence.

'They say the King's even goin' down one of Fitzbilly's pits! First time ever an' all!' some disbelieving miners related to each other.

Mary's sister, Betty, had confirmed, in her best whispering tone which suggested secrecy, that their Majesties would, indeed, be staying at the "Big House". Clarrie had revealed all the extra work that she and the other housemaids were doing in preparation for the historic visit.

'To think, our Clarrie will be under the same roof as King George and Queen Mary!' Betty had breathed, shaking her head in disbelief.

'Aye, she might even get a glimpse of 'em,' Arthur chuckled. 'In between all t' work.'

* * *

June 1912

Mary had tried her best to keep her promise. She helped Bridie as much as she could, running errands, seeing to Ben and minding baby Declan when Bridie was especially withdrawn and depressed. Maria was also a great help to her mother.

The fifteen-year-old girl shouldered a lot of the work required to run the household, as well as managing paid jobs cleaning in the more affluent Denaby houses.

A row of new houses had been built in Tickhill Square only two years previously. Built for the colliery officials, they were envied by many. The eight pairs of semi-detached houses had walled gardens to the front, side and rear of each house, with attached coal places at the back. The three rooms and scullery downstairs represented luxury to other Denaby residents, as did the three bedrooms and bathroom upstairs. Maria had gained a cleaning job at one of the houses initially, followed by the others, each housewife desiring the status of 'having a maid', even if it was only Bridie's lass for a few hours.

Louisa also helped her mother with the housework and taking care of her brothers. But there was an air of sadness and reticence about the eleven-year-old. She was a quiet, brooding girl, much like her father. She hated the constant grime and chaos in the house. She craved order and cleanliness.

Most of all, she hated the pall of aloof melancholy that veiled her mother. There was little laughter, few smiles and restrained affection from both her mother and father. She yearned for a happier family life.

* * *

Bridie gave birth to a girl, Lottie, on the last day of May. The labour had been short and swift, surprising Bridie and Aggie, the midwife, with the speed of the birth. The baby was very small and seemed quite weak, but Bridie was just relieved it was over. Eli had glanced at this new daughter and frowned.

'She's a little 'un, not like t' others,' he said.

Bridie had been irritated by his comment, but she knew he was right. She did seem so small and fragile.

* * *

The baby had proved hard to settle, grizzling and whimpering as if constantly protesting. Bridie would feed her and lay her down, but within minutes the crying would start again. She produced wailing bleats as if uncomfortable and exhausted.

Maria and Louisa took turns at rocking her, back and forth, willing her to settle and sleep, but it was Bridie who had to give her continual attention and nursing. Mother and baby quickly became impatient, exhausted.

Eli would scowl, slam doors and disappear outside, anything to get away from the crying. It didn't occur to him that he could help. Bridie was always so glum and gloomy, hardly wanting to even speak to him. He felt neglected and rejected. It was easier to go to work, go to the pub and go to bed.

His almost-black eyes would narrow and glaze over with his hurt and bewilderment. He didn't know how he could make her happy.

* * *

Mary's concentration was broken by her awareness that she was being watched. Her eyes lifted from the mound of dough that she was kneading and knuckling on the kitchen table. She saw Louisa standing in the doorway, her face impassive but her eyes fixed and staring.

'She looks so like Bridie,' Mary thought to herself. 'With the same chestnut-gold hair, the same grey eyes, and even the same sprinkling of freckles.'

'Mi mam says can you come quick – babby's had an accident.'

Louisa's monotone voice interrupted Mary's thoughts abruptly.

'Of course I'll come, love,' Mary said, wiping floured hands down her apron. Alarm made her movements jerky, but she mustered a smile for the poor girl.

'What's happened?' Mary began, but her question was lost to the departing girl, already striding out along the "backs", heading for home.

They reached the house within minutes. The scuffed, peeling back door was open, allowing pungent odours to escape and contend with the stink of the middens outside. The hot, still air only intensified the heavy stench that hovered everywhere.

Mary followed Louisa into the living room, adjusting her eyes to its shady dullness. A fire struggled to burn in the grate, casting flickering light around the room. The stench and squalor in the room never failed to shock Mary, despite her own humble background.

Hearty guffaws punctuated the air, followed by rhythmic banging and clapping. Ben had seen her, and this was his usual greeting. He was on the faded, red sofa, stained with patches of every shade of brown where dirt, sweat and a host of substances had been deposited.

It was Ben's chair, his bed, his life, except when older lads wheeled him around the lanes in his wheel-barrow chair. He waved to Mary, saliva dripping from his laughing mouth.

Pitiful, staccato whimpers were suddenly heard. Louisa stood watching as Mary turned to find their source. There, on the floor, lay baby Lottie. Her tiny hand was quivering in unison with her cries. Mary stepped closer, disbelieving, peering intently at the floor, where the flames flicked their light. Trickles of blood stained the floor. There, beside the baby, was a tiny fingertip, completely separated from the finger. Mary gasped in horror and scooped up the injured child, gently cushioning her to her breast. She looked up and was shocked to see Bridie standing in the shadowy doorway, silent but watching. In her hand was a rag, speckled with her baby's blood.

* * *

Baby Lottie was taken to Fullerton Hospital. Mary accompanied Bridie, who was still in a stunned daze, neither speaking nor crying. It was as if she was in suspended animation, removed from reality. The doctor and nurse had questioned her about the circumstances of the injury, and eventually she responded, shaking her head slowly.

'I don't know how it happened. I don't know,' she repeated, still shaking her head in bewilderment.

'Why on earth did you put the baby on the floor?' Dr Twigg demanded, peering at Bridie through his spectacles, waiting for a plausible explanation.

'I don't know why she was on the floor. I don't know who put her there,' she answered in a thin, flat voice.

Dr Twigg looked at Mary, then at the nurse before pursing his lips.

'You must take better care of your baby,' he stated in clear, clipped tones. 'You cannot put such a young baby on the floor in a house full of people and dangers. I will be supervising this baby in future.'

Bridie looked down at Lottie, now sleeping, her wound bandaged, and nodded slowly and glumly. Her dulled eyes shed silent tears of fear and remorse.

Chapter 86
Monday 1st July 1912

'Will the King be wearing his crown? And will the Queen be wearing a diamond tiara?' Violet asked her mother excitedly.

'Eeeh, I don't know!' Mary laughed. 'You'll have to wait and see, won't you!' They were sorting and "turning" clothes, ready for the routine of the Monday morning washday.

'I can't believe that this time next week, we'll be going to Conisbrough Castle to see the King and Queen!' Violet announced with a marvelling expression.

'I think that's the third time you've said that!' Mary teased, happy to see her daughter so thrilled and animated.

South Yorkshire folk were looking forward to the Royal Visit and anticipation was mounting. The children from the local Conisbrough and Denaby schools had been invited to attend the special occasion, so parents had also become very enthusiastic.

'Sam says that's all his customers are talking about at the shop,' Ivy said. 'And our Albert can't wait! It's a pity our Emmie is a bit young, but I'm sure she'll enjoy everything.'

'Our Annie can't wait either,' Gertie laughed. 'And Charlie's always on about it! Bet you lots o' folks will make it a red letter day and have a laiker!' she added with a grin.

'What with t' King and t' Queen coming and our Rose having the baby in a couple o' weeks, there hasn't been so much to look forward to for a long time!' Mary concluded.

'Aye,' Gertie grinned. 'It's not every day you get to see royalty or become a grandma!'

* * *

Monday 8th July 1912 – Wentworth

The excitement was almost palpable in the balmy air of the summer's day. The Royal Visit was imminent, the preparations were almost complete. The local people of Wentworth, Elsecar and nearby villages could hardly believe that the King and Queen would soon be arriving.

Amongst the stream of people striding towards the "Big House" were Betty and Arthur, glowing with pride and delight. Employees of Earl Fitzwilliam, or Fitzbilly as he was affectionately known, were invited to see the results of the enormous effort that the staff had made to ensure that the House and gardens were exquisitely beautiful for King George V and Queen Mary, as well as the other privileged invited guests.

As Arthur was still a miner at the Earl's pit, and Clarrie a housemaid at the mansion, they were doubly qualified to receive the honour of stepping briefly into the elevated world of their superiors.

Betty and Arthur shuffled in line as they were ushered down various corridors and through numerous rooms until they eventually reached the State Dining Room. The "Big House" looked impressively huge from the outside; it was, after all, one of the longest private houses in Europe, but the inside also caused people to marvel at what they saw.

As their eyes travelled the full length of the room, 'Oohs' and 'Aahs' escaped their lips. The furniture, the flowers and the tableware produced comments quietly chorused by the passing line of villagers.

'My word, I can't believe it! Look at that!'

'This really is fit for a king!'

They absorbed the beauty and unbelievable intricacy of the set tables, each storing a treasure of details. The golden sheen from the cutlery and ornamental dishes caressed the crystal decanters containing various wines.

The roses provided delicate perfume and rich colour, contrasting with the fresh green of the ferns. The sparkling drops of the chandeliers bathed everything in a luminous lustre. They could only imagine what sumptuous food would be served in such magnificent surroundings.

'Wait till I tell everyone about this,' breathed Betty with radiating relish.

'Aye, it's a fine spread they've put on, I'll say that,' granted Arthur. 'And to think our Clarrie is part of all this,' he concluded with a satisfied grin.

'Yes, Clarissa Maud is very lucky to work here,' declared Betty with overwhelming delight at her daughter's good fortune.

Although these employees recognised their feudal rankings as workers and minions, they appreciated being included in special occasions. The relationship with their employers created feelings of pride and respect rather than bitterness or disdain.

Betty and Arthur relished both the anticipation and expected special memories of the historic event about to happen in their village. It felt a million miles away from Denaby.

* * *

Monday 8th July – Denaby

A steady flow of people sauntered along the Denaby streets, all heading for Conisbrough Castle. The special day had finally arrived; the King and Queen would be arriving at the Castle in a matter of hours. Few people wanted to miss this momentous event, and the hot summer weather encouraged them to leave their homes early that afternoon, with plenty of time to walk the mile and a half journey to the Castle grounds.

Mary and Jim chatted with Rose and Joseph as they strolled towards Conisbrough. Although heavily pregnant, Rose had insisted on accompanying them.

'I wouldn't want to miss this! Don't worry, I'm fine,' she reassured everyone. Jim had even decided to miss his morning shift, stating that the occasion was too special to miss.

Gertie, Charlie, Sarah and Ivy walked behind them, taking turns to carry little Emmie, feeling unusually festive and light-hearted. Bob and Winnie completed their group.

Bob had been off work with a broken toe, but he felt the journey to Conisbrough would be well worthwhile and he would enjoy the gentle exercise.

John had refused to join them, adamant that he had no interest in seeing royalty. He couldn't understand what all the fuss and expense was all about. He had scorned what the newspapers had written about the reasons for the visit.

'Their Majesties wish to acquaint themselves with the lives, work, and homes of their industrial subjects.' He thought it was more likely that they knew it was time to listen to the many grievances of their "subjects" before unrest and trouble spread.

Nearer to the Castle, hundreds of people lined the route and crowded on the grassy slopes of its grounds. Colourful bunting and waving flags contrasted with the clear, blue sky and the grey stone of the ancient building.

The keep soared, high and mighty, solid and secure in its surroundings. Thousands of children stood inside the Castle gates, eager to spot their mothers and fathers as well as the expected royalty.

Excited chattering bubbled and flowed around the gathered crowds, like simmering water in a pot. High-pitched children's voices periodically spiked the air, followed by a steady hum of laughter and deeper voices exchanging opinions of what to expect.

'They say King George is short, wi' not much meat on 'im, a bit sickly-looking.'

'Aye, and that they're called George and t' Dragon 'cos Queen Mary's allus strict and never smiles.'

'Well, I think Her Majesty is a fine-looking woman from her pictures in t' paper.'

The strong sunshine and the density of the crowds combined to make foreheads perspire and cheeks redden. Everyone wanted a good view of the expected party, and gazes turned to scan the road that skirted the Castle grounds.

A white marquee had been erected in the area directly in front of the Keep's steps. Carpet and potted plants had been pegged onto the entrance, together with a muslin curtain that shielded the inside table, festooned with flowers.

'They say Earl Fitzwilliam sent the tent over from t' "Big House" so's King and Queen can 'ave a cup o' tea in there,' one old lady remarked.

'Aye, they'll be parched in this heat! I know I am!' nodded her friend.

There was suddenly the sound of distant roars travelling from the nearby Doncaster Road.

The royal entourage had been scheduled to travel from London to Doncaster by special train, then to proceed by motor car to Wentworth, stopping off at Conisbrough for a brief visit and refreshments. Flattened hands shaded squinting eyes, trying to spot a motorcade between the distant trees that lined the road.

'They're 'ere! King and Queen's 'ere!' shouted a group of boys standing on the stone wall that edged the road.

Hearts started beating faster and necks were craned as people watched the line of twelve motor cars slowly nearing the Castle.

Five of the cars turned up to the Castle gates, while the others continued on their journey to Wentworth. Deafening cheering began, together with the frenzied waving of flags, hats and hankies, all offering greetings to the special dignitaries. People stood on tiptoes, desperate to get a view of George and Mary.

The open Daimler glided to a stop and the King and Queen stepped out. There was a brief, stunned hush as though the people were shy and disbelieving that these monarchs, such remotely revered icons, could actually be within their sight and presence.

Then, just as abruptly, there rose a crescendo of cheering as Earl Fitzwilliam introduced Mr Lowry Cole to their Majesties. Mr Cole was the agent to Countess Yarborough, owner of Conisbrough Castle, and he would be conducting the royal tour of the ancient monument.

All eyes were on the royal couple as they led the cortege up the shingle path to the gate of the Keep. The King was dressed in light grey, with a red and black tie. His brown bowler hat was lifted and extended from side to side in continuous acknowledgement of the rousing cheers of the welcoming people.

As he bowed his thanks, the sun glinted from the gold watch-chain looped across his waistcoat, which folded neatly beneath his jacket. His white spats over brown boots brought admiring glances.

'They're right, he is short and slight,' one old man remarked.

'And pale-looking,' his friend agreed.

Queen Mary was exquisitely dressed in a pale blue fitted jacket with a ruffle-edged neckline. Her white-gloved hands held a closed parasol and gathers of her long, full skirt. Her wide-brimmed hat was festooned in silken roses, and perfectly balanced her statuesque, hourglass figure.

'My, she really is a fine-looking woman!' was heard many times.

The royal couple proceeded towards the Keep, Queen Mary bowing graciously in acknowledgement of the great reception bestowed on them. She paid special notice to the children, some ranged almost at her feet.

At the steps of the Keep, hundreds of local miners had been lined up to greet them. Jim was one of them. He saw the King's bagged eyes and even the lay of his beard and moustache, he was so close. He marvelled at his smooth, white hands, unmarked by scars or ingrained dirt.

The King toured inside the Keep, especially interested in its remarkable stone fireplaces and stone ovens. He also enjoyed the wide-ranging views when looking out from the top of the Keep.

A huge roar erupted when the Royal Standard flag was hoisted. It marked the first time the Castle had been visited by a reigning monarch since King John's visit in 1201.

Queen Mary had reluctantly declined the Keep's tour as she was recovering from a foot injury. Instead, she enjoyed refreshing tea in the marquee.

All too soon the visit was coming to an end. George and Mary stated their thanks and appreciation for such an educative, enjoyable visit, and gave their final bows. They stepped into their motor car and departed for Wentworth. The crowds gave final 'hurrahs' and enthusiastic waves until the Daimler was out of sight.

Then the school children mingled with their relatives, keen to relate their delight as they headed home. Violet, Albert, Annie and Maggie all voiced their utter enjoyment of the unique occasion.

'It was just like being in a dream, Grandma!' Violet said to Sarah.

The old lady looked at her children and grandchildren.

'It'll be something you'll always remember,' she said. 'I know it will stay in my memory for as long as I live!'

'Yes, Mam, it was a momentous day for Denaby and Conisbrough folk,' Mary agreed. Everyone smiled, nodded and agreed as they made their way home in the glowing heat of late afternoon.

* * *

Joseph was in a bad mood. His thoughts relived the argument he'd had with Rose before leaving for the night shift. Sullen anger was mixed with hurt and regret. The day had been so special. A holiday atmosphere had bathed Conisbrough and Denaby in an unfamiliar feeling of excitement and wellbeing. The hot, sultry weather had intensified the special feel of the day. Everyone had been so excited, especially the children.

The Co-op had done a brisk trade in Union Jacks and bunting, prompting good natured, sardonic grumbling from older folk.

'It's a good job King and Queen only come once!'

Joseph realised now, as he stepped from the cage, that he'd been carried along by the holiday atmosphere, and the few pints of ale he'd drunk earlier on.

He had wanted to stay at home instead of working his usual night shift, arguing it was a special day. Rose had disagreed; she had other ideas, saying they needed the money, especially as the baby was due soon.

Tempers had flared and harsh words had been exchanged, resulting in his stomping out without their usual goodbye hug and kiss. Regret and guilt had washed over him, even before he reached the pit.

'Your lass not lettin' you 'ave a laiker then!'

'Are you under t' thumb?' some of his mates quipped sarcastically as they headed towards their districts.

Joseph had grinned, but said nothing. The pit was strangely quiet. So many miners had decided to miss their afternoon and night shifts because of the special occasion.

'Not even half usual turnout,' Jack, the lamp man summed up.

Joseph was walking towards the east district when he was called back by Deputy Jackson.

'Change for you tonight, lad. There's that many off, we need you to work in t' South District. You can team up wi' Bert Sutherland.'

Joseph headed for the South District, a much longer walk than he was used to. He was keen to start his road laying duties. He wanted physical exertion to relieve some of his frustrations. How could he have argued with Rose like that? Shame and remorse oozed from his body along with sweat and dirt.

Sun, ale and excitement was a rare combination for him, and perhaps that was a good thing, he thought to himself.

* * *

'Not having a shift off for t' King then, John lad?' Willie Anderson laughed as he fell into step with his mate. They were crossing the bridge, heading to Cadeby pit for their night shift. The air was still heavy with a humid heat, even though the sun had dipped to leave only the faint light of dusk. Both men already had films of sweat on their brows.

'Not likely!' John retorted. 'Daft buggers them who went to gawp at him,' he added. The awe and mystique of royalty completely eluded him. He was a new breed of 'subject', the kind who viewed bosses and gentry as the enemy, out to fleece the workers for as much as they could.

Royalty, to John, was part of the unfair division of the classes, the unfair division of wealth and power. Willie shared the same views, both sceptical of the Royal Visit.

'All these strikes since he came to t' throne's put wind up 'em all right,' Willie agreed.

'Aye, just you wait. One day we'll all come out. Not just dockers or railway men or miners – all on us together!' John declared with conviction.

The men got their lamps and waited for the cage.

'It's so fuckin' quiet! Where is everybody?' Willie guffawed. Their descent completed, they began their walk to the South District.

* * *

Rose was feeling upset and restless. She, too, was feeling guilty and sorry for the harsh words she had exchanged with Joseph. He was always so caring and thoughtful, even when he felt upset with how his father treated them. She shouldn't have been so stubborn and thoughtless. Why couldn't he have a shift off now and again? He was always so hardworking and conscientious.

They had so enjoyed their day out at the Castle. It was a truly memorable occasion, a day of happiness and celebration to break the monotony of work and worry. She sighed deeply, frustration producing tears that she slowly wiped away.

It was the first time he'd left for work without saying goodbye and kissing her. She so loved him. She hoped he would forgive her. She stood up slowly, weary and deflated. It was time for bed, time to rest. She gently stroked her stomach.

The table tidied and the fire covered in slack, Rose started to climb the stairs. Her legs felt heavy, just like her bulging belly. Each step felt extra steep, almost winding her. She was surprised to feel a griping pain rippling along her body. She lay down on the bed, thankful to relax and sleep.

Chapter 87
Tuesday 9th July 1912

It was nearly two o'clock. The night shift was halfway through. Joseph and Bert had eaten their "snap" and were taking their welcome swigs of cold tea. The sweltering heat of the tunnel, together with the strenuous work of road laying, quickly resulted in profuse sweating and persistent thirst.

The two men were working on the extreme edge of the South District, well away from the other workers further down the plane. It was strangely quiet.

Both men were used to working alongside groups of miners, with the noise of banter and clanking shovels breaking the oppressive silence, cutting through the long hours of toil. The reduced workforce had resulted in the men being spaced out along the plane.

The only evidence of life in the darkness beyond were the muffled shouts and scrapings of the men further down the plane. It all felt unusual.

Joseph's thoughts had strayed to Rose again, when something strange and different happened. Both Bert and Joseph felt a "puff of air", a reversal of the air flow, and then a sudden increase of heat. Dust from the floor lifted, filling the air.

'Bloody hell!' Joseph cried out as he turned to look at Bert. They both stopped working, suddenly nervous and anxious.

'I don't fuckin' like this!' Bert boomed. Even though he was older and more experienced than Joseph, both men feared that something was wrong. They looked at their lamps and saw that the flames had changed. They were now thin and blue.

'I think there's been an explosion somewhere on the plane!' Bert shouted, but his voice was swallowed up by the dust and darkness.

Neither man could settle, both were on edge. They knew that the "puff of air" could indicate there had been an explosion. The air current was sent from the downcast shaft, through all the workings to the upcast shaft. The puff of return air suggested that there was something wrong with the ventilation system.

'You go and check the ventilation at top o' t' district,' Bert ordered Joseph. 'And ask anybody int' next district if they know owt. I'll stop 'ere.'

Joseph nodded, picked up his lamp and started walking. His heart, as well as his mind, was racing as he trudged his lonely trek along the plane. The creaking of the props and the heat of the blackness engulfed his thoughts as well as his body.

What if there had been an explosion?
Where had it happened?
Had anyone been injured or killed?

Such was the depth of his wide-ranging thoughts, that he almost stumbled into a man, Horace Green, who was heading further down the south plane

Green listened as Joseph recounted his concerns. The man's features set and his eyes narrowed.

'That sounds like a bloody explosion, all right. You go back to Bert and I'll go get Deputy Jackson and a couple o' other men. We'll come down to you, then we'll go and see what's 'appened,' Green said, already turning to walk back to his district. Joseph did as he was told and headed back to Bert.

* * *

The small party of men crept along the plane, further into the South District. Joseph and Bert had been joined by Deputy Jackson, Green, and two other men, Young and Jordan.

Thin blue flames flickered weakly in their lamps. Gas was in the air but the air was still good enough to breathe.

The men proceeded hesitantly, fearfully, but they were resolute. They knew they had to find out if an explosion had occurred.

Slowly, slowly, the men inched forward into the hollow stillness. All was silent apart from their heavy breathing and the clinking of their clogs. Deputy Jackson led the way, stopping at each of the ventilation doors to test the sweetness of the air. The free current of air was good and the roof sound, so the party of men progressed further along the plane.

Deputy Jackson suddenly halted, shocked at what he saw.

'God Almighty!' he groaned as his eyes scanned the scene in front of him.

Falls of dirt and stone mingled with twisted girders. Tubs lay smashed and scattered. Broken rails jutted from the floor. Props were crumpled, partly covered with lumps of rock. The pit was a shattered mess. The other men followed, fearful of what they might find, their clogs sinking into the deep piles of dust.

'Well, there's no doubt about it. There's been an explosion, all right. God knows what's further on!' Green stated, summing up everyone's thoughts. Deputy Jackson sucked in a deep breath, and expelled a long sigh.

'I'm goin' on,' he said. 'You stay 'ere if you want.' They all looked at each other, unsure and afraid, but every man raised his lamp, lifted his clogs from the dust, and carried on.

Within moments, the group of men stopped. They could see something pale and light stretched out in the deep, grey dust.

The weak light from their lamps revealed a man's body, his arm visible above the dirt, his head face down in the soft, piled dust. Deputy Jackson and Green quickly knelt down and carefully turned the man over, but he was quite dead. The other men watched with bated breaths and racing hearts.

'My God, it's Mick Rooney!' Joseph cried out. He knew the Mexborough dataller well. Deputy Jackson shook his head slowly.

'Poor bugger.'

The men looked at each other, each realising the possible, if not probable fate of the other workers further into the district. 'I can't see anybody surviving this, but we've got to go on,' Deputy Jackson said quietly, already stepping ahead.

Within yards, the men's hopes of finding life in the shattered ruins proved to be vain. Bodies lay all around. It was a terrible sight.

Deputy Jackson quickly ordered Joseph and Bert to stay with him, telling the others to go back to the pit bottom and raise the alarm. The departing men nodded their agreement and began their trek back to the shaft. The remaining men slowly surveyed the awful spectacle that met their eyes.

Some of the bodies were so crushed and broken it was hard to tell that they had been men. Others, like Mick Rooney, lay stretched out and buried in the dust. Many were badly burned, terribly scarred and scorched, with their arms shielding their heads in a protective stance against the sheet of flames.

One young lad lay with his arms still around his pony's neck, the hair singed from their bodies. Others were recumbent, bronzed and stiff, like statues, laying amidst the bodies of horses. Joseph could hardly bear to look at all the carnage. He had to bend and retch into the shadowy dirt.

'My God,' Bert uttered under his breath as the horrific sights overwhelmed him.

'You two are bloody lucky to be alive,' Deputy Jackson told them.

Joseph and Bert nodded, both dazed at the thought of how narrowly they had escaped death. Joseph closed his eyes and imagined Rose's beautiful face. He thought how he was soon to be a father. He then whispered his heartfelt thanks to God.

* * *

By daybreak, management and some men above ground had been alerted to the disaster that had occurred. Fevered activity sprang into action. The Denaby and Cadeby Rescue Teams were sent for, as well as Wath-upon-Dearne's colliery team, which was on standby.

Sergeant-Instructor Winch was called to supervise the rescue operations, alongside Mr Charles Bury, the recently appointed manager of Cadeby colliery, and Mr Harry Witty, now agent of the Denaby and Cadeby collieries.

Mr Chambers, managing director of the company, was summoned from Newcastle, and Mr William Pickering, Divisional Inspector of Mines, was called from Doncaster, together with his assistant, Mr Gilbert Tickle.

Senior Inspector Henry Hewitt began his journey from Sheffield, and two other inspectors, Mr Hudspeth and Mr Wilson, were called from Leeds.

* * *

The noise of rhythmic banging broke through Rose's sleep, alarming her even before she was fully conscious. The metallic cacophony of pokers striking grates travelled up and down the rows of thin-walled houses, then beyond.

It was a sound that produced fear and dread. It was a signal that there had been a serious accident at one of the pits.

Rose rubbed her eyes and heaved herself off the bed. She threw on her clothes as quickly as she could. Her fingers trembled and her actions were clumsy. She had to steady herself as she descended the stairs. Her mind was pushing her forwards, but her body was holding her back.

The dawn light brightened the gloom as she lifted the blind at the living room window, but worry and trepidation flooded her body.

'Please God, please God, let Joseph be all right,' she muttered to herself, already shaking with apprehension. Her mind was struggling to organise her thoughts.

Panic rose like bile into her throat. It was then that she felt the flash of pain chase through her stomach, followed by a warm trickle of water that fell from between her legs and gathered on the floor. Her waters had broken. The baby was coming.

The drumming of pokers had faded, cut short by urgency, as it travelled onwards around the village. In the relative quietness, Rose grasped her poker and struck the grate three times. It was a prearranged signal to alert her next-door neighbour, Ida. Within minutes, Ida was by her side.

'It's probably just a rumour that there's been an accident,' Ida began, thinking that was the reason for Rose's alarm. But Rose moaned and doubled up in pain before she was able to gasp. 'The baby's coming, and Joseph's at the pit, and it's all my fault!'

* * *

As the sun rose over Denaby, so did the worry and anxiety of its residents.

People hoped it was just a rumour that a major accident had happened; there had been plenty of false alarms in the past. Folk worried about relatives and friends, fearful for their safety. Explosions and fires had happened before, so there was good reason to be so concerned.

Men dressed quickly and headed outside for further information. Women fretted at home, ready to whisk babies into their arms and lead children by the hand to wherever they needed to go for more news.

By six o'clock, the Denaby and Cadeby Rescue Teams had arrived at Cadeby pit and were heading underground. Night shift workers were just finishing, leaving their districts and coming up, many only just aware that a disaster had occurred.

Word quickly spread that an explosion had happened in the South District. Men were missing, men were dead. The dazed night shift workers exchanged frightened looks and morbid comments, torn between yearning for safety up above, and the desire to help mates who were still below ground.

* * *

Mary was packing up Jim's snap when the dreaded rattling of pokers reached them. Jim stopped eating his breakfast, both of them instantly alarmed.

'Oh, no!' Mary cried out, immediately concerned that John was working his night shift.

Her heart started to thump as if it was trying to leap out of her body. She slumped onto a chair, staring at Jim, hardly daring to speak.

'Now then Mary, love,' Jim said, grasping her hand. 'It's probably another false alarm. I'll go and find out if anything's happened. Try not to worry.'

He stood up, ready to leave for the pit. Mary tried to smile, but an ominous foreboding caught her breath and weakened her body. She had seen the look in Jim's eyes and the set of his face. He was as frightened as her.

Jim opened the back door and found Ida on the doorstep, about to knock.

'It's your Rose,' she panted. 'She's started in labour. I've been and told Aggie the midwife and she's on her way there.'

'Thanks, Ida love,' Jim said and turned to Mary.

'She'll want you with her, love. You go to her.' Mary nodded, but her mind was in a chaotic whirl.

* * *

More men left their houses, unsure of which pit to head for, but with an urgency that showed in their postures. Their bodies leaned forward, clogs striking cobbles at a determined pace, their faces serious beneath hastily pulled on flat caps. Concern motivated their actions and words; they needed to know more.

'What's 'appened?'

'Does tha know owt?'

'Which pit is it?'

Shaking heads revealed their ignorance, so on they went.

Jim was one of these men, and Walter was another. They had both left their homes at the same time, both worried about their lads, both needing to know if they were all right.

Even in these circumstances, Walter stubbornly ignored Jim's call and avoided answering his questions. Then, they saw two miners who they knew worked on the night shift at Cadeby.

'What's gone off?' Walter asked them.

'There's been an explosion, on t' South District, they say.'

'Rescue teams have gone down,' the men answered.

Jim felt his blood almost freeze in his body.

'My lad, John, works on there. Do you know if he's all right?' Both men shook their heads solemnly.

'My lad, Joseph, works on t' east district wi' you,' Walter began, before he was interrupted by them.

'Deputy Jackson moved 'im last night, there were that many off work.' He paused.

'He were moved to t' South District,' his mate added.

Jim heard Walter's sharp intake of breath; it matched his own.

'Thanks, lads,' Jim muttered, and hurried on towards the pit. He was so worried that he didn't even notice Walter was walking in step with him.

* * *

Rumours had spread like wildfire. There had been an explosion at Cadeby pit in the early hours of the morning. The rescue teams were already underground, heading for the scene of the disaster, hoping there were still men that could be rescued, rather than only bodies to be brought up. But no one was sure.

Crowds soon gathered in the roads and on the bridges leading to the pit yard. The lack of accurate information frustrated them.

Men had been joined by women and children, all standing quietly, whispering conjectures to nearby people, anxious to quell their rising fears for loved ones and friends. They hoped and prayed that their husbands, fathers, sons and brothers were spared.

Some men pushed their way to the pit offices, eager to offer any assistance that they could. There was confusion amongst the officials there, with little organisation regarding the number of miners allowed to go underground to assist with rescue operations, but the men were desperate to help.

Many of them had relatives or friends missing. They had to help. Jim and Walter were two of these men, along with Bob. Despite his broken toe, when he heard the bad news, he was adamant that he should be allowed to help.

Some of the men were given respirators before descending, although the air had been assessed as being good, even in the South District. They went down and headed to the scene of the disaster.

* * *

Rose fell back against the pillows, her face filmed with perspiration. It was eight o'clock, and she had just given birth after two hours of straining and pushing.

Mary's tears of joy mingled with her own perspiration. The baby had been born safely, his lusty cries providing relief for everyone.

'Oh, Rose! My darling, Rose!' Mary cried. 'You have a son, a beautiful son!' Rose's delighted smile lit up the room as her own tears fell.

Aggie watched quietly as she performed all her necessary duties to the new mother and child, but she, too, was beaming.

'You have a fine-looking boy, Rose,' she confirmed. Just for a few minutes they had all been able to feel happiness, the joy of new life, but all too quickly reality washed over them.

'Where's Joseph?' Rose's anguished plea stabbed at Mary's heart. She felt her own breathing falter as she thought of Jim and Bob, as well as John. Word had been sent to Mary by a friend, that Jim and Bob had volunteered to help with the rescue party.

Mary tried to control her breathing.

'Ivy and Gertie are downstairs with Violet and Grandma Sarah. They'll stay with you. I have to go to the pit.'

* * *

Beads of sweat prickled Mary's skin as she slid her body through the silent crowds gathered along Pit Lane. Her thoughts were in utter turmoil; her stomach churned with anxiety.

Men stood in huddles, hands on hips or stuffed into pockets, their solemn gazes focused on the colliery, watching and waiting for news.

Women clustered in groups, hugging babies, holding infants' hands, or with arms folded across their breasts.

Their frowning faces were etched with worry and apprehension; they were all waiting for news.

Even the children stood still, quiet and bewildered as they watched and waited. Policemen stood alongside them, hands clasped behind their backs, looking at the people with sympathetic expressions. No one had to be reprimanded or controlled.

There was a sudden gasp of horror as all eyes turned to the long gantry. In full view of the alarmed onlookers, a corpse was being carried down from the pithead. There could be no doubt, men had been killed. Mary closed her eyes and felt her body sway. She could not bear to think that any harm had come to the people she loved.

She forced herself to head closer to the pit shaft, but police had cordoned off that area. Women begged for more information, but they were told to wait. Mary caught the whispers and laments of some close by.

'Please God, not my son. His father only died this last Christmas gone,' an old woman pleaded.

'What shall I do if I lose my husband? We've seven children and another one on the way,' asked another.

From nine o'clock, there began the awful procession of the dead. Bodies took their solemn journey down that tall gantry to the pay room, now a makeshift morgue.

* * *

Mr Bury, Cadeby manager, and Mr Pickering, Divisional Inspector of Mines for the Yorkshire and North Midland District, had descended the pit as soon as they arrived.

It was decided that Mr Witty, the agent to Denaby and Cadeby collieries, would stay above ground to supervise the many details that required instant attention, and to stem the rapidly rising confusion which threatened to overwhelm the officials.

The rescue teams and the many volunteer miners had already gone underground and cautiously proceeded to the South District.

The crowds swelled and more police arrived as Mr Witty made the many arrangements. After receiving a message from the pit bottom that twenty-two bodies had so far been located, he sent stretchers down.

The bodies were to be received in one of the pit offices, the pay room, where Fred Webster would be in charge. The message had also said that the ventilation was good, and the rescue workers didn't need to use their apparatus.

Mr Douglas Chambers, nephew of Mr William Chambers, and manager of Denaby Main pit, had arrived not long afterwards, as well as Mr Tickle, an assistant inspector of mines, and Senior Inspector Hewitt from Sheffield.

Mr John Chambers, managing director of Cortonwood colliery, and father of Douglas Chambers, also offered his immediate assistance. All of these noted mining officials descended and made for the South District. They were only too willing to offer their professional advice and help.

Joseph and Bert stayed underground with Deputy Jackson. They waited until the rescue parties arrived, informing them of earlier events and the location of the bodies.

Mr Bury and Mr Pickering joined them soon afterwards and issued orders to the men. The location of each body had to be marked and recorded for future evidence. After various tests, the officials informed the men that there was no fire, and breathing apparatus was not required. They began putting the victims of the explosion on stretchers, and the bringing up of the bodies began.

* * *

Jim descended in the cage with a feeling of dread, but his only thoughts were for his family.

Walter was in the same volunteer rescue party, and they all made their way along to the South District with a fierce determination to give any sort of aid and assistance that was required.

They saw and heard Mr Bury and Mr Pickering giving out instructions, together with other officials, some who they did not recognise.

Extreme concentration was needed from the rescuers, so there was little unnecessary conversation as they proceeded, but Jim imagined that Walter's thoughts reflected his own. They were both desperate to learn the fate of their sons.

The men progressed resolutely, their breathing affected by nerves and trepidation as they approached the location of the explosion. Jim's gaze was steady and intent as he registered the chaotic shambles of the workings which signposted the scene of the disaster, but there was no choice but to continue.

Within minutes, the group of men halted to allow other rescuers to pass by with three stretchered bodies that were being carried back to the cage.

Jim hardly dared look at the corpses, but he felt almost ashamed when relief surged through his body. All three corpses were old men. They were not John or Joseph. He looked at Walter, and for one brief moment, there was a sincere connection between them, an understanding that they shared the same feelings.

Walter quickly looked away, as if embarrassed to have revealed his emotions. The party continued further along the plane, but not before asking the other rescuers what they knew.

'Is anybody alive?'

'Have they reached all t' men further on?'

'Do you know who's dead?'

The other men shook their heads and pursed their lips before replying.

'It dun't look good.'

'Gaffers are saying they think everyone's dead.'

'Some o' bodies are in a bad tacking.'

Everyone became subdued at this news. There was a growing realisation that a major disaster had occurred. Jim's heart sank.

* * *

The bodies were steadily recovered, taken to the pit top, then carried to the pay-room mortuary, or the "dead house", as it became known. Relays of men carried them there, including Eli, who worked diligently for hours, using his strength and resilience to cope with the task.

Thankfully, the bodies were covered in sheets, but the experience had a profound impact on him. It was as if he'd only just comprehended that mining was a very dangerous job. The crowds of onlookers still waited for news.

*   *   *

Jim physically flinched as he saw the devastation on the plane. He and his party were making their way between the falls of stone, stepping between twisted rails and the piles of dust, when there was a sudden, anguished cry.

'Joseph!' The name burst from Walter's lips, haunting and plaintive in its tone.

Jim turned to look at him, but Walter was staring elsewhere. There, in front of them, was Joseph, walking towards them, his lamp held high, his movements slow and laboured as he picked his way through the debris.

'Joseph!' Walter shouted again, and this time Joseph looked up and responded, as if rousing himself from a dream.

'Dad! Jim!' he cried. Walter grasped his son's hand. Neither spoke for a moment.

'I thought you were dead!' Walter's voice was low and controlled, as if trying to contain his emotions.

'I nearly bloody were!' Joseph said. He closed his eyes for a moment, before hurriedly explaining what had happened earlier. The party of men listened intently, their features registering shock and sadness at his words.

'Do you know anything about John?' Jim managed to asked Joseph.

'I don't, Jim. Rescue teams are still searching down t' far end o' plane,' was his subdued reply.

Jim nodded but he couldn't speak.

'Gaffers have told me to go up top, now that other rescuers are down,' Joseph added quietly.

Jim suddenly remembered and blurted out.

'Rose's started wi' babby, lad. Mary's with her now.'

Walter seemed startled by his words. A gasp puffed from Joseph's mouth.

'You get back to her,' Jim added.

402

Joseph nodded quickly before shaking Jim's hand, then grasping his father's hand. Father and son looked each other in the eye, something they had not done for a long time.

Both felt the stirrings of renewed close feelings. Joseph turned and headed for the cage. He just wanted to get back to Rose.

'Aren't you going back wi' 'im?' Jim asked Walter.

'Nay, there's still work to be done,' he answered.

* * *

The men pressed on further along the plane. Rescuers mingled with officials, all working strenuously.

'That's Basil Pickering, Wath Main's manager. He's Inspector Pickering's son,' one man informed the others. 'All these top men down our pit.'

'Aye, they're all trying to work out what's 'appened. We could tell 'em. Where there's gas and gob fires there'll be explosions,' another man added scornfully.

Jim was listening to these comments when he saw two men carrying a stretchered body towards them. One of the men was Bob, who suddenly realised that Jim was only yards way.

'Jim,' he began, then his voice broke. 'I'm sorry, Jim.'

The two men stared at each other, but Jim knew. He looked at the covered corpse.

'It's John,' Jim said, a statement rather than a question.

Bob nodded slowly. Jim moved towards the body and lifted the sheet.

It was John, his precious lad, John. His body was hardly marked, but the skin was bronzed, his hair singed. He looked peaceful, as if resting. But he was stiff, lifeless, dead.

'Can I carry him back?' Jim heard his own words, but it did not sound like his voice.

'I'll take him,' Walter immediately offered, but Jim was decided.

'I want to take him,' Jim insisted. He replaced Bob, holding the stretcher with clenched fists. Bob nodded, turned, and headed back to the waiting bodies. The party of men followed him.

Walter turned to watch Jim and the other man walk in the direction of the cage.

'How can I tell Mary?' Jim thought. He felt numb. He had lost his only son.

* * *

'Twenty-two bodies gone up so far,' Bill Townsend, the onsetter, informed the weary men. It was eleven o'clock in the morning and Joseph was glad to be in the cage.

He longed to be up above, to feel fresh air, to see the sky, and most of all, to be with Rose. He felt the sway of the cage as it ascended; it jarred his weary body and increased the somersaulting of his thoughts.

His mind could barely fathom the sights he had seen and the events that had happened that morning. He knew they had been lucky, him and Bert. So far, they were the only two men on the South District that had definitely survived the explosion.

Thirty-five others were either dead or missing. He gave an involuntary shiver, as if death was brushing over him.

The cage bumped to a stop and the men stepped out. As they headed for the lamp room, they heard shouts from inside.

'Fuckin' hell! There's been another explosion!'

* * *

Walter opened his eyes but could not work out where he was. The air was thick with dust, black and choking. He tried to move, but something was weighing him down.

He pushed and strained until he was free. The corpse fell to his side. They were both on the ground, lying in the thick dust. Walter slowly came to his senses and began to remember. He had been lifting a corpse onto a stretcher when there was a blast of warm air, followed by a tremendous roar. He had been thrown to the ground and must have passed out.

He slowly realised that there had been an explosion, a second explosion, in the same place as the first.

He rubbed his eyes, hoping to see more clearly, but the air was thick and black. He ran shaking hands over his body, as if to reassure himself that everything was intact. His fingers met stickiness where blackened blood oozed from cuts and scratches. Stinging stabs of pain ran along his face, but he could move, he was managing to breathe; he was alive.

He started to crawl, hoping to escape the cloying blackness, but was unsure which way to go. Panic rose. He felt lost, afraid he would not be able to find his way out, afraid he was entombed.

Then he saw a faint light coming towards him. He heard footsteps and felt strong arms pulling him into a nearby siding where the air was clearer and purer.

Walter gasped with relief as he recognised his saviour, a young miner called Percy Royd, who had volunteered earlier to stretcher out the bodies.

'There's been another bloody explosion,' Percy said. 'On level fourteen, like t' first one. God knows what's 'appened to all t' men down there! I was sent back to recharge some lamps, or I'd have been there an' all!' he added, with a rising voice that signalled doom.

* * *

Joseph was torn between going to see Rose and returning underground.

The rumours of a second explosion had provided him with a dilemma. He longed to escape the pit, with all its terrible sights and awful devastation, but he could not. His conscience would not allow him to.

Confusion and panic surrounded Joseph as he hovered on the pit top. People couldn't believe there had been a second explosion; could not comprehend that there had been another disaster whilst still dealing with the first. He had been stunned to see the huge gathering of people around the colliery, silent; still waiting for news.

It was then that he saw Jim on the gantry. He was standing over a stretcher, the body covered with a sheet.

Eli Shaw and another man were there, waiting to receive the body and carry it to the mortuary. Joseph saw Jim's bowed head, then his pulsing shoulders as the sobs shook his body. Eli's cupped hand hovered over Jim's shoulder, then it lowered gently to pat the grieving father.

The men lifted the stretcher, and the body was carried away with protective care and solemn respect.

Joseph was so alarmed that he ran to the gantry, despite his aching limbs. Jim gazed at the crowds of people as Joseph reached him.

'Jim!' he panted, searching the older man's face with a beseeching look. 'What's happened?'

'It's John, Joseph lad,' Jim said, expelling a shuddering sigh. 'Our John's dead.'

'No!' Joseph cried. 'No!' Jim's sad stare and sorrowful expression answered Joseph's uncertainty. For a moment, he couldn't speak. 'Does mi dad and Bob know?'

Jim nodded. 'It was Bob who found him. Me and Walter met him on his way to t' cage. I wanted to bring John back up. Then I heard about t' second explosion. I 'ave to go back down. Bob and Walter are still there, but I 'ave to tell Mary first…about John.' His voice faltered as he anticipated that awful responsibility.

Joseph was absorbing all the information when they both heard a woman's piercing call.

'Jim! Jim!' It was Mary. Ivy and Gertie stood with her. They had seen everything on the gantry, but they needed to know more.

Jim and Joseph made their way down to the women. Mary stood rigid with fear, her sisters either side of her. Jim approached them, his gaze unwavering but his eyes brimming with tears. His heart was beating wildly as he gathered Mary's hands into his.

'Mary, love. It's our John…he's…'

'No! Not dead! Please, Jim, tell me he's not dead!' Mary begged. Jim clamped his lips and nodded imperceptibly, as if trying to lessen the devastating news.

Mary felt the loving arms of her husband and sisters as they supported her crumpling body. It felt as though her heart was shattering.

She had a sudden flashback to the night John was born, that sultry summer night when she and Jim had welcomed their baby boy with pure joy and happiness.

'Joseph, you have a son,' Mary somehow found the strength to say. 'Rose is waiting for you. Jim, you have a grandson, our first grandchild.'

The two men tried to take in her words as she began to sob.

* * *

Mr Witty was just about to send down a message to Inspector Pickering, saying that he should come back up to the pit top in time for his luncheon appointment with King George and Queen Mary at Hickleton Hall. The morning's events had altered Mr Witty's plans, but he still hoped to attend the royal function if the circumstances allowed.

'Come at once. Pit blown up again,' was the disastrous news.

Mr Pickering and the other pit officials were down there, helping to recover the bodies from the first explosion.

Defying his instructions to stay above ground to manage the situation, Mr Witty hurried underground to discover the extent of the damage.

Many other men also rushed to help, including Jim and Joseph, who had bid hasty but sincere farewells to Mary and her sisters.

They were all from mining families, and everyone understood the compulsion to give assistance, but it was hard to watch loved ones return once again to potential danger, or even death.

Jim placed a tender kiss on Mary's lips and they shared a meaningful look before he and Joseph headed back up the gantry to the waiting cage.

* * *

Joseph and Jim, together with other rescuers, were making their way towards the South District, unsure of what devastation and destruction they might find. As they neared the south plane, they were heartened and relieved to find men alive, still working to recover any victims of the explosions.

But their relief was short-lived when they were told about the facts of the disaster and the events leading up to it.

Fred Mansfield, a member of the Wath pit rescue party, briefly explained what had happened, as the other men listened intently.

He had seen the group of officials further along the plane, near level fourteen. The group included managers Mr Bury and Mr Douglas Chambers, and his inspectors Mr Pickering, Mr Tickle and Mr Hewitt. All were in the process of retrieving the bodies of men killed in the first explosion, and working alongside the other rescue parties.

'I were only one with a respirator,' Fred explained. 'It were my job to search in other areas in case of afterdamp. That gas is deadly after an explosion. All t' others were told that they didn't need apparatus as the air was good. But there was a sudden blast of hot air, then a tremendous roar. There was a massive fall of roof, hundreds of tons of it, brought down by another explosion. We're going there now.' He started walking ahead.

As the men followed him, Jim's thoughts were in chaos, especially fearful for Bob. Joseph was similarly stunned as he thought about the missing people, including his father.

They proceeded further along the plane, uncertain in their thoughts, but deliberate in their actions. It was Jim who saw him first.

'Christ Almighty! It's Walter!' he shouted. Joseph narrowed his eyes and was overwhelmed to see his father limping towards them, cut about the face, but alive.

'Dad!' Joseph cried out, before clutching his father's arm. 'Are you all right?'

'My God, Walter. We thought you might be dead!' Jim said. Walter stared at the two men, then turned around to go back down the plane.

'I'm all right. I'm comin' wi' you,' he said, limping as he retraced his steps.

* * *

Mr Witty reached the south plane at the same time as other rescuers, all advancing cautiously as they neared level fourteen.

They soon came upon bodies lying all along the plane, burnt and shattered by the explosion, some beyond identification.

A few men were still alive, but terribly injured. Instant aid was given to them, but some of them died minutes later.

Further along, the rescuers reached a huge roof fall that almost blocked the roadway. Men lay beneath it, cruelly crushed, and all dead, killed instantly by its massive weight.

The rescuers sighed and shook their heads as if disbelieving the sights before them, but still, they carried on, squeezing themselves through cracks in the chaotic jumble of broken girders, overturned tubs and heaps of stone.

Mr Witty was one of the first to crawl beyond the fall, to the spot where Mr Pickering's party had been working immediately before the second explosion.

The managers and inspectors lay on the floor, their bodies entangled, all appearing to be dead, gassed by the afterdamp that had circulated along the plane after the explosion.

Only the huge roof fall had stopped the gas spreading throughout the district. As Sergeant Winch arrived with the stretcher bearers, Mr Witty realised that Mr Bury was still breathing, barely alive, but not dead. He was immediately taken to a place where the air was purer, then taken back to the cage.

The rescuers with respirators advanced still further, and were saddened to find twenty-three bodies in a group, all gassed and disfigured, all dead.

Officials, rescue parties and volunteers were among the dead, wiped out while carrying out their duties.

Mr Witty realised that the death toll had significantly increased since the morning. He feared as many as seventy people had now died in the two explosions, but the actual cause of the disaster was still unknown.

There were personal tragedies too. Mr Edward Chambers, manager of Cortonwood pit, was hard at work helping at Cadeby pit when he was told he had lost his boy, Mr Douglas Chambers, manager of Denaby pit.

Mr Basil Pickering, manager of Wath Main Colliery, was among the rescuers after the second explosion, and helped to carry out the body of his father, Inspector Pickering.

The Denaby and Cadeby Rescue Teams were all killed, except for Sergeant Winch and one other man. They'd had remarkable escapes because they had been sent back to relay messages to the pit top when the second explosion occurred.

The waiting crowds still had to learn of their personal tragedies. As the day wore on, the bodies were brought up and received into the pay-room morgue. Soon, they would be identified, if possible, by their loved ones. They would be on the dead list.

* * *

People shuffled past the pit's general office, curious to read the many messages of sympathy that had been received and posted on the railings.

The first one was from the King and Queen, graciously expressing their sincere condolences for the tragic loss of lives at the colliery. After news had spread of the second explosion, the Home Secretary had wired a long, sympathetic telegram, referring particularly to the great loss sustained in the deaths of Mr Pickering and his colleagues.

The inspector was regarded as one of the leading authorities on coal mining in the world. It was especially poignant that, instead of lunching with the King and Queen at Hickleton Hall, as he should have been, he was lying in the ruins of the second explosion.

There were also messages from Viscount Halifax, Countess Yarborough, Lady Copley of Sprotbrough Hall, the Archbishop of York, the Mayors of Rotherham, Barnsley and Sheffield, as well as the Yorkshire Miners' Association.

By late afternoon, the crowds had swelled even more. Thousands of silent onlookers watched as more bodies were brought down the gantry. They made way for horse-drawn ambulances carrying the injured to hospital.

News had spread that Mr Bury was dead. Then there was a ray of hope as rumours contradicted this. They heard from travelling whispers that he was gravely ill, only just clinging on to life; the doctors were struggling to revive him at Fullerton Hospital.

There were also moments of optimism as the walking wounded appeared, blackened miners giving helping hands to injured workmates as they came out of the pit.

People strained to see their faces, hoping against hope that their loved ones were still alive, only to feel bitter disappointment when they didn't appear.

The heat of the day had increased, yet the atmosphere was cold and chilling. The headgears of the colliery rose dark and stark against the summer sky. Only a few remaining flags fluttered forlornly, so decorative the previous day, but so incongruous on such a terrible day of disaster. Death was in the air.

* * *

Mr Chambers, "King of Denaby", arrived at the pit at about 3.30 pm, hurrying back as quickly as he could from Newcastle.

He immediately took charge and consulted with the experienced mining engineers who had been sent for from the Midlands. After discussions, Mr Chambers, Mr Witty and Inspector Wilson decided that the proper course of action was to build stoppings to shut off the most dangerous affected areas in the South District.

Mr Chambers and his party of officials then went down the pit. They took great pains to make sure that all living persons were withdrawn from those workings, then marked off the places for the stoppings. A fourteen-inch dry brick stopping was to be plastered over, and when it was finished, another stopping, two feet thick, and constructed of bricks and mortar, was to be built in front of it.

Mr Chambers knew this would be necessary, as, in his time, he had dealt with fifty-six underground fires, thirty-five of them at Cadeby between 1893, when the pit opened, and 1912, the time of the disaster.

The Barnsley seam at Cadeby was very gassy and extremely dangerous. Everyone knew this, including the Company. Even Mr Chambers had the grief of losing his dear nephew, Mr Douglas Chambers. Death was no respecter of a person's rank. Their status could not save them.

* * *

It was 7.30 pm and the evening air was still hot and humid.

Two motor cars travelled into Conisbrough along Hill Top Road. In one car was King George and Queen Mary, accompanied by Earl Fitzwilliam. In the other was Lord Stamfordham, the King's Private Secretary, accompanied by Major Atcherley, Chief Constable of the West Riding of Yorkshire.

Their Majesties had decided to make a personal call to the offices of the Denaby and Cadeby Collieries Company as soon as their day's duties were done. News of the second explosion, an even greater disaster than the first, had prompted them to visit, in order to show their deep sympathies for all the bereaved people there.

The cars slowed as they approached the colliery offices, and the waiting crowds soon realised who the illustrious visitors were. All caps were doffed as the King and Queen stepped out of the Daimler, and some people started to surge towards them. They could not believe that their Majesties were there, so near, and cheering began.

King George quickly raised his hand, a gesture that immediately conveyed that this was a mistimed, inappropriate response. Those close enough to him could see his sorrowful, serious expression, and the cheering died away, giving place to murmured blessings.

The royal party was received into the pit offices by Mr Chambers and Mr Wilson, the only inspector to survive the second explosion. Both men were grimed in coal dust, still wearing the same dirty clothes from their labours underground.

Nevertheless, the King and Queen shook their hands and asked pertinent questions about the disaster, greatly interested in what it meant to the mining community.

The King asked particularly as to the fate of his faithful servants, the government inspectors, and was greatly touched when told what had happened. Mr Chambers showed the royal party plans of the scene of the explosions and explained their force, killing so many in an instant.

The King and Queen were saddened by what they were told, visibly shocked to hear of such terrible events and the enormous loss of lives. The King's face showed grief and concern, as if experiencing a great personal loss.

Queen Mary had tears in her eyes, as though thinking about all the poor widows, mothers, sisters and daughters affected by such a disaster. She had been especially touched when she witnessed the grief of a miner's wife who had come up to one of the enquiry offices to look at the list of the dead. The woman began screaming with distress when she saw the name of her husband on the list, and was led away from the Queen, who was descending the steps nearby.

A short time later, Queen Mary asked to see the poor woman, but was informed that she had gone. Queen Mary was unable to extend her solace and sympathy, which had been her intention to bestow.

The royal party left after quarter of an hour, heading back to Wentworth. King George had himself descended a mine earlier that day, Elsecar pit. It was the first time a monarch had ever done so.

He and Queen Mary had also toured surrounding villages that same day, meeting miners, their families, and even visiting a miner's newly built colliery house in Woodlands, Doncaster. This had added a particular poignancy to their appreciation and understanding of the disaster and how it affected their subjects.

The grieving people of Denaby and Conisbrough were humbled by the fact that their King and Queen had visited them and wept with them in their time of distress and bitter anguish. It made a lasting impression on them.

A notice was promptly issued from the colliery offices:

Their Majesties, the King and Queen, visited Cadeby Colliery today to ascertain, personally on the spot, all particulars of the sad calamity which has deprived many of those we love. They commanded me to express, to all who have suffered loss of any who were dear to them, their deep sympathy with them in their grief.

W. H. Chambers

Later that evening, Mr Chambers received a message, forwarded by Lord Stamfordham, from Wentworth:

'The King and Queen were shocked to hear all about the terrible accident at your colliery, today. Perhaps the fact that their Majesties were near to the scene, in the midst of so much rejoicing when they visited Conisbrough yesterday, brings home to them still more, the sorrow and sadness which now prevails among you. I am desired, once again, to express their Majesties' sympathy with the families of those who have perished, and with the sufferers in this grievous calamity.'

Mr Chambers read through the message several times. He still felt shocked by what had happened, still felt grief at the loss of so many lives, but he knew there was work to be done, despite the late hour. He sighed, adjusted his spectacles, and walked towards the pay-room.

* * *

Shortly after the King and Queen had left, Mr Frank Allen, District Coroner, arrived from Mexborough. He was organising the opening of the inquest on the men whose bodies had already been recovered.

It was an enormous responsibility for him, but he worked diligently, already appointing his jury, an even spread of men from Conisbrough and Denaby. Police Inspector Barraclough of Mexborough had been asked to take charge of the inquest arrangements.

Mr Allen and the jury went to the pay-room to view the bodies, sixty-five in total, outstretched on tables, each covered with a white cloth.

Some of them were identified, and Mr Allen went across to the colliery offices to sign the necessary death certificates permitting the removal of bodies. But not one body was removed that night; all stayed in the mortuary.

By ten o'clock that night, the Coroner, jury and army of newspaper reporters had left the inquest room and the colliery, but not so the waiting crowds. They stood for hours afterwards, staring at the pay-room's dimly lit windows, behind which lay their loved ones, stiff and cold. They could not bear to leave them.

Luckily, it was a hot July night, but they hardly noticed their environment, being so distraught and distressed with their plight.

Mary and Jim were two of those people. They stood quietly, almost spent with emotion. Their beloved son lay in the pay-room, and they did not even know where Bob was. Mary could not bear to think how her mother, Sarah, and Bob's wife, Winnie, would be feeling.

They too had wanted to keep vigil outside the pit, but had been persuaded to wait at home. Mary and Jim were shouldering the heartache, as much as they could, for everyone.

They thanked the Lord that Joseph and Walter had been spared, but could find little consolation when they thought of John and Bob.

Jim remembered what he had seen in the pay-room when he went to identify John. The images flashed through his mind.

Rows and rows of bodies, all still, all cut down as they laboured for a living wage. Some he recognised; some could not be recognised with such savage injuries.

His eyes settled on one of the outstretched bodies. It was John, his precious lad, John. Jim looked at his bronzed skin, his shorn hair, thankful that he was hardly marked. He remembered John as a baby and as a boy; quiet, calm but always determined.

Tears sprang to Jim's eyes as he realised how much he loved him, how proud of him he was, how he could not have wished for a better son. But, oh, how he wished John had stayed at home, had not worked his night shift, had not been struck down in his prime.

He also remembered the night he had identified his own father's body, also struck down in Earth's bowels. He touched John's hands, those hands he had watched build bridges and towers with the wooden blocks he had made for him as a baby. He then felt the bubbling sobs, the searing pain that was rising in his body. It was the excruciating pain of losing a son, his only son.

He was unable to contain his grief. Deep, painful sobs erupted from his throat, so powerful that he sank to his knees. His beloved lad was gone.

* * *

Joseph left the pit in the late afternoon, completely exhausted after so many hours of toil and distress, but thankful that he had been spared. He walked home with Bert. Both were aware that they had miraculously escaped death, but both felt anguish that so many honest, decent men had not.

Walter had gone home before them, limping and sore, but also feeling fortunate to be alive. He felt different, changed by the day's terrible events. He almost felt guilty that he had been spared.

Remorse washed inside him as thoughts of his past actions and behaviour prodded his conscience. He felt he had been given a second chance to appreciate fully his family and friends, but he did not know if he deserved it.

* * *

Joseph opened the back door and stepped into the kitchen. He closed his eyes for a moment, savouring how it felt to be home.

He heard voices coming from the living room. He opened the door. Ivy was sitting next to Sarah, her arm around her mother's shoulders. His mother, Esther, was filling the teapot.

They all looked up as he entered the room. Cap in hand, his expression was a mixture of relief and sadness.

'Joseph! Oh, Joseph!' Esther sobbed, falling into his arms. 'Your dad's come home and you've come home! My prayers have been answered!'

Joseph's gaze travelled to Sarah. Her eyes were red and swollen, her skin ashen.

'Joseph! Thank the Lord!' she whispered. 'Is there any news about Bob?'

'No news yet, Sarah,' he answered, shaking his head.

Sarah nodded and gulped, as if trying to find words. 'We know about John. We know he's gone…Ivy and Gertie told us. I just pray that Bob's all right,' she murmured, her voice faltering.

Ivy squeezed her hand, as if to transfer strength and support. Joseph looked at each woman in turn, unsure of what to say.

'You go to Rose and the baby,' his mother said.

'Yes,' Sarah agreed. 'God knows we want some happiness today!' she added, trying to smile.

Grief and joy battled within him, but he placed his cap on the table, wiped his hands down his trousers, and walked to the stairs.

Rose heard footsteps. She knew it was him, her Joseph, coming back to her, safe and sound.

Their eyes met as he stepped into the bedroom, and they smiled at each other through their tears.

'Joseph! You're all right!' she gasped. He nodded, but could hardly speak. They turned to look at the sleeping baby, the image of his father.

'I love you, Rose,' he whispered. He felt truly blessed.

* * *

Mary and Jim looked towards the pay-room. It was midnight, but they could not leave. The day, 9th July, the bleakest day in living memory in Denaby and Conisbrough, was over. They must now brace themselves for whatever the next days would bring.

Chapter 88
Wednesday 10th July 1912

There were crowds outside the pit, lines of people standing on the lanes and bridges near the pit yard. Many had been there since the day before. Family members had brought food and drink to sustain them in their vigil, but still they waited and watched.

By eight o'clock, the company of pressmen had returned, all eager for news and photographs that could be reported. Irritation was increasing, however, as the officials were reluctant to share information with them.

It was Mr Chambers who then agreed to inform them of further developments. He stated that the rumour that there had been a third explosion was, in fact, true, but there had been no resulting deaths as had originally been thought. At about 3.30 am, workers who were endeavouring to shut off the deadly area of the South District by brickstopping in the intake and return airways, had narrowly escaped another catastrophe.

The explosion had blown out the stoppings and the men had been forced to run for their lives. Two of them had sustained serious injuries, but all had been very fortunate to escape death. Mr Chambers confirmed that work had continued there, and by 7.00 am, the stoppings had been restored and were being periodically inspected.

Mr Chambers also granted an interview for a few, selected reporters. He was meeting with Mr Redmayne, His Majesty's Chief Inspector of Mines for Great Britain, and Mr Wilson of Leeds, who on the death of Mr Pickering, had become acting Divisional Inspector, to discuss the condition of the mine.

During the interview, Mr Redmayne had stated:

'The management are exercising every possible precaution to prevent air from getting to the affected area, and by that action, they hope to suppress the danger. The stoppings in the intake and return airways will be periodically examined by bands of skilled men. It is not a particularly hazardous duty, but it calls for the shrewd judgement of trained men. I am departing almost immediately for London, where I shall report to the Home Secretary, and will make arrangements for the Home Office Inquiry.'

All three gentlemen agreed that the disasters had been caused by explosions, although Mr Chambers stated:

'All I can say is that it is most mysterious.'

Mr Wilson also stated that he could not explain the accident, but there was no chance that it was linked to shot-firing or electricity; those being the usual chief dangers, but not in this case. He ended the interview by stating his profound sadness at the loss of his colleagues, Mr Pickering, Mr Tickle and Mr Hewitt, adding:

'Why I am not among them is because the telephone did not happen to work early enough yesterday morning.'

Mr Chambers concluded the interview by saying that seventy-one bodies had been recovered, but there were still others under the fall and beyond. It was expected that all could be recovered by the following day.

He had then excused himself, as he was required to meet with the distinguished visitors who had just arrived. Viscount and Viscountess Halifax had driven over from Hickleton Hall and were making enquiries about the latest developments.

Mr Buckingham Pope had arrived from London, and His Grace, the Archbishop of York, had motored over from Wentworth. The Vicar of Conisbrough, the Reverend Strawbridge, was also in the pit yard.

While bodies were being recovered underground and coffined in the mortuary, the Archbishop proceeded to the pit yard where he and Reverend Strawbridge conducted a short but extremely touching service, attended by any available officials and men who were close by. Prayers were offered for the solace and comfort of the bereaved, together with supportive counselling and guidance.

As the Archbishop and Vicar walked back to the pit offices, they witnessed a disturbing incident. Three women were returning from the mortuary, where they had been to identify relatives. All were distressed and weeping copiously, when a young press photographer stepped into their paths, sensing an opportunity for an emotional picture. He held his camera in front of their faces while he got a steady snap, showing no regard for their feelings.

Although the nearby crowds had been silent and subdued, the callous act ignited their temper. A group of furious people promptly grabbed his camera and smashed it to the ground, also threatening to smash him if he did not retreat.

The Archbishop and Vicar were reminded of the real, deep emotions of the crowd, despite their stunned lethargy of the past hours. The two clergymen had been given an insight into the true feelings of the community.

* * *

Mary and Jim had watched the morning's developments. Drays had appeared early on, carrying coffins, thirty or forty of them, supplied by the Company. Local undertakers had run out of stock, so high was the death toll. People heard that a group of sextons was hard at work preparing a special plot of ground in Denaby churchyard in readiness for the many imminent funerals.

The first body to be released was that of Inspector Pickering, being taken to his Doncaster home where his wife was waiting to receive her coffined husband.

Throughout the morning, other bodies were taken home by colliery ambulances, where grieving relatives waited in darkened rooms to receive their loved ones.

Mary and Jim were waiting for John's body to be released, waiting to have their lad home with them. Then they were called to the mortuary. They were asked to carry out a possible identification of Bob. Winnie had joined them, insisting that she should be there. Sarah was at home, waiting for news.

* * *

The police had earlier cleared a way for the motor car which had carried six nursing sisters who were coming on duty. Their offers of help had been refused the previous day, but now their services were definitely needed.

Jim, Mary and Winnie approached the pay-room and were asked to wait outside. Seated on a bench were five women, all clad in black, all crying piteously. They had just been to identify their husbands and could not be comforted, despite the kind efforts of the nurses.

Mary slipped her arm through Winnie's and Jim stood on her other side. She seemed so small and slight, but she was quietly calm, bravely keeping her emotions in check.

The smell of the disinfectant hit their noses, but it was preferable to the unpleasant stench that hovered around the mortuary. The sweltering July heat was creating ghastly conditions for the nurses and mortuary attendants, but they were doing excellent work in coping with the laying-out and coffining of the bodies.

The rows of bodies inside the mortuary took Mary and Winnie by surprise, overwhelmed by the sight of so many corpses. Jim knew what to expect but was still shocked by what he saw. All those men who had died doing their work, doing their duty.

A nurse led them to a body that had only just been recovered. One of the rescuers had passed on the information that he thought it could be Bob Cooper.

The body lay with a sheet over the upper half. The nurse's look conveyed that it was necessary, as the injuries were too severe to afford a facial recognition. Mary and Winnie gasped simultaneously. They both knew it was Bob.

They didn't need to see his face. On his leg was the pattern of raised brown spots in the shape of a donkey, something his family had always teased him about, considering his love of horses.

He also still wore the distinctive belt that his family had clubbed together to buy him for his last birthday. Lastly, his toe was black, the broken toe that had kept him off work.

Winnie could no longer keep her emotions in check. She started wailing, a sound that cut through Mary; a sound she would never forget. Winnie had lost her darling husband, the father of her daughter, the father of the baby growing in her womb, whom he would now never meet.

Mary had already lost a son, now she had lost her beloved brother. Jim looked at the two women and acknowledged that the valiant wives, mothers and daughters of miners suffered just as much as the men folk in the mining community. They now had to tell Bob's mother and sisters that he had lost his life trying to help others.

* * *

The streets of Denaby and Conisbrough were shrouded in gloom. Blinds were drawn at every house, blocking out the July heat, blocking out the sadness and desolation that had gripped the villages.

Men were not working, uncertain when Cadeby pit would open again. They leaned against railings or stood in groups, quietly discussing the terrible events.

Women stood on the streets, sharing thoughts and opinions. Occasionally they would halt their conversations when a coffin was transferred from the colliery ambulance to a house. They would then mutter supportive platitudes to neighbours in the hope of giving consolation.

The Archbishop of York and Reverend Strawbridge had earlier toured Conisbrough and Denaby, visiting some of the bereaved families, trying to bring comfort and hope to the poor people. Their words and actions were appreciated. It was a ray of brightness on such a black day.

The clergymen then met with the vicars of Denaby and Mexborough. They held a conference to discuss the impending funeral arrangements. It was anticipated that at least fifty burials would take place in two days' time, on Friday 12th July, in family graves or in the specially allotted part of Denaby cemetery.

Conisbrough and Mexborough interments would be taken separately, at a different time. If the relatives of the victims were agreeable, the coffins would be placed in Denaby Main Church, where a service conducted by the Archbishop would be held.

Seats would be allotted to each company of mourners. After the service, the committals would be taken in various parts of the cemetery by Reverend Hawkes, Vicar of Denaby and Reverend Bateman, Vicar of Mexborough, and their curates.

News of these arrangements gradually spread, but some people were still waiting to have their relatives' bodies recovered or identified.

* * *

Mary and Jim stood outside their front door and watched the men carry the coffin into the house. Mary clutched at Jim's hand for support; her other hand covered her mouth. The late afternoon sun was bright and glowing, but she felt as if ice was in her blood.

She looked at Jim. His eyes were vacant, as if refusing to acknowledge what they saw. His mouth was a tight line, as if attempting to stopper any outburst.

As the coffin was placed carefully onto the floor, a sudden whimper escaped his lips and he bowed his head, as if defeated. His lad was home. John was home. But he was dead.

Mary knelt down and stroked the wooden lid, trying to have some kind of contact with her son. She closed her eyes and her lips uttered quiet murmurs of love. Around her stood her family, their faint sobs breaking the silence, everyone trying to control their grief.

Sarah stood between Ivy and Gertie, their arms giving support and assistance. She looked so frail and fragile; only her eyes looked bold as she stared at the coffin of her beloved grandson. Memories of John flowed fiercely in her mind, pride and love giving her a few snatches of solace.

She thought of Albert, her grief still raw, and she wondered how she would cope in future. First the loss of her grandson, and now the loss of her only son, Bob. The news of his death had utterly broken her.

In the kitchen, Charlie and Sam looked on, their faces set with sadness. Behind them stood Bridie, her eyes wide and unsure as she witnessed the sad homecoming of Mary's boy. She felt the collective grief of the Walker household and felt moved by their solidarity and love for each other.

Chapter 89
Thursday 11th July 1912

A few groups of people lingered outside Cadeby pit, still wanting information about their relatives, or still waiting to identify the few remaining bodies in the mortuary.

Seventy-three bodies in total had been recovered since the disaster, and Mr Bury, Cadeby's popular and respected manager, was still fighting for his life in Fullerton Hospital.

Fourteen bodies remained underground, but it had been decided by management and inspectors that it was too dangerous to enter the sealed-off area of the explosions. Tests had confirmed that the risk was too high. It was hoped that the remaining bodies could be recovered as soon as conditions allowed.

Most of the recovered bodies had already been coffined and transported to their homes; only a few remained in the mortuary waiting first to be identified by relatives, then laid out by nurses and finally coffined by mortuary attendants.

Compared to the two previous days, the pit was quiet and almost deserted. Relatives of victims were at home, mourning the loss of their loved ones and making preparations for their funerals in the coming few days.

There was a general air of desolation and stillness about the whole district. No work was being done at either of the two pits, people were in a hiatus, still numbed by recent events, but anticipating the funerals and all the ensuing affairs that had to be sorted.

Bob's body had been taken home earlier in the day. Once again, his family and friends had gathered together to grieve, to pay their respects and to support each other.

Winnie clung to her mother and father, her sisters watching and waiting for their time to share hugs and kisses with her.

Sarah held onto little Maggie, Bob's pride and joy. She felt numb, but all the lasses were there: Mary, Ivy, Gertie and Betty, who had travelled from Elsecar to be with the family at such a sad time. Their menfolk stood outside in the back yard, sharing solemn comments about the havoc wreaked on their lives.

Sarah felt Albert's presence, as though he wanted to be with the family too. She looked at the coffin and felt the burden of her grief dragging her down.

She sighed deeply, but she knew there was nothing she could do. One by one, she was losing those most precious to her. She drew Maggie a little closer and kissed the little girl's hair as her tears flowed for her lost son.

* * *

Friday 12th July 1912

Many families woke up with feelings of gloom and trepidation. It was the day when funerals of the victims would begin, the others arranged to take place over the following days.

A few were to be held in Conisbrough and Mexborough, but the majority that day were the burials of Denaby residents cut down in the disaster. The service was to begin at 3.00 pm in Denaby Main All Saints Parish Church, conducted by the Archbishop of York, the Bishop of Sheffield and Reverend Hawkes, Vicar of Denaby.

One of the most prominent funerals was for Mr Douglas Chambers, manager of Denaby Pit, killed in the second explosion. His promising career in the mining industry was cut short at the age of twenty-eight, as well as his recent marriage. The popular, ambitious young man was regarded as "a man of the future" by his father and uncle, and would be sorely missed by the whole community.

There was a great gathering in the neighbourhood of the dead manager's house, 'Peveril', on Elm Green Lane in Conisbrough.

Two coaches led the hearse that carried his body, and a huge procession walked behind. They walked through Conisbrough, into Denaby, and on to the church. Many colliery directors and managers mingled with mine officials and workers, all wanting to show their respects for the many victims.

Thousands of people lined the streets in Denaby, all wanting to witness Mr Chambers's last journey. A hush fell on the great crowd at the sight of the cortege.

The array of distinguished mourners watched as the coffin was carried into the church, including Mr William Chambers, still grief-stricken at the loss of his nephew. The coffin was made of unpolished oak and bore the simple inscription:

'Douglas Chambers, died 9th July 1912, aged 28.'

Among the many floral tributes was a bunch of lilies from his young, heartbroken widow.

The Bishop of Sheffield's address was very moving and sympathetic:

'Only a few days ago, all seemed happy and smiling with your loved ones. Work was good, wages were good, the weather was good, everything seemed good. Then, in a moment, a cloud descended upon us, and we are plunged in the darkness of the shadow of death. For those who have lost their nearest and dearest, our hearts beat, and go out to them in prayerful sympathy that God may succour them in their time of trial and trouble.

'We have admiration and respect for the heroism which has characterised this terrible catastrophe. The silver lining of the cloud has been the rescue parties who descended the fire-stricken mine, and tried to rescue those who were doomed.

'While we cherish admiration for the heroism of those who are dead, we also offer our respect for the heroism of those who were ready to die, and who are always ready to die for those who are perishing.

'We cannot, at the moment, understand the mystery of this tragedy. At the beginning of the week, everything seemed to be inspiring and glorious. Our King and Queen have been in our midst, and we know how you value the sympathy of their Majesties. God moved in a mysterious way. That day will be revealed in the great day of revelations.'

Mary, Jim and their family listened to the Bishop's comforting words as they sat in the church, waiting for the committals to begin in the prepared areas of the cemetery.

They cast their eyes towards the rows of coffins placed within the chancel. Sunlight shone through the stained-glass windows, partially relieving the cool dimness within the church. They were thinking back to that morning, when undertakers' carts had collected the coffins for their final journey to church.

Assembled friends and neighbours watched on the streets with sad expressions and heavy hearts. Men lifted their caps as a token of respect for their deceased comrades. Women bowed their heads, pressing hands to their faces to stifle the tears.

There had been an eerie, chilled silence running along the streets, as if cold, relentless death was passing over. Most people had experienced similar circumstances before, as death was always lurking, ready to pounce on the unsuspecting, but the scale of the disaster had drawn new, unwanted boundaries of loss. People could not come to terms with it.

* * *

The large company of mourners moved slowly out of the church to the accompaniment of the sweet strains of Chopin's Funeral March. The heat of the mid-afternoon was sweltering, but dark thunderclouds had lowered and a storm threatened.

The coffin of Mr Chambers was taken to a corner of the cemetery and his body committed to Mother Earth. His plot was at the head of a long line of ominous looking trenches.

It seemed very fitting that the manager should be buried alongside his men. As the final notes of the stirring 'Last Post' travelled across the open grave, a terrible storm broke overhead. Thunder boomed and lightning flashed in great, blue, jagged streaks, as if God was illustrating what had happened down the mine; the flash of flame then the dull roar of the explosion.

Torrential rain fell for half an hour. It was one of the fiercest storms known in Denaby for many years. The deluge meant that mourners in the cemetery had to reach shelter or brave the elements at the graveside.

Mary and Jim watched the lowering of John's coffin into the wet earth, raindrops mixing with tears as their heads bowed in sorrow. Murmurs of plaintive crying travelled all around the cemetery, each family feeling the keen loss of a loved one. Mary felt the overwhelming pain of losing her son, and she knew that she must also somehow summon up the strength to watch the committal of her brother's body.

The storm had resulted in delaying, considerably, the remainder of the funerals. They must wait.

The clergy did not conclude their sorrowful work until half-past eight in the evening. The mourning families walked home, exhausted and bereft.

* * *

Saturday 13th July 1912

Inspector Pickering's funeral was held at Doncaster, conducted by his close friend, Canon Sandford, Vicar of Doncaster. Crowds lined the streets to watch the cortege proceed through the town to the Minster.

He was a greatly respected gentleman, as well as a brilliant mining engineer. Two years previously, he had been awarded the Edward Medal for bravery. He had risked his life underground to stay with a doomed miner, who was pinned by his legs, in an accident at a pit near Leeds. The man had died, but not alone.

There was genuine surprise that a man of Mr Pickering's wide experience and superior knowledge had lost his life underground, but no one doubted his unfailing professionalism and unstinting dedication to safety.

He had bravely led the rescue party after the first explosion, and had died a hero.

Inspector Hewitt was buried at Sheffield the same day, and Assistant Inspector Tickle's funeral had been held the day before at Glasgow. Several funerals were also held at Conisbrough, Mexborough and Wath.

The whole district was united in grief, but Mr Bury continued to fight for his life in Fullerton Hospital.

* * *

That same day, there was another death in Denaby, which many thought should be attributed to the disaster. A Denaby miner had spent Wednesday, the day after the explosions, stretchering out bodies, one of which was his brother-in-law. This had affected him so greatly that, on returning home, he told his wife:

'The sight was horrible. I shall never forget it if I live to be a hundred. I shall never go down the pit again.'

Three days later, he committed suicide by drowning himself in the River Don. At his inquest, his wife said that he had never slept in his bed after Wednesday.

He would just come home, take a cup of tea and say, 'I'll look sharp down to our May's,' where he would comfort his widowed sister. She also said her husband had never had any trouble before the colliery explosion.

The Coroner's verdict was, 'Drowned while mentally affected'.

* * *

Sunday 14th July 1912

More funerals were held over the weekend at Denaby, Conisbrough and Mexborough. One of the Conisbrough funerals was for a nineteen-year-old miner who had been back at work for only a fortnight, after illness. He had spent several weeks in Conisbrough Isolation Hospital, recovering from an attack of typhoid. Another funeral was for two brothers, aged nineteen and twenty. They were born in Oxfordshire but had moved to Conisbrough to work at Cadeby pit, alongside their father. They lived on Northcliffe Road, and were buried together in Conisbrough Cemetery.

* * *

That Sunday night, Mr Charles Bury, the hugely popular Cadeby manager, died in Fullerton Hospital. For almost six days, he had clung on to life, having fitful periods of consciousness.

He was a young man of thirty-five, slightly built, but fit and strong. It was hoped that he would pull through, despite the terrible effects of the explosion. But the deadly fumes of the mine had affected his brain so much that he had died whilst unconscious.

Father Kavanagh had been sent for earlier in the evening, and, in his dying moments, Mr Bury was received a Roman Catholic, with the prospect of a Roman Catholic burial. His death was bitterly lamented by all who knew him.

* * *

Tuesday 16th July 1912

One week after the disaster, a meeting was held at The Station Hotel, Conisbrough, to decide on the question of resuming work at Cadeby pit. It was attended by Mr Herbert Smith, President of the Yorkshire Miners' Association, members of the Miners' Inspection Committee and representatives of Cadeby Main colliers. After days of removing bodies and burying the victims, normal work of coal production had to be considered. Some work had already started at Denaby pit, and it was necessary to discuss when workers could return to Cadeby Colliery.

The Inspection Committee reported that they had made a thorough inspection of the Cadeby workings in all but the sealed-off area and they now recommended that work be resumed as quickly as possible, with the exception of the South District, which they regarded as not yet being safe.

The recommendation was unanimously agreed by the Cadeby men, and a resolution was carried in favour of the immediate resumption of work in all parts of the pit, except the district adjacent to the stoppings which sealed off the affected workings, as well as the bodies of their workmates.

Miners had to accept that they could not have more time to mourn, and must come to terms with their fear. In the battle to earn a living, coalmining was a hard taskmaster.

The total weekly income of miners who were union members was a standard "out-of-work" allowance of nine shillings per man and one shilling a week for each child. Non-Union members received no income except charity.

With so many men out of work at a large colliery like Cadeby, the cost to Y.M.A. funds would be a substantial amount of money.

It was, therefore, in the interests of Herbert Smith and the Y.M.A. to bring about a quick return to work, but only if conditions at the pit met their safety requirements. The meeting concluded with the decision that work at Cadeby would be resumed with the backing of the union.

* * *

Tuesday 16th July 1912

The funeral of Mr Bury took place on Tuesday afternoon. Crowds gathered to watch his body leave Red House in Denaby, where he had lived with his Aunt, Mary Bury.

Mr Bury had moved to Denaby more than twenty years previously, when he was a mining student, articled to Mr William Chambers. He had shown such promise that he was given charge of Denaby Main pit, as manager, at the age of twenty-three.

He was a greatly admired man, held in high esteem by his colleagues, his colliers and numerous personal friends. Mr Bury had earned respect for his exceptional abilities as a mining engineer, gaining a reputation as one of the cleverest mine managers in the north of England.

He was also liked for his happy, good-natured disposition and strength of character. His love of cricket and its sporting enjoyment also had endeared him to many hearts.

The cortege was watched by many villagers as it progressed to the Catholic Church, where rows of colliers stood at the back to witness the bestowing of the last rites on their respected manager.

The service was taken almost entirely in Latin, with all the ceremonial aspects of a Roman Catholic funeral. The people of Denaby said a respectful goodbye to their heroic manager, only one year at Cadeby, but greatly admired.

* * *

Wednesday, 17th July 1912

Miners returned to work with a mixture of anxiety and resignation. In some ways, life had resumed its normal course, but to many, life would never be the same again.

As a result of the disaster, over sixty widows and one hundred and thirty children would be potential dependants. Little time was lost in setting up a Cadeby Colliery Disaster Relief Fund for the maintenance of those women and children.

Contributions immediately started to pour in from all walks of life, including local churches, companies, breweries, pubs, theatres, shops, schools, collieries and private individuals.

The first contribution of £100 came from Charles Thelluson of Brodsworth Hall, followed by Mr Buckingham Pope's £1,000 donation. His Majesty the King donated £100 and many others, including £50 from the Archbishop of York, £200 from Whitworth's Brewery, £250 from the Co-operative Wholesale Society and £1,000 from the South Yorkshire Trade Association.

Even poor people scraped together donations. Miss Lily Finney, a servant girl, donated 2 shillings and 6 pence. Mr Middleton, a postman, contributed the same amount and Mr T Harris, a working man, donated one shilling. Contributions were even received from Canada and New Zealand.

It was decided that a meeting would be held in August for the purpose of appointing Trustees of the Fund, and also a committee to administer funds. The generosity of the contributors was greatly admired and appreciated.

* * *

Thursday 18th July 1912

Winnie opened the back door and guided Maggie into the kitchen. They had spent the afternoon next door with her own family, something she had been doing most days since Bob's death.

She felt as if she needed their constant love and support to help her through this awful time. She almost felt as if she was a child again, finding comfort from her mother and father's protective loyalty.

'Come on, let's go and see Grandma Sarah,' she said to Maggie as they stepped into the living room.

436

She could see Sarah's snow-white hair as it rested on the back of the chair. It was still called Albert's chair.

'Sshh, I think Grandma's asleep,' Winnie whispered, placing her forefinger across her lips. Maggie nodded and copied the gesture that she'd seen many times before.

Winnie stepped round the chair and glanced at Sarah, then quickly looked again, peering intently. She could feel a strange atmosphere, a cold quietness that enveloped the space.

Sarah was completely still. Her body was relaxed, as if weighed down, but her face was different. Her skin was pale but unwrinkled, the lines around her mouth were now smoothed away. There was even the hint of a smile etched onto her features.

Winnie touched her hand, and was not surprised to feel its cold stiffness. She opened the fingers gently and removed the pipe, Albert's pipe, that nestled in Sarah's lap.

'Come on outside, Maggie, we don't want to wake Grandma up,' Winnie managed to say as she controlled her ragged breathing. She knew Sarah would never wake up again, that she would never have to grieve for all her lost loved ones again. She had gone to join them.

* * *

Tuesday 23rd July 1912

Mary woke up with a heavy heart and swollen eyes. Her fingers traced the puffiness that stung her face, the soreness that stretched her dry skin. It even hurt when she blinked her eyes.

She sighed deeply. She felt as if she had done nothing but cry for days and days. First John, then Bob, then her mother. All lost in the space of less than two weeks.

The only moments of relief from all the pain, was the happiness of Joseph and Rose that their baby boy was healthy and thriving.

Joseph John was their longed-for son, a ray of hope and optimism in the midst of so much despair.

The events of the previous day rushed around in Mary's head, making her feel almost nauseous. The funeral had been so hard to bear. Everyone had felt such shock at Sarah's death.

The hardest part was that they had not had the chance to say goodbye. She had died on her own, in her husband's chair, clutching Albert's pipe.

At least the funeral had allowed them to say their own personal goodbyes, but, oh, how difficult it had been. Mary and Gertie had stood rigid and quiet with grief, Betty had been speechless in her overwhelming sadness and poor Ivy had been inconsolable, her sobbing and wailing wrenching at their hearts.

Other people had looked on, pensive and emotional at the loss of such a lovely lady. Sarah had always been a stalwart in her family, a kind, caring, strong matriarchal figure.

The doctor had stated that her death was the result of a heart attack, but everyone thought it was the shock of losing Bob and John so suddenly. She had never fully recovered from Albert's death. Her heart was so broken, it had given up. Many people believed she was yet another victim of the disaster.

* * *

Wednesday 24th July 1912

One week after the return to work, the Cadeby Disaster Inquest was held at The Denaby Main Hotel. The Coroner, Mr Allen, and his twelve-man jury were charged with investigating the deaths of the eighty-eight victims of the disaster on 9th July.

Mr Allen took his seat at 10.30 am, and amongst those present were the Home Office representative, Mr J. Wilson, Mr G. Poole, His Majesty Inspector of Mines, Mr W. Chambers, managing director of Denaby and Cadeby Collieries and Mr Herbert Smith, president of the Yorkshire Miners' Association.

Eight witnesses were called to give narratives on what they had seen and done on the fateful day, including Mr Witty and Inspector Wilson. Their narratives covered how the explosions were discovered, their possible causes, how the victims were found and the remarkable escapes of some men.

After their recounts had been heard, Mr Allen stated that any further enquiries would terminate for the present. He said they had ample evidence to assist them in finding out how the men had died, and also sufficient evidence to enable them to come to a conclusion to ascertain by what means they had died.

It was not within the province of the jury to go further than that. It was not their duty to apportion blame.

The Home Office intended carrying out a separate pending Inquiry and requested that the Inquest should keep their investigation short of the actual cause of the disaster, and so the evidence was freed from scientific terms and detailed, technical matters.

This lightened the burden of the jury considerably. The coroner instructed the jury not to attempt to express an opinion as to the cause of the disaster.

The jury retired and consulted for only twenty minutes, before returning a verdict of '*Accidental Death*, caused by two gas explosions in Cadeby Colliery on 9th July, 1912.'

Mr Smith showed immediate dissatisfaction with the verdict, stating:

'Is that all the finding of the jury?'

Mr Allen was surprised. 'Yes, that is all. You don't suggest that it is murder, do you?' he asked.

'But isn't something to be said about the people who were prevented from making enquiries?' Mr Smith retaliated.

'I think it is a very proper verdict,' was the coroner's reply.

'We have tried to keep clear of any future Inquest that may be made,' explained the foreman of the jury.

'They don't say that anyone is either to blame or is not to blame,' concluded the coroner.

Before closing the Inquest, Mr Allen thanked the jury for their services and stated that there would have to be another Inquest on the remaining fourteen victims still unrecovered.

Mr Herbert Smith was unhappy with this speedy, undetailed verdict. He decided he would take matters further in future.

PART ELEVEN

Chapter 90
August 1912

The Denaby and Cadeby miners were back at work, but there was still a strange, unsettling atmosphere in the nearby villages.

The Home Office Inquiry into the disaster was impending, but fourteen entombed bodies remained, waiting to be recovered from the stopped-off area in Cadeby pit's South District.

Anxiety and indecision hung in the air, as there had still been no formal explanation of how and why the explosions had happened. Miners offered their own experienced, pragmatic theories to fellow workers, but caution was necessary in the way they expressed and shared these personal opinions. No one wanted to lose their job, yet loyalty to the victims was keenly felt.

This tussle of emotions created restlessness and unease within the close mining community.

* * *

5th August 1912

The Inquiry began on 5th August, 1912 and lasted only three days, when it was adjourned. It was held at the Guildhall, Doncaster, led by Mr Redmayne, H.M. Chief Inspector of Mines.

The formal investigation into the causes and circumstances of the Cadeby Colliery explosions was adjourned until such time as the affected South District area could be safely inspected by Mr Redmayne.

* * *

18th August 1912

On the afternoon of 18th August, a member of the Manvers Main rescue party died underground at Cadeby Colliery. They were carrying out the task of advancing beyond the stoppings of the affected South District, to bring out as many bodies as possible.

Whilst carrying out a body on a stretcher, the man gave a pre-arranged alarm signal that he had temporarily lost the mouthpiece to his breathing apparatus. The rescue party immediately left the body and proceeded to assist the man in replacing his mouthpiece.

They walked as quickly as possible from the affected workings, but after only one hundred yards, the man lost his mouthpiece again when he fell. His workmates retrieved the mouthpiece and tried to fit it into the man's mouth, but his jaws were locked. They tried and tried, but could not open them.

The rescue party stayed with him some time, but then came to the conclusion that the man was dead. Their own oxygen was almost spent so they had to leave him and head for an unaffected area. The rescue party, and many other people, considered that this death should also be attributed to the disaster.

Yet another victim.

* * *

23rd August 1912

An advertisement appeared in the front page of *The Yorkshire Post*:

Cadeby Colliery Disaster Relief Fund.

Notice is hereby given that a meeting of subscribers will be held at the offices of Messrs. J. W. and A. E Hattersley, Solicitors, Mexborough, on Friday 23rd August, 1912, at 5.00 pm, for the purpose of appointing Trustees of the Fund and a Committee to administer the same, and of approving the draft of the deed upon the Trusts and subject to the provisions of which the Fund is to be held and applied, and of passing the necessary resolutions.

Mr N. Laidlow, Treasurer
Sheffield Bank Company Ltd. Mexborough

Trustees for the Relief Fund were drawn from the ranks of the noble and great with local or coalmining connections. At the meeting on 23rd August, it was resolved that the following be appointed Trustees of the Fund, and that the said sum of £7,045. 2s. 9d be forthwith paid over to them:
- The Right Honourable Charles Alfred Worsley Anderson Pelham, Earl of Yarborough
- The Right Honourable Charles Lindley Wood, Viscount Halifax
- Sir Charles Norris Nicholson, Baronet
- General Robert Calverley Alington Bewicke-Copley, - Esq.
- William Wright Warde-Aldam, Esq.

The working Committee for administering the Relief Fund was to be made up of ecclesiastical dignitaries, colliery management and professional people. These included Reverend Strawbridge, William Chambers, Mr Laidlaw and John William Hattersley.

Mr Laidlaw, the Mexborough Bank manager, submitted a list of potential dependents for an actuarial analysis, to the District Manager of the Commercial Union Assurance Company.

The one hundred and ninety-five potential dependents were divided into widows, boys and girls, and categorised by age. There were sixty-three widows, the youngest aged eighteen years and the oldest aged sixty-seven years. There were fifty-two boys from under one year to twelve years old, and eighty girls from under one year to twelve years old.

At least two more children were to be added when they were born. It was noted, however, that it was strange that children of thirteen and fourteen years of age were not on the list, as if twelve years of age was considered the upper limit for child maintenance.

The widows and children waited for any kind of support to ease their destitution.

* * *

21st September 1912

The bodies of all the victims of the disaster were finally retrieved from the pit in September. Mr Allen, the District Coroner and his jury met at the colliery offices on Saturday, 21st September 1912 for the purpose of taking evidence of identification of the last six bodies recovered.

The widows had been waiting for two long months to perform their identifications, greatly increasing their pain. For two of these widows, however, the suspense was not over, as they could not positively identify the last two bodies as their husbands.

Neither man had come home since the explosions, and they were both working night shifts at Cadeby Colliery on the fateful day, so the Coroner stated that there was no doubt that they had both died on 9th July.

However, it was deemed that the two husbands could have already been buried under another name. Mr Allen declared that it was impossible to tell where they were buried, and, if they started trying to get to know where they really were, it would upset the feelings of other families who had relatives buried.

He would, however, do his best to provide the widows with the proper death certificates. The grieving widows had to accept the sad mistake.

* * *

23rd September 1912

The last burial services in connection with the disaster were held at Denaby Parish Church on Monday, 23rd September.

The mourners included the widows and relatives of the two victims who had not been satisfactorily identified.

In these sad circumstances, the services had a special significance as the vicar addressed the congregation. He stated that they were gathered together for the purpose of committing to the ground 'the poor earthly bodies of two men, who, by whatever name they were known by in earthly life, had died nobly and bravely.'

He continued:

'We have been asking week by week that the men and women should pray for those who have lost the men they have loved, and they have been praying. Now, today, we have an added sorrow. There is doubt in the minds of those who are left whether they are really, this afternoon before the altar of God with the bodies of those whom they loved. And therefore, we want to ask ourselves, 'What are we praying for this afternoon? What are we doing?'

'We always do two things in a burial service. We commit the souls of those who have gone to God's love and protection. We commit the dust to the dust whence it came. We are, with no shadow of doubt, and with absolute confidence, gathered here today, before the altar of God, to commit these two souls with Christian reverence and Christian faith. There is an earthly body and a spiritual body. Whatever doubt some may feel about the first, there is none about the second.'

The congregation uttered united 'Amens' with tears in their eyes.

As they moved to the cemetery, they noticed that the graves had been prepared in close proximity to each other. The coffins each bore the inscription: 'Presumed to be…' before the name.

The widows listened to the vicar speak the committal sentences in turn, over each of the bodies. They had to accept that their husbands had gone, but it stung that they did not know where.

* * *

December 1912

Mr Redmayne had adjourned the Home Office Inquiry in August until such time as the work of extinguishing the underground fire and the recovery of the portion of the mine affected by the explosions, which had been walled off, had sufficiently advanced as to permit his making an underground inspection.

The workings were sufficiently recovered to allow him to make a partial inspection on 30th September, and he heard further evidence the next day, 1st October, but had again adjourned the Inquiry, hoping to be able to make a complete inspection within six weeks.

Circumstances had, unfortunately, not allowed him to carry out his intention. Mr Chambers had fully hoped to open up the walled-off workings, but on reconsideration, concluded that such a proceeding would present considerable danger, to which Mr Redmayne agreed.

The Inquiry was resumed on 5th December, when Mr Chambers explained:

'My desire is to get the coal still remaining in the explosion area, by working in another direction and not to go along the abandoned roads anymore. We can take the ventilation along a different course so that it does not percolate through the fire area.'

Mr Redmayne questioned if there would ever be a chance to inspect the affected area, but was reassured by other Mine Inspectors that they had carried out sufficient inspections, equipped with breathing apparatus, to provide valuable evidence that was of great importance in determining the cause of the two explosions.

Mr Redmayne decided that a second-hand report must suffice, and the Inquiry continued.

* * *

December 1912

1912 had been the blackest year in living memory for the mining community of Denaby and Conisbrough. People were anticipating the new year with relief and cautious optimism, hoping and praying that no new disasters and ordeals were waiting to pounce in the future.

The mining communities were tired, deflated and still grieving for all their lost loved ones, but life had to go on.

Winnie had moved back to live at her parents' home now that Bob and Sarah were both gone. Wilfred and Clara had welcomed their daughter and granddaughter with open arms, especially as Winnie was enduring the last few difficult weeks of pregnancy.

Everyone praised the way she was coping with the devastating loss of her beloved husband, Bob, but only she knew the depths of her despair.

She frequently crumbled in times of privacy, but, for once, she was thankful that she lived within a crowded, boisterous household. Moments of privacy were rare, yet she had only to close her eyes to feel the searing heartache and the crushing yearning for her Bob, the love of her life.

Only Maggie, and the new baby that she was carrying, provided her with the will to go on. She knew she had to be strong for them.

* * *

25th December 1912

Winnie gave birth to a fine, strong son on Christmas Day. She thought of him as her Christmas gift from Heaven. He was named Robert Wilfred, after Bob and her father.

People had reminded her that he would be added to the list of dependents, that he would receive a shilling a week, like Maggie, until the age of fourteen years.

As a widow, she received five shillings a week, unless she remarried. She wished, with all her heart, that she could have Bob back for the rest of her life, instead of charity from a Relief Fund.

Chapter 91
January 1913

Mr Redmayne sent his report of the Inquiry to the Home Office at the end of January.

It began by stating that, in compliance with the Home Secretary's instructions, he had held a formal investigation, in accordance with the requirements of Section 83 of the Coal Mines Act 1911, into the causes and circumstances surrounding the explosions which occurred at Cadeby Main Colliery on the morning of 9th July, 1912.

Eighty-eight persons lost their lives, thirty-five by the first explosion, and fifty-three by the second.

The Inquiry was completed in December 1912. The different interests represented were:
- The owners and management of the Denaby and Cadeby Main Collieries by Mr Gichard, solicitor of Rotherham.
- The Cadeby Main Branch of the Yorkshire Miners' Association, by Mr Marsden.
- The relatives of the deceased members of the Yorkshire Miners' Association, by Mr Herbert Smith, President.
- The Miners' Federation of Great Britain by Mr Smillie, President, and Mr Hartshorn.
- Twenty-four witnesses were summoned by Mr Redmayne, four of them at the suggestion of Mr Herbert Smith.

The report was divided into the following sections:
1. Description of Cadeby Colliery and method of working.
2. Description of the South District.
3. Conditions prevailing in the South District prior to and on the day of the explosions.
4. Narratives relating to the occurrence of the two explosions.
5. The sealing off of the affected portion of the mine.

6. The work of partial recovery of the sealed off portion of the district.
7. Conclusions.

Each section was reported in great detail, taking into account witnesses' recounts, scientific assessments and technical circumstances of the mine's workings.

Mr Redmayne concluded that there had been no breaches of the Coal Mines Act which contributed any cause to either explosion. He was, however, critical of many aspects of the Company's management of the Colliery.

As to the cause of the first explosion Mr Redmayne wrote:

'I think the fire originated some years ago, in the area around the fault, which had never been completely eradicated. There have been thirty-five fires since the mine opened. As more coal was extracted, a great cavity formed, and an accumulation of an explosive mixture, which was never fully sealed off. The conditions that Monday night provided just the combination of circumstances necessary to cause an explosion on a more extended scale.

'I believe Mr Chambers's earlier instructions were well conceived for effectively sealing off the affected area, but I do not believe these instructions were carried out in their entirety. Mr Bury, being dead, cannot appear in his defence, and I refrain from attaching blame to any one person.

'The second explosion seemed to have travelled wholly along the face and not divided. It may be that there was a large accumulation of gas on one side of the district after the first explosion, which, igniting at the fire, burnt more or less quietly up and down the coal face until an explosive mixture was formed.

'I have come to the conclusion that, as there had been a fire only days before the disaster, the affected area should have been completely stopped off, and all men should have been withdrawn from the district. Mr Chambers had stated that:

'If we withdrew working whenever we got fires, we should only have a pit to put gob fires out. We would get nothing else out. When the pit is standing, the fires are more liable to break out than when the coal face is advancing.'

'I disagree with this. It seems coal production and profit were put before safety preventative measures.'

Mr Redmayne was also critical of the organisation of the rescue work on 9th July, stating that too many rescuers went down the pit indiscriminately.

Mr Witty should have issued instructions prohibiting the descent into the mine of all persons who had no written authorisation to do so. Had this been done, the loss of life occasioned by the second explosion might have been much less.

Mr Redmayne even suggested that the management of a colliery may not be justified in allowing persons to risk their lives in order to recover and bring out dead bodies when there is a high risk of a second explosion, as was the case at Cadeby Colliery.

He did acknowledge, however, that there would be differences of opinion about that, and that sentiment weighs heavily when there is an intense desire on the part of the relatives of the dead to see and bury the bodies.

He concluded that the defective organisation by some of the officials resulted in there being great difficulty in obtaining the correct number of victims and casualties. This was very regrettable, and emphasised the necessity of strict discipline in these matters.

The official Inquiry was over.

* * *

February 1913

Mary panted as she lifted and emptied the bucket of dirty water. She had noticed, more and more, that the strain of lifting and bending made her easily become breathless. Her heart would pound and involuntary gasps would slowly settle the increasing weakness and fatigue that occurred when doing anything strenuous.

She tried to hide all this, and was grateful when Violet, although only ten years old, often offered to help with the continuous household tasks, but Jim was beginning to show concern.

His steady, intent gaze would track her tempered movements and register her frequent rests in-between the many chores.

'I'll just have a minute,' she would say, realising and remembering that her mother, Sarah, used to say the exact same words.

'Are you sure you're all right, Mary?' Jim would often ask.

'I'm fine,' she would answer breezily. 'I *am* nearly forty-one, and houses don't clean themselves!' she would quip, trying to deter his scrutiny.

'You're right, we're both gettin' on,' he would joke, trying to hide his anxiety. But they both knew each other too well to cover up their true emotions.

Although it was more than six months since the disaster, feelings were still raw and painful. Time could not diminish the agony of their loss.

John was missed so much by everyone. Mary could still sense his presence in the house, still detect his scent on his clothes that she had so lovingly washed and folded away.

She had so few physical souvenirs of her precious boy. But she comforted herself with her memories of him, his looks, his playful teasing and his intense desire for a fairer world.

The memories would drain her, so keen was her pain, but she would not be without them. They wrapped a warm blanket of love and pride around her.

Jim retained his grief inside, but there was a long shadow of sorrow cast on his life that could not be concealed. He had lost his only son, but he acknowledged Mary's even greater pain.

She had lost her son, her brother and her mother in one cruel fell swoop of time. He reasoned that her health and spirits were bound to be affected, but he was afraid. He just hoped that time would allow her to become stronger.

Their grandson, baby Joe, gladdened their hearts at this sad time. He provided some welcome respite from their grieving.

Rose and Joseph delighted in his placid, contented nature, thankful for his thriving, soft chubbiness and happy smiles. The baby also helped strengthen the reconciliation between Walter and Joseph, much to everyone's joy. Mary and Jim could not handle any more rifts in the family.

Gertie, Ivy and Mary had become even closer as they mourned, giving each other mutual comfort and support.

Gertie had become the dominant strength in the family, pragmatic like her father, yet resolute and dependable like her mother. Annie was the light of her life, a friendly, confident twelve-year-old girl, enjoying school life at the recently opened 'Council School' on Balby Street in Denaby. Charlie and Gertie still felt blessed to have a daughter, their only child.

Ivy really missed her mother, as well as Bob and John, but Sam had gently made her realise how lucky she was to have such a loving family; many had not. She and Sam led busy lives, running the shop, and looking after young Albert, now nine years old, and Emmie, almost five, but Ivy still pined for her mum and dad. They would always have a very special place in her heart.

Sister Betty had wept copious tears and felt such heartache at the loss of her loved ones, although she still always tried to be positive and resilient in her attitude to life.

She and Arthur had recently received thrilling news. Their daughter, Clarrie, had become engaged to be married, and even more exciting was that her fiancé, Sidney, was one of Earl Fitzwilliam's coachmen.

'Sidney has a very responsible position,' Betty had proudly informed everyone. 'He's responsible for looking after the Earl's coaches. He even has his own living quarters in the stable block!'

'Who'd have thought our Clarrie would end up livin' at t' Big House!' Arthur added, shaking his head.

'No one, Arthur, no one. Not in a million years!'

Betty just wished her parents and brother had lived to see Clarissa's good fortune.

* * *

March 1913

The *Mexborough and Swinton Times* reported on the sudden death of a Deputy who had been badly injured in the second explosion at Cadeby on 9th July.

The Last Victim. Deputy Suddenly Expires. Effects of Gas Poisoning. were the headlines.

The Deputy was said to have had a 'miraculous escape' when he survived the explosion, but was found dead in bed only months later.

He had managed to give evidence at the Home Office Inquiry, where he had stated 'I felt a scorching across my eyebrows.' But he was also left in a collapsed state.

Dr Ford had attended him when he was brought home by motor car early in the afternoon of 9th July. The doctor had given evidence that the man was suffering from burns on his arms, face, body and hips, had bruises all over his body, and was suffering from shock and gas poisoning. He had also complained of a burning sensation in his mouth and throat.

At the Inquest into the man's death, held at the Denaby Main Institute, Coroner Mr Allen stated to the jury that it would be necessary to listen to the evidence of how the man was found dead, as well as to consider if his death was due, or in any way connected, with the explosion.

The first witness called was the man's widow, who said that, before the explosion, her husband's health had been good. He had left home on 9th July for his usual 'day shift', 6.00 am until 2.00 pm. She next saw him when he was brought home at 1.30 pm, after the second explosion.

Dr Ford attended him that evening. Since that day, her husband had not been well, and kept having spasms from then on. He had been able to start work six months later, on 15th January, and had worked until a few days ago. He was found dead in bed the previous day and she had sent for Dr Ford that morning.

Mr Witty also gave evidence that the deceased, as Deputy, went down with a rescue party at about 6 am on 9th July. He saw him at the top of the pit in a somewhat collapsed state when he was brought up about twelve noon.

Dr Ford stated that he had attended the deceased for the next three months after the explosion. The man had complained of shortness of breath and weak action of the heart, known as cardiac asthma. He had last seen him alive on 10th February. The doctor stated that death was due to heart failure; he could suggest no other cause.

The form of poisoning, from which the deceased was suffering, was carbon monoxide.

In his summing up, the coroner said he had not considered it necessary to reiterate the details of the Cadeby mine explosion. What the jury had to consider was the cause of death. After a few minutes' deliberation in private, the jury returned a unanimous verdict as follows:

'Death was due to heart failure, following cardiac asthma, the result of breathing carbon monoxide in the Cadeby Main explosion on 9th July, 1912.'

The Deputy's widow and family heard this verdict, and believed that he was the third additional victim of the disaster, making a total of ninety-one rather than the 'official' total of eighty-eight.

Her husband died aged forty-five. What was not stated at the Inquest, was that their son was also killed in the second explosion. Their lad was nineteen.

* * *

June 1913

The women were seated around the table, sharing chatter and banter about recent news, both local and national, reported in the *Sheffield Telegraph* and the *Mexborough and Swinton Times*.

Mary liked to have visitors, liked to have a room full of people again. She hated being alone. It only made her even more aware of the missing people in her life.

Rose cuddled baby Joe as he slept contentedly in her arms. 'He's been trying to walk so much, it's tired him out!' she laughed.

'Yes, he'll be glad of a nap,' Mary agreed, gazing fondly at her grandson.

Winnie had baby Bob on her lap. At six months old, he was now much more aware of his surroundings and enjoyed being fussed over by other people.

'My how he's grown!' Ellen had remarked when she saw him. 'It's only been a few weeks, but I can see the difference!'

'Yes, everyone says that,' Winnie agreed. 'And how much he looks like his father.' Mary heard the catch in her voice and reached out to stroke her hand.

'Bob would be so proud of him,' she whispered to her sister-in-law. Tears sprang to everyone's eyes. It was so sad.

Rose sniffed and dabbed at her eyes. She felt she should try to lighten the mood, and began talking about the new "Picture House" being built in Denaby. She had read all about the details in the *Times*, and was looking forward to it opening in November. She read out a few of the reported plans.

'It's going to be called The Empire Palace and will be built upon the most modern lines, with every possible comfort for the patrons,' she quoted.

'It will be equipped with comfortable, continuous seating in the cheaper seats, and velvet tip-up seats in the better parts. A gas engine and dynamo will be installed so that the hall will be excellently lighted with electricity of its own making. The heating will be efficiently carried out on the low-pressure hot water system. The ventilation, which plays an exceedingly important part in an up-to-date cinema house, will be thoroughly studied, so that the health and comfort of the patrons will be ensured. Excellent, large entrances will give access to the hall, and there will be ample exits so that the hall can be cleared of people in a few minutes.

'To give a perfectly clear view of the pictures on the screen, the floor will be made to slope, so that every person will be ensured of a first-class view. The interior of the building will be tastefully decorated, and the operator's box will be absolutely fireproof.

'Generally, the scheme from the details and plan supplied to us, appears to be the outcome of a great amount of thought and experience, and should be a boon to the inhabitants of the district. It is certain to be greatly appreciated. Success is bound to follow in the wake of such a thoughtful and enterprising body of promoters, who evidently have a unique experience of cinematography.'

'Blimey!' Ellen cried. 'I can hardly wait for it to open!' Everyone smiled and nodded their agreement.

'If it's as popular as The Picture House at Conisbrough, it'll be full every night!' Winnie declared.

'Mr Buckingham Pope would have been proud to see it built in Denaby,' Mary mused. 'It was sad to hear that he died suddenly only last week while he was abroad in Tangier.'

'Well, he was seventy-five, and supposed to be in good health when he was last in Denaby only a few weeks ago,' Ellen remarked. 'His death was due to bronchial pneumonia, it said in The Telegraph,' she added.

'I read that his nephew, Captain Maurice Pope, is going to take over as Chairman of The Company,' Mary said. 'Let's hope he makes a good job of it.'

'I'm surprised you haven't mentioned anything about Emily Davison, Ellen,' Winnie remarked with a smile.

Ellen closed her eyes and shook her head.

'I just couldn't believe what she did!' she breathed. 'To think that she stepped in front of the King's horse, in front of all those people at Epsom Derby! Including the King and Queen!'

'But she died a slow death, four days later. All those internal injuries. The horse couldn't do anything to avoid her, they say,' Mary interrupted. Ellen's eyes glazed over, as if looking into the future and continued:

'Yes, but she was willing to die for The Cause. She believed so passionately that women should have the right to vote. She was even holding the Suffragette flag when she stepped in front of the horse. For years, she'd dedicated her life to supporting Emmeline Pankhurst's Women's Social and Political Unit. She became a radical and militant member, going to prison, even being force-fed when she went on hunger strike. The authorities didn't know what to do with her! In the end, she gave her life to try to bring about change. She believed that by disallowing women the vote, the state was classing them as second-rate citizens. I think she died a heroine!'

'Some people called her a mentally-ill fanatic though, and said she committed suicide,' Rose said.

'Well, it's true that the papers were more concerned about the King's horse and jockey,' Ellen observed. 'But there were still thousands lining the streets of London at her funeral!'

The women looked at Ellen's resolute face and absorbed her heartfelt words. They respected her fervent admiration for the Suffragette Movement, but they were undecided and uneasy about its concept. They were almost glad when baby Joe woke up and the conversation could revert back to babies and cups of tea.

* * *

July 1913

Many people viewed the prospect of the first anniversary of the disaster with trepidation. Distressing memories of that awful day would stir their buried sorrow, tormenting them with bitter regret and yearning for what could have been.

Emotions may have settled and calmed, but they still lay in wait, ready to erupt to the surface, ready to renew the pain and hurt felt so keenly by relatives and friends of the victims. Yet, for others, it would be a welcome time to publicly remember their menfolk with love and pride, an opportunity to feel their closeness, even from beyond the grave. So, it was with dual emotions, that the folk of Denaby and nearby districts awaited the date.

9th July, 1913

Special services were held at the local churches to mark the importance of this poignant anniversary. Many tears flowed, many thoughts revolved around the terrible events of that awful day, prompting some people to put into words their innermost feelings. One such poem was printed in the local newspaper.

Poem to Commemorate the Cadeby Disaster – 1913 (1 year anniversary)

In memory of those who lost their lives in the Cadeby Pit explosions, 9th July, 1912.

How soon a year has passed away,
Since that both glad and fateful day,
Which, first with joy, filled every heart,
And then disaster left its mark.

In Conisbrough district – oh, so fair,
Stand Ancient Castle ruins there,
This had our King and Queen impressed,
And caused them there to take a rest.

'Twas this that filled each heart with glee,
Our gracious Majesties to see,
And every voice rang out with cheers,
But soon to be subdued with tears.

That midnight shock was one of fire,
Which twisted men like ropes of wire,
One look sufficient to suffice,
That God knew best the sacrifice.

And still like wind the bosoms sigh,
And tears like raindrops fill the eye,
We feel afresh the pain and loss,
Which these few awful hours cost.

Time may blunt the sharpest sting,
But memories will for ever cling,
No one can ever fill their place,
They have left too wide a space.

Some of the bravest of our race,
Went down that mine to lend their aid,
Whose members should not be defaced,
But with true heroes take their place.

They may be black and charred with fire,
When brought out from the burning mire,
Dear Lord! It is to thee we pray,
That thou has washed their sins away!

Oh gracious God, who knoweth all,
Have mercy on those precious souls,
Whose noble lives were freely given,
And grant them perfect rest in Heaven.

(Written by Mrs W. Beardshall, 5, Station Road, Wombwell)

There was true admiration for this touching poem. Mrs Beardshall had encompassed and reflected the heartfelt emotions shared by many. They were moved by the poem's words and tender messages.

* * *

July 1913

As well as bittersweet feelings and memories, the anniversary of the disaster had awakened cynical, aggrieved emotions.

The mining community harboured private, furtive opinions that some degree of blame and culpability could be attributed to the Company's relentless management of the mines.

At the very least, people criticised and condemned the bosses' system of ruthless control, with many believing that negligence and a cruel disregard for the men's safety had been major factors in the cause and results of the explosions. But people were reluctant, if not afraid, to voice their opinions publicly.

The Company held a powerful vice on their freedom of speech. Miners had to remain silent if they valued their jobs. The union officials, however, could speak up. They could direct the contempt and blame that the miners felt towards their employers through more formal, wide-ranging channels.

* * *

July 1913

That same month, a remarkable parliamentary debate was held in The House of Commons, which addressed the Cadeby Main disaster of the previous year. During question time, Mr John Wadsworth, Labour Member of Parliament for Hallamshire, asked the Home Secretary, The Right Honourable Reginald McKenna, three questions:

1) Had he received a copy of Mr Smillie and Mr Hartshorne's report, which was sent from The Miners' Federation of Great Britain, regarding the Inquiry held into the Cadeby Main disaster of 9th July, 1912, in which report they alleged that there were breaches of the coal Mines Act?

2) Was he satisfied that such breaches of the Coal Mines Act did take place?

3) Was it his intention to take any action against the management at this colliery?

Mr McKenna replied that he had received a copy of the report from Mr Smillie, President of The Miners' Federation, and stated that he agreed with the Chief Inspector, Mr Redmayne, that there were points where the requirements of the Act had not been complied with.

However, Mr McKenna noted that Mr Redmayne had formed the opinion that the responsibility laid primarily with the manager, Mr Bury, who lost his life, and that, in view of the fact that the fire would have probably been got under control without accident if the directions of the managing director, Mr Chambers, had been carried out.

Therefore proceedings could not be taken with any prospect of success against Mr Chambers, as was desired by Mr Smillie and the Miners' Federation.

Furthermore, Mr McKenna stated that the report was not sent to The Home Office until 30th May, therefore the time allotted by the Act for the institution of proceedings, six months after the disaster, had expired in January. Time had run out for any further proceedings against the Management of Cadeby Colliery.

Mr William Brace, Labour M.P. for Glamorgan South and, like Mr Wadsworth, a Trade Unionist, retaliated by asking Mr McKenna if he was aware that Mr Chambers had declared he would not, under similar circumstances, withdraw the workmen from the mine, despite the fact that it was a grave violation of the Coal Mines Act not to do so, and despite the fact that more than eighty lives were lost. Mr Brace insisted that Mr Chambers had wholly failed to realise his responsibility for human life, and questioned Mr McKenna as to whether he considered Mr Chambers to be a fit and proper person to have miners' lives placed under his care.

Mr McKenna replied that he had consulted with Mr Redmayne on that point, and was informed that the Act stated that responsibility laid only with the Manager, not the Managing Director.

Actions to decide competency could only be brought against the Manager, who was killed. Consequently, both on the grounds of time and personal responsibility, there could be no possibility of action being taken.

Mr Brace was not satisfied with the reply, and the debate continued. He stated that the Miners' Federation of Great Britain was very aggrieved with the circumstances involved in connection with the disaster. Mr Chambers was regarded as a general manager, who took a very active part in the management of the colliery.

Mr Redmayne's report had shown that Mr Chambers accepted the responsibility of giving the orders, therefore he should also accept the responsibility of the outcome. They felt that the dead colliery manager was being made to carry the burden of responsibility for the disaster unfairly.

They noted that there had been a series of gob fires prior to the explosions which the management had wrestled with, yet still the miners were required to carry on working in such a dangerous environment.

It was also remarkable that the miners had remained silent about the condition of the mine. Mr Brace intimated that fear of the management dictated this silence. He stated that the Federation was making the serious charge that due precaution was not taken to protect the lives and limbs of the men working in such bad conditions. Also, no word had been sent to Mr Pickering, Inspector of Mines, about the condition of the mine. In the end, he had given his life to solve the problem of the fire.

Mr Brace continued his passionate criticism by stating that miners' lives should be sacred, but there was a callousness about the accident which absolutely appalled him. While thirty-five bodies had been lying in the pit, a new shift was allowed to descend the shaft without even knowing about the terrible disaster. Only when the inspectors arrived was the winding of coal put an end to.

Mr McKenna once again stated that technicalities of the Mines Act meant that only the manager could be held responsible, and no proceedings could be taken against Mr Chambers, or anyone else, except within six months of the accident. The Home Office had no grounds for proceeding against Mr Chambers before January 1913, and now it was too late.

Although the Mines Act was only passed in 1911, the accident had already disclosed serious defects in the existing law. New amendment of the law was required. It was acknowledged that circumstances had delayed the gathering of evidence for the Inquiry, which led to a delayed report.

Six months had proved insufficient time to carry out a thorough investigation. It was, therefore, proposed to introduce, at the earliest opportunity, an amendment of the Coal Mines Act, extending the period during which a prosecution may be begun to three months after the Inquiry into an accident had been completed.

It was also proposed that the Home Secretary might order an Inquiry to be held with a view to determining who was at fault for any accident.

Mr McKenna also recognised the fact that there was a defect in the Act as it stood, and the law should be so amended that a person superior to the manager, when he was really in truth the manager, must be liable to have his work certificate suspended just as if he was the manager himself.

Finally, it had been strongly recommended by technical advisers that regulations were provided to direct that the men should be withdrawn in all cases similar to those existing at the Cadeby mine prior to the accident.

Dangerous conditions should not be determined by a matter of opinion on what they constituted. Mr McKenna expressed his hope that the explanation he had given would suffice.

There was criticism, however, from Sir Arthur Markham, Baronet and Liberal Member of Parliament for Mansfield. This was directed towards Mr Brace and in defence of Mr Chambers.

Sir Markham, an industrialist and mine owner, as well as politician, stated that he regretted that Mr Brace had used his position in The House to make statements reflecting on men who were not there to defend themselves.

He considered Mr Chambers to be an outstanding authority on gob fires, as well as an honourable man who would accept all responsibility for orders he gave. He questioned why Mr Brace had not instituted a prosecution in a court of law on behalf of the miners.

Mr Brace's sardonic reply was to acknowledge that no one knew better than the Right Honourable Baronet that employees have no right to take action against employers.

The Baronet retorted that there had been considerable panic in the mine on 9th July, which rendered it impossible to know the exact facts and produce a calm judgement of what happened. He believed there was not a mine in Great Britain that was worked in total conformity with the Mines Act, such were the numerous, complicated regulations. Mr Brace should acknowledge that it was impossible that every detail in the regulations could be attended to.

Mr Norman Craig, Conservative M.P. for Thanet, supported him by pointing out that if men were withdrawn every time there was a question of gob fires, they were also withdrawn from the ability to work and earn, producing yet more problems.

Mr Ernest Meysey-Thompson, Conservative M.P. for Handsworth, Birmingham, stated that there were great difficulties owing to the varying circumstances under which accidents occurred in mines, and it was impossible to foresee in every case what ought to be done. He had numerous miners in his own constituency who showed concern for working in distinctly dangerous conditions, such as those at Cadeby Colliery, and he agreed with them.

He felt that many accidents had not been dealt with in a satisfactory manner by the Home Office, and hoped proper precautions would be promoted in future. He urged that the provision of life-saving apparatus should be compulsory in every district of all pits.

The vote was taken, and Mr Brace and Mr Wadsworth's motion was defeated. There was a mixture of prolonged 'Cheers' and Labour cries of 'Sold once more.'

Denaby and Conisbrough miners would have been fascinated, and angered, to have witnessed this debate.

Chapter 92
August 1913

Jim and Mary glanced at each other from time to time in the companionable silence. The atmosphere in their living room was calm and comfortable, but also pensive.

The heat of the day was finally cooling, and the brightness outside contrasted to the gathering dimness inside. Occasions to be alone, just the two of them, were scarce. Work, family commitments and visiting friends resulted in quiet times being rare, but appreciated and savoured. Mary admitted to herself that she needed longer periods of peace and quiet these days. Her body seemed to need more and more rest.

'Violet will be home soon. She's been out playing since tea-time.' Mary remarked, looking up at Jim.

She was holding a serviette and a postcard, both printed remembrance souvenirs of the disaster. The decorative keepsakes had poignant poems and lists of the victims' names printed on them. She could not resist carefully taking them out of a special box, handling them with a sad reverence, then replacing them with a gentle sigh until the next time.

They brought on fresh, flowing tears and overwhelming regret. Seeing the names of lost loved ones was painful, yet a feeling of connection, of continuing love, was also gained. John and Bob were sorely missed.

Jim looked up from his chair and nodded. He watched as Mary stood up slowly and walked to the window. Each day, he was noticing her slower movements, her concentrated expressions, almost frowns, while carrying out everyday tasks, as though they were becoming too difficult, too draining.

He also saw the flashes of white that streaked her chestnut hair, not grey, but white, just like Sarah's used to be.

'Well, what do you think about the report of the Inquiry, then?' Mary asked, breaking into his thoughts. She settled back into her chair, waiting for his reply. He, along with many other people, had been reading about the published report of the Inquiry in the *Mexborough and Swinton Times*, and mostly there was scornful derision from the miners at its findings.

'I think that if our John was still 'ere, he'd 'ave been rantin' and ravin' about a lot o' things. Company's got away wi' everythin' scot-free. Only Mr Bury's been blamed, and he's dead! Even t' union couldn't do owt to get justice!'

Mary saw and heard his passion.

'You're right. Our John would've spoken up – even if he got into trouble!' Mary agreed, not without a strong resonance of pride. She remembered how she used to chastise him for being so outspoken, but now she was glad that he had been true to his beliefs. Yes, she was so proud of him.

'At least there's some good news in t' paper. It's all about the men goin' to Buckingham Palace to get their medals. Honoured heroes, they are,' Jim said proudly.

Six months earlier, the community had been greatly pleased to hear the announcement that Edward medals were to be awarded in connection with the rescue work at Cadeby. Six men were to be honoured for their outstanding courage, although many more could have been equally praised for their bravery.

Amongst the six was Sergeant Winch, as well as deputies and assistant managers at Cadeby, many of whom were first at the scene of the explosion.

The men had recently travelled to London to be awarded their medals by King George V at Buckingham Palace. Each Edward medal, awarded to recognise acts of bravery of miners, in endangering their lives to rescue fellow workers, was pinned onto each recipient's coat by the King himself, and each received his congratulations.

On the front of each medal was stamped 'For Courage', and on the back was stamped the representation of a miner working underground. The owner's name was stamped on the rim.

Denaby folk were proud to read this recount, and were greatly pleased to hear that a number of other courageous rescue workers were to be awarded silver life-saving medals of the order of St. John later in the year.

The St John Ambulance Brigade was well established in Denaby and the surrounding villages. It would be the first time, however, that a reigning monarch would bestow these medals. The journey to Buckingham Palace would indeed be a very special occasion for the recipients.

'They deserve their medals,' Mary whispered. 'That's all I can say.' She bowed her head and sighed.

* * *

October 1913

Mary was pleased that Bridie had started calling round more often. She always welcomed a chat and a cup of tea with her, especially as she seemed happier and more content than before.

Declan, a sturdy two-year-old, was playing happily with his toys on the rug, while Lottie sat on her mother's lap. The one-year-old little girl was still small for her age, but she was alert and interested in her surroundings, especially touching and patting little Joe who was sitting and bouncing on Mary's lap. Bridie seemed different since Lottie's accident. It was as if the stress and upset had shaken her out of a stupor. She now seemed more relaxed and interested in her family life.

It helped that she had less work and hardship now that the other children were older. Maria was a friendly, hard-working lass, with a naturally happy disposition. Even her parents' relationship and Bridie's melancholy nature had not affected that.

The fifteen-year-old twins, Eddie and Billy, had been working at the pit for over a year and brought in welcome money.

Louisa also helped around the house when not at school, but the twelve-year-old girl was still quiet and aloof, watching rather than participating readily in family life.

Ben, a solid, strong twenty-one-year-old man was a concern, as he had recently become louder and more impatient, almost aggressive in some instances.

His frustration had created unpleasant episodes, as though the tussle of having a child's mind in a man's body had increased his strength and determination. He would not stay as still or as quiet as he had before. His thrashing arms and noisy retorts would not cease at certain times.

He had succeeded in throwing himself around on the sofa in such a way that he fell to the floor, almost up to the fire. Bridie had confided in Mary that they had been forced to tie him to the sofa with a length of rope. It was for his own safety.

'Let's swap,' Bridie said, punctuating Mary's reverie. The two women smiled and reached out the two babies to each other.

'You'll find Lottie much lighter than Joe!' Bridie exclaimed as they cuddled the infants. Mary smiled and nodded, but her mind was registering something else.

She had definitely caught the smell of alcohol on Bridie's breath, and it wasn't the first time. It was strange because Bridie had always insisted that she hated the smell or taste of any alcohol. Her memories of the passing boarders in her family home were always associated with stale beer-and-spirits breaths, especially when they had been so close to her.

Mary studied her friend as she chatted to Joe.

'You're such a bonny lad,' she crooned. 'A blonde-haired bonny wee lad.'

'Yes, he's a darling little boy,' Mary agreed. 'And we're all so proud of him. Esther and Walter adore him. It's wonderful how little Joe has brought our two families closer together.'

She stroked Lottie's hair and kissed the little girl's hand, the one that still bore the marks of the missing fingertip. Dr Twigg had kept his word. He had monitored baby Lottie's health and thriving with continued diligence.

* * *

4th November 1913

Crowds of people streamed out of various exits of the building and began walking home in differing directions. They were happy and excited to have been the first audience at Denaby's brand new cinema, The Empire Palace.

The cold, black night could not stifle the ripples of opinionated chatter that flowed around the appreciative crowds. It was such a new experience for so many of the audience of over one thousand, an experience that had transported them into a thrilling, unknown world of moving pictures.

'Oh, I so enjoyed it!' Rose declared as she walked home with Ellen and Violet. 'The story and the characters seemed so real, and the screen is so big!' she enthused.

'I've never seen anything like it!' Violet exclaimed. 'I'll want to go there all the time now!'

'Well, we finally got to see a film and it was such a good choice – *Ivanhoe*,' Ellen announced with satisfied glee. 'Even after last night's disappointment!'

Almost two thousand people had gathered outside the cinema on Doncaster Road the previous night, expecting The Picture House to open its doors for the first time, as advertised.

They had been disappointed to hear that, due to an oversight, the licence to open and operate had not been granted. It was hoped to gain the relevant licence from Wakefield as soon as possible, and hopefully the following day.

'Well, I think it was worth waiting an extra day,' Rose insisted. 'It was marvellous!'

Ivanhoe was an American silent adventure film starring well-known actors William King Baggot and Herbert Brenon. It was a screenplay based on the 1819 historical novel written by Sir Walter Scott. Set in the Middle Ages, the chivalric romance included the characters Ivanhoe, Athelstane, Lady Rowena, Richard the Lion-Hearted, Prince John, Friar Tuck and Robin Hood.

Walter Scott's association with Conisbrough, especially the castle, gave the audience added interest. The production company of the film was Independent Moving Pictures, and it was distributed by the Universal Manufacturing Company.

Released only in September 1913, the film had a running time of 48 minutes, which equated to four reels, and it was silent but with English intertitles. The same Company had also recently released a short horror film, *Dr Jekyll and Mr Hyde*.

'I hope that film comes to Denaby soon!' Violet exclaimed.

'If you dare go and see it!' Rose laughed at her younger sister, pulling a scary face. Even Ellen laughed at them.

* * *

December 1913

A week before Christmas, the *Mexborough and Swinton Times* reported that, on 16th December, His Majesty the King had presented the Silver Life Saving Medal of the Order of St. John to seventeen men for gallantry displayed in Cadeby Main on 9th July 1912 and successive days.

The names included two local doctors, the manager of Wath Colliery, deputies from Denaby Main Colliery and the Vicar of Denaby.

The medal was originally instituted in 1874 as a reward for deeds of gallantry in saving, or attempting to save, life on land. It was granted to a person who knew there was danger at the time, but had still saved or attempted to save a living person.

An eyewitness had to guarantee this deed, and there had to be a counter-signature from his employer, clergyman or magistrate. No amount of heroism in the recovery of dead bodies would count.

The medals were not applied for by the recipients, it was The Order itself that first moved on the matter. The Secretary-General of The Order of St. John approached the Archbishop of York, who had close associations with The Order, as well as having been a frequent visitor to the stricken district of Denaby during and immediately after the explosions.

The Archbishop had promptly appointed a local committee to investigate the conditions of the disaster, and to watch the proceedings of the Inquests and Home Office Inquiry. The seventeen names chosen, who fulfilled all of the necessary criteria, were then approved by The Order.

The recipients travelled to London the day before the awards ceremony, and lodged in a hotel. The next day, the men were driven in a motor-bus to the gates of Buckingham Palace, where they were met by the Secretary-General of The Order.

They were conducted into a large hall within The Palace, and each person had a fastener placed on the lapel of his coat. They then walked into a smaller room where the King was waiting, and they formed a line in front of him and stood to attention.

After speaking a few words suitable to the occasion, the King reached for the medals, which were arranged on a nearby scarlet cushion, and pinned one onto each recipient's jacket. He shook each man's hand then thanked them for the bravery they had displayed during the disaster. He remarked that he was pleased to present the medals himself as he remembered the occasion all too well himself.

When the ceremony was over, the party marched out of the room and outside to the gates of The Palace. They were besieged by press-men and photographers, and were happy to have a group photograph taken.

Dignitaries from The Order then took charge of them, giving them a bus tour of some London sights, and treating them to a special luncheon at The Holborn Restaurant. Each man brought away a copy of the menu as a memento of a very happy occasion. After a few hours of further tourist wanderings, the party caught the train at 5.45 pm and arrived home in Denaby at 10 pm.

During the journey, the men were able to examine and admire their medals. On one side was an engraving of the Maltese Cross and lions, the emblems of The Order. The inscription read: 'For service in the cause of humanity'.

On the other side was an engraving of the wort plant, another emblem of The Order, with the inscription: 'Awarded by the Grand Priory of the Hospital of St. John of Jerusalem in England'. Each man's name was inscribed on the edge.

The men agreed that it had been an unforgettable experience and would value the medals and photographs as lasting keepsakes. The memories of the work they had done during and after the explosions would also be eternally in their minds. They had lost good workmates and honourable friends in the disaster. They would never forget them.

PART TWELVE

Chapter 93
January 1914

The people of Conisbrough and Denaby were beginning to settle down after the trauma of the disaster, but there were still persistent problems and worries that affected many residents.

The miners were grumbling and holding regular union meetings over the ongoing fight for fair minimum wages. They were even ready to strike as they felt they were being harshly treated compared to other regional collieries.

Each meeting was more and more heated, more and more belligerent. They even objected to the press being present and reporting the contents of the meetings. The continual accidents and regular mining fatalities only strengthened their determination. The company listened, but did not agree with their requests. Tempers started to fray.

Another, more immediate concern was that diseases and infections were rife in the community. There was a continual, increasing flow of cases of scarlet fever, enteric fever and diphtheria. The Conisbrough Isolation Hospital was so full, Mexborough patients could not be admitted. The dearth of beds and nursing staff became the main subject of debate at the Hospital Board Meetings. Again, tempers rose.

* * *

'Oh, Gertie, love, try not to worry, I'm sure she'll be all right.' Mary's words did nothing to stem her sister's tears. Gertie was shaking with distress. She could not bear to think of Annie in The Isolation Hospital, so sick but away from her family.

'She'll be so unhappy, and I can't even be with her!' Gertie wailed, bringing on more anguished sobs.

'I know,' Mary soothed, clutching Gertie's hand, 'but she's a strong sensible lass. She'll get through this.'

Thirteen-year-old Annie had been diagnosed with scarlet fever, and the doctor had insisted that she should go to Conisbrough Isolation Hospital. The disease was highly infectious.

She had complained of a sore throat, together with a headache and fever. Only one day later, the dreaded red rash appeared on her face and chest, quickly spreading to her arms and legs. Her 'strawberry tongue', red and coated with raised bumps, had confirmed the diagnosis.

'It might be weeks before I can see her!' Gertie continued, shaking her head as if to cast off this awful news. 'I don't know what we'd do if…if…' she continued, unable to voice her worst fears.

'Don't think like that, love,' Mary implored. 'Lots of people get over it.'

'Aye, but some don't!' Gertie cried out, dissolving into shuddering sobs.

Mary knew about the symptoms and different stages of the illness because the local doctors had vehemently informed the local community about the importance of assessing and reporting the disease swiftly.

She knew that the red rash made the skin feel like sandpaper, and when it faded, usually after a week or two, then the shedding of the outer layers of the skin began, lasting several weeks.

The real worry, however, was that some patients suffered complications that caused kidney disease, rheumatic heart disease, or even death. Sadly, it was usually children between the ages of five and fifteen who mostly contracted the disease.

'Please, God, help our Annie to get better,' Mary whispered to herself. Gertie was still crying.

* * *

February 1914

'You stink o' booze!' Eli settled his almost-black eyes on Bridie as she swayed and turned away. A hint of a sneer played around her lips, but her eyes were vague and unfocused.

'Sure, that'll be yerself you're talking about!' she chided, her voice playful but cold.

'It's not me, it's you!' he answered. The assertive tone in his voice was unfamiliar, unusual for him. Few things nudged him into positive speech. 'I've come straight from t' pit. It's only half-past two, I 'ant even 'ad a drink today! It's you! You allus smell o' booze nah!'

He stood, tall and scrawny, his dirty hands cupped round his skinny hips. 'Yer never used to,' he stated in a flat, sad voice.

Bridie turned to look at him, but he had already sat down, frowning, rolling up his coal-stained shirt sleeves. She wanted to talk to him, to explain how she was feeling, but his blank expression silenced her.

Ben was on the sofa, staring at them, then the tugging and the lunging and the pulling began again. He did not like the rope. He hated the rope.

His shouting began, booming incessant howls that so grated on Bridie that she had to narrow her eyes and clamp her lips into a sad, defeated line. She felt the usual, oppressive hopelessness that regularly engulfed her. *Would it ever go away?* Her dry eyes produced no tears.

* * *

March 1914

The sisters were gathered together at Gertie's house, and, for once, the mood was happy and celebratory. Annie was home! Mary, Ivy, Betty and Gertie frequently glanced at the young woman, delighted that she was recuperating from her illness so well, looking stronger each day.

'We'll soon have you fit and healthy again, love,' Gertie said, gazing fondly at her daughter. 'All that meat your Auntie Ivy keeps bringing us should do the trick!' She smiled with relief and joy.

The past weeks had been a nightmare for her and Charlie. They had been so worried that they might lose their precious daughter.

'You'll soon be back at school!' Mary declared, beaming at her niece.

Annie smiled and nodded. 'Yes, I've missed all my friends, and even the teachers!' she joked. But she had found the whole experience of being ill, and in hospital so long, very frightening and overwhelming. She knew, though, that she had been luckier than many of the other patients there. Some of them would never go home, never return to school again. Her sad, pensive expression prompted Betty to speak of happier things.

'Clarissa, or should I say the new Mrs Sidney Heppelthwaite, sends her love to all of you,' she began, pride and delight coating her words. 'It's such a pity you weren't able to get to the wedding. All that snow practically cut off Wentworth. We had to tramp there all the way from Elsecar! It was worth it though.' Betty's dreamy gaze lifted as she recalled the special day.

'The Earl and Countess were so generous. They gave Sidney and Clarissa a whole day off for the wedding, as well as sending a signed card of congratulations. Some of the staff were allowed to attend the wedding breakfast, and they even allowed Cook to prepare the joints of meat and pastries. As for the cake that she made, I don't know how many pounds of fruit were in it, but it was beautiful!'

Betty shook her head, unable to convey how lavish the special occasion had been. It was beyond her wildest dreams. She would always remember the look of pride and incredulous delight on Arthur's face as he witnessed his daughter's special day. He couldn't believe his lass was so fortunate.

'It all sounds wonderful. I hope the couple will be very happy,' Ivy declared.

'She's a very lucky lass, all right,' Gertie agreed.

Mary linked her arm into Betty's and whispered, 'You must be so happy and proud.'

Betty nodded, blinking back her tears of joy. She felt so blessed. Gertie looked at her Annie and she, too, felt blessed.

Chapter 94
April 1914

Bridie opened her eyes and blinked slowly. The tap-tap-tap of the knocker-upper's stick reduced in volume as progress was made along the row of houses. It would soon be time for the morning shift to get ready for work.

Her mind told her that she should get up and begin all the chores, but her body resisted. She felt warm and cosy, but also heavy and limp. Her parched tongue tried to moisten her snuff-dry mouth. She needed a drink.

Declan and Lottie lay at the other end of the bed. Their soft, rhythmic breathing informed her that they were fast asleep.

The space beside her reminded her that Eli was working the night shift, something he had only recently started doing. She didn't mind, though. It gave her more space and freedom. His almost-black eyes could not watch her and track her as much.

I must get up, she told herself. Eddie and Billy would soon be wanting their breakfasts and their snap tins packing up for work.

She dressed quickly and quietly and made her way downstairs. She didn't want to wake the two lasses. Maria and Louisa would soon be disturbed when the twins got up. The thin curtain that divided their room could not cushion the noise.

She opened the living room door as quietly as she could. She didn't want to wake Ben. He was usually fast asleep on the sofa. The room still felt warm as she stepped inside, even though the fire had been banked up overnight.

I'll soon have it blazing, she told herself. She lit the candle that was on the mantelpiece. She decided to light the gas lamp later.

Bridie stretched and yawned, still heavy with sleep. She knew she had consumed more beer than usual last night, but she liked how relaxed and calm it made her feel.

She glanced over to the old sofa, her eyes adjusting to the flickering light. For a moment, her brain did not register what she saw. She stepped closer to the sofa, as reality and comprehension struck her like a hammer.

Ben was sprawled and hanging over the side of the sofa. His arms sagged, limp and still. His head was contorted to one side, as if straining to look around. But his blood-specked eyes stared, unseeing, into the shadowy dimness of the room.

Bridie gasped as she saw the rope. It was meant to protect him from danger, to keep him safe. But it had not. It was coiled and twisted around his neck, squeezing and pressing like an evil snake, relentless and determined.

'No! No! No!' Bridie screamed as her trembling fingers plucked at the rope. 'No! No!' she wailed as the rope remained tight and unyielding.

She pulled Ben further onto the sofa, hoping to ease the tension of the ligature, to reduce its vice-like grip around his throat, but the knots were too tight, the pressure too great.

Bridie stared at her first-born son, now a man, but still with a child's mind. She saw his bloated face, his open mouth. She felt his hands and shrivelled legs. His body was cold and dead.

It was then that she started to wail: deep, keening howls that erupted from her innermost being. The images of her grandmother, poor Liza and the dead baby in the sack flashed before her eyes, almost blinding her. She rubbed her eyes viciously, she wanted to rid herself of all the memories of death.

But she could not escape from the sight of her poor, dead son. She rocked back onto her heels and slowly looked up.

There, in the doorway, stood Louisa, silent and staring, her face impassive. Bridie felt herself sway, felt the sensation of floating and weakening, but she did not feel the impact of her body as she collapsed to the floor.

* * *

The glowing embers comforted Bridie as she sat, alone, allowing her thoughts to drift. It seemed an eternity since she had found Ben; she could hardly believe it was still the same day.

She swivelled her gaze to the old sofa and once again experienced the pain of seeing it empty. Ben was no longer there. She sipped at her beer, greedy for its soothing effect on her bruised body and battered mind.

The onslaught of distressing experiences had left her exhausted, almost numb. The day had passed with a mixture of crystal-clear recollections and vague, elusive conversations that fogged her mind.

Her eyelids drooped as the pain and guilt and sorrow flowed through her entire body, weighing her down and crushing her. She blamed herself for Ben's death, and she knew others would too. She had been the last one to see him last night, when he was smiling and wriggling beneath his blanket, ready for sleep.

She was the one who had tied him up, as usual, around his waist and legs. At least, she thought she had done that. She could not really remember clearly, but she would not admit that to anyone else.

Ben must have squirmed and twisted around so much that the rope had coiled and tightened and knotted around his neck relentlessly, she told herself. But she still felt guilty.

Once again, she tried to order the startling flashbacks that streaked through her mind. She remembered feeling faint, then strong arms lifting her up and worried faces staring down at her.

The twins had tugged at the rope frantically, finally managing to loosen its deathly grip. Maria was crying and moaning. Louisa was still, aloof and watching.

'I need to get the fire going and light the gas lamp,' she remembered herself repeating over and over again, until Maria suddenly took control and issued orders.

'Sit down, Mammy. I'll see to everything,' Maria had said. 'Louisa, go and get Dr Twigg!' Those last words had alarmed her, she recalled that clearly.

She felt frightened. She knew he already considered her a bad mother. He would blame her for everything. But she could not change anything. She could do nothing.

She sipped yet more beer and recollected how Eli had looked when he came home from his shift.

'What's goin' on 'ere?' he had asked as he walked into the room. His coal-blackened features had shown confusion, swiftly followed by dismay as he followed their gazes to the sofa. He stooped his lanky body over his son's, his almost-black eyes peering intently.

Then he saw the rope, the red-brown marks around his son's neck and his lifeless expression.

'What's 'appened?' he shouted. 'What's fuckin' 'appened?'

'He must've moved around so much that t' rope got all twisted round 'im, round 'is neck,' Billy began.

'We managed to loosen it,' Eddie said. 'But it were too late. Mam found 'im when she got up.'

Eli looked over to her, his eyes narrowing and blinking slowly as he filled the room with his towering body.

Bridie shook her head slowly from side to side, holding out her hands, palms upturned, trying to convey her utter bewilderment.

'Yer shun't 'ave tied 'im up! Yer know he din't like it!' he boomed.

She had visibly jumped, startled by his raised voice that she had rarely heard.

'It was for his own good!' she had retorted, stung by his accusations. 'It's a bit late for you to suddenly be concerned for him!' She felt hurt and aggrieved, but she was doubting herself. She felt she was to blame.

She recalled her rising panic as the doctor had arrived. Louisa led him into the room, her eyes wide but her face expressionless.

They had all stepped back respectfully as he strode purposefully to the sofa.

'Why is this rope here?' he immediately asked.

'We 'ave to tie 'im up every night or he'll fall on t' floor,' Maria answered.

'He sleeps on t' sofa but he's allus tryin' to get off it. He nearly fell on t' fire once,' Billy explained.

'It's to keep him safe,' Eddie said.

'We only ever tie 'im round t' waist and t' legs,' Maria whispered.

Bridie remembered that she had not spoken; she could barely breathe. Dr Twigg paused momentarily before leaning over Ben more closely to begin his examination.

They watched in silence as his steady gaze passed over Ben, observing and assessing. His experienced hands carried out varied, rapid procedures as they touched and travelled over the body. He moved even closer to inspect the marks around the neck.

Finally, he had straightened up, taken off his spectacles and sighed sharply before addressing them.

'I am afraid to say that all life is extinct. As there are suspicious circumstances, I will be informing P.C. Pashley and the coroner. There will be an inquest into the circumstances of the death. Do not touch or move the body before the police arrive. She had then felt his focused, piercing glare as he continued in a cold, professional voice.

'I will be providing a death certificate. I will be instructing the undertaker to remove the body. I will let myself out.'

They had all watched blankly as he clipped shut his bag, put on his spectacles and walked out. She remembered Eli's stooped shoulders and defeated expression, and the bleak faces of her children. She remembered that her hands would not stop shaking.

The policeman arrived not long afterwards. She recalled that he had studied Ben's body and where he'd been found, making copious notes in his pocketbook. He had asked many questions, some of which had blurred in her mind.

Bridie had been questioned the most as she was the last one to see him alive and the first to find him dead. P.C. Pashley had tried to be understanding when her tears choked her, halting her words, but he had been rigorous in obtaining all the information that he required. He wrote everything down. He would remember everything even if she did not.

Eli had responded to questioning with brief, almost dismissive words. His almost-black eyes had constantly sought hers, as if wanting to avert any difficult responses to her. *He blames me*, she told herself over and over.

P.C. Pashley's stringent questioning finally ended. She was relieved. Her head ached; she could barely concentrate.

'I will be handing my report to the coroner. You will be informed of the details of the inquest and who will be required to attend as witnesses,' he said as he stood up to leave.

She remembered that the undertaker had arrived as P.C. Pashley was leaving. She had to stand and watch as Ben was taken away. She heard her children's muffled sobs. She wished Eli would comfort her, but he did not.

The rest of the day passed in a blur. Disbelief jostled with anguish. As news about Ben had spread, friends and family had visited, all trying to offer their sympathy and condolences.

Bridie could only remember a series of indistinct conversations, as though people were speaking to her through a thick fog. She had nodded or shaken her head as she thought appropriate, but only occasional words penetrated the haze.

She clearly remembered Mary's visit, how her dear friend had hugged her, whispering comforting words through her tears, that were meant to soothe and reassure. She had tried to please Mary by nodding and fashioning a weak smile, but her heart was frozen with grief, regret and fear.

The beer was all gone. It was time to bank up the fire. She cast one last look at the empty sofa then climbed the stairs. The house was silent. Everyone was asleep. She hoped she could sleep. She had to end this terrible day, but she was fearful. She dreaded the inquest where others would probably blame her, but no one could blame her as much as she blamed herself.

* * *

Bridie clenched her fingers and looked straight ahead. Eli was to one side of her and the twins, Maria and Louisa to the other. No one spoke as they waited for the inquest to begin. It felt strange being in The Drum for such a formal, serious event. She sucked in a ragged breath and steeled herself for the ordeal of being a witness at the inquest of her son's death.

The jury members filed in and were seated, followed by the coroner, Mr Allen, who stood at the front and formally opened proceedings.

'The purpose of this inquest is to establish the cause of death of Benjamin Shaw, aged 21 years, of 75, Cliff View, Denaby Main. It is not the role of the coroner to decide any question of criminal liability, or to apportion guilt, or attribute blame.'

Bridie heard his words, but could hardly register that he was referring to the death of her son, her Ben. She willed herself to focus and concentrate on the proceedings.

The first witness called was Dr Twigg, who informed that he had been summoned to attend the deceased at 75, Cliff View. After examination, he had concluded that life was extinct, and that, in his opinion, the cause of death was ligature strangulation by rope. He had informed the police and the coroner of the circumstances of the death.

P.C. Pashley was the second witness called. He informed the inquest that he had been notified by Dr Twigg of the death of Benjamin Shaw of 75, Cliff View, and had immediately attended the house.

On entering the living room, he saw the deceased lying on the sofa. There was a rope around his neck and ligature marks were clearly visible. He noted details of the body and where it was found.

He ascertained that it was a regular occurrence that the deceased was tied every night to the sofa where he slept, in order to prevent him from falling to the floor and further possible dangers in the room.

The deceased had a reduced mental and physical capacity, and could not walk or talk. The family stated that the rope was always tied around his waist and legs in order to prevent him from harm.

The deceased's mother, Bridie Shaw, had found him in the morning when she got up. He was lying over the side of the sofa with the rope coiled around his neck. She attempted to remove the rope but could not.

She pulled the body so that it lay on the sofa in order to ease the tension of the ligature, but she realised the deceased was already dead.

Her cries alerted other members of the family. Brothers of the deceased managed to loosen the rope, but it was too late. Dr Twigg was sent for and, on examination, pronounced that life was extinct, and notified the police and the Coroner.

Bridie was called as the next witness. She cleared her throat and breathed in deeply before beginning her recount of events.

Her heart was pounding as she answered the Coroner's questions. She heard the rigidity in his voice as his questioning continued and she translated his persistence and probing into criticism and condemnation.

He interrupted her frequently as she gave her evidence. Bridie imagined his increasing reproval as she gave her answers and finished her statement.

'I will ask you these very important questions once more, Mrs Shaw,' the coroner continued. 'Why did you think it necessary to tie your son to the sofa with a length of rope every night?'

'Sure, it was for his own good, to keep him safe. He'd started thrashing around, wanting to get down onto the floor. He never used to do that, it's only lately that he couldn't settle and be still. He couldn't walk or talk, but he was strong. I did it so he would be safe,' Bridie asserted.

'And it was you who tied him up that night? If so, how did you tie him?' Mr Allen questioned.

'I've told everybody – over and over again – that I only tied him around his waist and legs, like I did every night,' Bridie insisted, her voice rising with increased tension and frustration. 'Everyone had gone to bed, except my husband who was working the night shift. Ben was all right when I left him,' she added.

'And how do you think the rope ended up around his neck, a ligature so tight that it caused strangulation?'

'I don't know!' she cried. 'He must have wriggled around and pulled at the rope so much that it got twisted and knotted round his neck! When I found him the next morning, he was cold... and dead.'

Her voice faded and stopped. She could not contain her sobs. She cried in anguish.

'Thank you, Mrs Shaw. You may sit down,' the coroner stated. As she returned to her chair the doubts and suspicions rolled around in her mind.

I knew they'd say it was my fault! I knew they'd blame me! she told herself.

She stared with fixed eyes and a sinking heart as the inquest continued. Eli, Billy, Eddie and Maria each gave evidence in turn, recounting what had happened and responding to the coroner's questions. Bridie just wanted the ordeal to be over and was glad when Louisa, the last witness, was called.

The young girl stood calm and erect, gazing at Mr Allen with unblinking eyes. She described what she had seen when she came downstairs that morning, how her mother had tried to loosen the rope, then how Bridie had fainted.

'Have you seen your mother faint before?' the coroner asked.

'Only a few times. Usually when she's 'ad too much to drink,' Louisa replied in a clear, confident voice.

'Do you mean when she has been drinking alcohol?' Mr Allen asked sharply.

'Yeah. When she's 'ad too much beer. She hides it in t' kitchen cupboard. I've seen 'er.'

Piercing stares turned towards Bridie.

'You were sent to summon Dr Twigg,' the coroner continued. 'Is that correct?'

'Yeah,' Louisa replied, 'he knows me Mam well 'cos he saw to our Lottie when she 'ad 'er accident. She lost tip o' her finger when she were a babby. She were on t' living room floor and someone trod on 'er.'

'Thank you, Louisa. You may sit down,' Mr Allen instructed. He turned to Bridie.

'Mrs Shaw, I need to ask you one further question. Had you been drinking on the night of Benjamin's death, the night you tied him up?'

Bridie licked her lips and swallowed hard.

'Yes... but not much. Sure, I wasn't drunk or anything!' she insisted.

Mr Allen gave her a long, sustained stare before addressing the jury.

'I must remind you once again, that the purpose of this inquest is to establish the cause of death of Benjamin Shaw. It is not the role of the coroner and the jury to decide any question of criminal liability, or to apportion guilt, or attribute blame. Please bear this in mind when you consider your verdict.'

Within fifteen minutes the jury returned and the coroner resumed proceedings.

'The verdict of the jury is that Benjamin Shaw's death was accidental, and the cause of death was ligature strangulation by rope. The foreman of the jury has asked it to be noted that it was agreed that there were dubious, uncommon circumstances attached to the death, mainly regarding the custom of tying the deceased to the sofa with a length of rope. It will be for the deceased's mother to decide whether this was a justified, appropriate action. The inquest is now closed.'

The coroner and the jury stood up and left the room. The rest of the people who had attended then stood and began to file out. Bridie sat rigid, her mind repeating the coroner's last sentences. She felt the hurt and pain wash over her as the condemnation of the coroner and jury penetrated her fragile state of mind.

'They've blamed me. They think I'm a bad mother,' she told herself. Eli turned his almost-black eyes onto her stricken face.

'I telled yer not to tie 'im up. I telled yer not to drink so much.' His accusing words cut through her like a knife.

Even he blames me, she thought. *I was only trying to do my best.*

Louisa looked at her mother, and, for once, smiled.

* * *

Bridie stared at Ben's coffin on the undertaker's cart. It was time for the journey to church.

It had been comforting to have the coffin in the living room for one last night before the funeral. She sat beside it, gently stroking the wooden box, muttering whispered words to her first-born child, even though she knew he could not hear her, Eli hovered in the background, watching, perplexed, unsure of what to do or say.

Bridie had hardly spoken for the last three days since the inquest, and the more she withdrew from Eli, the more he withdrew from her.

Kind neighbours looked after Declan and Lottie, but the older children had seen their mother's vacant stares and blank expressions as she tried to deal with her emotional turmoil.

People tried to comfort her, assuring her that it was not her fault. Ben's death was a tragic accident. Bridie listened but said little.

Even Mary's passionate insistence that she was not to blame, that she had been a caring mother despite the many difficulties that Ben's condition had presented, all fell on deaf ears; all was quietly disregarded by Bridie.

'I know everyone blames me,' she had repeated simply.

The undertaker's cart pulled away and the silent cortege followed.

Bridie felt the spring sunshine warm on her face, she heard the clip-clop of the horses' hooves on the cobbles, she saw Eli's long legs striding out in front of her, but inside, she was numb. Neighbours stood on the street, watching the solemn procession, whispering remarks to nearby folks.

Bridie saw the women, arms folded across their breasts or nursing children. She felt their penetrating stares as she passed by, but such was her self-condemnation, she believed they were whispering words of censure rather than sympathy.

The church was cool and quiet, the service reflective and consoling. But Bridie could feel no solace. The bright daylight stung her eyes as they stepped outside and walked to the cemetery.

She saw the freshly dug grave, but could barely watch as the coffin was lowered into its dark, damp depths. She remembered the day Ben was born, her beautiful son.

'Goodbye, my love,' she whispered as the committal prayer was spoken.

Bridie heard the thud of the soil as it hit the coffin, but she could watch no more. She turned to the comfort of Mary and Maria's arms.

Eli was busy wiping his own tears as he gazed down at the coffin. Billy, Eddie and Louisa were solemn as they walked away from the grave.

* * *

The house was silent as everyone slept. Only Bridie was still downstairs, alone in the living room. She was so relieved that the funeral was over, so thankful that people had at last gone home. She yearned for peace and quiet. She consciously relaxed her body, not realising how tense she had been all day.

The silence wrapped around her, soothing her anxiety, allowing her to wallow in her own thoughts. Her family and friends had meant well, lavish in their sympathy and condolences, but she just wanted to be alone.

She was glad that Eli had decided to go to the pub earlier in the evening. She could see that he wanted to escape the highly-charged emotional atmosphere in the house.

'I'm off to t' Pig,' he had announced.

She had said nothing. She was none too steady herself, but she could not refrain from her beer. She was glad Mary was looking after Declan and Lottie. She could relax.

Eli had looked at her with hooded eyes and a sad expression when he came back home.

'I'm off to bed,' he muttered.

Again she said nothing.

The warmth from the fire and the effect of the beer calmed her into an almost soporific state. The relief of having the inquest and funeral over was bathing her in a trance-like stupor, removed and distant from the harsh realities of life.

She felt as if she was floating, until the sight of the empty sofa, Ben's sofa, suddenly triggered an unwelcome stream of images that surged before her dazed eyes.

'No! No!' she whimpered, incapable of blocking their assault on her senses. So many times she had relived the ordeals she had suffered, so many times she had blamed herself for everything. She felt suffocated by guilt and sadness.

She gasped as she snatched her old brown shawl from the chair and rushed to the back door. She needed air.

The dark silence along the "backs" seemed to clutch at her stumbling body. It was deep into the night. People slept. She was entirely on her own.

But the images of poor Ben, poor Liza and the poor baby in the sack still paraded before her eyes, dizzying her as she staggered along the streets.

'No! No!' she whimpered again. She felt like a little girl, confused and lost, being touched and mauled by uncaring hands that wanted to hurt her. Those hands had sullied her, cheapened her, damaged her.

Yet, she had told no one. The memories of the abuse were locked inside her. They had festered and infected her with shame and humiliation. She felt worthless as she pushed through the darkness.

Bridie suddenly became aware of her surroundings. She was on the canal towpath. The moon shone glinting lights on the water that attracted her and drew her closer. The night suddenly felt protective, and the water appealing.

The shimmering lights mesmerised her, blotting out the awful images and memories Her mind was empty and peaceful. She felt like a good person again. She sighed and abandoned herself to the water's compelling draw.

* * *

The sharp series of raps startled Louisa as she tended the morning fire. 'Nobody usually uses t' front door,' she thought to herself as she went to open it.

P.C. Pashley stood on the step. She noted his serious expression and hesitation.

'Mi Mammy in't in, she must've gone round to Mary Walker's, for our Declan and Lottie. She's been lookin' after 'em since we 'ad t' funeral yesterday,' she said, to fill the moments of silence.

'Is your dad in, Louisa?' P.C. Pashley asked quietly.

'He's still in bed. He's on t' night shift tonight, and he got drunk last night,' she explained. 'Our Eddie and Billy are on afters, so they're still in bed, and our Maria 'ant got to get up till eight o'clock. There's only me up for school.'

'Go and get your dad, Louisa,' P.C. Pashley requested as he stepped inside the living room. Louisa regarded him with inquisitive, assessing eyes.

'Is summat up?' she asked.

'Go and get your dad,' the policeman repeated gently.

A few minutes later, Eli appeared in the doorway, his black hair on end, his dark eyes blinking as he struggled to shake off his sleepiness.

'What's up?' he asked.

'I need a word with you, Eli, alone,' began P.C. Pashley.

Eli stared blankly as Louisa walked into the kitchen.

'I'm afraid I have some very bad news for you, Eli. A woman's body was found in the canal this morning. Mr Bisby, the lock keeper, sent for me and I identified the body. I'm sorry, lad, but it's your Bridie.'

Eli's almost-black eyes drilled into the policeman's kindly gaze. He heard the words but his brain could not fathom their meaning. First puzzlement, then confusion and, finally, disbelief tracked swiftly across his features. His pale skin blanched. His long fingers raked through his unkempt hair.

'No, no, that can't be rate!' he croaked. He swallowed hard, shaking his head. 'No that can't be rate!' he repeated.

P.C. Pashley pursed his lips and continued. 'Dr Twigg was sent for and he confirmed that it was Bridie. She drowned, Eli.'

Eli's body suddenly sagged and slumped onto the old red sofa. His long legs stayed extended as he remained silent and still.

'The undertaker was called and he has removed the body,' P.C. Pashley continued. 'I will need to question you, and other members of the family, concerning the circumstances relating to Bridie's actions and state of mind during this recent period.'

'Why? You don't think she killed 'er sen, do you?' Eli's anguished voice resonated within the room.

'There will be an inquest, given the circumstances, Eli. I'll inform you of the details when I've given my report to the coroner.'

Eli looked at him blankly. 'What will I do wi'out Bridie?'

He blinked his heavy lids slowly, grasped his knees with his cupped hands and bowed forward. His quiet sobs were sustained and sincere. Louisa listened from the kitchen. P.C. Pashley then began his questioning.

* * *

Mary was still in shock. She just couldn't believe that Bridie was dead. They had always been so close, almost like sisters. Her thoughts retraced the morning's events, as if to help her confirm that her long-time friend was indeed dead.

She had been feeding Declan and Lottie their breakfasts when there was a knock at the door.

'I bet that's your Mammy coming to see you,' she smiled. 'Go and let her in, please, Violet. I don't know why she's knocking.'

She heard voices, then was surprised and shocked to see P.C. Pashley standing in the doorway, with Violet and Maria hovering behind him.

'Is there something wrong? It's not Jim, is it?' Panic surged through her. Her heart raced and her legs weakened.

'Mrs Walker,' P.C. Pashley began. 'I'm investigating a very sad occurrence. A woman's body was retrieved from the canal earlier this morning. I'm sorry to have to tell you that it's been identified as that of Bridie Shaw. She was found drowned.'

'No!' Mary gasped, then she saw Maria's red eyes and tear-stained face. 'Oh, my God! No!' she cried, as she reached for a chair to sit on, then burst into tears.

Declan and Lottie didn't like all the crying and the big man with the hat on. Their lips trembled and they, too, started crying. Mary reached to cuddle Lottie, rocking her back and forth as she absorbed the terrible news. Maria picked up Declan, holding him close as her tears flowed.

Mary had answered P.C. Pashley's questions, explaining that she had last seen Bridie at the funeral tea the night before. She had offered to take the children for the night and Bridie had agreed.

'The last words she said to me were, 'You're such a good friend, Mary. God bless you.' I'll always remember that,' Mary said tearfully.

'What state of mind was she in when you last saw her?'

Mary answered honestly.

'She was exhausted and obviously very sad. Ben was her firstborn, and she always looked after him, even though it was hard. She always tried her best.'

'Did she ever say anything about wanting to end her life?'

'No!' Mary insisted. 'No! She's always been a quiet, thoughtful girl, and the inquest and funeral really upset her, but she wouldn't kill herself!'

P.C. Pashley closed his pocket-book, thanked her and let himself out. Mary turned to Maria and they fell into each other's arms for comfort.

* * *

The inquest was held two days later at The Station Hotel. Many people attended, saddened by the tragic circumstances of Bridie's death, especially so soon after the loss of her son.

The coroner and his jury heard the statements of witnesses called to give evidence. Their first was Mr Bisby, the lock keeper. He stated that he was doing his early morning inspection of the lock when he noticed a shawl lying on the towpath.

The brown shawl was close to a body that he saw floating, face-down, in the canal. He managed to retrieve the body, which was fully clothed, although no coat was present. He asked his wife to inform the police, and P.C. Pashley had arrived shortly afterwards, immediately identifying the body as that of Bridie Shaw, a local woman.

P.C. Pashley was next to give his recount. He confirmed that the body had been found drowned. There were no visible marks of violence. He identified the body as that of Bridie Shaw, someone whom he had only recently been involved with, due to the death of her son, Benjamin Shaw. There was also a handkerchief found close to the body. He had then sent for Dr Twigg.

Dr Twigg confirmed that he had been summoned to the lock where a body had been found drowned. He had identified the body as that of Bridie Shaw, someone he knew well from recent, frequent meetings.

On examination, the body showed no marks of violence. The presence of alcohol could not be confirmed. In his opinion, the cause of death was asphyxia due to drowning.

Statements from Bridie's family members were next to be given. All had stated that she had been very quiet and subdued since Ben's death, but that she had remained stoic during his funeral.

They had all gone to bed before Bridie on the night of the funeral. She was on her own after Eli had gone to bed. He was the last one to see her. She had seemed calm and composed. They all stated that she had never talked about harming herself. They did not believe that she would want to kill herself.

The coroner thanked them all before asking the jury to retire to consider their verdict. The people attending waited anxiously. Mary squeezed Jim's hand as they sat, stony-faced and tense. Eli looked straight ahead, unmoving.

Willie, Bridie's father, had a sombre countenance. *Another child gone*, was his overriding thought. *Another of my wee bairns gone.*

The jury returned the verdict of 'found drowned'.

The coroner stated that there was no evidence to show whether Bridie Shaw had drowned accidentally or not. There were no witnesses.

He expressed his condolences to the family who had endured the loss of two loved ones within such a short space of time. He then thanked the jury and closed the inquest.

Mary closed her eyes and sighed. *My poor Bridie*, she thought. *My poor, darling Bridie.* She clutched Jim's hand and bowed her head in sorrow.

Eli looked down at his cupped, calloused hands. He felt bereft and alone. It did not occur to him that he would have to support his children at such a sad time, and in the future. That had always been Bridie's responsibility.

* * *

The mourners watched as Bridie's coffin was lowered into the grave. She was now reunited with her son as they shared their final resting place.

Tears flowed as people whispered earnest laments, their last, sad goodbyes. Bridie's family and friends were still in shocked disbelief that mother and son had died only days apart.

As the committal ceremony came to an end, Jim hugged Mary closer to him. He knew how much she was grieving for her friend. He hugged her even closer as he thought of all the people he had loved and lost. Death was so heartbreaking, so final.

Chapter 95
June 1914

The days and weeks following Bridie's death were hard for everyone. Her father, Willie, sixty-seven years old but still working down the pit, seemed like a changed man. He said little, so different to the days when he was always laughing and joking. But the loss of his beloved wife, Hannah, his three children, Liza, Michael and Bridie, and his grandson, Ben, had subdued his happy nature. He felt robbed, yet he was thankful that he had children and grandchildren who were still living, still loving.

Mary missed Bridie so much. She took to frequently thinking back to their shared childhood, easily summoning the bright, clear memories. She could scarcely believe they would never see each other again.

She had comfort from her increasingly close relationship with Maria. The seventeen-year-old girl was lost without her mother, and Mary was humbled that she confided in her, mainly about the difficulties at home.

'Declan and Lottie keep asking where their Mammy is. I've told them that she's gone to look after Ben, and that I'm their Mammy now, but they still cry for her,' Maria said sadly. 'My Dad hardly speaks to us, and he's always in a bad mood. He flies off the handle about everything. Billy and Eddie are fed up, he's always finding faults with them. He just wants to get away from us. He's either working, sleeping or at the pub. He doesn't care about us.'

Mary listened to her rising resentment, saddened but not really surprised by her words.

'Oh, Maria, love, try not to get too upset. Eli's always been quiet and unsure of himself. He's missing your mother, and it's his way of dealing with it. You're a strong, capable lass. You're the woman of the house now. You'll cope. Things will get better with time.'

Mary stroked the girl's hand and leaned closer to give her a fixed, reassuring gaze. 'You know your mother always adored you,' she whispered.

Maria nodded and sighed. She knew she had to be strong, but she so missed her Mammy.

* * *

Mary paused as she felt the familiar heavy, dull chest pains, followed by racing palpitations. The kitchen and living room floors were now clean, but at what cost? The scrubbing and mopping left her feeling exhausted.

She slowly stood up, her body complaining at the physical exertion, but she would not be deterred from doing the usual domestic chores, the same ones she had done all her life. She stubbornly refused to accept that, at the age of forty-two, she was ailing, and did her best to disguise the symptoms of her poor health.

She had allowed Violet to take on more of the lighter household duties but was determined not to overload the eleven-year-old with responsibilities; they would all come soon enough. Violet was still a child, and Mary wanted her to enjoy her childhood.

Jim's anxious looks and concerned words could not be avoided, however. He saw her reduced energy, her slowing movements and heard her muffled breathlessness.

'You should see the doctor, Mary,' he suggested frequently, his face revealing his worry.

'Oh, I'm fine, stop worrying,' she always insisted. 'I'm just a bit short o' puff. I'll be as right as rain in a few minutes.'

She tried to reassure him. But the few minutes were extending to many minutes, the sitting down periods lengthening. She had even recently taken to sleeping propped up on pillows, rather than lying down.

'I can breathe better this way,' was her standard excuse.

She had just tidied up when Rose's tinkling laugh heralded her arrival. She was pretending to chase Joe into the house. The little boy giggled as his sturdy legs afforded him a little run.

'Find Grandma!' Rose laughed to her son. Mary was happy to receive his hugs and kisses.

'We're goin' for a walk and wondered if you want to come wi' us. It's such a lovely day, and Joseph won't be back till later on,' Rose greeted her.

'Well, maybe after a cup o' tea and a sit down,' Mary replied. 'Now, Master Joe, tell Grandma what you've been up to.'

'You sit down, Mam, I'll make the tea,' Rose offered.

Joe climbed onto Mary's lap. She could feel his chubby robustness and see his healthy face. She thanked the Lord and felt blessed at such good fortune. She so loved her daughter and grandson.

As they sipped their tea, Mary noticed a special smile playing around Rose's lips, a bloom of happiness. Rose was aware of her mother's scrutiny.

'Mam, I can't wait to tell you! I'm sure I'm pregnant! Joe's getting a little brother or sister!'

'Oh, Rose! That's wonderful news!' Mary exclaimed, genuinely delighted. 'Your dad will be thrilled!'

Rose was beaming happily, when they heard the back door open, and in walked Joseph.

'Joseph! What are you doin' 'ere at this time?' Rose blurted out in surprise. Joseph stood in the doorway, cap in hand, staring at them.

'There's been an accident at t' pit…mi dad's been killed. A few others are injured. Mary, one of 'em is Jim. I've been and told mi mam already, a neighbour's wi' 'er.' He became silent again, still rigid, his face set.

'Oh, Joseph!' Rose cried as she ran to him.

'Where's Jim?' Mary managed to ask as she struggled to stand.

She did not hear his answer. Her body was engulfed by a crushing pain that squeezed the breath out of her. She saw the room dim, then blacken. Her body swayed as she collapsed to the floor. Not even Joseph's strong arms could break the fall.

* * *

Mary peered at Jim's worried face and squeezed his hand. She was so thankful to have him home, safe and sound.

'I keep tellin' you, I'm all right, I just went a bit dizzy. It was t' shock of hearing about poor Walt, then not knowing about you. I thought I'd lost you,' she whispered. 'Poor Rose has 'ad too many shocks today.'

Jim patted her hand reassuringly.

'I was the lucky one today, Mary,' he said, remembering the day's events. 'Walt was the unlucky one. That fall o' coal was so big and so sudden, he didn't stand a chance. It's a miracle nobody else was killed.'

Jim had not told Mary all the details of the accident; he didn't want to cause her any more anxiety and upset. She looked so pale and frail. Even her voice sounded different.

He knew his cuts and bruises would heal, but he worried about her. He looked at his hands, scratched and torn. They had all tried to get to Walter, fear increasing their strength and energy as they dug with their bare hands.

The second, smaller fall had halted all their efforts. Some of the rescuers had been injured. Jim had received a blow on the head, dazing him, but he knew no one could survive being buried beneath that weight of coal.

His mates had helped him to the pit top, where fresh air had relieved his stupor, but not his spirits. Walter had not been saved. He was gone.

'Poor Esther and Joseph,' Mary sighed, as if reading his thoughts. She felt weak and drained, both physically and mentally.

Yet more blood on the coal. Another soul lost.

She remembered that awful pain that had caused her to crumple to the floor, but she would keep that to herself. She could already feel the soreness of the bruises waiting to colour her body. She had taken a heavy fall, but Esther's pain would be immeasurably greater.

* * *

Walter's funeral was held a few days after the inquest into his death. As expected, the verdict was *Accidental Death*. Walter was just another miner killed whilst working his shift, one more statistic on the list of colliery fatalities.

Mary insisted on attending the funeral. She walked slowly, holding on to Jim, weak in her body, but strong in her desire to show her condolences.

Esther and Joseph were part of her family now, and Walt's sister, Ellen had always been a good friend. The two families, the Smiths and the Walkers, were united in their grief and sadness as the funeral rituals were carried out on the hot, summer's day.

Mary was glad that Esther was going to live with Rose and Joseph. She could be with her adored grandson, Joe, and the expected new baby would give everyone something to look forward to. There had been so many recent deaths. Birth would be a welcome, joyous occasion.

Jim watched as Walter's coffin was lowered into the grave. He thought back to all he had shared with his friend, both the good and the bad. He was thankful that many secrets had also gone to the grave. At least they had parted as friends.

Chapter 96
July 1914

The heatwave was sustained and brutal. Day after day, it stifled energy and enthusiasm. People sweated and gasped as the scorching temperatures stilled unnecessary movements and slowed even the fittest of people. No cooling breaths of air comforted perspiring bodies. Barely any relief could be found from the glaring heat.

'I've never known it as hot! How much longer 'ave we got to suffer!' was the repeated, complaining refrain. Yet people still had to light fires to enable cooking and washing, still had to toil above and below ground. They longed for the respite of cooler temperatures.

Mary was secretly pleased that the heat was so relentless and all pervading, relieved that she could attribute her increasing lethargy and frailty to its persistent pressure. She had an excuse to sit and rest, easing her tired limbs into relaxing stillness, replenishing her ragged panting with calmer breathing.

She could suffer the heat much better than her ailments. She was aware of Violet's worried glances, the little girl's frequent hugs and willing offers to carry out chores, anything to help her mother.

Mary was also aware of Jim's frustrated anxiety. She saw the fear in his eyes. She knew that she could not hide her own growing fears much longer. She was fearful that her body was failing, afraid of future consequences. But she wanted to ignore the unpleasant realities, even if only for a little longer. She had Jim, she had her family. That was all she wanted.

* * *

All four men downed their beer in greedy gulps. These first pints had slaked their thirst, but they were ready for their next round.

The tap room in The Drum was cooler than the blazing heat outside.

'By, that were grand, I were ready for that! It 'ardly touched t' sides!' Charlie declared, swiping the back of his hand across his mouth. 'I swear them bloody furnaces at t' Kilner's get hotter every day, and in this heat too! Gertie says there'll be nowt left on mi soon if I keep on sweatin'. I've already 'ad to take mi belt in a notch!'

'Don't know how you do it,' Sam said. 'I can only just about stand all this heat in t' shop. It's a good job we've got one o' them refrigerators. Makes world o' difference to 'ave an ice-box, keeps all t' meat longer,' he added.

'I remember when Mr Revill on West Street at Conisbrough got one years ago, he were first butcher round 'ere to 'ave one. It were even in t' paper about it!' Jim said. 'I'd never even 'eard of 'em before then.'

'This heat can't last much longer, it's got to break some time, then we'll be moanin' about summat else,' Joseph observed.

'Best get suppin' then,' Charlie quipped. 'It's been a good excuse to come to t' pub.' The men smiled, nodded and carried on drinking. Their conversation was relaxed and amicable. It was good to enjoy time away from worries and sad events, although recent news abroad had become more significant.

'Things are getting' a bit nasty since that Archduke Ferdinand and 'is wife were shot in Bosnia last month. T' papers are full o' their assassinations.' Sam frowned. 'They say it might start a war over there.'

'Too far away for us to be bothered about,' Charlie replied, savouring his ale.

'It'll bother us if Germany and Russia get involved. It'll all kick off then, you mark my words,' Jim warned.

'I'm more bothered about us gettin' one over on t' bosses about t' minimum wage,' Joseph added.

He was still thinking about his father as he supped his beer. He would never know his grandchild waiting to be born, and that saddened him. Walter had died too young.

* * *

The cricket pavilion provided welcome shade for some of the crowd watching the match between Denaby and Cadeby United Cricket Club, and Hickleton Main Cricket Club.

The heat was still intense as the Saturday afternoon fixture progressed, but it had not deterred a good turnout, eager to watch and support their clubs.

The Denaby ground was one of the finest in the district. Only recently the *Mexborough and Swinton Times* had written that visiting cricketers always enjoyed playing there as there was always a perfect wicket, a friendly handshake and generous cups of tea, not to mention a sporting crowd.

Mary was enjoying watching Jim play. He was one of the oldest in the team, but his experience and enthusiasm was highly valued. She felt proud as she watched him concentrate on his wicket keeping, bravely facing the oncoming fast balls, hoping for the opportunity of a catch from a nick off the bat.

Rose, Winnie and Ivy sat alongside her, and the children, Violet, Maggie, Albert and Emmie, sat on the grass with toddler Joe. She was glad she had made the effort to attend the match, even though the walk had exhausted her.

Mary was heartened and refreshed by the sight of the cricketers demonstrating and enjoying their sporting prowess. Applause and comments from the appreciative crowd rippled around the hot, summer air, in tandem with the thwacks of the bat and the spins of the ball. Everyone was enjoying the match.

'It's still hot, but it feels a bit different today,' Rose observed. 'Like there's a storm brewin'.'

'Those are the first clouds I've seen in ages,' Winnie said, gazing at the distant, greying sky.

'I never thought I'd want it to rain, but I wouldn't mind after all this heat,' Ivy laughed.

'Just so long as the match gets finished first,' Mary said. 'It would be a pity to get rained off.'

'I can't wait for tonight! I don't care if it rains or not!' Violet announced.

'Why's that?' Winnie asked as she cuddled baby Robert on her knee.

'I'm goin' to t' Empire Palace wi' Annie and Auntie Gertie. We're goin' to see a Charlie Chaplin film. All t' papers say he's rate funny.'

Mary smiled at her younger daughter. It was so nice to see her happy and excited.

* * *

Jim was feeling jubilant. They'd won the match, even though it was only by ten runs. Everyone agreed it had been a good match, exciting and entertaining. Hickleton Main was considered a very good team, so victory was sweet. Denaby folk had wandered home in high spirits, pleased with their village club.

Mary and Jim walked home slowly, arm in arm, while Violet ran ahead. Dark clouds had been steadily building. The atmosphere was strangely still and hushed, as though waiting for something to happen. The first splashes of rain were felt as they arrived home.

'I'm so glad you came to watch the match, Mary,' Jim said, smiling down at her.

'I enjoyed it,' she said, as they walked into the living room.

'I've not got much time for tea, Mam!' Violet called, racing upstairs. 'Auntie Gertie and Annie will be here soon!'

Mary smiled at Jim.

'It's nice to see her excited and rushin' around,' she said. 'I'll get her a sandwich before I sit down.'

Jim nodded as he sat down and opened his paper. It felt good to relax and reflect on the day's events. He was pleased with himself, he didn't think he'd played too badly, in fact, he had surprised himself with his catches. *Life in the old dog yet.*

His thoughts were interrupted abruptly when he heard a loud crashing sound.

'Mary? What was that?' he called, standing up. He stepped towards the kitchen, then saw the awful sight. Mary was on the floor, still, her eyes closed. Fragments of cups and plates lay scattered around her.

'Mary! Mary, love!' he cried, dropping to his knees. 'Mary!' he cried again, gathering her hands in his.

A thunderous boom, followed by a crack of lightning, ripped through the room as the storm finally unleashed its power, but Mary lay unresponsive, unmoving. She was breathing in soft, shallow pants. He gently cradled her, his mumbled, frenzied words willing her to open her eyes and speak, but she did not.

'Mam!' Violet screamed as thunder roared and lightning flashed again. The girl stood in the doorway, rigid with fear.

'Violet, go and get Dr Twigg! Quick!' Jim ordered.

She nodded in stunned silence, her eyes wide with panic. Jim watched as his little girl ran out into the lashing rain.

'Don't leave me, Mary,' he whispered through his tears, rocking her tenderly in his arms. 'Please don't leave me.'

* * *

Jim gazed down at Mary as she slept. Although it was only one week since she had collapsed, he had to acknowledge how much she had changed.

It was as though she had shrivelled in both size and vitality. Her once softened features now showed angular contours of prominent cheekbones and sculpted jawbones. White streaks flashed through her faded chestnut hair. But she was still beautiful to him. He was still so thankful that she was alive.

His thoughts churned over the events of that awful, stormy evening when he thought he had lost her. His memories still struggled to gain some degree of order and comprehension. Mary had regained consciousness only moments before the arrival of Dr Twigg. She had stirred and opened her eyes.

'Jim,' she had murmured with a mixture of relief and bewilderment.

'You're all right, love. You've had a fall,' he tried to reassure her, tightening his arms around her.

'You're crying,' she whispered, trying to reach out to his tearstained face, but she was too weak.

He smiled down at her, relieved to hear Violet's voice as she opened the door. Dr Twigg had followed her in, immediately taking charge of the situation.

'Now then, Mary, let's take a look at you,' he began in a steady reassuring tone, kneeling down.

Jim and Violet had watched as he carried out his examination and questioning. They had lifted Mary onto a chair and listened to her faltering words, punctuated by bouts of breathlessness.

Jim felt growing fear and alarm as she admitted her long-established symptoms of chest pains, racing heart beats and overwhelming fatigue.

He could hardly believe she had suffered so long and concealed so much. He felt guilty that he had not realised the severity of her illness, but he knew she was trying to protect the feelings of others. That was the kind of selfless, caring person she was. Violet had crept nearer to him, needing his support.

'Violet, you go round to Rose's while I speak to Dr Twigg,' he gently suggested. 'Then you can both come back to see your mother.'

The little girl looked over to Mary, her eyes brimming with tears. Mary smiled and nodded.

'You do as your dad says. I'm all right, love.'

Violet sniffed and nodded before leaving.

There was a brief silence before Dr Twigg removed his spectacles, cleared his throat and delivered his opinion. He looked from Mary to Jim as he spoke.

'I believe that you have a disease of the heart, Mary, and it is probably advanced, considering your symptoms and their duration. You must have complete rest. That is the only thing that I can prescribe. Your symptoms may be alleviated to some degree, however, I must emphasise that this is a very serious illness, and especially at your relatively young age. I will attend you daily to monitor your condition.'

There was silence in the room as his words were digested. Dr Twigg gathered his belongings and repeated his warning before he left.

'Mind what I say. You require complete rest, no work whatsoever.'

Mary and Jim looked at each other blankly. They did not speak, but just held hands.

Jim had seen the change and deterioration in Mary's condition over the past week. All vibrancy had diminished. She had little energy and neither complained nor protested at having to permanently rest. Jim understood the implications of her compliance. She was unable to be active. She was an invalid.

The rest of the family, together with friends, had offered their immediate help and support. Ivy and Gertie shared domestic duties, Winnie and Maria ran errands, and Rose and Ellen sat with Mary.

They all loved her. She had always helped them. Jim was grateful, but also saddened that his darling wife was so frail and unwell. He yearned for her to be healthy and strong again, but she was steadily weakening.

Chapter 97
August 1914

Mary watched the flames frolicking along the cobbles, rising and falling as if dancing. She liked this quiet time, when her memories could wander without constraint. Her mind still had freedom, even if her body had its limitations.

Moving from her bed in the corner of the living room, to the chair in front of the fire, was the extent of her mobility, but she was grateful for the loving care of her family and friends.

Filmed eyes travelled to her hands, once strong and capable. Her fingers found comfort in the band of gold, once her Grandma Annie's ring, that spun gently round her bony finger.

She remembered the first time Jim's hand had touched hers. She knew she had loved him from that moment. Flowing memories, still bright and warmly secret, softened her dry, stiff mouth, both soothing and exciting her.

An involuntary gasp puffed from her throat, surprising and embarrassing her. She could recall the fluttering pulsing, the confusion of shyness and passion, at a moment's recollection. But things were different now.

Each day she felt the steady, progressive weakening, the sustained ebbing of energy that left her exhausted, gasping for breath. Each day she saw increasing worry reflected in people's faces, though they tried to hide it with encouraging platitudes of optimism and cheerfulness.

Eyes seemed to be always watching her, assessing her, which resulted in her trying to show false bravado and confidence, when, really, she felt as if she was diminishing, fading away. She felt she was like her mother, in looks and demeanour.

Strangely, it was Gertie with whom she could talk most openly. Kind, practical, steadfast sister Gertie, who seemed to have a sixth sense in knowing what to say and do.

She would wash and dress her frail sister in a matter of fact but sensitive way, idly chatting to create an air of normality. Mary confided her innermost thoughts and fears freely, without reserve, relinquishing any pretence of confidence or optimism, declaring her anguished, frustrated emotions.

'I know, I know, love,' Gertie would murmur gently, patting Mary's hands slowly, as if transferring strength and compassion.

'Just like Mam used to do,' Mary would think, reminded of her mother's sincere, caring manner.

This renewed feeling of coping nourished her, enabling a more positive attitude to others, even if only briefly, before melancholy triumphed again.

Violet had taken to snuggling up to Mary at any chance. The little girl's mouth trembled.

'I love you, Mam. Don't worry, you'll be better soon,' she whispered.

Mary squeezed her hand and gulped back tears.

'Aye, love. We'll soon be able to do things together again. I'll be able to go to t' Empire with you to see a Charlie Chaplin film. You're allus tellin' me how funny he is.'

Violet nodded and smiled, cuddling closer to her mother. Jim watched them, his solemn face attempting a weak smile.

Mary knew how much he was hurting; she knew every expression of his face, but he was always reassuring and optimistic in his words, and loving in his behaviour.

She felt blessed to have such a caring, loving husband. She had always thought that, which made her illness even harder to bear. She didn't want to leave him.

* * *

People were reading the newspapers with growing interest and bewilderment.

'I can't fathom out what's 'appening o'er there,' was a much-repeated refrain from puzzled residents of Denaby.

Events abroad had suddenly escalated until it was difficult to keep pace with the latest news reports. The assassinations in June of the Archduke Franz Ferdinand and his wife, Sophie, had set off a rapid chain of events involving major powers, who argued and blamed each other for hostilities.

On 28th July, 1914, Austria-Hungary had declared war on Serbia. On 1st August, Germany had declared war on Russia; on 3rd August, Germany had declared war on France, then on 4th August, Britain had declared war on Germany.

The British people had only just heard that they were now officially at war with Germany, and the news was both shocking and alarming.

'Bloody Hell, din't see that comin'!' was the opinion reverberating around many towns and villages, including Denaby.

'Might be summat and nowt,' was the hopeful verdict by many.

* * *

Dr Twigg had been attending Mary regularly since her collapse, and each time, her family observed his sombre expression and prolonged scrutiny as he examined and gently questioned her.

Mary gazed at him with tired, subservient eyes, obediently answering his probing enquiries in a hushed, resigned voice.

Her appetite had steadily decreased until she was barely eating. Her body had weakened until she could no longer move to her chair. She lay in bed, thankful for the warmth and comfort it afforded her weary limbs. Only her mind felt strong and alert.

Only one week after Britain declared war on Germany, Mary's condition suddenly deteriorated. On that fateful Tuesday morning, 11th August, severe pains gripped her exhausted body. They tightened and attacked her chest until she could hardly breathe.

She writhed in agony, in a feeble attempt to escape the intense suffering, but she found no comfort.

Jim and Gertie heard her muffled gasps.

'Jim, Jim,' she managed to pant.

'I'm here, love, I'm here,' he whispered. 'Try to keep still.'

'The pain, Jim, the pain,' she moaned.

'I'll go for Dr Twigg,' Gertie said, already on her way out.

Jim lay beside Mary and held her close. His tears wet her hair as she rested on him.

* * *

Mary lay still, panting muted, quickened breaths. The pain had gone, but there was a curious heaviness that burdened her body, a pressure that weighted and relaxed her, sinking her into a state of peaceful restfulness.

She remembered the doctor telling her to rest and relax. She could do nothing else, but was relieved to follow his instructions. She allowed herself to drift off to sleep, waking for short periods, thankful to be pain-free and comfortable.

All day, there had been frequent visitors, shocked and disheartened at Mary's sudden decline. She heard their hushed, murmuring voices, concerned yet fearful of disturbing her, but she was pleased to watch them and listen to their words. They comforted her as she lay in her dream-like condition.

Rose sat by her bed, holding her hand and gently stroking the streaked hair that fanned the pillows. Mary saw her daughter's rounding stomach.

Rose bravely assured her mother that she would soon have another grandson, or maybe a granddaughter. Mary was silent, allowing the expression in her eyes to speak for her.

'You go back to sleep now, Mam, you look tired.'

Rose kissed her forehead and tiptoed away.

Mary was surprised to see Betty when she next woke up.

'Hello, love. How are you feeling, Mary?' she asked. Mary gazed at her eldest sister, lowering and raising her eyelids in answer, but she could not hold back the silent tears. She was surprised to see that Betty was also crying. Their impassioned gazes needed no words.

Esther, Ellen and Maria stood watching, together with Winnie, each bereft of words, wiping the tears from their cheeks.

Jim was never far away as she wandered in and out of consciousness, bravely smiling at her, whispering comforting words. Lines were etched around his eyes and mouth, his pain and anguish could not be hidden, but he tried.

'I thought you might like to look at this,' he whispered. He held the wooden rose. 'This flower will last forever. It will never die, just like my love.'

She remembered the words he had told her, all those years ago. Mary saw the love in his eyes, and he saw the love in hers. She smiled as she relaxed into sleep.

She woke up feeling different. The heaviness in her body had lifted. She felt as though she was floating. Only her breathing caused discomfort.

Deep, sucking gasps raked through her body. She could not control them. She looked at the faces around her – all the people she loved.

Jim was on one side, Rose on the other. Violet lay on the bed with her, her face pressed against her, her arms around her, gently weeping for her. Her beloved sisters stood arm-in-arm, their sorrowful faces wet with tears. Dejected sobs were stifled as they all witnessed the distressing sight. Their Mary, their lovely Mary.

She felt Jim's hand on hers. She still remembered that first touch, long, long ago. The touch of love.

'You just go to sleep now, Mary. My darling Mary.'

She felt his fingers caressing her cheek as she breathed a long, low breath.

Mary closed her eyes and was thrilled to see the faces of those she had loved and lost. Her mother and father, Grandma Annie and Grandad George, her brother, Bob, her adored son, John, even Bridie was there, all smiling at her, beckoning her, welcoming her.

She smiled back and sank into a world where she no longer had to fight for breath. She did not hear the heartrending sobs of those she had left behind.

Chapter 98
September 1914

Life would never be the same again. Jim still felt raw, heartbroken that Mary had gone. He missed her so much, yearned for her with every fibre of his being, but he had to carry on. Shifts still had to be worked, coal still had to be hewn, money still had to be earned. But it all felt so futile and superficial without Mary.

The day of Mary's funeral had been the worst of his life. He tried not to think about it, but flashes of memories could not be suppressed. His last touch of her beautiful face, his last tender kiss, his last look before the coffin lid was closed.

Family, friends and neighbours had stood by the graveside, numbed by grief and sadness, cold, even in the August sunshine.

Everyone felt the poignant loss of such a kind, loving, caring person. She had been a wonderful wife, mother, daughter, sister and friend. Many tears were shed that day, and afterwards.

Jim would never forget the sound of the earth as it hit the coffin in the grave. Mary was finally leaving him.

Yet, he would always remember the glowing tributes, the sincere condolences from so many people. She had been truly loved and would be sorely missed. Rose, especially, was heartbroken, so close had been the bond between mother and daughter. People worried that her pregnancy might be affected, but she possessed a steely strength of character and determination to be resilient for her family.

Jim's main worry was Violet. She had taken her mother's death very badly. Tears were never far away for the young girl, even in her dreams. She would wake up crying, her pillow damp with tears.

Jim was thankful when Gertie suggested she stay with them for a while, especially as she was so close to Annie. They were like sisters. Violet agreed to stay with her Auntie Gertie and Uncle Charlie. She loved them and needed them. She looked forward to being with Annie more, too. It was nice to think of happier things. She so missed her Mam.

Jim acknowledged that he, also, needed time and space to grieve. He had lost his father, his son, and now his wife. Each had taken a piece of his heart with them, and he felt the pain.

Chapter 99
October 1914

Jim walked along the "backs" carrying his flask and snap tin. The pleasant autumn weather made the prospect of another eight-hour afternoon shift down the pit harder to accept, but he had to work and earn.

In some ways he was glad to be at work, when the physical toil and required concentration relieved his sadness for a while. He was still fighting depression, still mourning his Mary, but the routine of life continued.

The times when he was at home, lonely and alone, were the hardest to bear. His thoughts would roam, but he gained little solace. He would gaze at the wooden rose that sat on the mantelpiece, and tenderly grasp Mary's wedding ring in his hand until his tears blurred his sight and dulled his touch.

Memories of Mary were both his comfort and torment; he missed her so much, still loved her so much.

'Hey, wait for us, Jim! We'll walk to work wi' thi!'

Jim looked round and saw Billy and Eddie striding towards him.

'Eh-up, lads,' Jim said to the twins. 'It's too nice a day to be goin' to work, in't it?'

'No, we're glad to get out o' t' house,' Billy complained. 'Mi father's drivin' us mad!'

Jim paused before asking, 'Is Eli still drinkin' as much?'

'Drinkin'!' Eddie shouted. 'He gets pissed every night! He does nowt but get drunk and get on to everybody. He's allus moanin'!'

Jim knew that things were difficult in the Shaw household. Maria was always complaining about Eli.

'He's never been rate since mi Mam and our Ben died,' Billy said.

'And he's gettin' worse,' Eddie added. 'What wi' our Maria and Louisa moanin' about all t' work they have to do, and never havin' enough money, it's like a hellhole in our 'ouse! We feel sorry for our Declan and Lottie, they're only babbies.'

'Yeah, we're both fed up!' Billy declared. 'We'd be better off joinin' up and fightin' in t' war o'er there. Can't be any worse than livin' and workin' 'ere!'

'You mean you want to sign up for t' Army?' Jim asked sharply. 'You're not even old enough!'

'Dun't care. We'll lie about us ages if we 'ave to. We reckon it'd be fun goin' off abroad. Furthest we've been is Sheffield!' Eddie scoffed.

'Yeah, goin' to France'd be a bit of an adventure,' Billy agreed with his brother, grinning. 'Mind you, can't see this war lastin' much longer. We'd better sign up quick!'

Jim shook his head as he listened to their laughing banter, but he understood their feelings. If he was younger, he'd think about signing up himself. Life was empty without Mary.

The three men walked along Pit Lane. Another day toiling underground. The warm sunshine was left behind.

Sources

- *A Photographic Record of the 'old' village of Denaby Main* by John A. Gwatkin.

- *The Terrible Yorkshire Pit Disaster, Cadeby Main Colliery 1912* by James Beachill.

- *The Bag Muck Strike* by J. E. MacFarlane

- *Your Blood on The Coal* by J. E. MacFarlane

- Coal Mining History Resource Centre – articles supplied by Ian Winstanley.

- *The Great Struggle* by Reverend Jesse Wilson.

- *A Railway History of Denaby and Cadeby Collieries* by A. J. Booth.

- *Wentworth – A Brief History* by Graham Hobson.

- Conisbrough and Denaby Local History – website.

- *Mexborough and Swinton Times* (archives).

- *Sheffield Telegraph* (archives).

About the Author

Carol Ann Bullett was born and raised in the South Yorkshire mining community of Conisbrough and Denaby Main.
Her father and both grandfathers were miners at Cadeby and Denaby Main pits.
Carol's mother and aunts worked at the local Sickle Works and Powder Works.
She is a retired teacher. Carol's first teaching post was at Rossington Street School, Denaby, and later at Station Road School, Conisbrough.

Printed in Great Britain
by Amazon